Backstage Secrets

Backstage Secrets

Michelle Shingler & Vincenza Astone

AuthorHouse™
1663 Liberty Drive
Bloomington, IN 47403
www.authorhouse.com
Phone: 1-800-839-8640

The characters and events depicted in this book are fictitious. Any similarity to actual persons, living or dead, is purely coincidental.

First published by AuthorHouse 11/21/2011

ISBN: 978-1-4670-0782-5 (sc)
ISBN: 978-1-4670-0783-2 (ebk)

Printed in the United States of America

This book is printed on acid-free paper.

Michelle Shingler Vincenza Astone/IPMTV International Programme Marketing 15 Skylines, Limeharbour, London E14 9TS
Email: degasb@talktalk.net

We raise our glasses to the conference and events industry!

You've served us well with both laughter and tears
Missed cues and dramas and lots of fears.

Through thick and thin we've pulled together
With some of us sometimes being at the end of our tether.

Sleep deprivation and endless script changes
Equipment updates and technology ranges.

Faultless shows with the turn of a page
Little do they know what goes on backstage.

But all good shows must come to an end
So we take a bow with our colleagues and friends.

Chapter One

"Ladies and gentlemen, this is your captain, Charles Mead speaking and I'd like to welcome you aboard this British Airways flight to Nice. Our flying time today will be approximately one hour and fifty-five minutes. The weather forecast is looking favourable, with good visibility and beautiful clear skies. We'll soon be taxied to the runway and it looks as if we shall be taking off slightly ahead of our allotted departure time. The cabin crew will shortly take you through our safety procedures and we would be grateful if you would give these your undivided attention, even for those frequent fliers of ours. In the meantime please sit back, relax and enjoy your flight."

Now, just how many times have I heard a flight captain's announcement? And yet here I am again, jetting off to foreign parts and getting paid for it! Perfect. I often wonder if life can really get any better. Well yes, of course it can! I fly an average of two to three times per month, sometimes more and sometimes less, but it goes with the job. This perfect job of mine!

"Hey Martha, remember the time we were coming back from that gig in Dubai and you had a bust up at check-in, because: *'Madam, you have way too much luggage with you'* he says, imitating the check-in attendant. "In the end you literally shoved everythin' into the 'old except your mobile, passport and boarding pass. Fuck! You were fuming. Still makes me laugh, your face was a picture!" The voice belongs to Mickey Prowse. Mickey's a fabulous industry colleague and also a very special friend. Not special in the sense of jiggy jiggy, sex special, but simply special. So, how best to describe him? Cheeky and an outrageous flirt! Plain and simple. He's a sound engineer and one of the conference industry's real characters and now he's sitting directly behind me, which of course unnerves me somewhat!

"Of course I remember! That attendant was a complete bitch! She had it in for me, the moment I arrived at check-in. Oh, but then of course, the best of it is, we arrive into Heathrow and every one of you rushes off, once your bags have come through, for which I don't blame you, after all, I would have done exactly the same, but I was left there, like a right idiot, without any bags. Not one! And where were my car keys? Yep, in with my luggage. Oh, that was a fucking nightmare!" I cringe, just thinking about that trip. I had to stay at the airport for another four hours, until my luggage was redirected from Charles du Gaulle Airport—quite how it ended up in Paris, I have absolutely no idea. Then the battery went flat on my mobile and my purse was in my handbag, which, yes of course, was in the hold too! Never again will I be parted from my beloved handbag. I will fight to the death for it to be with me at all times, irrespective of how much the bloody thing weighs!

The cabin crew have completed their safety demonstration and are now walking through the plane checking passenger seat belts.

"Excuse me Madam, please could I ask that you tighten your seat belt?" asks one of the air stewardesses.

"Honey, not without liposuction I can't. No!" comes an immediate reply. Each and every one of our crew bursts into laughter. Tears are rolling down our faces, as many passengers turn around, to see what all the commotion is about.

The stewardess blushes, but giggles too, not sure that she is being politically correct at laughing at a passenger's misfortune. I am sitting next to Mel, Mel Arethusa, Show Caller extraordinaire! Mel is one of the funniest girls on the conference circuit, with a sense of humour second to none, but always a true professional. She is a larger than life, in every sense! Cuddly of mass proportions, kind and a very attractive girl and of course, crew just love working with her and her never-ending wit.

"I can't believe you just said that!" says Belinda, tears of laughter still running down her cheeks. Belinda is sitting on the other side of Mel. Belinda Edwards, the fun loving production assistant. She's young, slim, blonde and oh, so pretty. We always call her by her full name and never shorten it to Bel. A previous boyfriend once referred to her as 'Swell Bel' when she put on a little unexpected weight and from that day to this, she refuses point blank, to be called Bel. The crew boys simply love Belinda, together with her partner in crime (and I stress here, 'partner in crime' relates to her working relationship, not sexual relationship), Ellie Harman. Ellie is a real butterfly, extremely beautiful and full of life. Belinda and Ellie have carved out a real niche for themselves, as Production Assistants and they really are the best in the business. Efficiency beyond, when sober, of course!

Ellie is sitting in between Mickey and Dan, Dan Williams. Dan is a video technician in his early thirties. He's married, but of course adores the opposite sex and he has had his eye on Ellie for several years! Ellie, needless to say, is not in the slightest bit interested, but always enjoys playing up to him when they work together. No harm in flirting now, is there? Besides which, Dan is extremely handsome, with a six pack to die for! We all adore him, especially when he discards his top!

The remainder of the crew are scattered around the plane. There are fifteen of us travelling out on this particular flight, with more crew due over the next couple of days. The six of us—me, Mel, Ellie, Belinda, Dan and Mickey are definitely the naughtiest of the bunch! We are excited at the fact that we are seated together, as it's always good to catch up on what's been happening and, of course, with whom!

We are even more excited that we have escaped sitting within the vicinity of Ingrid Lorne-Harris, aka 'Producer from hell'. Ingrid is one of those people who just fall on their feet, time and again. She's in her early forties (reputedly, but I beg to differ, as I suspect she must be fast approaching fifty!) with short brown hair, limited dress sense (she's verging on the edge of the twin-set and pearls brigade) and to top it all, possesses a really hideous laugh. A laugh that is so totally over-the-top and totally embarrassing—she sounds like a bloody hyena! But the only saving grace of course, is that she doesn't laugh very often!

Ingrid is a total control freak. She is two-faced and above all, must always, always, be the centre of attention. She is sickly sweet and fawns over male members of crew and client alike. She despises women, as she sees every woman as competition, vying for attention. Sour, very sour! Ingrid has worked for Angel Productions for about eight years. We all work on a freelance basis for Angel. Business is tough, so therefore we cannot be too choosy as to which companies we work for, but in fairness to this production house, they are prompt payers, settling their invoices on time, and that's what we freelancers like, especially with the economy as it is!

We are travelling to Cannes, South of France, running a show for KAYSO Inc., the largest fashion retail outlet in the United States. They are an extremely successful organisation and are now rapidly expanding into Europe and Australasia.

We settle down into our seats, as the plane begins its ascent. Finally, we're on our way. Thankfully, flying doesn't bother me. It never has and hopefully it never will. I recall a time when we hit the most horrendous turbulence, trying to land in Barbados and I honestly thought my time was up. I prayed like I've never prayed before and thankfully my prayers were answered. I think this was probably due to the fact that I offered a lot more than I was really going to give to the good Lord—namely: limited sexual activity, limited alcoholic consumption and more frequent visits to his 'house'! However, a stiff drink once we landed, helped me clean forget all of my promises! I was not ready to depart this world; after all, I was only twenty three years old at the time—I'd still got a lot of living to do!

Closing my eyes, I smile to myself, as I recall how I entered this chaotic world of conferences and live events.

I had popped round to surprise a friend with champagne and flowers on her birthday and I caught her in the middle of decorating her kitchen.

We chatted away, as she carried on painting. I opened the bottle of bubbly, not wanting it to go warm of course and it sprayed, quite literally, all over the kitchen units, so I quickly grabbed a newspaper from the side to mop up the spilt champagne, before it reached the floor and whilst pulling the newspaper sheets apart—the spillage was, after all, a pretty big one—I pulled out the Job Search section. And, of course, the advert caught my eye immediately:

Travel the World...

Freelance Prompter required for events industry. Must possess good typing skills, excellent command of the English language, great levels of concentration and be able to communicate with people at all levels. Hard work and plenty of travel...

Well let's see—my typing is good, after all I achieved exam results and have certificates to prove it. Quite an achievement; let me tell you! I can speak English excellently, even though I am of Italian origin. As for concentration? Well, if I really put my mind to something, I can usually achieve the required result. And, of course, communication—Yep, I, can communicate—I have been told I am a real 'people person!'

In fairness, when I read the ad, I had no idea what a Prompter was, but I kept re-reading those lovely three words 'plenty of travel'—I love travelling; after all, life is an adventure, especially when travel is involved.

I knew that my darling Pops (my father as he is affectionately known by his children and all of our friends) would go berserk, with yet another job change—he is very much of the generation that thinks a person should join a company, make progression and continue working there until it is time to retire—on a handsome pension.

Now, originally I had wanted to be an air stewardess, but Pops refused point blank to entertain such a notion. The thought of his daughter waiting on people was just too much for him to comprehend, especially after such an enhanced and costly education.

I then decided that the police force would be my vocation. I would pound the streets, making our country a better and safer place! Needless to say Pops once again, poo-poo'ed the idea. Potentially, far too much violence for his little girl to endure and he didn't think I would be able to tolerate the discipline or take orders easily!

So, what was I to do? Can you imagine being in the same job for all of your entire working life? Fuck me! No way—it would send me nuts and there would be no doubt that I'd be living in a padded cell, rocking in the corner! And my only couture would be strait jackets, which, let's face it, aren't terribly flattering!

So there it was; the ad that was to change my life—I had nothing to lose, so I carefully folded it up and popped it into my handbag, knowing that on Monday morning I would be making a phone call.

Victoria, the birthday girl and I, clink glasses to toast the fact that she is now 31 years young, but secretly I am toasting my new job. OK, OK, I have no idea what the new job really entails, but it is going to be mine, after all, it involves travel!

Monday morning soon comes round.

"Good morning. I'm calling about the job you have advertised in the Oxford Times," I say, in my best polished English accent.

"Who's calling please?" asks the receptionist. "My name is Martha, Martha DiPinto."

"Hold one moment Martha and I'll put you through to Tom Kremner," she responds.

I wait, like an excited child.

"Good morning Martha. Tom Kremner speaking," the voice is velvety and strong, with a slight London twang. "You'd like to know more about the job then?"

The more he describes what the position entails, the more intrigued and excited I become. I just know this is the job for me, I just know it. Travel within the UK and abroad, a team player, meeting people from all walks of life, working hard, but playing hard too—what more could I ask for? Oh yes, a decent rate of pay maybe!

Tom asks me what I currently do for a living, but there is only so much I can 'fluff up' about being a personal assistant, although it has to be said, I am a rather good one, even though I do say so myself! But let's face it, it's mind-numbingly boring and I know that I am ready for a change.

Tom invites me to attend an interview. I try to picture what he looks like and I'm opting for mid-forties, dark hair and a toned physique.

I arrive at Kremner Audio Visual the following day, at nine o'clock sharp. My heart is racing and my mouth is dry.

"Hi, Martha DiPinto for Tom Kremner," I beam, at the receptionist.

"Ah yes, you're here for the Prompting job, aren't you?" she smiles.

The receptionist hands me an application form, which she asks me to complete and after dotting the 'i's and crossing the 't's, I dutifully hand it back to her. Shit! Fuck! Bollocks! This is it, my life-changing opportunity!

The door behind reception opens and there he is, the man who is indeed going to change my life. Handsome? Definitely! And yes, in his late thirties or early forties, cute smile and a firm handshake and yes, toned as well! He is positively sexy, with a capital S!

We walk through an open plan office, where the phones are ringing and the atmosphere is buzzing. I overhear a telephone conversation:

"OK, so just to confirm. That's a crew of eight flying out to Phoenix on the fourteenth, returning on the nineteenth. Crew comprising: two sound, two vision, two lighting, one graphics and one prompt. Consider it booked and with your preferred crew, if I can get them of course..."

I can't believe my ears. That could actually be me going to Arizona one day! One day soon, hopefully. Now, all I have to do is impress the rather gorgeous Tom Kremner.

The décor of Tom's office is minimalist. A large barrister's mahogany desk, with green leather inlays and a large green leather captain's swivel chair, with a bookcase to one side and a filing cabinet on the other. On the bookcase is a photo frame. Now, who do we think will be in the photo? Let's guess... Wife and children or just children, as he's possibly divorced or just wife, as he's not the parenting kind? Too early to ask, but I crane my elegant neck to check out the image. Well, surprise, surprise, I am wrong in all cases—no wife, no children, but a photograph of gorgeous Tom, shaking Nelson Mandela's hand.

My mind starts to wander; as it does every so often. Just what would it be like to straddle Mr Tom in that swivel chair? Inappropriate thought I know and way too early to be thinking along those lines! But he is seriously sexy!

Adorning the walls are several photographs of events that have been staged by Kremner AV; events which have taken place all over the world—London, Paris, New York, Milan, Sydney, Oman, Dubai, to name but a few.

Tom motions for me to take a seat. "So then Martha, you want to be a Prompter, also known as an Autocue Operator or Teleprompter? Got patience, have you? Because let me tell you, you sure as hell need it in this game. Clients change their minds constantly and we end up pulling rabbits out of hats to meet their demands. You always do it with a smile, but what you mutter under your breath is entirely up to you! I'll be honest, Prompting particularly, requires high concentration levels and masses of patience. Graphics and Prompt always get the bum deal, be mindful of that. You could be working with Heads of State, politicians, film stars, celebrities from all fields, or Joe Bloggs from the factory floor, who has to give a presentation to his colleagues. So tell me, first off, does any of that faze you?" he asks, a smile spreading across his oh, so handsome face.

'Scares me shitless,' I think to myself, as still I don't really understand what the job is all about. After all, if I were to say to you right now, hey fancy becoming a 'Prompter' would you know what the heck I am on about? No, thought not!

But can you imagine Heads of State, and celebs relying on me? Fucking hell! Just imagine!

"I'd be lying if I said 'no' to this fazing me, but it's only because it's new and of course, I'm a fast learner," I smile.

Tom smiles back, leaning into his chair. His eyes are penetrating, hopefully penetrating through my tight-fitting shirt!

'Pull yourself together Martha, right now!' I say to myself. I just know that at some stage, Mr Tom Kremner and Miss Martha DiPinto will enjoy rampant, uninhibited sex! It's only a question of time. The connection has already been made! And he's bloody gorgeous!

"OK, so let's give you a hypothetical situation Martha. You are in London and have just finished a show, after having worked until the early hours the night before. You have to pack up your equipment and load it into a vehicle, you then have to drive to the next venue, which is, let's say Bristol, where you have to off-load and then assemble the equipment in readiness for the show in the morning. Got a problem with any of that?" asks Tom.

He really is to the point, so forceful and commanding.

"No, no, I'm certainly not afraid of hard work. In fact, the harder, the better, if you ask me," I continue, a smile spreading across my face, as I realise what I have just said.

After studying my application form and asking a few searching questions, the interview is interrupted by a telephone call. Tom excuses himself and picks up the receiver. Whilst he's on the phone, I take a moment to look at the photographs displayed on the walls of his office. It's a pretty impressive sight. Pop stars, rock bands, celebrities presenting awards—Martha, note to self, do not fuck up this interview!

After finishing his telephone conversation and once again apologising for having taken the call, he asks if I have any questions before he takes me (not takes me in the sense of sex, you know, over his large, impressive desk—more's the pity) to see the prompting equipment, in what he calls the rehearsal studio.

I am so overwhelmed by everything, I can't think of any appropriate questions, so we head out of his office towards the studio.

So here it is; my future. There's a lectern, or podium, positioned in the middle of the room, (basically it's a stand from where people present) that is flanked by two pieces of angled glass. Now rumour has it, that words can be seen on these glass panels when the prompting equipment is switched on. Boy it's technical! Too technical for me! The glass panels sit on long poles. So far, so good!

There are two monitors resting on metal bases facing upwards towards the glass, but when you look directly at the monitor, the image is the wrong way round. Now, here comes the technical bit! Ready? When you look at the glass, the words are the right way round—the principle is the same as holding writing up to a mirror, giving you a back to front image. (Apparently, a lot of people mistake these glass screens as bullet-proof protectors, as prompting is a favourite tool of politicians!). It's magic! Magic it may be, but totally fucking baffling to me!

Tom calls me forward. "Now Martha, only the prompter and the presenter can see what's on the prompting glass," explains Tom.

Eureka! So that's what this job is all about! Autocue; like they use on the TV when they're reading the news! You know, when the news reader looks directly at you, but is really reading the autocue words. Hence the description of news readers as Autocuties! My God, do you remember the holy debacle that was the sham of Fox (as in Samantha) and Fleetwood (as in Mick), when they got all the script mixed up on the Brit Awards? That really was such a mess. Of course, if I'd been there, it would have worked perfectly! Talk about jumping the gun, I am thinking as though the job is already mine... OK Martha, let's get back to the interview!

"So does that mean if the speaker is a real pain in the butt, I can type in a rude message whilst they're speaking?" I laugh, suddenly thinking that was not the smartest comment to come out of my mouth!

"Don't think that hasn't been done before!" says Tom, laughing.

The interview and demonstration come to an end and Tom tells me that he has another three candidates to interview and that he'll let me know by the end of the week if I've made it through to the next round. My heart sinks, after all, I want to know right now that I have been successful.

"Ah, before you leave Martha, I nearly forgot. Would you mind completing a typing test? You'll find a document on the desk over there," he says, pointing to a single table with a computer and printer on top of it. "There are some errors in the content, so please could you re-type it, word and grammar perfect?" he throws me a wink, coupled with that fabulous Kremner smile.

Once I have finished the task in hand, in double-quick time, I might add, I leave Kremner AV with a gut feeling that I'm going to get that call, very soon. That call, which is going to change my life, forever.

The following day, late afternoon to be precise, my mobile rings. To my surprise it's him, the gorgeous Tom Kremner.

"Martha, hi it's Tom Kremner." My heart starts beating like a big base drum. It feels as though it's going to burst.

"Thanks for coming in yesterday. I just want to say that after seeing the other candidates I've decided to offer you the job. I don't have time for second round interviews, and I know that you will be able to cut it. So, if you're interested, when can you come in to get started with training?" he asks.

"Interested? I'm over the moon Tom. How about Monday? That gives me time to sort out my resignation," I giggle. I knew it! I bloody well knew it!

"Perfect and eager, now that's what I like. See you then. Bye for now," he says and with that, Tom is gone.

I am elated. I have landed my dream job, even though I still don't really understand what it's all about, glass panels, monitors, and backward words—just how hard can it be though? But, hey I am on my way to a whole new life and, of course, the big wide world.

I work really hard during my training, but of course, I don't mind, as I love every single minute of it. I have several months of intensive training. Role playing every possible scenario. It's intense! It's exhausting! It's brilliant!

Tom Kremner hasn't lied about needing patience and concentration; Prompters need it by the bucketful! And I have to admit, that there are times when I think that I will never be able to handle doing a show on my own, without a trainer by my side. However, that day does eventually arrive and it's out of the blue.

But am I really, truly ready? Of course, I am!

I receive a call from one of the staff who works on the hire desk at Kremner AV. She explains how she has rung round all of the regular Prompt operators, but they are all busy with other shows, so Tom suggested calling me, as he thinks that I am ready to 'fly solo'.

So this is it; I have agreed to undertake my first solo event,. Sweet Jesus! I am gripped by fear. I know I can do it, but there is still an element of self-doubt.

Victoria Gardens Hotel in Buxton, Derbyshire is my event location. I am due to arrive at ten am tomorrow morning.

People say 'don't worry, you'll be fine'. How can they say, 'don't worry?' I am absolutely petrified. What if I fuck up? My only saving grace comes in the guise of Peter Falcroft, who is the Production Manager and by all accounts he is really nice, well, according to the girls on the hire desk, that is. Peter will be my contact on site. I will befriend this man from the moment I arrive and hope (and pray) that he likes me—likes me enough to get me out of a mess, should I fuck up!

The journey to Buxton takes just short of three hours. As I drive, literally up hill and down dale, over the Derbyshire moors, I mentally go through the things I have packed. Pencil case (a new job gift to myself—Burberry, no less), scissors, dictionary, toiletries, hairdryer, make-up and underwear, both functional and sexy, just in case! Hey, you never know! And most importantly crew blacks. Everyone in the industry wears blacks. Black shoes, black top, black trousers, black skirt and black jacket. Yes, I have packed everything.

I eventually arrive at the very grand Victoria Gardens Hotel, where I park up, take a deep breath and pray, to myself.

'Father, please let everything be alright on this, my first solo job. I apologise for all my ongoing, inappropriate sexual thoughts and antics and I also apologise for all my bad language and, of course, for not coming to visit you in your 'House' as often as I should. I also promise to make a real effort and not boss You around and question your teachings; as my mother always reminds me that You cannot be bossed around. Sorry for everything, but please don't let me, fu…, um, you know, make a mess of my first show. Thank you and Amen.' I make a sign of the cross and hope for the best.

I enter the hotel and make my way to the Woodward Suite, where the rig (fancy word for build) is taking place.

I push open the doors and there are the crew, off loading the lorry and bringing equipment into the suite. There are flight cases (boxes that the equipment is transported in) everywhere. It would appear that I am the only girl on the crew today. Can't be bad—this job has its perks! How I love being a girl!

"Hi. I'm looking for Peter Falcroft," I say, as I enter the suite. Everyone looks at me—yes indeed, I love being a girl!

"Over there lovely, the one with the big voice and no hair, drinking coffee—typical production manager!" replies one of the crew, smiling.

I walk over towards Peter.

"You must be Martha," Peter shakes my hand and offers me a cup of coffee. We chat for a few minutes and then he points to a set of flight cases that are just being off-loaded from the truck.

"That's your gear. Grab yourself a trestle table, a six-footer from over there and you can start to rig here. This will be the backstage area. Scripts will be here in about twenty minutes," smiles Peter, as he walks away and helps himself to another cup of coffee.

I walk over to where the trestle tables are stacked up against the wall and pick off the first one and drag it, yes drag it, as it is way too fucking heavy to lift. But hey, hang on just a minute, let's just take stock. Where is the international travel that was promised? 'Travel the World' it said. Not hump tables, come on, get real, this is not what I signed up to! But nevertheless, I drag the table to where Peter has told me to position it.

I unpack the flight cases containing the prompting gear and proceed to put it all together. I am so engrossed in making sure I have all the cables plugged into the right connections, that I don't notice a very tall, skinny man (and not a particularly attractive man) standing in front of me.

"You must be Martha. Barney Shaw pleased to meet you," he shakes my hand and gives me a memory stick.

"These are the scripts. I want them formatted and ready within the hour, client will be here at three o'clock and I want to run technical rehearsals before they arrive. There are only two of them using prompt, so you will have an easy time," he says, without a smile or an ounce of encouragement.

Once I'm set up, I sit at the prompting computer and get on with the scripts. Finally, all the 'i's' are dotted and 't's' are crossed. The crew are well into the rig now and the staging has been brought in and the lectern is position. I don't really notice the time.

"Martha, can you go on cans please? I need to check something out," shouts Peter.

Cans, how cool—I am finally on cans! 'Cans' this is the industry word for headsets. These enable the show crew to speak to one another during the show, without being overheard by the audience.

"No problem!" I reply.

I dutifully oblige and await further instruction. In the meantime, I continue to check every sentence for spelling and punctuation, as I don't want to fall at the first hurdle!

The palms of my hands are starting to feel a bit sweaty and I am feeling hollow inside, partly from nerves, but mainly due to hunger. Hell, I love food, but I didn't eat anything before leaving home, as it was way too early for breakfast.

Now, I would kill for something to eat, anything. I rummage around in my handbag, it holds everything, but alas there's not much going on in there today! We have an empty Tic-Tac box, a toffee, which looks a little hairy, a soft apple, which is obviously past its sell by date and a Penguin biscuit, which has obviously been in the bag for weeks, as it is crushed, and I mean crushed!

What I wouldn't give for a gin and tonic and a slice of cheese on toast, with a sprinkling of chillies, oh, how bloody perfect!

Around half an hour has gone by since Peter asked me to go on cans and now, I desperately need to visit the Ladies cloakroom. I lift one of the headphone muffs from my right ear, to determine if I can hear anything, as the suite seems to have gone rather quiet. Shit! My bladder is near to bursting point. I seriously don't want to wet myself on my first solo job, after all, what kind of reputation would I get?

I wonder if I dare take the cans off and peek out from backstage. Sod it! I just have to, as soon I'll be past the point of no return and I will be standing in a puddle. I remove the headset and peer around the corner of the set.

"Care to join us Martha?" asks Peter. All the crew are laughing, as they tuck into their sandwiches. "Ah, is this your first show love?" asks one of the carpenters. I am so embarrassed; they have got me good and proper. I laugh, then trickle!

"Yes, well thank you gentlemen, very funny," I say, as I make a dash out of the suite, straight into the toilets across the foyer.

The relief is so welcome I can't begin to explain. It's a bit like a never-ending orgasm; yes, I suppose that would be the closest description! Although in fairness, I've never had a never-ending orgasm, a multiple one yes, but not a never-ending one, as it would still be going on now, wouldn't it?

I come out of the cubicle and wash my hands, oblivious to my surroundings. I look at myself in the mirror. You know what? I'm not looking too bad today. My hair, unruly as it is—big, curly hair, is behaving itself and my make-up looks polished and professional. Yes indeed, I look reasonably well groomed. Whilst I'm marvelling at the image in the mirror, I notice something unusual. Not unusual about me. No, unusual about my surroundings. Shit! Fuck! Bollocks! There are urinals behind me!, In my desperation to get to the loo, I've walked straight into the gents' toilets! And to my absolute horror, Peter has obviously followed me in, as is taking a pee, dick in hand, smirk on face.

Oh, good Lord above! Please don't let me carry on acting like a complete fuckwit. I feel my skin changing colour to crimson red and thankfully, it's not a hot flush, it's just out of sheer bloody embarrassment!

Head up high and shoulders back, I open the door and head out into the foyer, where the two receptionists are giggling at my misfortune.

"I always say I'll come back as a man, but having had a look in there, I'm not so sure!" I laugh, as I walk back into the Woodward Suite.

After a few moments, Peter arrives back in the suite. "Better?" he asks, smiling. I grab a plate and take some food from the serving platter.

"Yes, thank you, much better. And thank you for being so kind to me on my first solo job. Oh, but before I forget, don't ever let anybody tell you that size doesn't matter!" I wink, as I walk away, chuckling to myself.

"Call it your initiation into the business as a qualified Word Bird," laughs Peter. "The first show should always be one to remember!"

Suddenly, I am jolted back to the here and now. Mel is shaking me, "Hey Martha, time to wake up and strap in. You've missed breakfast, but no worries as I ate yours!" she laughs.

"Ladies and Gentlemen, welcome to Nice International Airport" announces the voice over the plane's intercom system. I glance down at my watch—we've landed, just ahead of our scheduled time.

Chapter Two

We finally make our way into Nice Airport, terminal two and after clearing passport control we head towards baggage reclaim. Our flight is full and the hall is bustling with passengers from other destinations, all of them waiting in anticipation for their luggage to arrive. After all, life doesn't really get any worse than arriving in a foreign destination minus luggage—let me tell you, it's a total nightmare, having experienced this situation several times!

"Oh, how I could do with a cigarette. Is there a smoking area in here, or, have we, the unclean, got to go outside?" grumbles Mel.

"Unfortunately I think you'll have to wait a while," replies the polished English accent of our Production Manager, Hugo Barrington. He is completely charming, clever, witty and oh, so well mannered. Old school, through and through.

Ingrid has had her eye on Hugo for years. She doesn't think that anybody is aware of her attraction, but everyone knows and of course, we all take the piss out of her behind her back, as it would be very rude to do it face to face! Hugo has yet to reciprocate Ingrids' advances and in all fairness, she will certainly have a long, long wait. Hugo no more fancies Ingrid, than he fancies a night in bed with a prickly porcupine, although he would never admit this to her, as he is definitely far too well mannered to offend.

Ingrid hates staging shows and events without Hugo, as she is fully aware of his eye for meticulous detail and technical know-how. If the show is seamless, then it's deemed a success and of course, if it's deemed a success, then Ingrid is praised. Sweet!

Although the conference industry is totally amazing fun, full on and fucked up, there are downsides and one of the downsides is crew consideration. More often than not, we are forgotten. Some clients, not all in fairness, tend to think that they 'buy' the crew for twenty-four hours a day, whilst we are on site and there is no real need for us to eat, or drink, or for that matter, sleep, during this time. At least with Hugo on the job, we know that we are going to be fed and watered. Happy crew, ultimately equals a happy and successful show.

Suddenly, we are all aware of the buzzer and the light flashes on number five conveyor belt, our belt, with our luggage, hopefully. People start scrambling to the yellow markings around the belt to collect their luggage. As usual, there are those passengers who think it's a good idea to push their trolley right up to the line, at the same time bashing luggage hunters' legs and giving insufficient room for people to collect their cases and turn round without inflicting pain. Airport travel is never, ever, fun and I defy anyone to tell me differently.

I can stand it no longer and I slowly turn around to the rather portly, well—dressed gentleman standing at an angle to me, thrusting his trolley into my leg. We should, of course, be thankful for small mercies, for at least it's his trolley, rather than a part of his mid-region anatomy, thrusting into me.

"Could I kindly ask that you remove your trolley from my leg or I will be forced to embed my heel into your foot?" I ask, very politely. He looks at me blankly.

"Io non capisco, e la un problema?" the portly gentlemen responds. I smile sweetly, as I fully understand this mad Italian.

"Sposti per favour il vostro carrello." And as if by magic, his trolley moves and we smile, well, not so much a smile, more of a grimace.

We gather our belongings, delighted that everything has arrived, including tool kits, display graphics and all the equipment added to the job at the last minute, which of course, did not make it onto the truck, before it departed the UK. The excess baggage charge was around nine hundred pounds and that was with a cheeky smile and a smooth talking Hugo Barrington discount!

Belinda, Mel and me, make our way outside to the front of the terminal building where we eagerly light our cigarettes. A few of the other crew join us, fumbling in their bags and pockets for cigarettes and lighters. I suppose the only saving grace is that now about only fifty percent of the conference industry crew smoke since the introduction of the smoking ban! I am of course slowly giving up, but you've got to understand that I have a really stressful job and smoking can help alleviate this stress. After all, I think there are two, well, possibly three, (if you include sex) things that eliminate stress—smoking and drinking, but of course, it would be inappropriate for me to be totally pissed on site, so smoking, in my eyes, is the lesser of two evils. Although, if I was to be perfectly honest, I would like to have lots of sex to alleviate my stress whilst on site, but that is really inappropriate, isn't it?

"Fuck me! Dan, take a butchers at that! Holy Maloney! Now that's what the French Riviera is all about! Cor! Bloody Cor!" exclaims Mickey.

There, in front of us, are two sun-kissed, blonde beauties, pushing their luggage trolleys across the road, up towards the car park. One young girl (yes, she's a girl not a lady, after all ladies don't dress in such a manner do they?) is clad in nothing short of a belt for a skirt and the skimpiest top you could possibly imagine, which of course barely covers her breasts, pert breasts at that. The other girl, is wearing the smallest pair of hot pants I think I've ever seen, together with a tiny halter neck top. Both outfits leave little to the imagination, but as they say, 'if you've got it, flaunt it' and boy oh boy, do these two have it. For a moment, I try to imagine myself in such an outfit and then swiftly dismiss this vision—what the fuck is wrong with me? I've easily got fifteen years on them and yet, I think I'm actually jealous—well, at least I'm jealous and not horny like the boys!

"We've been here less than ten minutes and you two have already started letching. What in God's name is wrong with you both?" giggles Ellie, 'You are totally unreal and of course, totally married, let us not forget that.'

"Oh come on, take a look at those wiggles, they really are somethin' else. They're well fit, bloody perfect, but of course, not as perfect as you beauties," laughs Dan.

"Doesn't do it for me Dan! I'm pleased to say!" replies Ellie.

Mickey and Dan continue drooling and share their admiration with the rest of the crew boys. Of course, they all start wolf whistling. The two scantily clad girls in question, don't bat an eyelid, after all, they are used to such reactions and aside from the fact that the boys are not jumping into high performance cars, or chauffeur driven limousines, they don't warrant a second glance!

"Get a grip Mickey!" I chuckle.

"South of France is just the best for hot, gorgeous, totty," Hugo chips in, much to everyone's surprise.

"Hey Hugo what's the schedule looking like? Do we have much time for R&R on this show, after all it would be such a shame to let opportunities slip away, if you know what I mean?" asks Dan.

"Well we're up against it at a couple of points, especially with the reset for the fashion show—so my apologies in advance for that." Hugo is always so damned polite, 'but thankfully we get this evening off and then we've got a couple of additional free nights later in the schedule, whilst client is off doing their own thing.'

"Fantastic! I know a great little watering hole on the front, overlooking the 'arbour, great place and buzzin', so, perhaps we should give that a go tonight?" shouts Mickey excitedly, 'and it's not too far from our hotel either.'

"Thank God for that!" I exclaim.

I absolutely hate going out with crew when there is a long walk involved—the boys stride out, and when you're wearing four inch heels, invariably you are twenty paces behind, as you can't keep up with them!

So, here we are in the South of France, the land of beauty, fabulous weather and extravagant wealth, but do we have a fleet of cars collecting us? No, of course not, we're not that important! Our coach draws up alongside the kerb, bags and kit are loaded into the side luggage holds and we pile on, all of us being extremely careful not to get landed sitting next to Ms Lorne-Harris.

Belinda, Ellie, Mel and me, clamber to the rear of the coach, quickly followed by Mickey and Dan. Hugo being his ultra efficient self, is waiting until the last bag is loaded and the last crew member is seated before he boards, but sadly for Hugo, the coach is rather full and although there are a couple of spare seats dotted around, Ingrid has saved him the seat next to hers, which she pats, as Hugo boards the coach!

We arrive at our hotel, Le Maritime and we make our way to reception. The foyer is vast, with magnificent chandeliers and highly polished marble floors and it is adorned with the most beautiful flower arrangements. There is one in particular, which is standing on the central large circular table; it must be at least five metres high, full of white lilies and red roses—it's truly magnificent.

Once checked in, we compare room numbers and wait for the concierge to allocate room tags to our luggage and then we all go to the bar. This is a ritual when working with Angel Productions, the bar bit—when attending an overseas event, all the crew get together upon arrival, to toast the success of the event (let's face it and let's be honest here, any excuse for a drink and we're there!). The toast is only ever one drink, but as rituals stand, this is a pretty good one. I order a Bellini, simply because we are in Cannes. Ordinarily, I would be ordering a large gin and slim line tonic, over ice, ideally three cubes and a squeeze of fresh lime juice. Total perfection! I was introduced to gin and tonics by my gorgeous older sister, Amelia, at the tender age of twelve and although I was thoroughly ill for forty-eight hours, after having consumed far too many, the fabulous taste has remained forever!

Amelia is so much more level headed than me now, but if truth be told, I'm not completely sure that her life has turned out the way she wanted it to. Don't get me wrong, she is totally happy, so very happy, but I suppose it is a, oh, I don't know, what would you call it? I suppose it's a normal life she has now. She used to be a complete and utter party girl, whereever there was a party, Amelia was sure to be there. She is completely beautiful and looks so Italian from her dark mysterious eyes to her alluring lovely long legs and head of perfect black curls. Then, out of nowhere, she met Edward. Now, don't get me wrong, Edd (as he is affectionately known within our family) is brilliant, he absolutely adores Amelia and for him to slot into our wayward Italian family so easily, was a welcome relief, as we are not the easiest family in the world to understand and we don't readily accept outsiders either!

Within a matter of six months, Amelia and Edd were engaged and then within a year, they were married and Amelia was pregnant. Gone was my party buddy, she literally transformed her life within a matter of weeks after meeting him. In fairness, I hated Edd when I first met him, as I knew, just knew, that he would take my darling sissy away from me, but now, after some time, I love him too. He is so pompously cool, a brilliant husband, a fantastic son-in-law and above all, a dutiful hands-on dad.

I always imagined that Amelia would party forever and eventually would die, not of old age, but exhaustion. But I was wrong—for now, she is happily married, two children, a perfect husband, but an ordinarily quiet life and quite a lovely job—as a nursery teacher, which absolutely suits her down to the ground, at this point in her life!

So, here I am at Le Maritime, one of the largest and most prestigious hotels in Cannes and it's located right on the sea front. The majority of crew are staying here, whilst the remainder have been allocated rooms at Le Chateau Noir next door.

Room 102 is mine for the entire week; Mel has been allocated room 106, Belinda room 107 and lovely Ellie, room 108. All girls together, just how we like it! Ingrid thankfully, has been allocated a room on the fourth floor, far, far, away from us. I believe the fourth floor provides suites rather than rooms, but Ingrid is the boss so she deserves to feel special, doesn't she?!

Hugo has asked that we all meet at the venue, the Palais du Roscoff, at four pm. The majority of us have worked at this venue before and as far as buildings go, it's fundamentally a pretty faceless, large, purpose built 'convention city' type building. Despite being completely soulless it does have one saving grace, namely it's location—it is fronted right on the sea-front, not that we have much time to bask in the sun or swim in the sea, but during the few breaks that we do get, it is fabulous to go outside into beautiful warm sunshine and look at the glistening waters.

You know what? I cannot wait to get to my bedroom. Irrespective of which class you fly and I've done them all, travelling always makes me feel dirty—not dirty in the sense of inappropriate sexual thoughts and actions, but dirty in the sense of grubby, smelly and unclean. I desperately desire a shower and I need one now!

We have ninety minutes before we are expected at Palais du Roscoff, so time enough to unpack, shower and pick up my messages. I am obsessed with my mobile phone and I am completely lost without it.

My bedroom is perfect. It's light and airy; cream silk drapes adorn the windows, with matching throws on the bed, together with Egyptian cotton sheets. How perfectly civilised. The view out of the window is gorgeous. To my left, is the main promenade, ideal for people watching (As if I have any time for that!) and the glistening Mediterranean sea is to my right. Now, don't get the wrong impression, not all crew accommodation is as luxurious as this! I remember once, working on a show in London where a rat had made its home in my bedroom!

D-I-S-G-U-S-T-I-N-G!

I grab my wash bag, don the 'Oh so flattering' shower cap before doing anything else and jump into the shower and there I remain for ten luxurious minutes, lost in my own world. I always find it amazing how easy it is to simply jump on a plane and arrive in another country within a matter of hours. By and large, everything runs like clockwork on travel days and the format is always the same, irrespective of what time I am travelling. My alarm goes off, followed by my iphone alarm and finally my dressing table alarm. Three alarms might be considered somewhat excessive, but sometimes, when I've only three hours sleep in between shows, these three alarms are the only things that stir me from my slumber. From alarm clocks to bathroom, in strict order: toilet, shower, floss, electric toothbrush, mouth wash, drying of face, applying moisturiser, drying body, applying Prada body lotion, applying make up and back into my bedroom.

I always have two travel cases packed, which include black crew clothing, evening wear, underwear, both functional for day wear and not so functional for evening wear, after all, you just don't know who might turn up! Shoes and lots of them (they are, after all, my ultimate guilty pleasure) and my wash bag and make up bag. Do I really need two fully loaded travel cases? Well, yes, actually I do. One is for short trips, the other for longer trips. As my motto goes, 'She lived, she laughed, but she was always prepared!' Thankfully, key preparation is paramount in my world, after all, I need some form of stability!

I have my routine down to a fine art and calculate that forty minutes is all I need, from first alarm, to key in the ignition.

I always carry two passports; one UK and one Italian. With the amount of travel I do, on a month to month basis, sometimes it's essential to send a passport away in order for visas to be allocated and you can bet your bottom dollar that the day it's sent away, is the day I get a call to do a show overseas! At all times I will have a passport in my handbag, which sometimes comes in very handy, like the time I met a rather gorgeous Parisian gentleman in London, whilst having cocktails at Claridges (I don't do that often, honestly, but it was a friend's birthday so it seemed like a bloody good excuse at the time), only to be whisked away that evening for dinner in Paris... my birthday friend totally disapproved and didn't speak to me for over a year!

Suddenly, I am aware that my skin is tingling. Have I overdone the massage function on this shower? I wrap a thick white towel around myself, then go into the bedroom. Time to unpack, which for me, is always a chore. In a previous life, I am sure that I must have had maids! I loathe packing with a passion and I absolutely despise unpacking, but now I've unpacked, of a fashion, I jump on the bed to check my iphone messages. I have a text message from lovely Amelia, inviting me to supper this evening and two missed calls from Theo, my wayward, totally beautiful gay brother.

I text Amelia back: *Hi darling, thanks for dinner invite. Have you forgotten, I'm in Cannes for a week? I'll call you when I get back. Give the kids a big sloppy kiss from me. Mxx.*

I scroll down my phone list until I come to T for Theo. Theo is my younger brother who works in fashion. Not only does he work in fashion; he is totally obsessed with it. His life revolves around fashion shows in New York, Paris, London and Milan and he designs, non-stop. His mobile rings once and he picks up immediately. We chat relentlessly, each trying to get our words out before being cut short by one another.

Then, he makes me smile, more so than usual.

"Darling sister, guess where I am going to be in two days time? Not that I wish to make you jealous!" he gloats.

"Tell me, my darling spoilt little brother, where in the world are you going to make me so jealous?" I ask, inquisitively.

"Cannes, cara mia, Cannes. KAYSO are showing and as I've been instrumental in designing their new collection, I will be there taking the majority of the credit" he laughs.

Yep, he's gloating.

"Well, 'Golden Balls', perhaps we can meet up for cocktails, or maybe dinner one evening, as I too am in Cannes and I too, will be at the KAYSO event, so sweetheart what have you got to say to that?" I giggle, knowing that secretly he will be delighted.

"Mamma mia!, That is absolutely fantastic! I can't believe it. I'll call when I arrive. Ciao e un grande baci." And with that, he is gone. In hindsight, that was rather a long conversation for Theo—he simply doesn't have time for anything, other than fashion and talking to him is such a waste of time!

I take a look at my watch and time is ticking by, but within minutes, I am dressed in a pair of rather gorgeous Capri pants, skimming my ankles and a matching navy and cream top (an absolute bargain, well, in my mind it was, from a fabulous boutique in Oxford) and a pair of completely over the top sunglasses, and now, I am ready to face the world again.

The time is now three forty pm and I am on my way to Mel's room, room 106. Arriving at her door, I knock loudly, "Hey you old trout are you ready to go?" I shout, knocking a couple more times more for good measure.

I wait a moment or two, then the door opens and to my absolute horror there is a grey haired, very elegant, old lady staring back at me. I step back to check the number on the door, as for sure this lady is not Mel Arethusa!

"Goodness me! I am so frightfully sorry, I thought my colleague was staying in this room." I stammer, completely embarrassed.

At that precise moment, Mel appears out of Room 101 and not Room 106 as I had written down. She is beaming from ear to ear and winks, mischievously.

"That's alright my dear," says the elderly lady in a soft American accent. 'there has been a mix up with rooms and your friend very kindly offered to move. So very sweet of her.'

"Well, I am very sorry to have disturbed you," I say, sheepishly. She closes the door just as.Belinda and Ellie come out of their rooms. Mel at this stage is doubled up, completely helpless, laughing, at my expense!

"You might have fucking phoned me and told me you'd swapped rooms, you dozy mare," I manage to verbalise, through my own laughter.

"And spoil the fun? I don't think so, you old tart!" laughs Mel.

Once we gain a hint of composure, we make our way to the lift, still giggling about my misfortune with the old American lady.

We pile out of the hotel and turn right towards the Palais du Roscoff. It's a bright, sunny afternoon and the promenade is busy. It's lovely to walk along by the sea, with a gentle breeze just about moving the leaves on the abundant palm trees that line the esplanade.

Out of nowhere, Ellie is grabbed around the waist and lifted up into the air, legs akimbo; it can only be Mickey or Dan.

"Gotcha sexy! You're so bloody gorgeous, go on darlin' tell me you'll be mine!" says Dan, as he spins her round.

"Not in your lifetime Dan and certainly not in mine!" chuckles Ellie.

"You're such a spoilsport Ellie, go one, just once" he continues.

"Dan, do you really think for one moment I will succumb to be but another notch on your bedpost? Think about it, you prat. I am young, free and single. You, on the other hand, are married. No competition! But of course, if you weren't married, well, then maybe, just maybe... Hold on a moment, let me just have a little think..." Ellie stands in front of him with her hands on her hips, looking up, towards the sky, and starts to giggle: 'Never in a million years Dan, will you and I do 'jiggy jiggy!"

"Yeah, but babe..." laughs Dan, kissing her cheek tenderly.

"But babe nothing! You can keep trying and I'll just keep on saying 'no!'" replies Ellie.

She loves flirting with Dan and secretly dreams of perhaps, just once, shagging him senseless, the chemistry between the two of them is electrifying, but she knows that it will never to be. After all, she knows that just once would not satisfy and the temptation to continue would be too great and Ellie, being Ellie, would certainly never jeopardise Dan's marriage.

"Like me to carry that 'oldall Belinda?" Mickey is referring to the large black holdall that Belinda is carrying over her shoulder.

"Oh thanks, Mickey," says Belinda, struggling to hand it over to him.

"Fuck me! Dan! Over there.! Quick! Over there! Just look at the arse on that!" says Mickey, rather loudly.

"For God's sake! Don't you ever stop? Please, just for once, behave!" smiles Mel, rolling her eyes.

"You know me Mel; the day I stop admiring these pretty ladies, is the day that I am six foot under!" chuckles Mickey.

"You might just want to go six foot under now in that case then," laughs Belinda.

"What d'ya mean?" asks Mickey.

"That phwoar was aimed at a guy!" says Mel, roaring with laughter.

Mickey stares in disbelief at the rather beautiful bottom in front of him.

We all laugh at his expense. In fairness, the long blonde hair, the long legs, the tight jeans, shoulder bag and boots, do look as though they belong to a female, but when 'the person' turns around, the beard is a definite give-away!

We finally enter the venue and make our way to the main auditorium, where the other crew members have gathered. The only person missing is Ingrid, as per usual. But of course, she likes to make an entrance, for this she is renowned!

Hugo calls out to Mickey and Dan and asks them to join him, as he wants to confirm the access route for the load in of equipment, which is scheduled for tomorrow morning. The 'get-in', as we call it, will begin at five am with local crew being employed to help off load the truck and assist with the rigging of equipment. I love watching rigs. It's amazing how you can start with an empty space and watch it being transformed into something different, something special that you become a part of.

Belinda and Ellie have set up a temporary work station and start to unpack the holdall that Mickey kindly carried in. It's full of printed production schedules—our event bibles. These provide all the details of the event, from crew contact numbers, to meal times, to crew call times for each day, to rehearsal times; in fact, all the information we need to execute the show, from start to finish. Ellie starts to hand them out.

"Got any swag then, my darling?" Dan asks Belinda.

"Oh yes. Just wait until you see what we're wearing! Angel has a new design for their polo shirts!" giggles Belinda.

Belinda proceeds to open a box, which has been delivered earlier in the day, and smirking, she pulls out one of the crew polo shirts. She removes it from its plastic bag and then holds it up, for all to see!

"You have got to be bloody joking! Hey, Mickey take a butchers at this!" shouts Dan, in disbelief.

Everyone is looking round and there it is, in all its glory, the most ridiculous polo shirt we've yet to wear!

Belinda is right. Angel Productions have indeed changed their design and it is quite simply, hideous. The colour is spot on, black, nothing unusual in that, but there is a large embossed purple outline of an angel over the back and then, as if that wasn't bad enough, in the middle, from wing to wing, is the word CREW in blocked purple lettering. The right hand sleeve reads KAYSO Cannes and to add insult to injury, they are made of... wait for it... polyester. Good God! Who, in their right mind wears polyester these days? No one. Absolutely no one, especially in this sweltering heat. The really sad thing is, that we are working with KAYSO, a fashion house and we are wearing polyester! What in the world were Angel thinking of, when they chose this ridiculous, hideous, item of clothing?

Production companies on the whole, aren't too bad where crew 'swag' is concerned. However, there are some companies who expect one shirt to be worn on consecutive days (how utterly filthy) and then there are some, who expect you to wear it again, if you ever work for them on another show, which could be months down the line! They forget, that none of us have wardrobes large enough to accommodate all the crew clothing we are provided with along the way, as we work for countless companies, not just theirs! However, charity shops do benefit, as do car cleans, as they are great for wiping down vehicles—minus buttons of course!

Belinda grabs the shirt back from Dan and puts it back into the box, just as Ingrid walks into the auditorium.

"Hello everyone. Sorry I'm a bit late. Everything is always go, go, go. Clients are just so demanding. Hugo can you take this bag please?" Hugo, dutifully lifts it from Ingrid's shoulder and carries it over to the makeshift workstation.

Mel nudges me and smiles. "It's arrived!" she is of course, referring to Ms Lorne-Harris, aka 'Cruella D'Angel.'

All of us assemble in front of the table where Ingrid has now positioned herself.

"Now then, please gather round, as I'd like to go through the production schedule. Does everyone have a copy? Then we'll begin," smiles Ingrid.

"Fuck! Sounds like we're getting a rendition of bleedin' Jackanory!" whispers Dan to Mickey.

Slowly, we run through the production schedule. Ingrid has spoken to every department, sound, light, video, graphics and last, but not least, it's now my turn—prompting.

"Martha. Speaker rehearsals will be in the same suite as graphics, obviously. I would like your equipment, together with one of the plasma screens to be set-up. Hugo will assist you with this, should you need his services, of course," finishes Ingrid.

"And will the kit be moved again, apart from when it's brought backstage into the main auditorium?" I ask.

"I'll let you know in due course. We'll see what the client wants, shall we Martha?" replies Ingrid, obviously annoyed at me having posed a question. I have to say, I did it for devilment really. I couldn't care less whether we move it, or not, but I do like to be awkward on occasion.

"That sets the level for the show then," whispers Mickey, 'client says 'jump,' and Ingrid coos 'ooh how high, how high!'" we all snigger.

Ingrid continues. "Now, I'd like to mention crew dress code. You will each be given Angel Production polo shirts and you will notice that you have been allocated an extra one. You are required to wear it tomorrow, for the rig day. And I might add, that there is no negotiation on this matter. Please can you collect them from Belinda and Ellie before you leave? We have a new design, which I am sure will appeal to you all."

Dan catches Ellie's eye and winks at her, before tucking his elbows into his sides and waving his hands like wings—Belinda struggles to keep a straight face.

"And so on that note, apart from Hugo, Belinda and Ellie, the rest of you are stood down for the evening. Thank you."

Mel walks up to Belinda to ask for her polo shirts,

"Got any XXL then, birdie?"

"Behave Mel. When have we ever managed to satisfy your desire for a polo shirt that actually fits? I am pleased to inform you, that we have medium, large and extra-large only; if it helps, that means that Ellie and I will be wearing dresses all week. I was advised that we were getting smalls, but it wasn't to be," laughs Belinda.

"You two will be wearing dresses and I, my darling, will be wearing a sausage skin!" chortles Mel.

After Mel, Mickey, Dan and me have collected our wonderful new attire, we make our way out of the Palais du Roscoff and head back towards our hotel. It is now six pm and we have all agreed that an early supper is a good option, as we have a feeling that this is just the start of what is going to be an extremely long and arduous week. Little do I know that this is going to be a week of pure hell, but for all the wrong reasons!

"Let's just dump the polo shirts and meet back here. We can then walk up to the restaurant and stop off for a beer on the way, it'll be cheaper and more fun than staying at the hotel," says Mickey. 'We'll text the others to say where we are, 'opefully they can join us too.'

Having dumped our shirts in our rooms, we meet up in the hotel's reception and go to a small bar, just opposite the Palais du Roscoff. We choose a table outside, as it gives us a good vantage point of the venue's entrance, so we can see the others coming out, after their meeting with Ingrid.

As we sit there, we chuckle and laugh, as we recount our experiences since we last worked together, with Mickey and Dan taking full advantage of the 'people', or in their case, 'totty watching' position, we have found at this pavement bar.

After a couple of drinks, we catch sight of Belinda and Ellie coming out of the venue. Dan shouts and gives the loudest wolf whistle imaginable, catching not only their attention, but that of several passers-by as well.

"'Ello darlins'. We're just off to the restaurant for a bite. Do you want us to wait until you drop yer bags back? And where's Hugo?" asks Dan.

"We'll come as we are. Poor Hugo is still with Ingrid, talking to the venue people, so I said that we would text him, to let him know where we are. They'll be ages yet. You know what Ingrid's like. Oh, by the way, Ellie and I will be giving those rather gorgeous, long legged models, (yes we've seen their agency cards), a heads up on you both, so your cover will be blown!" giggles Belinda, looking directly at Mickey and Dan.

"Out to spoil our fun Ellie? Or is it coz you're jealous that my attentions will be aimed at the leggies? Ha, I knew it, you likes me, don't ya?" chuckles Dan.

Having paid the bill, we head off to the restaurant for dinner, which thankfully is quite literally just around the corner, as we are far too tired for long walks across Cannes this evening.

Dinner is delicious and it's now ten pm, but there's still no sign of Hugo. I call his mobile phone, but it's switched off, which can only mean one thing; he's still stuck with Ingrid.

We leave the restaurant together and stroll back towards the hotel.

There's a Jaguar XK8 parked on the corner of one of the the streets, with a particularly stunning looking, well dressed female standing next to it. Mickey and Dan can hardly contain themselves.

"Don't bother boys—you won't stand a chance, she's after money, not a fun time!" laughs Belinda.

The XK8 lady smiles at us, as we walk by.

"Very expensive and out of your league boys," chuckles Mel.

"Leave it out, Mel. Didn't you see the way she was looking at me? She wants some, I can always tell!" Mickey laughs, with a wry smile.

We enter the hotel foyer and rather sadly, there is still no sign of Hugo.

"Night then girls. I'll see you all in the morning and hopefully with a big smile on me face. Mickey and I are going to the bar for a nightcap. You can join us, if you like," smiles Dan.

We look at each another but decide that an early night is a far better idea, especially as the schedule is so full-on for the rest of the week.

"Breakfast is at the venue by the way. So don't hang around the hotel in the morning," announces Belinda, as everyone wanders out of main reception and off to their respective rooms or bar stools, in the case of Mickey and Dan!

Chapter Three

"Okay. Okay. For fucks sake.! I'm awake!" I shout out loud. I fumble for the remote control, which of course, has fallen between the bedside table and bed and finally switch off the TV alarm—Sweet Jesus! How I hate, absolutely hate, staying in hotels.

I know that I now have ten minutes before the next alarm goes off on my mobile phone, pure bliss. I have slept really well and in fact, I've had a full eight hours, which I badly needed.

I lie in bed listening to MTV, contemplating the days' activities. I have a feeling this is going to be a very long week. Never mind, after all I'm in Cannes. I love Cannes, almost as much as I love Monaco. Weather, men, money, designer shops, men, oops did I already say that? I love men full stop. No matter where in the world I am, men and shoes are my favourite and guilty pleasures...

My second alarm starts to beep. Fuck! Now it's definitely time to get up. I stretch, I wriggle about and then I step out of bed, hunting for my slippers. I know, I sound like a little old lady, but let me assure you, I am definitely not one of those—yet. I do, however, have an absolute aversion to walking on hotel bedroom floors; floors that have been trodden on by hundreds of others. I would rather die, than walk bare foot on a hotel bedroom carpet!

After I locate my slippers, I walk towards the bathroom—same ritual every morning: toilet, shower, floss, electric toothbrush, mouth wash, drying of face, applying moisturiser, drying body, applying Prada body lotion, applying make up and back into the bedroom.

Now occasionally the routine may change, but this is only when I have to do something with my wild hair—it takes an age to dry, so I tend to wash it during the evening and rarely in the morning, after all, who has two hours to sit under a hairdryer? Not me, that's for sure!

And another thing, I always, but always take a shower rather than a bath when I am staying in a hotel. Why? I hear you ask. The answer is simple. The mere thought of lying in a bath that has been used by a stranger, absolutely freaks me out.

My iphone is ringing—it's Mel.

"Morning Slapper! You awake?" she asks.

"Morning Old Trout! Of course, I'm bloody awake. Give me half an hour and I'll meet you in reception!" I chuckle.

I check my emails on my iPhone and then quickly get dressed in crew blacks—black trousers and of course, my wonderful Angel Productions polo shirt! Lordy! Can you believe that I am in Cannes, where beauty and glamour prevail and I am dressed in such appalling daywear? I should be dressed in Prada or Gucci and certainly not in fucking polyester!

I grab my laptop bag, briefcase and Prada handbag (I love handbags) and head off to meet Mel in reception.

"So, did you have a good night's sleep?" I ask Mel, as I approach her.

"Honey, I slept for England. You?" she responds looking very awake.

"Like a log. I feel great this morning. Doubt I'll be saying that at the end of today though!" I smile.

"Belinda and Ellie are already at the venue. Their call time was seven o'clock, so it's me and thee, shall we... ?" asks Mel, as she moves towards the revolving doors.

We arrive at the venue and make our way to the auditorium, where the crew are rigging.

"Morning you two," shouts Mickey 'Breakfast is in the room on the opposite side of the foyer. Not a bad 'un either!' he carries on wheeling a flight case towards his newly erected workstation.

We enter the Fleur Suite which has been designated for crew catering. There are a few technicians chomping their way through croissants, cheese, ham and a whole host of other goodies. The thing I love most about France, aside from handbags and men, is the wonderful morning coffee, served with hot milk. How civilised. Perfect, in fact!

As we help ourselves to the breakfast buffet, Ingrid walks in.

"Not too long Mel please, I need to go through the show book, as we have changes already," she barks.

"No problem Ingrid. Oh and good morning," replies Mel sweetly, with just a tiny hint of sarcasm in her voice. Mel looks at me, rolling her eyes; she does the rolling of the eyes so brilliantly. She absolutely hates Ingrid, God help us; it will be a miracle if she doesn't end up arguing with her during this show. An absolute bloody miracle!

We sit down and start to tuck in to our breakfast and it's not long before Hugo joins us at the table.

"Well it's all going swimmingly. Some of the video kit hasn't been put on the truck and one of the crew has missed his flight from Gatwick. Fuckwit! Anyway, how are you both? Sorry I missed supper last night, but as you know, I was landed with Ingrid and we didn't finish until late, but thanks for the message Martha," he smiles, whilst drinking his coffee.

Hugo tells me that my equipment is in the auditorium and he'll get it moved by one of the local crew to the rehearsal suite, together with the plasma screen for graphics. As he's telling us, our graphics operator, Jerome walks in.

"Good morning all. Fantastic venue isn't it?" he remarks.

"If you like that sort of thing," replies Mel, with a big grin across her beaming face.

"Right, best get on and go and see the 'Old Bag.' I'll see you later." And with that, Mel grabs her belongings and walks off with a wiggle in her step.

Hugo's walkie-talkie begins to shriek:.

"Eric to Hugo. Over. Hugo, are you taking a leisurely breakfast? If so, we need you in the auditorium. And if not, we still need you in the auditorium—we've got a problem. Over" Something must be going down...

"Hugo to Eric. I'm in catering and just for the record, I've finished my coffee, so I'm on my way. Over," he smiles, throwing me a kiss as he leaves to attend to whatever it is Eric needs him for.

Jerome and I carry on chatting. I haven't seen him for quite a long time. He is such a good laugh. He has long hair and wears a pony tail, which I really don't like on men, but it suits him. Occasionally, he wears a bandana, much to the disgust of Ingrid. Without fail, Ingrid repeats the same comment every time he wears it:

"Now Jerome, we're not going to wear that on show day are we?"

He is great at his job and his graphics always look amazing and clients really like his easy-going manner, so he can get away with pretty much anything he wants to. Within reason of course!

"Have you seen how many speakers there are Martha?" he asks.

"Go on..." I mutter, hoping that he isn't going to say twenty plus.

"Well, not that many, considering I've been programming for weeks. There's only four. But there's one guy who has been a complete pain in the arse, goes by the name of Danny Mendosa. Watch out for him, I think he is quite likely to be the biggest shit on God's earth for you and me. I am currently on draft twelve of his graphics and no doubt, when he arrives, there will be more changes" says Jerome.

"I haven't seen a thing yet. I expect Ingrid will give me all the scripts once we've set up," I respond, with fingers crossed.

Suddenly, we hear an almighty crash coming from the auditorium.

"What the fuck was that?" shouts one of the crew still chewing on a croissant.

We all get up and run towards the auditorium. Hugo is standing in the hall, together with Dan and some local crew.

They have been erecting racking, on which big projectors sit and whilst they were lifting one of the projectors, unfortunately one of the local crew lost his grip and it went crashing to the floor.

"Well, that's the f'ing back up gone then," says Dan, turning to Mickey who has now joined them.

"Fucking Muppet!" exclaims Mickey

"I'm looking forward to explaining this one to Ingrid!" says Hugo, wryly.

"Forget Ingrid. It's Tom Kremner I'd be worried about!' says Dan.

Belinda has rushed over, not to see what all the fuss is about, but to check that we are on our way to the rehearsal suite, as Ingrid has been asking, well shrieking, for us. Thankfully, Mel is already upstairs with her. And fortunately for the crew, the rehearsal suite is up on the second floor, so Ingrid isn't in the vicinity of the projector incident—she will undoubtedly blow a gasket. Can't wait for that one!

"How's it going Belinda?" asks Jerome, giving her kiss on each cheek.

"Don't ask. 'She, who must be obeyed,' is in overdrive at the moment, so I wouldn't tell her about the projector; let Hugo handle it. He does it so eloquently," she laughs.

We arrive at the rehearsal suite with Ingrid huffing and puffing about our lateness. Jerome and I quickly move two tables into position and start to rig our equipment.

"Oh, for goodness sake, I haven't said how I want the room set out yet!" barks Ingrid.

"I want you there, Martha and you there, Jerome and the plasma screen there and the prompting glass there!" she shouts.

Fuck me! This woman is pernicious. There is about half a metre difference to where we had placed the tables originally. Belinda wasn't joking when she said Ingrid was in overdrive. We move the tables as instructed and carry on rigging.

"Ellie is collating the scripts that have been sent over. Oh, and before I forget Jerome, Danny Mendosa has emailed some further powerpoint changes. Some of the others have changes too, I understand," she bellows. I wonder if she was dropped at birth or brought up in the wild by a pack of wolves. Ingrid Lorne-Harris is a real piece of work—her manners and people skills are utterly disgraceful!

Jerome shoots me a look, as if to say 'told you so', but at least we have a full morning to get the presentations into some sort of order, prior to the clients arrival.

"And one further thing, I fully appreciate that this is the rehearsal suite, but I'd like all the cables tidy and taped down, please."

Reverting back to Mel, Ingrid continues:

"OK Mel I think we're there. Have you any questions?" But before Mel can answer, she carries on: "Fine. Good. Well, I'm off to the auditorium," and with that remark, she gathers her papers and leaves the rehearsal suite.

Mel looks at Jerome and me and starts to laugh in disbelief.

"Well she doesn't bloody change. She's such a control freak!" sniggers Mel.

"Wait until she gets downstairs, she'll go completely mental!" laughs Jerome.

"Why, what's happened?" asks Mel, inquisitively.

"One of the local crew lost his grip on the back-up projector and now it is no more!" I say, putting my hand to my mouth.

"Fucking hell! Run for your lives!" laughs Mel.

Ellie arrives with memory sticks containing scripts and graphics.

"Here's what the client has sent over so far. However, it will all change, as we know. I've got some coffee and tea being sent up, together with some water. I think you're in for a long old day." And with that, she leaves, picking up Ingrid's stopwatch that was inadvertently left behind, during her hissy fit.

The rehearsal suite is a vast room with panoramic windows to two sides. To the right, is the marina with moorings for large luxurious, 'I want one of those,' yachts. There are lots of restaurants and brassieres scattered around too. And to the left, is the promenade with its palm trees, boutiques, and pavement cafes. The Cote D'Azur really is, heaven on earth in my book.

Time passes quickly and soon enough it's lunchtime so Jerome and I leave our computers and go back down to the Fleur Suite, where lunch is being served.

Mickey, Dan and Hugo are already in there, discussing the unfortunate circumstances surrounding the project incident.

"Well, hopefully that's today's only bit of excitement and mishap," says Hugo, 'I've got another projector on its way, together with the balance of kit that's been missed off the job.:

"Cor Jesus mate," laughs Mickey "I wouldn't want t'be in the persons' shoes who fucked up there! Missing kit? Tom will have their balls served up on a plastic plate, forget the silver!"

"Probably make the poor bastard pay the cost for getting it here too," laughs Dan.

Both Mickey and Dan served their apprenticeships at Kremner AV so they are well versed in the ways of Tom Kremner and they also know that he runs a really tight ship.

"Good job I hired it in from Tom, he's so efficient, he simply deals with shit when it happens. He did say that he might try to pop over during the week, just to check that everything is running ok," continues Hugo.

Belinda joins Jerome and myself at the table, swiftly followed by Mel and Ellie. We are enjoying our lunch when Ellie's walkie talkie lets out a squawk.

"Ingrid to Ellie. Over."

"Yes Ingrid. Over."

"Where are you Ellie? I've got problems with the printer—I need it sorted NOW. Over"

"On my way Ingrid. Over"

Ellie puts down her walkie-talkie and starts to mimic Ingrid, perfectly "*I need it sorted NOW.*"

The crew are in fits of laughter and even more so, when Ingrid sticks her head round the corner. Ellie turns a subtle shade of beetroot red, but fortunately Ingrid has neither seen, nor heard her mimics!

Mel is laughing so much she is choking at the same time. Hugo is trying desperately to suppress a laugh, as Ingrid demands to be brought up to date with the projector and missing equipment situation. Mickey and Dan make a swift exit.

Jerome, Mel and me, having finished our lunch, head back to the rehearsal suite. We enter the glass lift and press the button marked second floor. The lift starts to ascend. We chatter amongst ourselves and then notice that the lift hasn't stopped at the second floor—we simply carry on to the fourth floor, but the doors do not open when we arrive at the fourth floor either. Of course, we think nothing of this and press the button marked second floor again. This time, we go directly to the ground floor and once again the lift doors don't open. Sweet Jesus! What the fuck is going on? This lift has taken on a life of its own!

Hugo and Ingrid are standing in the foyer talking. Ingrid has her back to the lift. Mel is frantically waving at Hugo; as once again the lift ascends, but it is definitely not stopping on the second floor. Well, you can just imagine can't you? The giggles are starting. The lift once again ascends to the fourth floor. Doors firmly shut!

There are people waiting to take the lift on the third floor, but having pressed the second floor button again, we simply sail right pass them on our way back down to the ground floor. Mel is now completely uncontrollable, she is laughing so much, that she's either going to burst or pee herself. Alas, I think it's the latter, as she has strategically places a hand between her legs. Jerome is banging furiously on the lift walls—he's now desperate to get out. We arrive at the ground floor once again and still the doors do not open. Not surprisingly, the lift is going up again. I am mouthing to Hugo who is looking on in sheer amazement at our helpless antics, "Help us, the lift won't open, help." These antics are definitely not our doing. Mel is now firmly on the floor, I am giggling so much that my mascara is starting to run down my face and Jerome eventually grabs Mel's walkie-talkie.

"Jerome to Hugo. Over."

"Yes Jerome. You can probably tell that I'm watching in disbelief. Over."

"Hugo, we're stuck in this bloody thing. It doesn't seem to want to stop; I'm neither kidding, nor joking. Can you please do something? Over" laughs Jerome.

Once again we arrive at the ground floor. Now Ingrid is looking at us, in disbelief, her arm is moving furiously, beckoning us out of the lift. Her face is a picture, a picture of total, pernicious annoyance.

Of course, we are all laughing hysterically.

"Let's all wave," I suggest.

As we ascend again, we wave, but Ingrid, of course, is not waving back!

"Hugo to Jerome. Over. I've spoken with the venue and the maintenance people are on their way. Hang tight. Over"

"Hanging on boy, definitely hanging on. We'll see you soon. Over," responds Jerome, through his hysterics.

Eventually, we come to a stop on the first floor where the maintenance man and Hugo are waiting for us. The doors open and I have to say, I am absolutely delighted to get out, terra firma has never felt so good!

"Nice of you to join us," comes that dreaded shrill voice, as Ingrid climbs the stairs. I think that was her attempt at humour.

"Now perhaps we can resume work rather than messing about, after all, that's clearly not what we're paid for, is it?"

"Bitch," mutters Jerome, underneath his breath.

"Ingrid, yes we're fine thanks and we're safe. I'll get straight to it, after I've been to the gents if that's okay?" smiles Mel.

Ingrid looks a little sheepish and embarrassed, but still doesn't ask after our well-being. But did we expect her to? No, of course we bloody didn't!

Word has soon got around about our lift plight and we are delighted that our experience has given the crew a laugh. A laugh at our expense!

Ellie comes into the rehearsal suite with another memory stick, with yet more script and graphic changes.

"You don't need to ask who these are from and worse still, he's arrived in Cannes and is at the hotel as I speak. Just an hour to go and they'll be here. They are driving Belinda nuts already. Mary-Jo Capelli is the client link and her assistant is Rochelle Schneider, both New Yorkers by the sounds of it. And Belinda and I reckon Mary-Jo is the perfect match for Ingrid. So let's hope when there are fireworks, it will be a real 'handbags at dawn'!" giggles Ellie.

Another hour passes and scripts and amends are all sorted and client should be arriving very soon. Mel is looking out of the window and remarks on how she's going to place a bet that the group of people walking down the promenade are from KAYSO. I walk over to join her quickly followed by Jerome.

"That's got to be Danny Mendosa—ten Euros says it is. Just look what he's wearing for Christ sake!" remarks Jerome.

The man in question is rotund to say the least. He is wearing an Hawaiian shirt in yellow and orange together with matching Bermuda shorts and he is puffing on a cigar, a large one. Boy he is one ugly dude.

"I could do with a cigarette before we start this marathon session. Does anyone wish to join me?" I ask.

"Too right, c'mon quick before they get up here," gushes Mel.

We race down the stairs, as quickly as we can and go out through the staff entrance at the rear of the building.

The weather is fantastic; sunny, very warm and beautifully bright. We finish our cigarettes in a hurry and race back up the stairs, arriving just ahead of Ingrid and the client.

"Hello team. I'd like to introduce you to Mr Howard Johnson III, Mr Danny Mendosa, Ms Mary-Jo Capelli and Miss Rochelle Schneider," smiles Ingrid, accompanied by her sickly coquettish girlie grin.

Jerome has won the bet.

Chapter Four

After the client introductions and general small talk, Ingrid escorts them downstairs to see how the auditorium is shaping up. Now that the client team is out of sight, we take another quick break. Oh, come off it now—are you really rolling your eyes? Yes, I know that it appears that we don't do a lot, other than eat, talk and smoke cigarettes, but let me tell you, when the work starts, then our down time no longer exists.

The three of us are enjoying our coffee in the Fleur Suite, when Ellie comes rushing in.

"Here you go guys, sorry it's so late, but we were waiting for KAYSO to give us the details— speaker rehearsal running order. Shouldn't be too late finishing tonight, but it looks like hell for the rest of the week. Sorry!"

Mel, Jerome and I scan through the rehearsal schedule. We have Howard Johnson III and Danny Mendosa this afternoon, with the remainder of the speakers tomorrow, starting at eight o'clock in the morning. Life is never easy—back to work we go, via the stairs of course, as the lift is totally out of bounds!

We're ready to start our afternoon of torture. Mel, with her stopwatch for timings and Jerome and myself are cued up with Howard's presentation. We just need Ingrid. Well, that's a matter of opinion. Of course we don't need Ingrid, but Ingrid thinks that we need her—two very differing opinions!

"Shouldn't be too bad," remarks Mel.

"Don't hold your breath Mel. We've got Mr 'Tango' Mendosa after Howard."

Jerome is making reference to Danny Mendosa's dress sense and fake tan, and 'Tango' is such an apt nick-name for now, at least. I am sure it will get worse!

Howard Johnson III, Senior Vice President of KAYSO Inc. one of the world's largest clothing manufacturers and retailers, with branches in the USA, Australia, Europe and South East Asia. At a guess he is about forty-five years old. He's tall, ruggedly handsome and immaculately dressed. He's wearing chinos, beautiful leather shoes and a crisp white shirt and sporting his designer sunglasses on his head. Well, so here's the question. Would I, or wouldn't I? My guess is 'yes,' I would, but I don't make it a rule, or habit, of sleeping with clients, unless of course they are tall, ruggedly handsome and immaculately dressed!

"Okay guys. Where do we start?" Howard is pouring himself a glass of water.

"I think it would be a good idea, if you just check through your graphics first, with Jerome and then, over to Martha for script. If you have any changes to your script immediately though, perhaps Martha could be getting on with them, whilst you are with Jerome? And then afterwards, we'll go for a run through" says Mel, in her 'oh-so-professional' manner.

"Yes M'am." Howard's eyes are sparkling. I can hardly contain myself! I glance over at Mel and she knows exactly what I'm thinking. Thankfully, there are some perks to this job of mine! And a handsome client is one of them.

Ingrid enters the room, full of apologies and fretting about what is going on, in the main auditorium.

"I am so very sorry to keep you waiting Howard. I was just sorting out the auditorium," she coos.

"No problem Ingrid. But is there a problem downstairs?" asks Howard.

"Oh, we don't do problems Howard, we view them as challenges, but it is all sorted out now," Ingrid responds, smiling sweetly.

Sweet Jesus! How I hate this woman: absolutely hate her with a passion, '*oh we don't do problems*', what a load of baloney; she doesn't do problems, because it's down to everyone else to sort them out for her! Stupid cow!

"Well, if you need to be elsewhere, it's not a problem for me. I am more than happy to run through my presentation with these guys; they seem to know what they are doing." replies Howard.

Ingrid blushes, "Oh, no Howard, I'm sure they can cope downstairs without me, for a while."

"I'm sure they can!" mutters Howard, and winks at me. This man already has the measure of Ms Lorne-Harris. Perfect. I think Howard and I are going to be friends. Fingers crossed!

Howard hands me a copy of his script, with a few amendments made in red ink. Well, at least his writing is legible, which is something I have to say, is sorely lacking these days; and as for grammar, well, I don't think that they teach it in schools now. It never ceases to amaze me, how many people holding really senior positions within large corporations and earning serious amounts of money cannot actually spell and have the grammatical aptitude of a two year old. This job is a real eye opener.

I complete the changes and Jerome has made a few alterations to graphics that are supporting each of Howard's presentations. He has three slots so far. The opening speech of the conference, the Senior Vice President's overview and a closing speech, and we know that the closing speech is only a skeleton draft at this stage, as he wants to see how the conference pans out, before completing the final copy.

We are now ready to rehearse. Howard stands at the lectern and I reset the lectern glass. Originally, I had them set for my height and with Howard being about a foot taller, he can't see a thing.

I explain that we have motorised prompting poles for the show and these static ones are just for rehearsal purposes. We use motorised poles to compensate for the varying heights of presenters. So, in theory at least, we programme the poles to adjust to the height of a speaker. I say in theory, because sometimes they jam and quite frankly, they are a complete pain in the arse, my arse! It's just another piece of technology that's all well and good, until it goes wrong.

We are half way through Howard's opening speech, when there is a knock at the door and Danny Mendosa appears.

"Excuse me Howard. I've just taken a call from Clarke Clarkeson in Detroit and there's a problem, he's asked to speak with you personally," says Mendosa.

Mel stops her stopwatch and Ingrid smiles weakly. It is immediately noticeable that Howard is irritated by this interruption.

"Tell him I'll call him back, when I'm finished," replies Howard, authoritatively.

"Sure thing, but..." starts Danny.

"I said, when I'm finished Danny," Howard is visibly annoyed by Mendosa's persistence.

Danny, aware of having annoyed Howard, draws back and closes the door.

We carry on rehearsing the opening speech. Howard is a natural presenter. He uses prompt as it should be used. Not sticking to each word verbatim, but throwing in the odd ad lib and paraphrasing sentences too. Speakers like this, are true professionals and a dream to work with.

After rehearsing, we take a break, while Howard goes off to find Danny and to make the phone call that seems so vitally urgent.

"This guy is great—knows exactly what he wants. Just hope the rest are the same!" says Jerome.

"Fat chance of that!" I respond, rather cynically.

Howard returns and rehearses his second script. We make the necessary amendments and then start to discuss his closing address, which he agrees will be pointless rehearsing at this stage, as he's not sure what he's going to be saying and depending on the outcome of the week, he may deliver his speech, 'off the cuff.'

Ingrid asks Mel to check the rehearsal time for Howard for tomorrow. It has been scheduled for four pm.

"So, you've got Danny next. I am going back to the hotel, as I sure am tired. Hope he doesn't give you too much of a hard a time!" says Howard smiling, showing off those real white American sparkling teeth. 'Thank you for all your help and hard work. Will you all be in the bar later?'

"You bet!" beams Mel.

"Well, it depends on what time we finish here Howard," says Ingrid, rather sourly.

"A drink would do you good you know, Ingrid," says Howard, and again winks at me. He definitely has Ingrid summed up perfectly! And with that closing comment he leaves.

"One down, one to go, for today at least," sighs Mel.

"Yeah, but what a ONE!" chuckles Jerome.

"Sweetheart, are you secretly gay, or what? Do you have the hots for the lovely Howard? Because you're going to have to join the queue and something tells me, you are definitely going to be disappointed, especially when he opts for me first!" laughs Mel.

I giggle like a child, for Jerome is no more gay than I'm a virgin, although it has been a few weeks now since male contact. Perhaps this is why I am feeling so very horny, especially around the likes of Mr Howard Johnson III!

Now comes Danny Mendosa; late thirties with a vast, unattractive waistline. His position within the KAYSO group is Group Operations Director and it is so very obvious that he is in awe of Howard and wants to impress at every opportunity, by making his presence felt. Danny is typically the type of character crew really dislike. Rude, aggressive, self-centred and one who certainly doesn't care about who he has to tread on, to get what he wants. The three of us don't like him and we've only just met him!

Danny walks into the rehearsal suite as if he owns it.

"Is there any coffee in this place?" he asks.

Mel dutifully walks over to the table and pours a cup of coffee for him.

"How do you take it Danny?" she asks.

"Black," he replies.

Once again, manners seem to be a thing of the past, such a rarity these days. I always maintain manners cost absolutely nothing, but they sure go a long way, especially with crew. If we are treated properly and with respect, then we will give 150%, but treat us badly and, well, I am not at liberty to say. Somehow though, I have the distinct feeling that this man is going to give us a very, bumpy ride.

Mel is quite clearly pissed with him. Is that why she has poured his coffee into a cup that has already been used by someone else? Oops, he's definitely started off on the wrong foot with her.

"Okay guys, let's get going. Paula I've got some amends to my script."

I look around, but I assume he's talking to me.

"Hi Danny, good to meet you and just to let you know, my name is not Paula, it's Martha. Now then, your amends please, if I may?"

"Well, Martha these are for you then." He doesn't even look at me, as he hands over his amended script. There are crossings out and additions all over the place; it looks as though a spider has crawled across the pages, having dipped its legs in black ink.

Fuck! Didn't we just know that this toss-pot was going to be a complete pain? There is always one. 'What a prize wanker!' I am of course smiling sweetly, as this thought enters my mind.

He sits down, next to Jerome. Mel glares at me and then pulls a funny face. I smile and giggle. Danny looks up, irritated. I carry on giggling. After all, I am doing no harm, other than perhaps annoying this horrible, vile, little man.

Oh Lordy! Oh no! No! He's now started to sweat, rather profusely. How attractive this man is!

I text Mel, even though she is within ten feet of me: *Don't fancy your fat fuck much! X.*

I carry on making the changes to the script, as Mel's phone beeps with my text and just at that very moment, in walks Ingrid and scurries straight over to Mel.

"Mobiles off Mel, or at least switched to silent. You should know better, you're not a novice are you?" Ingrid treats us like children, how endearing. Mel dutifully switches her phone to silent, but not without reading my message first and giving me the finger!

"So, is everything OK Danny?" enquires Ingrid.

Mel kindly responds to my text message with:

I wonder what he's like in bed, my guess is pretty hot, after all he's sexy!

My iphone is silent, but I see the message and giggle. Danny looks over, inquisitively and smirks. I smile. Ingrid too is glancing over and I smile sweetly at her, as well. It's amazing how quickly the human body is programmed to respond to text messages and my return message simply reads:

Do you think his penis is also orange?

Ingrid continues to fuss over Danny, making sure he has more coffee and water and that he is happy with everything. Now, I wonder if he was to say to Ingrid 'drop to your knees honey and suck it like a baby' whether indeed she would. My guess is no, but well, who knows?

I decide to text Theo, whilst waiting for Danny to start, to ask if he knows of the infamous Mr Howard Johnson III and his stupid side kick Danny. Theo simply responds with:

Cara mia, call me later, there is much gossip x. I, for one, cannot wait.

An hour or so ticks by and Jerome eventually finishes the changes to Danny's presentation and I have completed his script changes. We are now ready to rehearse. Finally. Bloody hell,! This industry drives me fucking mental sometimes and I am oh, so desperate for a cigarette. Danny, the short arse, is standing at the lectern and as I manoeuvre around my table and over to the prompting glass, he takes it upon himself to make the necessary adjustments.

I'm shouting now, as I rush over. "Excuse me I'd prefer..." I start to say, but hey, too fucking late, the sound of cracking glass can be heard in the room.

What an arsehole. At the lectern, I explain to Dickhead Mendosa that there is a reason why I prefer to make the adjustments. I am used to the torque of the pole head, which quite clearly, he is not. I go outside to get a replacement glass from one of the flight cases, which have been stacked in a room adjacent to the rehearsal suite. He does not say a single word, no apology, nothing, but simply shrugs his shoulders and starts looking at his wrist watch—the bloody cheek of this man! Before the week is out, I am sure we will, without doubt, fight. I hate him. I really do hate him.

I replace the glass and adjust the poles to suit this stocky, little, short arse in front of me. I smile. Right, let's get on with this please.

"The glasses are too far apart Paula," Danny growls.

"I'll bring them in. No problem" I respond, but I am secretly seething, I have welts in my tongue—my way of thinking—if I bite my tongue hard enough, the bad words will not come bouncing out of my mouth, but they do create welts!

"Danny, please can you tell me when you are happy with them?" I say, with a smile.

Well, he has them so close together they look bloody ridiculous. But, whatever myself, or Mel suggests, falls on deaf ears, even Ingrid has a go at telling him, but he simply shoos her away. I leave them set, as per his instructions.

Danny starts to present. We are about three minutes into his script, when he stops.

"You're going too fast Paula, I can't keep up," he shouts.

My patience is now beginning to wane, with this fucking twit.

"I follow you Mr Medusa—at your pace—you're in charge."

Well, at least that is what I want him to think. He clearly does not appreciate me telling him this, as he has a scowl on his pug-ugly face.

"The name is not Medusa, it is Mendosa. And it's OK to call me Danny."

He speaks very slowly—ah, now he thinks he has the measure of me, he obviously thinks I am a little slow!

"I apologise. But if I could just point out, my name is Martha, M A R T H A, as I previously mentioned and I have to say I do mind being called Paula. I had an aunt called Paula and she really was a frightful woman, so the less we mention that name the better, as far as I'm concerned," I say, with a smile, trying to make light of this awful situation.

Mel clearly senses that I am on fire and about to explode, so rightly interjects.

"Right then ladies and gents, can we re-set please and go from the top?" she says, a little too loudly and anxiously.

Danny continues to drone through the script and reads it word for word. He is definitely not a natural presenter and I am sure as hell, that he is not a natural lover, either!

After he finishes, he asks Mel for script timing. She explains that he is currently running at thirty one minutes, but his slot allocation is only twenty minutes, therefore we should look to make amendments and lose some time, wherever possible.

Then, the prat mutters the immortal words, which at this moment in time, I cannot bear to hear; "I'll do it again and see what I can cut," he's smiling. I want to cry and slit my wrists.

This is going to take forever. Darling Danny, no scrub that, Dickbrain Danny, no, not that either. Fuckwit Mendosa, that's far better, has clearly not rehearsed his script before coming on site, he lacks authority and he lacks presence, all in all, he is a total fucking disaster.

He has clearly concentrated on his PowerPoint graphics—well, at least the screen will look good, if nothing else, because let's face it, he certainly won't look good...

We run through his script again and he makes amendments as we run through. It is so painfully slow. But thankfully, after the run through is complete, he decides to delete around fifteen graphics from his presentation. Praise the Lord! That will save us at least seven minutes of his sad little voice, echoing around the room.

It's now seven o'clock in the evening and we still haven't had a proper rehearsal of Danny's newly amended script. Version twenty eight, I believe! There's a knock at the door and Mary-Jo Capelli enters the room.

"Hey, hi guys. So, how's it going? Danny, you are scheduled to be meeting with Howard and Dwight. You haven't forgotten have you? I've reserved a table in the hotel's restaurant for eight o'clock," she smiles.

"Yep, I've forgotten for sure," he looks irritated.

"Okay, I'll have to finish tomorrow. I'll be here at nine in the morning," he says.

Mel quickly checks through the rehearsal schedule, for the following day.

"Excuse me Danny, your allocated time is two o'clock tomorrow afternoon, for rehearsals and I'm afraid we have other presenters coming to rehearse their presentations, from eight o'clock. This rehearsal schedule, is really tight," advises Mel.

"Give me a copy of the schedule, I'll decide who rehearses when," he growls.

Mel walks off to the production office to take a copy of the schedule, for him.

When she re-enters the room, he simply takes it from her, without a word of thanks and leaves, swiftly followed by Mary-Jo, who smiles and waves on her way out.

"What a waste of space that man is!" I say, shaking my head slowly, from side to side.

"I told you he was going to be trouble. There's always one and he is it for this show. Let's just hope that the others aren't in the same category!" adds Jerome.

We are all completely drained. We have only had two speakers this afternoon—one being a true professional, with the other being a complete and utter, self-centred, fuckwit. Time with Mendosa this afternoon, has felt like an eternity. From the years of experience we have between us, we know that this does not bode well, for the rest of the week.

We go downstairs, to take a cigarette break and have a quick drink. As we are making our way to the ground floor, (still no lift for us, after the escapades of our previous lift experience), Belinda comes running up the other way.

"Be aware Ingrid's on the war path! Knickers well and truly knotted! The models have arrived and have been told that they are sharing just one dressing room and it's handbags at dawn, across there! It's complete chaos! I've just come back for my file. The agency swear they weren't told about these arrangements, but I have it in writing, at least I think I have, so my arse is covered! See you later." And with that, she bolts back, into the fray.

Mel turns to me, "I'd hate to do Ellie and Belinda's job. I know they're freelancers, but my God, they earn their money. But it's not just that, they have to work at the beck and call of Ingrid, pre show, during the show and post show. Shit! How do they do it?"

"Both of them are really efficient. Belinda is Producer material, but she says she's happy being a really good Production Assistant. Mind you, Ingrid knows that both of them will scoop up any crap that she creates! She's not stupid in that respect!" I remark.

We walk outside to have our cigarettes and Hugo is there with Mickey. Hugo is happy that the rig is going well now and all things being equal, they should be able to break for dinner by eight o'clock, as per the schedule.

"Belinda to Hugo. Over." comes over the walkie-talkie.

"Hello Belinda. Over." replies Hugo.

"Hugo I'm sorry, but Ingrid has mislaid her walkie-talkie and wants to have a meeting with you and the client, about the turnaround for the catwalk scenario, in ten minutes, in the auditorium. Are you free please? Over."

"See you in ten then. Over." Hugo continues, turning to Mickey. "No rest for the wicked." he smiles.

We head off back indoors and thankfully catering is open and ready to serve crew dinner, as lovely Hugo heads off to find 'Cruella' Lorne-Harris!

We are the first to arrive in the Fleur Suite, which is always a good thing, when there are plenty of hungry crew around!

"Hello darlin" how're you doin?' asks Zak, putting his arms around my shoulders. Zak is another of our 'old school' crew—he's a lighting technician and a bloody good one.

"We're OK. I think we're done for the evening, but I daren't say too much. This is an Angel show after all! So, how are you, it's been an age?" I smile.

"Too right it's been an age, but always in my thoughts girlie," smiles Zak.

The banter continues throughout dinner. Crew drift in and out, until everyone has been fed and watered. However, there is no sign of Dan, Ingrid or Hugo.

Mel and I are clearing our plates away, when we hear the words:

"Psst Psst Cor! Cor! Cor!" It's Dan, expressing how delighted he is to have been introduced to Rochelle Schneider, an introduction he has gained before Mickey—one upmanship!

"Mickey! Yowza! The American girlie from KAYSO! Rochelle. What a babe!" enthuses Dan.

"Thinking with your head again, Dan?" laughs Mel, with a hint of sarcasm.

"Behave girl. Course I'm not, I'm thinkin' with somethin' else, she's bloody gorgeous!" he retorts.

Dan sits down with Mickey and Hugo joins them at the table, having returned from his meeting with Ingrid. It's great to be working with these boys, most of the time they are true professionals where their work is concerned, but ultimately, they just want to have fun and get paid for it! After all, don't we all?

There are however, production houses that actually won't employ them all on the same event, as they know that it can be 'dangerous!'—hysterically dangerous!

So, let's talk about Rochelle, Rochelle Schneider. She is exceptionally tall, blonde and extremely pretty with large breasts. She is Mary-Jo Capelli's assistant and I have a feeling that a competition will now certainly develop, between Mickey and Dan and quite possibly Hugo. As to who can make inroads into Rochelle? Well, we'll just have to wait and see!

We sit in catering for a while longer, laughing and joking, until Ingrid comes in and announces that she would like a meeting with all Heads of Department.

Everybody openly sighs, to which she shakes her head impatiently, but then goes on to say, that the models are in the auditorium taking a look around.

Rochelle and now, the models? Bloody hell1 The boys will think that all their Christmases and birthdays have come at once!

Chapter Five

The auditorium is really starting to take shape. There is still al lot of technical rigging work to be done, but the stage area is more or less, complete. There are large flat white felt panels at the back of the stage, with two entrances either side, from where the speakers will make their entrances. One KAYSO logo had been fixed into position, on the right hand side of the panels, the other hasn't yet been rigged—but will match the opposite side.

The set designer has incorporated the KAYSO logo into a large polystyrene clapperboard. It looks really effective. The lighting truss is up and in position, together with the video projectors and speakers. Mickey, still has the sound desk to sort out and Jack Lacey, our lighting designer, still has to plot the lighting states, which by all accounts, will be absolutely fantastic—after all, Jack is regarded as the best lighting technician on the UK conference circuit, together with Zak, his number one technician. Jack spent many years globe-trotting with the biggest rock bands in the world, but now, has decided to take it easy, especially as his new wife has told him to!

Backstage, Dan is sorting out his projectors and the rest of the video crew are plumbing in more cables into various pieces of equipment.

Backstage is a vast area. Currently, there is a catwalk lying on its side, which will be rigged for the fashion show. Part of the floor is bedecked with plants. The catwalk is made of reinforced Perspex and the plants will be placed within it, to create a greenhouse effect. There will also be some lights amongst the foliage, which will make it look fantastic.

"Hey Dan, look left, look left, quick!" says Mickey, with a sense of urgency.

The models are gathered in a circle talking amongst themselves. There are twelve of them. Now even I have to admit that they really are gorgeous, some with long hair, some with short, some red, some blonde, some brunette and all with long legs and fabulously slim figures. Mickey and Dan are drooling.

"Twenty Euros, Mickey. Which one?" chuckles Dan.

"Twenty Euros, you're cheap, but I'll take the red 'ead," replies Mickey, smiling.

"You're on mate!" Dan is almost drooling. Sad really isn't it?!

"All crew front of stage please," comes the voice of God (from someone holding a microphone and making an announcement). It's Hugo.

We respond immediately and make our way to the stage area, where Ingrid is standing, waiting to hold court, once again.

"Right. Now we are all here, I am going to say this only once..." she starts.

"Here we go. Why the fuck does she do this? It's so bloody patronising," squirms Mel.

"Makes her feel powerful, is my guess," I reply.

"Is there something you would like to share with us, Martha?" asks Ingrid, as she overhears my remark to Mel.

I shake my head, smiling, although I can feel my face reddening a little, with sheer rage. Mel is digging her elbow in my side, as a warning not to blow a gasket, which I've done on previous shows, with our producer from hell.

"Just remember, you are all ambassadors for Angel Productions. KAYSO is one of the largest clients on our books and this is a very important show. I do not want to hear any member of crew swearing, within earshot of client. There has been a lot of foul language today and it is simply, not acceptable," she instructs.

Mickey and Dan are not listening they are too busy ogling the models.

Mickey asks Dan a corker of a question:

"Would you, you know with Ingrid?"

"Not even with a paper bag on its 'ead, no-way!" whispers Dan.

Ingrid continues with her list of do's and don'ts and gives a reminder that crew have to be clear of the venue by midnight and with that, she hands the microphone to Hugo.

At least we know that there is a cut off time tonight and that most of us will get some sleep and if we don't, then it's our own fault! The briefing is over and everyone disperses.

Mel, Jerome and I decide to go back to the hotel. The other crew still have a couple more hours to get through, this evening.

As we walk along the promenade, there is a light breeze, which is most welcome, as it is still rather warm in the evening air. There are now, quite a number of people enjoying an evening stroll. A handful of tourist shops are still open, with people hunting for souvenirs to take home, from their visit to Cannes.

"Fancy a quick drink then, guys?" asks Mel.

"Not for me, thanks Mel. Danny Mendosa has finished me off today, I need to get some shut-eye, ready for tomorrow, but thanks all the same," says Jerome.

"You lightweight!" I joke. "Mel, I'm up for a drink, but first I must, absolutely must drop the computer off and change out of this horrible polyester polo shirt, it is not befitting for a young lady, such as myself, to be seen out in such a garment! And also I need to give Theo a quick call, it would seem that he has some gossip on KAYSO!" I chuckle.

"You're on then girlie. Sounds like a great plan," smiles Mel, linking my arm.

Arriving back at the hotel, I rush into my room, eager to rid myself of the polo shirt, but more importantly, I want to speak with Theo. Top off, squirt of deodorant, squirt of Dolce & Gabbana and then I grab my iphone. T, T, T, scrolling down I finally come to Theo. It's ringing, still ringing, come on Theo, please pick up. Damn, it's gone to voice message. I head off to the bathroom, a quick brush of the teeth and then I try him again. Immediately, he picks up, "Ciao bella, come stai? How was your day today? Are you enjoying your time with KAYSO?" he asks.

"Theo listen honey, my time with KAYSO has been mixed. Howard Johnson III is a delight, but Danny Mendosa is driving me to the point of distraction, he is a complete and utter fucking nightmare. It's quite beyond me how Howard entertains such an idiot. So, what's the gossip?" I ask eagerly.

"Cara mia, you are not going to believe what I am about to tell you. But first, my time is limited, as I am in the middle of a shoot, but brace yourself. Very quickly and in a nutshell, Howard was, I repeat, was, married to an American socialite for a couple of years, no children; but he really did love her. Anyway, she was a bit of a wild child and it transpires that she was caught having sex with a Presidential aide in the Whitehouse and a well known aide at that! And well, you can imagine how that would have gone down if it had hit the papers. It would seem that the delightful Danny Mendosa, who was working as Howard's assistant, gofer, call him what you may, became involved and somehow successfully managed to keep the story out of the papers. Howard is currently going through divorce procedures and of course, he feels indebted to Danny, hence Danny's new position within KAYSO," gushes Theo, finally coming to a stop.

"Fucking hell! Theo, how do you find out such stuff? You seem to know everyone and everything?" I question.

"Cara mia, firstly such language from a lady such as yourself is not necessary thank you, but in answer to your question, I have an inside line at KAYSO, I have, well let's say, I have a special friend, who keeps me abreast of situations within the organisation. Anyway my darling, I will be seeing you very soon, in Cannes, truly cannot wait,. Must dash, ciao for now. Baci," and with that, Theo is gone.

There's a knock at my door—it's Mel.

I grab her eagerly and pull her into my room.

"Oh my God, you are not going to believe what Theo has just told me." My eyes are as wide as saucers and my mouth remains open, akin to a fish seeking air!

I recount the entire conversation, word for word, well what I can remember, whilst Mel sits there, with her mouth open, almost as wide as mine.

"Shit, who would have thought that Danny Dickbrain Mendosa could ever be a hero? Not me, that's for sure," laughs Mel.

We are both looking at each other, giggling. Mel finally grabs my arm and we head out of the room, still giggling like two school girls.

The hotel foyer is bustling and I dare say a lot of them are KAYSO employees, but it's way too busy for my liking, so we make our way outside.

"Good evening Ladies. Have you both finished for the day?" an American accent enquires.

We turn around and there is Howard Johnson, the oh so lovely, Howard Johnson III, with Danny Mendosa and a couple of other people, sitting on the hotel's terrace.

Shit! I can feel myself blushing, but why the hell am I blushing? Oh, I just want to scoop him up in my arms and do inappropriate things with him.

"Hello. Yes a few of us have finished, others are still at the venue, but Mel and myself are just popping out for a quick stroll, before we turn in," I smile, warmly.

"Well, I hope you both have a nice evening and we'll see you in the morning," he smiles, throwing me a wink.

Oh shit, my knees are about to buckle!

"God, he's bloody gorgeous, Mel—such a gentleman!" I pant like a dog on heat!

Mel and I walk down the road and stop at the first bar we come to.

"Here do?" asks Mel.

We find a table outside and order a glass of red wine and a large gin and tonic. We chat for a while occasionally stopping to 'people watch' and then Mel notices the woman with the Jaguar XK8, whom we had seen the night before. She gets out of the car and walks into the bar, where she finds an available seat and orders a drink; she is certainly very attractive, with very expensive taste in clothes.

We have a couple of drinks and then having had enough of 'people watching' but to my mind, not quite enough of gin and tonic, we head back to our hotel.

Arriving back at Le Maritime, I spot Howard, (oh my Lord, this man is perfection) and Danny Dickbrain Mendosa, in reception. Howard looks up and waves, I wave back and smiling, I link arms with Mel and head up to the first floor.

Lordy! You know what? I think that maybe, just maybe, I might be getting to know Howard just a little better over the coming week; well, in fact, I shall make it my business, to get to know him better!

I air kiss Mel, (well we are in Cannes) and bid her goodnight.

No sooner am I in my room, than the phone rings. I reach for my iphone, but it's not ringing, it must be the landline. I lunge on the bed and make a grab for the phone, "Hello" I say a little breathless.

"Oh, hi Martha, it's Howard Johnson, have I caught you at in inopportune moment?" he asks.

"No, not at all. How can I help?" all the while I'm smiling like a Cheshire cat and the butterflies in my stomach are doing somersaults!

"Well, I was wondering whether you would like to join me, us, the group, for a nightcap?" he asks, rather sheepishly.

"That would be lovely. See you in the bar in five." And with that, I put the phone down. Oh my God! I must behave, I must totally behave. He is a broken man, especially after what his whore of a wife has put him through. I must not sleep with the client. I really must not sleep with the client. But of course, it would be rude to decline him, should I be asked!!

A quick dab of lip gloss and I make a dash for the lifts. Surprisingly, my heart is pounding a little. Sweet Jesus! What is wrong with me? Arriving in the bar, I spot Howard immediately and walk towards him. Danny is in heavy conversation with Rochelle. Well, I think he's in heavy conversation with her, or at least, with her breasts!

The next hour passes very quickly. I smile, I laugh, I engage in conversation, but most of all I flirt outrageously, with Howard. We hold our gaze just a little too long, we both make for the olives at the same time and did he really just brush his knee against mine? All of a sudden, I feel as if I am in a Mills & Boons novel, all we need now, is for him to take me in his arms and kiss me passionately.

Anyway enough of this stupidity! I pick up my room key wallet, which has been clearly displaying my room number for the past hour and bring the evening to an end. Not through choice, but maybe, just maybe, Howard might follow me upstairs? Well, a girl can wish! I bid goodnight to one and all and I sway, seductively, out of the bar.

My head is spinning as I think about Mr. Johnson. In truth, my head is spinning because I have had too much bloody gin. Fuck! What is wrong with me? I quickly shower and lavish Prada body lotion onto my soft, gorgeous, olive skin (vain aren't I?). I make sure my teeth are especially clean and then I wait. Not quite sure I know what I am waiting for, so I flick on the box and watch Fashion TV, my favourite European channel. After an hour of waiting, I figure that Howard Johnson III, is clearly not visiting Ms Martha DiPinto's room this evening. What a dreamer I am!

Suddenly I am woken up by the incessant banging on the door. Oh my God, I must have drifted off to sleep. Is it Howard? Shit! What does my hair look like? Too late now!

"Martha, Martha, Martha, wake up!" Nope, that's definitely not Howard.

I look at the clock it's two thirty-five am. I lie still for a moment and then the voice shouts my name again. Shit! It's Mickey.

I walk over to the door. "What do you want Mickey? I'm not interested, so just bugger off will you?" I hiss.

"No Martha, I'm in trouble. Quick, open up," comes his desperate plea.

I grab my robe, my personal robe, as I don't like hotel ones—they've been worn by others—and I make for the door. Mickey pushes his way passed me, his face is covered in blood and his white shirt, is thoroughly stained.

"What the fuck happened?" I ask slowly, horrified at what I am witnessing.

"Don't ask, just take a look at this, will you?" pleads Mickey, almost in a whisper.

He removes his blood soaked handkerchief from his face and there is a massive gash, to the side of his nose.

What the hell has happened? I grab my face cloth, from the bathroom and tell him to hold it over the wound, whilst I find my first aid kit. Always prepared, that's me!

"What the fuck happened, Mickey?" I ask, heading to the mini bar, to grab a couple of spirit bottles—purely medicinal, of course!

I hand a whiskey to Mickey and I swig the brandy, after all, I'm in shock too!

"Promise you won't say nothin' to nobody?" he says.

"You know me better than that Mickey," I smile. Mickey is clearly, visibly, shaken.

"Well, we finished at about 'arf eleven, so Dan, Zak and me decide to go for a drink. The others were still finishing off. We stop off at that bar next door."

I smile, yep, that's the bar Mel and I were in earlier.

"Well, that girl was there from last night, the one with the Jag, so I got chatting, as you do. The others were taking the piss, so after we finished our drinks we decided to call it a night and 'ead back to the hotel. Only I decide to have a quick wash and go out again, to carry on chatting to me new friend. Well, we has a couple more drinks at the bar and then she suggested we go back to 'er place for a nightcap, as it's just around the corner, in fact, it's within walking distance. Course, I make a joke about taking the car out to go 'undred metres" explains Mickey, quite clearly in pain.

"Well, we got back to this flat and I have to say it was a right stunning place. She pours some drinks and 'eads off into the bedroom to put on something more comfortable. Her English is right good, so when she gets back, we continue talking. Then, things start to get a bit friendly and a bit hot, if you get my drift?" Mickey is trying to laugh a little now, but I suspect the pain is still at the forefront of his mind.

I get his drift all right. Mickey is a great guy, but let's face it, he thinks with his dick, not his head! Mickey and I had an incident some years ago. I had fallen for the Prowse charm and was only too aware, of how good he is at turning it on, but thankfully, we have managed to remain firm friends, over the years.

"Well, I start to fumble and..." he pauses, 'this is so fucking, embarrassing', he says, blushing.

"Come on Mickey, spit it out. This is me you're talking to," I say.

"Well, she wasn't a fucking she. She had a cock!" he shrieks.

I am too stunned for words. But then, I manage to ask what he did next.

"I fucking thumped it and it fucking thumped me back. I grabbed me jeans and legged it. But bloody hell, he packs a punch!" he says, pointing at his face.

I start to smile and then my smile breaks into laughter, uncontrollable laughter. Only Mickey, the great Mickey Prowse, could fall for a man!

"It's not fucking funny, Mart!" chuckles Mickey.

"Not funny? It's bloody hysterical! You absolute prat!" I laugh, with gusto.

When the bleeding finally stops, I take him into the bathroom, to wash his face. Hey, is this my new vocation? Nurse Martha? No way! I rub on antiseptic cream and place a big plaster over the cut. Without doubt, he'll have a black eye in the morning, of that, I am sure.

Mickey thanks me for patching him up, giving me a big hug, before he leaves.

Meanwhile, I get back into bed. It's now three fifty am. Ten to fucking four! So much for my early night! I have to be up in two hours! Never mind. I switch off the light and snuggle down, laughing out loud, at Mickey's misfortune.

Well, another day, another dollar, as the saying goes. Getting up this morning is a little difficult. But then, it all comes flooding back to me—my flirty session with Howard and of course, my nursing duties with Mickey. I giggle to myself, as I get ready for the day.

Down in reception, at six forty-five am and Mel is already waiting for me.

"Morning. Did you sleep well Slapper, you're looking a little on the tired side?" Mel enquires.

"Kind of... I was a little restless," I reply, not divulging the details of last night.

Arriving at the venue, we head for breakfast; some crew are already tucking in, Zak included.

"Hello girls. Alright? Have you seen Mickey this morning?" he asks.

"No, we've just arrived. Why what's happened?" I ask.

"You should see him. Slipped in the bath last night and hit his head on the tap, as he went down, not a pretty sight this morning!" he chuckles.

"Really? Well Ingrid will love that, accident or no accident!" replies Mel.

Belinda arrives, swiftly followed by Hugo.

"Morning troops. How are we all? Better than the sound department, I hope," smiles Hugo.

Mel and I explain that we haven't seen Mickey yet, but Zak has filled us in with the details.

"Stupid twit. How much had he had to drink?" Belinda asks.

Zak explains that in actual fact, they had only had a couple of drinks and decided to call it a night. However, he did add that Mickey had tried chatting up the female with the Jag, but to no avail. Little did they know.

"Well drink or no drink, he must have gone down with a bang, because his nose and cheek are really, quite swollen" says Belinda, with some concern.

Just then, Mickey appears with Ellie and Dan. The others definitely were not joking. Mickey's nose is swollen and he hasn't removed the plaster I stuck on a few hours ago.

We offer our sympathies and of course, the obligatory piss take, but thankfully, Mickey takes it all in good spirit. He grabs some breakfast and joins us.

Hugo tells us how yesterday had been a bit tedious, with the models moaning about the dressing room arrangements, Ingrid having a hissy fit and the loss of the back-up projector, but then that's what this industry is made up of—problems. It's just a matter of how quickly and efficiently each problem is dealt with.

You certainly need to possess the ability to cope in a crisis in this game, as well as being able to think on your feet. And never lose sight of the fact, that a crew member—is only as good as their last job. Having said that, despite the length of time we have all served in the conference world, we have all had some disaster along the way, but we are all, thankfully still on the circuit. Fucking miracle, if you ask me!

Hugo calls time on breakfast and says that it would be prudent for everyone, to get on with what they need to be doing, thereby, not giving Ingrid any reason to start the day off, on the wrong foot.

Mel, Jerome and I head off to the second floor, ready to power up the equipment and await the arrival of the presenters. I tell them that I will meet them up there, as I need to pay a visit to the Ladies. Mickey catches up with me.

"Thanks so much Mart, for last night—I really appreciate it," he whispers.

"You owe me Mickey!" I say jokingly, 'I need all the beauty sleep I can get, these days!"

"Well, you look OK to me darlin'. Always have and always will. You're a true star." The Prowse charm is still oozing.

"Go and do some work Prowsie—see you later." And with that, he gives me a peck on the cheek and we go about our business.

Climbing the stairs to the rehearsal suite, I hear that wonderful American voice:

"Good morning Martha and how are you today?" It is of course, the one and only, Howard Johnson III.

"I'm very well, thank you," I reply, beaming!

"I hope Danny didn't give you guys too much of a hard time yesterday—he is such a perfectionist," smiles Howard.

"Not at all, after all, we get good presenters and the not so good presenters, with whom we have to work our magic," I smile.

"Well, thank you for working your magic on Danny. I am sure he will be perfect now. In return, why don't you allow me to buy you and Mel a drink later and Jerome too? We could meet in the hotel bar, or at another bar, if you have a preference?" continues Howard.

Now normally, crew don't like mixing with client, we like to do our own thing, but I think on this occasion, Mel and I could make an exception. I agree, providing we finish in time—of course!

He follows me into the rehearsal suite and Mel remarks that he is very early, as his rehearsal time is not until four o'clock, this afternoon. He explains that he wants to sit in on a couple of the presentations, to see what the other presenters are saying and to view their graphics, as he hasn't seen anything from them.

Jerome and I power up our computers and get ready with Bruce Shannon's presentation. Bruce Shannon is Vice President of KAYSO Australia. Meanwhile, Mel is chatting to Howard, whilst pouring coffee for everyone.

Bruce Shannon arrives. He is very tall, skinny and wearing the most outrageous spectacles I have ever seen on a man. They are bright lime green and magenta, frames. Mel shoots me one of her 'clock those goggles girlie' looks and smiles. However, I have to say, after working with Bruce we all warmed to him, as he knows what he wants and has obviously put a lot of preparation time into getting his presentation ready.

We take a break and Mel and I run downstairs for our much needed cigarettes. It is really warm now, in fact, about thirty degrees and there are a lot of people on the beach and needless to say, rather a lot of bikini-clad beauties, although some of them are not beauties, despite wearing not very big bikinis.

Hugo spots us, as he is by the loading bay and walks over. He divulges that Ingrid is in a meeting with Mary-Jo, Rochelle and Belinda and as far as he is concerned, that is a good thing, as he can get on with other jobs, like standing around talking to us in the sunshine, I suppose! He too, spies the bikini-clad lovelies—naturally.

"I think I'd better inform Dan and Mickey, perhaps they too, should be surveying the land and taking a break," he muses.

"You'd like the rig finished this morning, wouldn't you Hugo?" says Mel.

Hugo nods in agreement, "Then I should keep it to yourself!" smiles Mel.

Too late, Mickey appears by the door, his nose and eyes are now turning yellowish purple, they look really sore. We enquire as to how he's feeling and if Ingrid has passed comment. He tells us he's heeding Hugo's advice and keeping out of her way, so she hasn't seen the state of him—yet.

"Hugo—two o'clock, brown and turquoise swimsuit— clock that!!" Mickey exclaims, excitedly.

"WOW!" responds Hugo enthusiastically.

There is an amazon of a girl, standing up admiring the view, taking a drink of water from a bottle. She is tall, tanned with long blonde highlighted hair and she is gorgeous. A bronzed Adonis, who is sporting brown and turquoise shorts to match her swimsuit, gets up from his sun lounger and places his arm around her waist and pulls her towards him, kissing her on the cheek.

"Still reckon you two are in with a chance?" I giggle, as I finish my cigarette.

"One can look Martha, one can look!" Hugo sighs, despondently

"I think that's all you'll be doing on this job Hugo, time isn't really on your side," I reply.

"Not necessarily, Martha. You don't know what I know..." he says.

Mel then presses Hugo to spill the beans. He confides that KAYSO, or rather Mary-Jo Capelli, has dropped a bombshell on Ingrid this morning, by explaining that tomorrows' afternoon rehearsals are cancelled, hence Ingrid being in a meeting with KAYSO now. It would appear that Howard has decided to take all the Vice Presidents of the various continents, golfing at Le Parc, followed by dinner, so that means free time, all being well, for the majority of us. However, an earlier start in the morning was being planned, so that we can do rehearsals prior to them leaving, at about two pm. This would mean that it may turn into a long day today, but did we mind? I don't think so!

With that news under our belts, Mel and I return to the rehearsal suite—what a result! We don't care how late we have to work today, as it looks as though we have a free afternoon and evening to look forward to tomorrow! And I don't even mind that our hoped for evening drink with the gorgeous Mr Johnson is in jeopardy.

When we arrive back at the rehearsal suite, Ingrid is waiting for us.

"Can we press on please?" She asks, in a rather irritated manner.

Howard is still in the room and he asks if I can strip naked and make out with him. No, no of course he doesn't ask that, he asks me to print out a copy of the next speaker's script, more's the pity. Our next speaker is Marcus Driscoll, Vice President, KAYSO Europe. Well bugger me, he is lovely too! What is it, with this company? Believe me, not all corporate clients are gorgeous like this lot! He is Irish, with impeccable manners and a real "gentleman" in all respects. He is more traditional than Howard in his dress, but so very classic and smart. He's certainly a cutie and of course, if Howard eventually blows me out, then I could switch my affections to the Irish gentleman!

The day is turning out to be long and hard, which we are of course used to, but we do not mind in the slightest, as we know that tomorrow afternoon, we will be in for some R&R.

Marcus finishes his presentation, when Mary-Jo knocks at the door and enters.

"Excuse me Howard. Just wanted to confirm that the arrangements have been finalised for tomorrow afternoon. The course has been booked and tee off times confirmed. Cars will leave our hotel at two pm and the dinner reservation is confirmed." She smiles seductively—hey what's going on here. Is she? You know, is she after my man?

"What would I do without you?" Howard says, smiling and winking at Mary-Jo.

Mel and I glance over at each other, acknowledging the fact that we now know for certain, that we have some time off tomorrow.

With the mornings' rehearsals complete, we stop for lunch. However, what do we have after our break? Well, it's Mendosa time again! This, I cannot wait for, well I can, but hey, let's get this shit over and done with!

Lunch today is well and truly delicious; wonderfully filled, savoury and sweet crepes, fantastic pastries.

Rather reluctantly, the time has come to climb the stairs (we are still rather dubious about using the lifts) to the rehearsal suite, where, once again, we will be faced with Danny Dickbrain Mendosa. We are all feeling a little despondent at the thought of having to spend the afternoon with him, but hey, he might surprise us and be a total sweetheart—did I really just think that? No, I thought not!

I make a dash for the Ladies (not because I am feeling unwell, but I need a pee-pee before we start) and wham bam, I find myself flat on my back. I sit up shaking my head slightly, what the heck happened there? And to my surprise stood directly above me is, wait for it, no not Howard, but Tom Kremner. His hands have automatically cupped his mouth, now why is it that people do that, is it to suppress a scream? Who knows? Tom quickly bends down, to help me up.

"Martha, forgive me, I didn't see you, but I must say, it is good to see you, even if you do greet me, lying on your back!" he laughs.

"Tom, what can I say? For sure, I'm not going to thank you for knocking me to the ground, but hey, what are a few bruises between friends?" I smile giving him a big peck on the cheek and a hug.

"So, how are you doing? You're looking well. Cannes obviously suits you! Have you met a man?" Tom asks, inquisitively.

"Me? No. I've just dropped a couple of a Es and half a gram of Charlie to help get me through the afternoon," I reply, rather too seriously.

Tom is simply starting at me. "Martha, tell me you're joking, right, you're joking right, yes? Since when have you had to take drugs to get through the day?" he seems to be a little freaked now.

"Behave! I would no more take drugs than walk on a hotel carpet bare foot!" I thump his arm.

At this point, we both start laughing and Tom gives me a hug. I finally manage to step back, after Tom loosens his grip and then... Oh shit! Why does it always happen? I look up and see the lovely, the perfect, Howard Johnson III, watching us. Bollocks! Have I blown it with him now? Will he think that there is something going on, between Tom and me?

Chapter Six

I am lying on my back; I seem to be doing a lot of that today, but for all the wrong reasons! However, we have decided to take a break from rehearsals for an hour, before tempers really fly and bad things happen. Yes, we are still rehearsing Dickbrain Mendosa. So, I dash back to the hotel, as I just need a little 'me' time and also, Theo has texted, to say that he has arrived at Le Maritime hotel. Yippee! We are staying in the same hotel.

I text Theo, to ask where he is. He is only ever going to be in three places—a fashion boutique, a designer's studio, or a bar. He's in the bar, but is now on his way up to see me, in my room.

Within minutes he arrives, banging loudly on my door. We hug and giggle. Theo is looking absolutely, fantastic. He is wearing a silver grey suit, with an open neck, black shirt, with big pointy collars. His shoes are to die for, and that's coming from a female! They are black crocodile, with silver, leather laces. He looks too beautiful for words.

"Cara mia, I need to know what is happening—look at you, you look as if you have been up to no good. It has to be a man! Who have you fallen for now?" gushes Theo.

"I am not in love, I am simply in lust. Lust is easier to cope with. But if you promise to keep a secret, I will tell you. Actually, I don't know if I can tell you or not, because you know him. OK, OK, after three and I'll tell you. One, two, three... I am in lust with Howard, Howard Johnson III. There I've said it." I'm holding my breath now, waiting for Theo's reaction.

"Dio mio. Did you really just tell me that you are in lust with Howard Johnson, Howard Johnson III of KAYSO?" screeches Theo, in a rather high pitched voice. Oh Lordy! I thought he might freak out and sure enough...

"Yes. He's just so gorgeous. I mean after all, he's not just Howard Johnson, but Howard Johnson III—I know, I know, I'm shallow but, so what?" I say, pulling a stupid face, trying to make light of the situation.

Theo is just looking at me, mouth agog.

"Theo, what's wrong? Say something, I thought you would be delighted that I desire someone in the fashion industry." I laugh, but sense that all is not well.

"I am just shocked. He's a lovely man, but hey, he has lots going on in his life at the moment. Business is booming, but his divorce, although very quiet, is a nightmare for him. I don't want to see you hurt and also, there is something else you need to know, which is important, very important," says Theo, in a rather concerned, grown-up tone, which is most unlike him.

"Theo, what is it? I am simply in lust with him, nothing has happened and if you say 'stop', of course, I'll stop," I smile, taking his hand, as if he is going to tell me something dreadful.

"Well, you may be in lust with Howard, but, well, I'm in a relationship with his brother, Jefferson. We've been seeing each other, on an exclusive basis and have been together for around six months now. He's funny, creative and so very different to Howard, after all he's gay and Howard is definitely not gay," confesses Theo.

"Sweet Jesus! Tell me you are joking—Howard has a gay brother? No way, what does he do?" I'm the one screeching now.

"Jefferson is Creative Director at KAYSO and oversees the fashion shows; his eye for detail is faultless, he is a genius, a little like me, my darling. We are not public in our affections, many believe that I am his design and concept consultant, but behind the scenes of course..." he responds, smiling.

"OK enough now, there is only so much I need to know about your sexual designs. But my God, how weird would it be, if both of us were dating members from the same family? That is just like, unreal. But hey, you know what? I think I am kind of jumping the gun a little, after all, I am only in lust with Howard and nothing has happened. Does Howard know Jefferson is gay and more importantly does he know about you?" I ask, anxiously. Just how weird is this life we live?

"Yes, on both counts—of course Howard knows that Jefferson is gay and yes, he knows of me. We meet up at their headquarters and I've been over to his place, he's cool with the situation. Shall I introduce you to Jefferson?" he's smiling again, so I think the shock has subsided!

"I don't think I've ever been introduced to one of your, you know, friends, as in 'friends' before, so bring it on. Where is he now? Shall we go meet him before I have to get back to rehearsals?" I'm begging now. Unattractive I know, but an inroad to Howard! Fuck! Talk about keeping it in the family!

"We're sharing a suite, so come on up to Suite 401," he says, grabbing my hand. I grab my bag, as we head out of the room and make our way to the fourth floor.

We duly arrive at their suite and there he is; Theo's boyfriend. Jefferson Johnson. I'm not sure whether I should shake hands, or hug, so I hug and he hugs me right back. He's lovely, so trendy and really easy on the eye; it's frightening. They make a perfect couple.

We chat for a short while, Jefferson is charismatic and I can clearly see why my little brother thinks he's special. Conversation flows with ease and before I know it, my iphone is ringing and I am being summoned back to the 'hell hole' that is the rehearsal suite.

I hug the boys goodbye, but not before Jefferson invites me to dinner this evening.

"What a lovely idea, but I think we are in for a late one with rehearsals this evening, but if we do manage to get away, with a little of the night remaining, I will track you down and join you for a nightcap, if that's OK?" I smile.

Heading back to the venue, I text Mel: *Oh my God! You are not going to believe what just happened xx.*

OK, clearly I am a little late in returning to the rehearsal suite and everyone is waiting, including Howard. I smile a great big fuck off smile, as I walk in, my confidence oozing.

"So sorry to keep you all, but guess who I bumped into?" They all look at me in amazement. 'Give up? Well Howard, I just met your brother, Jefferson, what a great guy.' I smile, a wide, happy smile.

Ingrid is clearly pissed off that I have met Jefferson, as I suspect she has yet to meet him. Mel is sitting with her mouth open—not looking quite as attractive as she normally does!

"Well Martha, tell me the truth now, am I the better looking brother?" asks Howard, with a hint of questioning in his voice.

"Mr Johnson, I don't know if I am at liberty to say—one clearly got the looks and well, the other, I am sure got the brains, or maybe the brawn!" I reply, looking directly at him, not losing eye contact, not for one moment. My heart is racing. Why am I such a flirt?

"Hey guys are we going to stand around making small talk for the rest of the night, or what say you we get down to why we're here," sighs Danny, breaking the moment.

I catch Howard looking at Danny and immediately sense that he is not happy with either his tone, or his comment.

"Right then Danny, shall we go from the top, so that we can run through the additional changes that have been made today?" I'm feeling confident now, bolshie even. Fuck Mendosa, I've met Jefferson and Howard is soon to be mine—I just know it!

"Sounds like a plan Paula. Remember, let's run at my pace and not yours," he snipes.

"Danny, might I suggest you try a little harder to remember names—it's Martha, not Paula. Try to understand that she, after all, has your life in her hands, so to speak," quips in Howard.

Howard is clearly getting bored, as after an hour he bids us 'good evening' and throws me a wink, before he makes his exit and returns to the hotel. Sweet Jesus,! I really am falling for him and boy, what a catch!.

The moment Howard is out of sight, Danny turns into a complete and utter monster. If he barks once more, that I am going too quickly... If I was to go any slower, I would stop—is he just plain stupid? Actually I believe, he is! What a prat and I bet he has a really small 'tango' cock! Good job I don't have a 'speech bubble' above my head for my thoughts! Can you imagine?

Some three hours later, we finally call it a night. Thank fuck! It's now nine thirty pm; we have been on the go for the entire day, apart from an hour's downtime. We are scheduled to meet up with Mr Mendosa again early tomorrow morning, so for now, I can erase him from my mind. As soon as he leaves the room, Mel comes over and hugs me to within an inch of my life; boy she's a big bird, but such a lovely big bird!

"Fuck me! That took some control, so well done for keeping your cool." Mel is genuine in her comments.

"So, tell me what happened? Come on, I can't wait a moment longer," she pleads.

"Well, what can I say? Only that my darling brother, Theo, is dating Jefferson, Howard's brother! What are the chances of that?" I whisper, smiling the world's biggest smile!

"Fuck right off! Theo is with Howard's brother? Good God!" repeats Mel in disbelief.

"Right then, it's now nine thirty, what is everyone else up to? How's the rig going, downstairs? Shall we check it out and see if anyone is around for a bite to eat and perhaps a drink or two, as I, for one, bloody well need a drink this evening. I need therapeutic medicine, in the guise of Bombay Sapphire." I say, very quickly turning off all the equipment and eagerly wanting to leave this faceless, bloody awful building.

In the auditorium, Hugo, Mickey, Dan and Zak are admiring their work; finally, it seems as if everything is pretty much complete. The majority of crew have left for the evening, with only the four boys remaining on site. Tom is also there.

"Hi Hugo. Wow this is looking pretty good now, is everything complete?" I ask.

"Everybody's worked their socks off today and I think a couple more hours' tomorrow morning to run through a technical rehearsal and we'll be there," he replies seeming genuinely pleased with the achievements of the past couple of days.

From nowhere, Ellie and Belinda come bounding into the auditorium,

"Hello happy people, how are you all? It seems as if we haven't seen you all day, everyone OK?" asks Belinda, a little too eagerly.

"Yep, shit day from hell, but in fairness, Ingrid has been well behaved. Have you girls been spiking her drinks, or has she been popping pills?" asks Mel, with a smile on her face.

"What can we tell you? We have both been to hell and back and need to exit this building, as quickly as possible, just in case Ingrid tracks us down again and asks us to do yet more checking and re-checking," sighs Belinda.

She's in a bad way. Ellie takes her arm,

"I think we're going to call it day, or should I say night? We are both a little tired and frazzled and there is still so much to do, so if you don't mind, we won't join you this evening—is that OK?" asks Ellie, in a concerned 'oh please don't think we are party poopers' tone.

"Girls, you've both done a fabulous job today, well done. You'll be missed this evening; however, we fully appreciate that your beds beckon—enjoy room service," responds Hugo, kissing them both, before ushering them towards the exit.

"So then, ladies and gents, what shall we do this evening, other than of course, change out of these hideous, height-of-fashion—maybe not, polyester polo shirts?" I ask.

"Hugo, what time d' ya want us in the morning? How drunk can we get tonight? That's what I'm asking," winks Mickey.

"Well I have good news, very good news and a little bad news. Firstly, the good news—the main board from KAYSO have alternative plans scheduled for tomorrow afternoon and evening. Therefore, we will be standing down all crew members from two pm tomorrow. So, to balance out the good news, I would appreciate everyone being on site from seven thirty am tomorrow morning, in order that we can finalise the build and run technicals and of course, Martha, Jerome and Mel, you three, can then be ready for Mr Mendosa's proposed arrival at eight am. I know it's a relatively early start, but just think of the fun you can have tomorrow afternoon and evening," smiles Hugo, encouragingly.

"Well, I for one cannot wait for two o'clock tomorrow— sun, sand, fun. So, what shall we do this evening—eat out, eat in, drink out, drink in?" asks Mel, in her 'come on, let's get on with it' voice.

"There is a really nice bistro around the corner from Le Maritime, we could see if they have a table free," announces Tom.

"Perfect! Come on everyone, let's get out of here, deposit our gear, change our tops and then head for the bistro and a drink, or two, or three," I order.

On route back to the hotel I text Theo to see where he is, as I would like to meet up for drinks with him and Jefferson later.

Arriving back at my room, I pull off my polo shirt and my trousers and quickly change into black, skinny jeans, which are very tight, very sexy and very uncomfortable, not much food for me tonight and a black vest top that shows off just enough cleavage. I spray Dolce & Gabbana, just as my iphone beeps. It's a text from Theo: *Ciao bella, at Alfredo's on La Croisette, are you joining us? Howard is here xx.*

Fuck! I cannot believe that Theo is having dinner with Howard. Totally unfair—so what do I do now? Dinner with Theo, or dinner with my lovely, adorable friends. Theo? Crew? Theo? Crew? No contest.

I respond to Theo: *Hi honey, I'm going to have a quick drink with the crew and then I'll come join you, see you in about 30 mins xx.*

Does that make me a bad person? No, of course it doesn't. I quickly pull off my jeans, not an easy task, let me tell you, being as they're so bloody tight, but now of course, my underwear needs changing, just in case... Well come on, a girl should always be prepared, shouldn't she?

I rush downstairs to meet everybody and quickly pull Mel to one side,

"Honey, do you love me?" I ask, with my head tilted slightly to one side, in a child like manner.

"What the fuck are you on about now, you dozy moose, of course I love you, after all, why would I constantly be watching your back, if I didn't love you?" responds Mel, chuckling.

"In that case, one quick drink and then I'm off. Theo is in town and has invited me to join him for dinner. Do you mind? It's just that Theo is with Jefferson and not only is Theo with Jefferson, but Theo is with Jefferson and Howard. Yes, Howard Johnson III!" I smile, pleadingly.

"Oh I see, don't want to hang out with the crew now eh? What's this, not good enough for you?" giggles Mel.

"Fuck off trout!" I wink.

"OK Slapper. Now listen here, no hanky panky with any strange men! I'll meet you in reception around seven fifteen tomorrow morning, unless of course you need rescuing during the night. And if that's the case, be sure to phone me," she smiles as she orders another drink.

We all arrive at the bistro and within minutes, I've guzzled down my rather large gin and tonic. Kissing Mel and waving to everyone else, I head off to Alfredo's restaurant on La Croisette. The night air is warm, there's a slight breeze, which is perfect. Beautiful people amble casually along La Croisette. In Cannes it seems as though there are only beautiful people, odd looking people simply wouldn't fit in.

I'm here, Alfredo's restaurant. My heart is pounding, just a little too quickly—is it anticipation? Anticipation of spending time with Howard perhaps? Actually, no it's probably because I hurried way too quickly in bloody high heels! Oh, and of course, I guzzled my gin & tonic too!

I enter the restaurant and look around anxiously. “Ciao bella, over here,” beckons Theo.

“Hello my darling. Wow, look at you! Pops would be proud,” I giggle.

Jefferson jumps up and hugs me and then I turn to Howard and smile.

I blush and then finally he speaks.

“So, earlier, you inform me that you’d met my brother, but you can’t decide who is the better looking, but did you forget to tell me that Theo is your baby brother? Boy, this is one hell of a small world.” His lips part, no, not to bloody kiss me, but to smile his big, gorgeous, kissable smile.

I giggle, like a naughty child, naughty enough to lean in for a kiss on both cheeks, from the gorgeous Howard. The boys have already eaten, but I’m starving, so order a salad nicoise, together with a large gin and tonic, for additional Dutch courage.

For the next two hours, the four of us laugh, joke and above all, have an amazing time.

It’s fast approaching half past midnight and Jefferson is the first to make a move.

“Right ladies and gents, we can of course stay here all night and get horribly drunk, but my guess is that (a) Martha you’re probably working tomorrow morning, as I hear you’re doing Danny, poor you and (b) Howard you’ve probably got emails to deal with, before you get your much needed beauty sleep. And as for you Theo, you do as you are told, understand me?” says Jefferson, swaying slightly. Oh my, I think he’s probably had one too many whiskey sours.

“You are of course completely correct, I am doing Danny in the morning, so I can ill afford to get any drunker than I am already, although it would probably make my job a whole lot easier. So, who is going to walk me back to my hotel please?” I ask, swaying, as I stand. God! How very unladylike!

With that, all three men jump up, out of their seats. Howard gets the bill, whilst Theo takes me by the arm and leads me outside. The air is still warm, but there is a hint, just a hint, of coolness. I shiver slightly.

“Theo look at me,”

What?” he asks.

“What do you mean, what?” I respond, with a puzzled look on my face.

“What—what, you want my cardigan—no way honey, I’m not getting a chill for you, capisci?” he looks away, clearly, I am not getting Theo’s cardigan, which is not a bad thing, after all he is so very slim, with no padding to keep him warm! I wish I had been the one last to the dinner table, when I was young!

“Here, why don’t you slip my sweater around your shoulders, it’s only a short distance back to the hotel, or would you prefer we grab you a cab?” asks Howard, sneaking up behind me.

“A cab? Not necessary. After all, the walk will clear my head and thank you for your jumper, most kind sir.” I smile, my most dazzling smile, hoping all the while, that I don’t have the odd piece of salad lodged in between my teeth.

Theo and Jefferson walk ahead of us, laughing really deep, belly laughs. They are clearly well suited, two very beautiful people, so at ease with one another.

So, do I? Don't I? Do I link arms with Howard, or not? It seems wrong to, after all, he is a client, but on the other hand he is practically family. (Although Pops would go fucking mental if ever he knew that Theo, his only son, was gay. Lord! It would finish him off!) Family wins over the situation and I link my arm through Howard's. It feels natural and it feels good. I can feel the warmth of his skin against mine. I'm tingling, almost having an orgasm—later Martha, later!

We make small talk, all the way back to the hotel. Now, comes the moment of truth. Will Howard come to my room? Shit! Why is life so fucking complicated at times?

Arriving back at Le Maritime, Theo gives me an almighty hug, as does Jefferson, planting a big sloppy kiss on my cheek. Howard leans down (after all, he is quite tall) and kisses me on both cheeks, squeezing my upper arms delicately. We head to the lifts and arriving at Floor One, I bid the boys a goodnight and step out, all the while wanting Howard to step out with me. But he doesn't. Up to Floor Four the lift travels, without me. Oh, well. I'm feeling disappointed, but the evening has been fun and I am sure there will be other opportunities, especially now that Theo is firmly ensconced in the family!

Within minutes, I receive a text which simply reads:

Suite 444, sweater?

Suite 444? Oh shit! Was that Theo's room? Fuck! I can't remember, no it can't be Theo's room—surely he would have sent me a text from his phone, this text is from a number I don't recognise—is it Jefferson?

No, it must be Howard. Shit! What do I do? What a fucking ridiculous question. Well, what do you think I do? Let me tell you. I rush, like a whirling dervish into the bathroom and I take a huge swig of mouthwash and then of course, pull my heels back on, my sexy, tarty heels and I am at that lift before you can count to ten in Italian. I am jabbing the lift call button a million times.

Finally, I am in the lift, arriving at the fourth floor, but I need to rid myself of this mouthwash, so what do I do, swallow it? (Perhaps I should save the swallowing for later, if you get my drift.) No. I deposit it, in the first plant pot I find—that poor plant now has two chances, live or die! Secretly, I do have the manners of a pig and let me tell you right here, right now, if ever my daughter was to display such manners (not that I have a daughter at the moment of course, but who knows) I would ground her for a year. Filth, utter filth!

I don't even think of the consequences, before I knock on the door belonging to Suite 444, if I stopped to think about what I was doing, I would surely be hot footing it, back down to my room.

The door opens, and yes, it's Howard Johnson III. Thank you God. Thank you! Thank you! Thank you!

"I didn't take you for a man who would be so attached to his sweater, but hey, if needs must, here you go," I laugh, handing Howard the sweater, he had so kindly draped across my shoulders earlier.

"I get easily attached to certain things in life and currently this sweater is one of my attachments, but that could be because it was draped over the shoulders of a beautiful girl, earlier this evening," responds Howard.

"Dolce & Gabbana has such a distinctive air about it and you Martha, wear it so well," he continues, stepping forward and slowly moving the hair from my neck, breathing in the fragrance of my perfume.

My knees have quite literally, gone weak, I take hold of his arm to save myself from falling and in that moment our gaze meets; eyes fully locked on. I keep repeating over and over in my mind, kiss me, kiss me, kiss me. And, as if by magic, our lips meet. Very gently at first, so soft, so sweet and yes, I do believe that I can taste a hint of mouthwash, he's definitely a man, after my own heart. Wonder if he flosses too?

I pull back, holding his gaze. "So, tell me, what does a girl need to do around here, to get a drink?" I wink.

"Carry on doing what you were just doing and I might just crack open a bottle or two," replies Howard. He raises his hand and beckons for me to follow him.

In his sitting room, is an ice bucket and in the ice bucket, is a bottle of Krug, Jesus! I love this guy. Krug is my absolute favourite champagne, my most favourite ever, since I quaffed a couple of bottles, whilst at a private party, in Monaco. I adore Monaco, almost as much as I adore Krug!

Howard expertly opens the bottle, which releases a sigh and as my grandmother always says, a good bottle of champagne sighs when opened, like a satisfied woman.

Handing me a glass, Howard proposes a toast "here's to fate". We clink our glasses and head out onto the terrace. The night air is still and standing behind me, Howard wraps his arms around me tightly, spilling my champagne "oops" I say, trying to sound sophisticated, no bloody chance of that then, when I am a little on the nervous side. Nervous for what reason, I have no idea. Ordinarily faced with a situation of man, champagne and sex I excel, but tonight I just don't know what is wrong with me!

I try to wipe the spilt champagne from my top, but, as if by magic, Howard's handkerchief appears and he starts to wipe my chest. I can bear this no more, within moments we are back in his suite and heading for the bedroom, kissing frantically, as we make our way around the obstacle course of furniture.

Finally, his bedroom awaits—I am minus my top and one shoe. Oh my God! My bare foot has just touched hotel carpet! Seductively, Howard unfastens my bra, all the while kissing me passionately. I am ready to explode, but refocus, as it's far too soon for any explosions!

Next, he delicately takes off my bra, cupping my breasts with his hands; I am holding my breath, as this sensation is just too perfect. Need to breathe, need to breathe, otherwise will feint. Eventually, I let out a gasp, fuck that was close, could have been total blackout!

He lifts up my leg to remove my one remaining shoe. His lips find mine again and I am in seventh heaven (what is this seventh heaven that people refer to? I am none the wiser, but fuck, I definitely like it!). I can feel his hands around my waist, oh fuck, oh fuckity fuck, tell me, just tell me why did I put these jeans on? They are so bloody tight, we have no hope of getting them off seductively and certainly not without a struggle!

His hands find the button, I suck my belly in as far as it will go. Slowly, he unzips the zipper and then very gently, he starts to remove them. Oh shit!

He is doing it too slowly and far too delicately. He is having another go, using just a little more force this time, but no, they aren't budging.

I step back. "Howard, skinny jeans hug a woman's body and the only way these babies are coming off is with a good old yank. So I suggest you yank from the front and I'll yank from behind."

We struggle, but finally I am rid of my bloody jeans—just remind me that they are for the bin, unless I manage to lose a bit of weight!

Thank God I changed my underwear. I'm not into thongs, but I do like a good pair of lacy mini shorts and that is just what I am wearing. In fact, that is all that I am now wearing. I am feeling sexy, really sexy.

Within moments, Howard has rid himself of his clothes, including his shorts—boy, he's certainly not shy. Gazing at his cock, I am pleasantly surprised; it's huge, enormous in fact. Oh my God! I did not think for one moment he would possess such a large one!

Shit! Howard catches me looking;

"Martha is that a look of disappointment on your face?"

"Most certainly not, on the contrary, Sir!" I respond, eyes agog.

Well, what can I say? The next few hours are absolutely out of this world. He is everything a girl could wish for and more. 'Satisfaction Guaranteed,' should be KAYSO's new strap line. There is not one part of my body that he has not explored. He is so erotic and sexual that I feel as if I've known him forever.

Lying in each other arms, the moment seems perfect, but I know I can't stay here forever. "Howard, as much as I would love to fall asleep in your arms, I need to get back to my own room, before anybody spots me." I say.

"I quite agree Martha, but as your client, I would like you to stay for a short while longer. And as they say, the client always gets, what the client wants," he says, smiling.

He kisses me tenderly and then within moments, he is thrusting his wonderful, hard, large cock inside me, as if our lives depend on it. I come quickly and he groans, as he comes too.

"Fuck me! That was amazing," I say, with a shortness of breath.

"I aim to please!" responds Howard, as he strokes my breasts tenderly.

I struggle to get up, but get up, I must.

"Howard, I need to get out of here. I don't want to be spotted heading back to my room," I say. 'Oh shit! I don't think I can pull those bloody jeans on again. Let's hope I don't bump into anyone on the way back," I giggle.

I pull on my knickers, bra and top. A pair of high heels and I look the part—the part of a whore, but I don't care. I need to get some sleep.

I head for the door. We kiss passionately and I seductively tug his manhood—Sweet Jesus! He is just too perfect for words.

"Thank you," he whispers.

"My absolute pleasure," I respond.

Thankfully, I am not observed wandering the corridors and make it back to my room, unnoticed. I feel absolutely amazing. He is one hell of a lover. Now the big question is; will he be embarrassed in the morning? I certainly hope not.

But come to think of it, will I?

Chapter Seven

Fuck! I haven't slept a wink all night. Well, I say all night; of course, I didn't sleep whilst I was with Howard, for obvious reasons, but then after getting back to my room, I felt sure I would drop off immediately, through sheer exhaustion. But no, I lie in my bed, running through the previous few hours. What a night! Not only do I feel sexually liberated again, but, I've been liberated by a totally gorgeous gentleman, in the guise of Howard Johnson III. THE Howard Johnson III, multi millionaire, extraordinary businessman and man of genius fashion—just how lucky am I?

Although totally exhausted, I am still smiling. I prise my aching body from this perfectly divine bed and head towards the bathroom. My iphone beeps. Who could it be, at this time of the morning? Oh my God! Please, please, please let it be Howard. Opening up the text, I notice that it's the same number as last night:

Good morning Martha, hope I haven't woken you, but am having trouble sleeping. I don't suppose room service is on the cards? Hx.

How the fuck do I respond to that? Of course, I would dearly love to rush up to Suite 444, but let's think logically here: (a) too many people are around at this hour (it's fast approaching six thirty am), although it is still relatively early (b) I don't have time for sex, shower and rendezvous with Mel, at our allotted time and (c) I look like a fucking witch—my hair is almost matted, which to me, is always a good sign of fantastic, rampant sex!

I'm delicate with my response, as I would rather like a second helping of Howard... and a third and fourth, come to think of it!

After a few moments, I text back: *Good morning to you too! Unfortunately room service only runs during evening hours, union rule don't you know! See you soon. Mx.*

Fuck! I hope I haven't offended him. Of course, I really would prefer to be in his arms, rather than in the rehearsal suite, but I have work commitments and I mustn't let Howard and his gorgeously, sexy, large dick come between me and my work now, must I?

I am running late, but anxiously looking at my iphone, hoping and praying, for a response. And, as if by magic, it arrives: *I must review these union rules—remind me, when I see you later. Have a good morning. Hxx*

Oh my goodness! He's definitely got the hots for me, after all, I've got two kisses in his last text. I store his number under HJ III and run around like someone possessed, to get downstairs to meet darling Mel, on time.

Not bad going, arriving in the hotel's main reception at precisely seven seventeen, I spot Mel immediately; after all, let's face it, even a blind man would spot her!

"So, young lady, you have a smile the size of the Cote D'Azure spread across that filthy face of yours. Spill the beans and don't hold back!" giggles Mel, grabbing my arm, as we head out of the hotel's rotating, front door.

"You are so not going to believe, what I am about to tell you. But if I must, I will! After leaving you all last night, for which I am really sorry, honestly I am, I met up with Theo, Jefferson and of course, Howard. I eat by myself, as they had already eaten and then we drink. We drink lots. Conversation flows and, oh my God Mel, he is just so perfect. After that, we walk back to the hotel and he puts his jumper around my shoulders, as it's a bit chilly. We arrive back at the hotel, I get out on the first floor and they all head up to the fourth floor. Howard, then texts me. He wants his jumper back. So I rush up to his suite, spitting mouthwash out in a plant pot on route, hand him back his jumper and then have the most fabulous sex imaginable, with his enormous cock. Quite simply, fucking brilliant!" I gush, almost out of breath, but still beaming.

"You have got to be kidding me?" Mel's mouth is agog.

"He wanted his jumper back?" she giggles.

I play punch her on the arm, still grinning like a Cheshire cat.

"Mel, I cannot believe that I had sex with Howard Johnson. Howard Johnson III and it was bloody brilliant, no inhibitions. Fuck! I feel totally..., totally..., oh I don't know..., totally wow!" I coo.

"'Loose' is an appropriate adjective for you right now, after all, what gives you the right to bag Howard over me? Surely he would have wanted the more experienced of the two? Surely he would have wanted the curvier of the two? But no, you manage to steal him from right under my nose. Shame on you, Slapper!" beams Mel, hugging me.

As we head into the venue, I start to giggle,

"I simply cannot believe that I got to him before you did! Oh thank heavens we're here, I am in desperate need of a large intake of caffeine and food. Bloody starving, that's great sex for you!" I smile.

The majority of the crew are already in the Fleur Suite. Scrambled eggs, smoked salmon, cheese, ham and fantastic croissants. I pour a coffee and down it, almost immediately, slightly burning the roof of my mouth and the tip of my tongue. I then pour another and pile my plate high.

"Steady on Mart, you'll pop," smiles Mickey. "Did you 'ave a good time with your bruvver and his mate?" he asks.

"Mickey, I had a fantastic evening, thank you for asking. But of course, I am now in need of food to sustain me, through this dreadful morning. And, of course I need caffeine. Lots and lots of lovely strong coffee." I wink.

"Hair of the dog is what you need, girl. Although in fairness, you're still looking good, even if you are nursing an 'angover. I don't know how you do it!" replies Mickey, planting a kiss on my cheek.

I eat my breakfast with gusto and head up to the rehearsal suite, to await the arrival of Danny Dickbrain Mendosa. He won't faze me today, after all, I've slept with Howard, his boss, his superior and I am over the moon. Plus, we all have a free afternoon and evening, which means plenty of drinking and plenty of partying. Fanbloodytastic!

Mendosa is scheduled to arrive at eight am. It's now eight thirty five am. Bored. I am so very bored, waiting for this idiot. I head off outside with Mel, for a cigarette and we bump into Belinda and Ellie.

"Morning girls. How are you both? Hopefully this morning will not be quite as stressful as yesterday. What are the plans for later? Are we all meeting up to drink Cannes dry?" I ask, eagerly wanting to know what we have in store for our downtime.

"Good morning. How are you both? Well, today is definitely not going to be anything like yesterday. That was pure hell. Also, Ingrid is not feeling well, so won't be coming over until after ten am. Apparently, last night's food did not quite agree with her. Fucking brilliant! The one morning we do need her, she's not here. But not to worry, I'm sure we will still be stood down at lunchtime, with the rest of the crew hopefully and assuming we are, then we have very special plans arranged," announces Belinda, smirking.

Two cigarettes later, Mel and I wander back upstairs to the rehearsal suite. We are still taking the stairs, as the lift broke down again yesterday and we certainly don't want to be stuck in it. It is now eight fifty three and still no sign of Dickbrain.

My iphone beeps: *Are rehearsals running to plan? Hxx*. Sweet Jesus! This man really has got it bad.

I respond, quickly, just in case Dickbrain arrives: *Rehearsals? What rehearsals? Still waiting for Danny to show, he's definitely slacking. Mx.*

Howard responds immediately: *Want me to chase him up for you? Hxx.*

Don't you dare, I don't want him knowing that I have direct access to the boss, as lovely as that access is! Mx. I respond.

And, as if by magic, his response is almost immediate: *But I kind of like you having direct access to me. xx.*

I know exactly how to get access to you, Mr Johnson! However, now is not the time. First floor or fourth floor later? Mx, I respond cheekily.

Shit! Is this going to lead to text sex? Darn dirty text sex? Let's hope so!

No, definitely no sex text for me, as Mendosa comes crashing through the door, closely followed by Mary-Jo and Rochelle. Obviously, they have been having some sort of argument, as all are wearing frosty faces.

"Morning Danny, Mary-Jo, Rochelle. How are you all this morning? Hope all is well?" I ask, rather sarcastically.

"Honey, things just keep getting better and better," responds Rochelle, throwing me a wink.

"Well, you know I have some serious rehearsals to get through this morning, so Mary-Jo, go see what's keeping Howard and why he hasn't responded to my messages yet. OK? Go on, go!" barks Danny.

"Whatever you say Danny, but Howard cannot be at your constant beck and call. You understand he needs to prioritise," responds Mary-Jo, rather sternly.

"Right then Pau... , I mean Martha, can you try to run to my time today? Yesterday was a complete disaster and Jerome, shall we try and keep up with my slides? You know what I'm saying buddy?" growls Danny. Fuck me! He is in a seriously bad mood. What an arsehole! God help us all!

"Yes, sure thing Danny. Mel, are we running from the top?" asks Jerome.

"Yes, everyone from the top please. Danny we're going to try to beat the record today. Let's try and get it under twenty seven minutes, if possible," smiles Mel, ever so graciously.

Well, what can I tell you? It was long, it was hard and it was—now stop right there, before your imagination runs away with all those sexual thoughts you're having, I'm not talking about Howard's manhood, although yes, it is long and oh, so hard. No, now stop. I am talking about the first ninety minutes of rehearsal with Mendosa. This man, well, this man is such a pain in the arse and such a poor presenter. There is zero flow in his presentation and still, we are averaging thirty to thirty three minutes. What exactly is wrong with this fucking fruitcake?

We decide to take a ten minute break, as Dickbrain needs to get hold of Howard, in order to 'discuss important issues,' don't you know!

Mel and I rush downstairs. I check my iphone and I am just a teeny bit disappointed, as I haven't received any text messages from Howard. Has he forgotten about me already? Surely not, but I am still wondering if it's his suite this evening, or mine? Mine? Just listen to me! Mine's just a normal hotel room! Anyway, hopefully it will be his—plenty of Krug there, I'm sure!

I do, however, have a text message from Theo: *Hey baby girl, great time last night. What are your plans later? Jeff & I out to dinner with continent reps for KAYSO, are you joining us? Howard will be there. Baci xx*

Oh no! Do I tell Theo that I have slept with Howard, or not? I think I might have to, but face to face. Text after all, is a little too impersonal, even by Theo's standards.

The second half rehearsals have gone equally badly. There is no denying that Mendosa and I will never be the best of friends. I have been called many things in my time, all of which I have accepted graciously, but to be called and I quote, 'a complete incompetent' and 'crap at your job' is taking it, just a little too far.

Ingrid, who at this point has joined us, leaving her sick bed, actually defends me. Wonders will never cease. Perhaps I've read her all wrong? No. Perhaps not!

Dickbrain Mendosa storms out of the suite, with Ingrid chasing him. Rochelle, who is sitting in on rehearsals, comes over and embraces me, which of course, I am really not expecting. And I am slightly taken aback.

"You kept your cool, girl, that's good. The guys a true dick, don't let him get to you, right?" drawls Rochelle.

"It will take a lot more than Danny's words to offend me. And that's for sure," I smile, feeling well and truly pissed off, with such a prick of a presenter having the balls to belittle me.

Hugo has now arrived and, after seeking Ingrid's approval (whom he found sobbing in the venue's main reception) it has been agreed that everyone is to be stood down. Tempers, it seems, are fraying somewhat. Hugo has obviously heard of Danny's outburst, and it appears that Belinda and Ellie have been having problems with the models' agents, again. Thankfully, the models are off site today, as they are on a photo shoot; how lovely—such an easy life! Pose. Pose. Smile. But for the fact, that their intake of food is limited!

At precisely one forty eight pm, all the crew, including Ingrid, Belinda and Ellie, leave the venue. There are smiles all round. Even Ingrid, is trying to crack her face!

I have another quick peek at my iphone, but still no response from Howard.

Oh fuck! Perhaps I was a little too forward in assuming that we would have sex again, this evening. I so don't want it to be just a one night stand. I was rather hoping for more.

Some of the crew have already made their own plans for their down time. Mel, Dan, Mickey, Belinda, Ellie, Hugo, Tom and I head back to the hotel for a quick drink, as instructed by our two lovely production assistants. These two are obviously up to something, but I'm not quite sure what. Unfortunately, Ingrid is too busy to join us, but hopefully will try to catch up with us later, for dinner. Yah, yah, yah, as if she would ever make plans to socialise with us. Never has and indeed, never will. And a good job too, if you ask me, I really wouldn't know how to socialise with her!

Drinks all round at the hotel bar and then Tom announces that he is returning to the UK, later this afternoon. He's had a memorable time, but his job here, is now done. The equipment is all in place and as much as he would love to extend his stay, he cannot justify it, even if he is the boss!

Drinks in hand, Ellie and Belinda announce exciting news.

"Right then, I have arranged for a mini bus to collect us from the hotel at precisely fifteen hundred hours, that's three pm for those of you who have yet to embrace the twenty four hour clock. We will then travel to Nice Airport," starts Belinda, all the while grinning from ear to ear.

"Bloody hell girl! We're not going back to Blighty, are we?" interrupts Mickey.

"Mickey quiet, stop interrupting!" scolds Ellie, in her very best school ma'm's voice.

"As I was saying, we will arrive at Nice Airport, from where we will take a helicopter ride, into Monaco. It's only a short ride, around seven or eight minutes. Then, my friends, the party will really begin. Now, before I forget, if anyone wants to gamble at the casino, you know, the main casino, then it's no shorts, no polo shirts and no t—shirts. Above all, definitely no trainers and if you are gambling, please do make sure you bring your passport for identity."

"Wicked! Liking the sound of this!" smiles Dan, throwing a wink at Mickey.

"Right then, I for one am going to my room to change. Oh, before I forget, our call time for tomorrow morning, just in case we get split up, for whatever reason, which I certainly hope does not happen, but hey, you never know, is seven thirty am for breakfast at the venue and then into the main auditorium, by eight fifteen. As you know, we are having a full dress rehearsal tomorrow morning, so all I can say is, God help us!" announces Belinda, giggling as she rushes off to change.

"Ellie, can I hitch a ride to the airport, please?" asks Tom.

"Of course you can. It's sad to see you go Tom, but we will willingly boot you out at Terminal Two. No worries. Does us leaving at three, allow you sufficient time to check in?" asks Ellie, reverting to the role she plays so well—namely, that of a top notch, super efficient, production assistant.

"Plenty of time, my flight is not until five thirty, thanks," responds Tom.

Everyone starts to leave the bar, to rid themselves of the fucking awful Angel Productions polyester polo shirts.

"So, Hugo, are you looking forward to our time in Monaco? Now, that is where the real totty can be found," I smile, linking my arm through his.

"Martha, between you and me, I have alternative plans, so I won't be joining you," responds Hugo, rather secretively.

"Hugo, now what's the likelihood of you divulging the details, if I were to ask very nicely?" I ask.

"As it's you and I am sure you are a lady of the utmost discretion and keep this to yourself, I am planning to meet with Eleanor, one of the model agents, overseeing the fashion show. I've worked with her before; and well, you know, she finds me irresistible, so, what can I say? I can hardly turn the lady down now, can I? We are off to Juan les Pins, away from prying eyes, especially those of Ingrid," smiles Hugo, leaning in to give me a peck on my cheek.

"Your secret is safe with me. And Hugo, I hope you have a perfect time, but be sure to tell me all about it later, OK?" I giggle, responding with a hug.

Rushing to my room, I quickly jump in the shower and when done, I plaster Prada body lotion all over my body before changing into an all-in-one black jumpsuit, which is absolutely fantastic, totally, totally wow. I feel a million dollars when wearing this jumpsuit, which is simply perfect for Monaco. Slipping into black strappy, incredibly high mules, I grab my Gucci bag and load it up with iphone, lip gloss, tissues, wallet, etc, all the things a girl might need for a few hours in Monaco.

I ring Theo, but it switches directly to voicemail, so I leave him a message:

"Hi honey, sissy here, how are you? Great time last night, thank you. Danny pissed me off today, but hey, what do you expect from a fuckwit? I am going into Monaco with the crew this afternoon, so, not sure what time we will be back. If I'm back in time, let's rendezvous. Love you oodles. Ciao for now and big kiss to my little bro."

Shit! I've still not received a text from Howard. Do I text him, or should I leave him be? I grab a coin from my purse, heads I text, tails I don't. Up goes the coin into the air and down it comes. Fuck! It's tails. OK then, best of three. Second time up it lands on heads, yes! Here we go, third time lucky and it lands on tails. So, therefore I shouldn't text him, right? Wrong1 I grab my iphone and decide to send a little text, nothing major, just a little one:

Hi Howard, hope you have a great afternoon on the golf course, hopefully with plenty of birdies and maybe the odd albatross! But for now, I'm off for a drink in Monaco, hope to see you later x.

I check the time; it's now two forty. I am exhausted. Maybe I should lie down for ten minutes? Well, what a bloody stupid idea that is! Chances are, I will fall into a deep and glorious sleep and miss my trip to Monaco. I think not. After all, it's party time, so sleep will have to wait!

Chapter Eight

Down in the hotel's reception, we are waiting for our mini bus to arrive and there is definitely a buzz of excitement, after all, we have sun, laughter, the glitz of Monaco and the thrill of a free night; well, free in the sense of not working, not free in the sense of not paying for anything and of course, of untold naughtiness!

The mini bus arrives. Belinda, who I think is already a little drunk, is waving her group list around enthusiastically, encouraging us to board in an orderly manner. One by one, she ticks us off. She really is quite hilarious when she's tipsy!

"Mel, squeeze yourself on, there's enough room for two seats each. Mickey, now you behave. Dan, come on, move yourself and keep your hands to yourself, at the same time! Ellie, it's back seat for you. And Tom, come on Tom, we're so sorry to see you go. Finally, Martha, come on cutie we have a schedule to keep, hey, loving the outfit. Hang on, oh no, I'm missing one! Hold on, let me just count. Oh, it's OK, it's me and I haven't ticked myself off yet!" slurs Belinda.

Yep, she's definitely pissed, but then, in fairness, after the few days that she and Ellie have had to endure, I can hardly blame her for knocking it back, be it all a little too quickly!

The driver has loaded Tom's suitcase, and we are finally off. Off, on our adventures in Monaco.

Ellie hands out little miniature spirit bottles, which she has managed to snaffle from the concierge. Now obviously, he has a little soft spot for her, but then don't they all?

We are each handed two bottles, one vodka and one brandy—nice mix! Mickey proposes a toast,

"Ladies and Gents, let me 'ear your cheers for a corking twelve hours. Bring it on, I luv ya all."

We cheer and clink our bottles with one another, giggling like excitable school children, on a school outing. There seems to be an awful lot of love running through this small group and from nowhere, I suddenly feel a tad emotional. Now, I'm not quite sure why I'm feeling this way, but rather surprisingly, I allow tears to spring to my eyes. I never cry in public, it's just not done, besides which, mascara running down ones' cheeks, is never a flattering look, is it? I am being way too foolish for my own good, at this moment in time...

I am blinking quickly, trying to dispel the tears, but still they keep coming. I take a swig of vodka, in the hope that it will help and help me it does. However, it doesn't help in the way I want it to help, when it goes down the wrong tube and I start coughing, well actually choking; obviously, vodka is not the answer to my tears, but it sure does taste good!

Suddenly, Tom is by my side, patting my back gently.

"Are you OK?, Did it go down the wrong way?" he asks, in a very concerned, almost a fatherly tone.

"I'm not quite sure what happened there, but thankfully, I seem to be back in working order again—thank you." I smile.

My heart is pounding. What the fuck is wrong with me—has someone spiked my drink? Of course not, who would do such a thing? Maybe, I'm just high on emotion, not a bad thing, especially when I look around at this bunch of mad, crazy people, I am lucky enough to have in my world.

We manage to finish the entire quota of miniature bottles, just in time for our arrival at Nice International Airport.

We head to Terminal Two initially, to drop off Tom. One by one we hug him, even the boys, and then we wave and whistle, as we head out of the drop off zone for our short drive to Terminal One.

Our HelliAir representative is on hand to meet the arrival of our mini bus and as we all clamber out, Mickey bets Dan that he can get a date with the 'copter bird, twenty Euros apparently, says it's a done deal.

We are led to the HelliAir departure lounge. Mickey is deep in conversation with our representative and all I can say, is thank heavens she can speak English, as Mickey's French is not up to much. In fact, it's non-existent, it's just hilarious to watch the Prowse charm in action and believe me, it doesn't matter in which language he tries to speak, it always works...

It would seem that Mickey is actually getting somewhere with the rep, there is much laughter and flirting, between the two of them.

We board our helicopters, obviously not a helicopter each, because that would be totally greedy! No, there are two helicopters allotted to our group and rather surprisingly, our lovely lady rep is travelling the seven minute flight with us, obviously, she has succumbed to the Prowse charm!

In the first helicopter we have our rep, together with Mickey, Ellie and Belinda. In helicopter two we have me, Dan and Mel. Thankfully, our weight is distributed evenly, with Dan and I huddled on one side and Mel on the other.

"Sweet Jesus1 I hope this helicopter can take off, with me in the back!" Mel half jokingly, says to the pilot.

"Madame, you is no weight at all. I haz flown zee men twice your size and never wiz difficulty!" winks the pilot. Hey! Hang on just a minute, is he flirting with Mel? Boy, these men are like bees round a honey pot with her. There is a lot to be said, for carrying a few extra pounds.

Up in the air, we swoop across the waves and then fly high like a bird. The coast line looks amazing from up here and, within minutes, we have arrived at Fontvielle heliport, in Monaco.

Exiting our helicopter, I note that Mickey is exchanging numbers with the rep—boy, he's a fast mover; it's got to be said. They say their goodbyes and she is off, with a sexy wiggle.

"Well, Dan my boy, this is how a true pro gets the girl—want me to teach you a few moves?" asks Mickey, flicking his hair and lifting the collar on his shirt.

"And for the record mate, 'er name is Marie and she might just be joining us later, yeah baby!" continues Mickey, thrusting his pelvis back and forth.

"Mate, you just got lucky. Obviously, if the tables had been turned, she would 'ave said yes to me, but mate, rather than her flying back to Nice, she would 'ave stayed with me—boy, you're losing your touch Prowsie!" responds Dan, laughing.

"Right then everyone, the time is now four thirty five, what say you we grab a cab and hit the casino, next to the Café de Paris? We can grab a table at the Café, have a bite to eat, a few drinks and see where the night takes us!" shrills Ellie, in a really high-pitched voice. I think she is rather excited to be here, or it may be that she is excited to be rid of Ingrid, albeit for just a few hours!

"Brilliant idea. The only draw back of course, is that you can never find a cab when you want one, here in Monaco—everything is chauffeur driven, blacked out windows, pre booked, etc. We could walk, it will only take us fifteen minutes, or better still, watch a true professional in action!" I giggle, a little too enthusiastically. God, how I love Monaco! I always feel totally alive here, my favourite place on earth, other than Venice, of course.

I head over to a gleaming blacked out Mercedes mini bus, which is clearly displaying a sign for Hotel Hermitage. As I approach, a driver appears.

"Mademoiselle, Bonsoir, transferez-vous a l'hotel Hermitage?" he asks.

"Oui monsieur, il y a six de nous." I respond.

"Pas probleme, Mesdames et messieurs satisfont montent a bord du mini autobus!" He indicates to the group to board the mini bus, helping the ladies (I use the term very loosely) on first.

"You, my darling have the cheek of the devil. You do realise that he will now escort us into the Hermitage and then what are you going to do?" asks Mel, in astonishment.

"Have faith my darling, have faith. As I said, watch this true professional in action," I reply, leaning forward to hug my darling friend.

Arriving at the hotel, sure enough we are led into the Hermitage and straight to the main reception desk. I thank our driver, shaking his hand, so that our palms cross with a twenty Euro note. Nodding his head appreciatively, he departs.

At the reception desk, I confirm that we are from Angel Productions and wonder whether it might be possible to have a look around their conference facilities.

The reception host is very apologetic, as unfortunately there is a conference already running in the main suite, but it should be finished in the next sixty minutes or so. I assure her it is not a problem, as we will return, when we find ourselves in Monaco again.

Within minutes, we are out of the hotel and into the beautiful sunshine, which is still surprisingly hot, so late into the afternoon.

The Café de Paris is just around the corner from the hotel. We find a table easily, which is a rare feat and within seconds, we are people watching. Needless to say, Mickey and Dan are ogling the women, but in fairness to them, there are some seriously, beautiful women in Monaco.

Mel and I ogle cars, well not the cars, but more specifically their drivers! Just how many Ferraris, Bentleys, Aston Martins and historical E-type Jaguars, are there in Monaco? Loads, in fact more than loads, shit loads! In the blink of any eye, I counted seven Ferraris and six, with rather hot looking drivers! The seventh driver, unfortunately, has been tickled with the ugly stick!

Ellie and Belinda cannot contain themselves and immediately head for the casino next door. Thankfully, they are not destined to lose the shirts off their backs, as this casino is definitely for the novice!

"We'll only be a few minutes, I promise. But I'm starving, can you order us some food please and of course a bottle of white wine?" beams Ellie.

We order drinks, beers for the boys, gin and tonics and of course, a bottle of white wine for the girls, together with club sandwiches all round. Hunger has gripped us.

I watch in disbelief as people stand next to parked Ferraris, having their photograph taken by their loved ones. I must say, I have never really understood why you would do such a thing? After all, you're hardly going pull out the photo album at a dinner party and announce that 'this is my Ferrari'. If that was the case, you would go out to the garage and show them the Ferrari, but to show a photo of you standing next to something that clearly is not yours, is like, well weird.

I always remember attending the Monaco Grand Prix, when I was seeing Alexandre, God, how I love that boy, I love him too much and if truth be told, I do still love him, especially as he lives in Monaco and has all the trappings of wealth, old money, pure money, proper money. Such a perfect man, well, in my eyes he is. Such a shame that he is already married and that his two small children, absolutely hate me—I don't understand why, but ultimately, they were just too much to bear, even over a weekend!

Anyway, as I was saying, I remember coming to the Monaco Grand Prix, having a brilliant time, FIA passes, which allowed us into the pit lane, first class hospitality at the Rascasse and of course evenings at Amber Lounge, but the thing that stands out most of all, is when we were stopped by a couple (nice couple, dressed in shorts and Ferrari polo shirts and walking boots—sorry, but what is that all about?) Anyway, they wanted their photograph taken. Nothing wrong, or improper about that, I hear you say, but they wanted their photograph taken next to an Armco barrier, a barrier that had been used during the Grand Prix.

Now call me simple, but surely with all the famously, fantastic sites, housed in this tiny principality, one might find a more suitable backdrop for a photograph? But no, they definitely wanted it taken next to the Armco—and so it was, happy memories for them, I hope!

Mickey is busy texting, too engrossed, to notice a bevy of young, hot Russian girls walking by. Dan is almost fitting; his eyes are out on stalks.

"Ladies, excuse my language, but fuck me, do they get any more perfect than them beauties?" announces Dan, very slowly.

"Oh mate, put down the bloody phone and take a look at them girlies, what do you reckon, do we stand a chance?" continues Dan.

"Shit man! What did I miss? Look at the cute backsides on 'em, bloody 'ell, worth a shot or not?" asks Mickey.

"Boys, I hate to disappoint you, but I suspect that they are no older than fourteen, maybe fifteen at a push, but certainly not of a legal age to be messing about with the likes of you, two married men. Understand?" smiles Mel.

"Anyway, who are you texting? Oh no, don't tell me, not that bird from the 'copter—are you mad?" says Mel, punching Mickey's arm.

"Mad? Definitely not! Up for a bit? Definitely yes!" responds Mickey, laughing.

"You lucky bugger. What's the plan then? Where are you meetin' her?" asks Dan.

"You mean where are WE meetin' her? Dan my friend, she 'as a mate who is free this evening, so they're both coming into Monaco. Her mate's name is Chantelle, sounds sweet," continues Mickey, looking rather smug with himself.

"Oh my good Lord! What are you like Mr Prowse? And as for you Dan—he's a bad influence. Am I to assume therefore, that you will be leaving us stranded in Monaco this evening, to fend for ourselves?" I ask, in a childish voice.

"Martha DiPinto, if I didn't know you better, I'd definitely say that there's an 'int of jealously brewing 'ere. What's up chick, bothered that we've pulled and you ain't?" laughs Mickey.

"Behave, I was just rather looking forward to getting pissed with you both, but it seems we are three camps now—the boys' camp, the 'gambling' camp for Ellie and Belinda and the 'up for anything' camp, for me and Mel. Well, so be it!" I say, slightly aggrieved.

"Babe, we ain't gonna leave you and them naughty gambling girls here in Monaco alone, are we now? No, the girls, Marie and Chantelle are going to join us, they can be our tour guides for the night and any ways, they ain't gonna be here until after ten, so we'll be four sheets to the wind by then, hopefully," replies Mickey, with a wink.

With that, our food and drinks arrive. Dan is encouraged to go and find Belinda and Ellie, as we start tucking into our club sandwiches. Bloody hell, I am absolutely starving.

Dan seems to be taking his time; he must be struggling to get the girls out of the casino!

Some twenty minutes have passed since we received our food, but still no sign of Dan, Ellie or Belinda. Where the hell are they?

"Listen guys, I'm going to pop into the casino, to see if I can find them, otherwise, I might be destined to eat their food and quite possibly quaff that bottle of rather nice Chardonnay!" I smile, as I take a large swig of my gin and head off in pursuit of our missing friends.

The casino is lovely and cool. I stop off at the tabac, housed within the casino, to purchase some cigarettes and then head in. I veer off to the left, towards the slot machines, scouting every aisle, but to no avail. I head off to the back of the casino, where the gambling tables are set up. I walk round slowly, neck craned and then finally I spot them, way over in the corner, all huddled around a gambling table, Black Jack, I think.

I head over to them purposefully. They appear to be huddled around a guy, who seems to be winning big and the girls, it would appear, are his lucky charms. Now don't get me wrong, I have nothing against old men with young girls, but just for the record, it isn't going to happen with Belinda and Ellie and this rather, shall we say, portly chap, seems to be stroking Belinda's backside, from what I can see.

"Hi everyone, how's it going?" I ask. 'Your food has arrived, come on, let's go and eat.'

"Oh, Martha look! Serge is winning loads and his luck only changed when we arrived, didn't it Serge?" says Ellie, giggling like a love-struck teenager.

Serge looks over. He's obviously irritated that I've appeared. Did he think he might strike lucky with the girls? Well, his luck just bombed!

"Dan, have you also turned into a lucky charm?" I ask, sarcastically.

"Of course not, just didn't want to leave the girls with 'im did I?" responds Dan, tilting his head towards Serge.

"Come on you lot, say your goodbyes, I am sure Serge will be here later, if you want to pop back," I say, taking Ellie and Belinda by the arm.

"Oh, do we have to?" asks Ellie, in a child like, girlie, wimpish voice.

"Move it!" I respond.

"Bye Serge and good luck!" giggle the girls, in unison.

What the fuck have they been drinking? I didn't notice them holding drinks when I arrived, but something has obviously made them excitable.

We head outside, back to the Café de Paris.

"Fuck! It was untrue how much money was being lost and won in there and that isn't even the proper casino. The proper casino is over there." points Ellie.

"I think Serge is going there later, he said we could join him if we want to and he would pay us to be his lucky charms, but I think I would much rather get drunk with you lot!" says Belinda, flopping into her chair.

"I think he would be expecting a little more than just a rub of your arm Belinda, in return for his hard cash, if you get my drift..." answers Mel, shaking her head slowly.

It's now six thirty and everywhere you look, people are starting to venture out, dressed in their finery. Ladies dressed in Gucci, Chanel, Hermes, Prada, Celine, to name but a few! And girls in exceptionally short skirts and incredibly long legs and high strappy sandals.

In fact, it is really easy to distinguish Europeans from the British, especially the men. British men are very conservative in their evening attire—cotton or chino trousers and an open neck short sleeve shirt, coupled with the slightly daring sandal or 'fashion' shoe and sometimes the odd union jack t shirt. Ouch! How horrible!

The Europeans on the other hand, are completely different. They are dressed in linen, with a jumper casually draped across their shoulders, beautiful soft leather shoes and sunglasses, elegantly perched on the tops of their heads. Such style and class.

The nationalities of the women are somewhat harder to distinguish, as they flaunt themselves. The Danes, French, Italians and Germans possess great style and elegance. However, you can always identify Russians, as they fall into two categories—tall, beautiful and incredibly slim, or short, plump and plain!

For the next hour or so, we drink, we smoke, we eat ice cream. We drink a little more and then finish up with a round of shots, which quickly becomes three rounds of shots! Within the space of two hours, we have become hilariously drunk and manage to spend four hundred and forty Euros. Not bad going between the six of us, only an average of seventy five Euros each. A bargain at half the price!

Next, we head off to Slammers, a bar down the road, but this time there is neither a mini bus to take us, nor any taxis for that matter. No worries! It is a short distance away and definitely no more than a ten minute walk. Well, ten minutes if you are not drunk and in a group, so, more like twenty minutes, which I think is pretty good going.

Arriving at Slammers we order two jugs of mojitos and some beers. We are definitely in for a boozy night, there's no doubt about that.

There is a karaoke machine set up, so we ask the owner of the bar, a Yorkshire girl as it happens, whether we can use it. She is more than happy for us, to entertain her guests.

Within minutes, I am singing 'Fly Me to the Moon,' by Julie London. I am swiftly followed by Mel, who gives us a rendition of 'Fever,' by Peggy Lee; she sings it so well, that she actually gets a standing ovation and shouts of 'more, more'. So, being the obliging soul that she is, Mel has another go, this time she sings 'Always Something There to Remind Me,' by Sandie Shaw, which again, she sings brilliantly.

Next up, are Ellie and Belinda, who sing a duet—'Summer Loving,' from the movie, Grease. Well, they are both so drunk, that it's difficult to actually make out what they are singing.

The locals are well into the entertainment we are providing; so much so, that some of them, want a turn on the machine. No way, we are the entertainers!

Next up, it's Dan, singing 'Mac the Knife,' by Bobby Darin. Sweet Jesus! That boy can sing, even if he is so drunk that he can hardly stand!

Finally, we have Mickey up on stage, singing 'Let There be Love,' by Nat King Cole. Mickey is absolutely hilarious on stage, and I am sure he is making the words up. Of course, it was bound to end in tears, our tears, not his! He is swaying about so much, that he inadvertently sways off the end of the stage and lands, face down, whilst still managing to sing!

Once Mickey is up on his feet, we all take a bow and then have drinks on the house. The atmosphere has definitely changed since we arrived, loud music is now playing, people are laughing and there is definitely much merriment. Bring on the 'Midas Touch,' of the professional, conference freelancers!

Having spent the past two hours in Slammers, we decide to head off for more food. I, for one, am starving again and I think we definitely need more of a lining on our stomachs, if there is any hope whatsoever that we are to make rehearsals tomorrow morning—shit, if we all manage to make it back this evening, it will be a bloody miracle!

"I know a great bar and restaurant in the harbour, called Stars & Bars, and they have music, so we can dance too!" I giggle, linking arms with Dan and Mickey. "Shall we go there and have some food?" I say. 'I'm bloody starving.'

"Sounds like a plan to me babe. Is it OK for the 'copter girls to meet us there too?" asks Mickey, a little sheepishly.

"Of course it is. After all, it will be interesting to see how the mind of a French tart ticks, especially if she has designs on you, you daft bugger," sniggers Mel.

Bloody hell! Mel is so pissed. I really hope she doesn't fall over en route to Stars & Bars, as we'll need a bloody hoist to get her back on her feet again!

Some fifteen minutes later, we arrive at the Harbour; it is bustling like you cannot believe. People everywhere. We make our way to Stars & Bars and head straight to the bar and order drinks.

"I'll go, reserve us a table, alright?" says Mickey, staggering away.

Within seconds he's back. "Bloody 'ell, the waiting time for a table is around an hour and 'alf. We'll be completely bollocked by then. Shall we go somewhere else?" he asks.

"Once again my lovely, leave it to the professional..." I say, swaying towards the reservations counter.

"Bonsoir and how are you this fine evening Claudette?" I ask the lady behind the desk.

"Oh my God, I don't believe it, is that you Martha? Jesus girl! It's been far too long. Why don't you come and visit me any more?" asks Claudette, hugging me, as only a good friend can hug.

"Oh Claudette, you know what it's like, I am not with Alexandre any more, so I only come to Monaco occasionally, but as I am here tonight, I would really appreciate it, if you could find us a table. My friends and I are starving. I think Mickey came over to you, but we'll be dead if we have to wait any longer than twenty minutes," I say, hugging her and kissing her, in a begging kind of way.

I have known Claudette for a few years, having met her on the numerous occasions I have been to Stars & Bars. It was a meeting of great minds, as when I first met her, I had only just started seeing Alexandre and I wasn't sure whether he was the one for me. Anyway, I bumped into her one day, when I was out shopping in Monaco and we became firm friends. I know therefore, she will feel obliged to find me a table!

"Martha, it is so good to see you, really it is. Give me ten minutes and I will come and find you!" she smiles, hugging me affectionately.

"Thanks Claudette." As I walk away, I have a teeny moment of sadness. I miss Alexandre and I miss the friends I made in Monaco. Oh shit! I really do miss Alexandre, with all my heart. Fuck! Come on, pull yourself together girl. He's been and now he's gone and when all is said and done, he is a bastard of the first order!

"Hey guys, the true pro has once again worked her powers, and we should have a table within the next ten to fifteen minutes," I giggle, high-fiving Mel.

Within minutes, we are all drinking huge cocktails, even the boys and needless to say, we are dancing around, without a care in the world.

Mickey has gone outside to text Marie, his 'copter friend. I don't suppose it will do any harm in them joining us, as they say, the more the merrier.

I head off to the Ladies to powder my nose. As I am taking a pee, I realise I've not checked my iphone for a while. Most unlike me, my mobile is a permanent feature in my life, unlike men!

Oh my, I am Miss Popular. Not one, not two, but three missed calls and four text messages.

Missed call one—my father, just checking how the show is going and am I behaving and eating properly? Be sure to call home occasionally. Blah, blah, as only fathers do!

Missed call two—Theo, checking up on my behaviour in Monaco and telling me to stay away from Alexandre, no matter how drunk I get!

Missed call three—Fucking marvellous! It's Howard Johnson III asking how my free time is going. Golf apparently was good. Also, he is wondering what time I will be back in Cannes later.

Ha, ha, he loves me! And now the text messages, let's see...

Text one from Theo: *Ciao bella, why are you not answering your phone, please tell me you are not with HIM. Call me, when you get back to Cannes xxx*. I respond quickly, confirming that I am totally drunk, but definitely not misbehaving with Alexandre!

Text two from Hugo: *Hello Martha, just checking that you and the gang are having a mighty fine time in Monaco. Please remember, we do have rehearsals in the morning!* I text back to tell him we are all very well behaved, and sipping our drinks!

Text three from Howard Johnson III (yes he definitely loves me): *Hi Martha, not sure if you picked up my message. I can only deduce that you are having a ball. Hope to see you later. Hx*. I text back and tell Howard that we are indeed having a wonderful time, but that it would be even more wonderful, if he were here too. I send it with four kisses and a promise to knock on his door when I get back. What a perfect slut I am!

Text four from... I don't believe it! It's from Alexandre. Oh sweet Jesus! My body is going into melt down! My finger hovers for a moment, before pressing the 'read' button: *I hear you are in town. Call me, if you have time, I would love to see you x.*

Shit! Oh my God! I don't believe it! How do I respond to him? I still love him, so much in fact, that it hurts! I remain sitting on the toilet. I need a moment to think. Right, come on let me think about this. Thankfully, I am too drunk to send a grown up response, which means of course, if I do respond to him, I will no doubt put ridiculous things like, 'love you', 'want you', 'miss you', 'need you.' So, I should just ignore it, shouldn't I?

I jump, when suddenly there is banging on the door. To my horror, I notice that I am still sitting on the toilet and have been for some time with my jumpsuit around my ankles, together with my knickers! Shit! I've been here an age.

"Slapper, are you OK? What are you doing for fucks sake? You've been ages!" enquires Mel, from the other side of the toilet door. 'Your mate, who runs this place, has been over and we've got a table, so move it.'

I can think of nothing more, than to respond to Alexandre. I can't even focus on pulling my knickers up, let alone hoisting myself into my jumpsuit! Should I meet him? Should I invite him over to Stars & Bars? No, I simply send a kiss via text and leave it at that. Fuck! I miss him, despite him being the biggest bastard on God's earth!

Within moments, I am sitting with everyone (having of course finally got dressed and washed my hands), looking over the menu. I decide on pasta—a fantastic lining for the stomach, especially when laced with meatballs!

We order more beers, more gin and more wine.

Mickey keeps looking over towards the door. Ah, he is obviously awaiting the arrival of Dumb and Dumber, the helicopter girls!

"Mickey, what time are your lovely ladies arriving?" I ask. "Shall we order them some food too?"

"Mate, I don't know. I have texted her to let her know where we are, but she ain't responded yet, so they can order food when they get here," responds Mickey.

"Boy we're gonna have some fun tonight," chips in Dan, who now seems to be swaying a little, even though he is sitting down!

At precisely eleven pm, our food arrives and we all tuck in, picking off of each others' plates, in an annoying manner. We have ordered a mountain of dishes and the drinks just keep flowing.

It is not even midnight and I can't remember being this pissed, for such a long time. I feel brilliant. We all eat with gusto and finally our feast comes to an end. With the table cleared, we order yet more drinks and three rounds of shots. These shots, of course, will be our downfall. Of this, I am certain.

Chapter Nine

Well, as I thought, the last round of three shots has completely destroyed us. Ellie and Belinda are so drunk, they are now dancing on the table. Yes, quite literally on the table. Crowds have formed, mostly guys, as they seem to be dancing a little too erotically, for their own good! The gathered crowds are jeering them on and in return, the girls are gyrating, just a little bit more than is really necessary. They are absolutely loving it. It's a bloody worry what alcohol does to you!

Dan, on the other hand, is getting a little agitated by all these guys, watching his beloved Ellie and suggests to Mickey that they might get the girls down off the table and in fairness, Mickey is quick to agree and act. After all, the last thing we need is a broken bone or two, before the show!

Reluctantly, Ellie and Belinda agree to climb down, but carry on dancing around the bar, as Mel and Dan join them. The place is rocking, the music is loud, the beat is thumping and all around, beautiful people are laughing, drinking and dancing.

I lean close into Mickey, "Hey Mickey Pickey, what's up? You're looking sad," I slur.

"What is it with birds, eh? I thought I was getting on with Marie but she ain't even bothered to text to say she ain't coming, I mean what's all that about then?" responds Mickey, putting his arm around my shoulder.

"Well, all I can say is, good job she didn't come, because I have you all to myself now, just the way I like it!" I say, planting a big sloppy kiss on his cheek.

"You know what Mart, you and me, we could 'ave been something a little bit special, if we 'ad tried 'arder," says Mickey, looking a little too serious now.

"Now, Mr Prowse, behave yourself. What fun would it have been, if we were together? Our friendship is and always will be, very strong. But the chemistry between us isn't the 'permanent' kind now, is it? I love you, just the way you are, as my friend. My friend, who I can rely on, always." Fuck! I am so very pissed, as I am rambling and then kiss him on his lips quickly, as I don't want this affection turning into a full-on snog!

"Come on, I want to dance," I say, pulling him up out of his seat.

For the next three hours, we dance and drink with each other and pretty much everyone else, in Stars & Bars. Claudette is almost encouraging our naughtiness, by plying us with more and more shots. There has to be a limit to how much the human body can take, and I think I am fast approaching it!

Mel, Belinda and Mickey are dancing to 'Ain't Nobody,' by Rufus & Chaka Khan; all three of them are lost in the moment. It is, as the world would say, 'a wicked tune!'

Ellie and Dan seem to be getting a little too close for comfort they are locked in each other's arms. Now, I am not sure if this is because they are feeling the love, or simply, that if they were to release their grip, they would both go tumbling to the ground, through alcoholic meltdown!

I nip outside to check my iphone and get some much needed, fresh air. I've got three text messages, but I am almost too scared to open them up. What if Alexandre has been in contact again? Although, let's face it, I secretly hope he has!

OK, deep breath... Let's do this, so I can get back to the dance floor and the flowing alcohol.

Text one is from Theo: *Cara mia. Are you not back in Cannes yet? Are you still behaving? xx*

I respond simply, by saying: *Thank you for being you. Still behaving xx.*

Text two is from Howard, no surprise there! His reads: *Perhaps we can organise our own night out in Monaco, just you and me? Knock three times when you get back, I'll be waiting xxx.* He is just so perfect.

I respond eagerly: *I look forward to me and you in Monaco. Still here—are you still up? xx.*

Text three. Here we go again. It's from Alexandre. Now, let's just think for a moment. I could just delete it, without reading it, couldn't I? I could, but guess what? I'm not going to!

I note he sent his response at 00:17 hrs. Will he still be up? After all, it's after three am now. God only knows. Oh fuck it! I read his text: *Let me kiss you in person, where are you? xx.*

At this point I should simply turn off the handset, but of course I don't. Before I've managed to engage my brain, I am hitting the reply button. This of course is a big, huge, fuck off mistake. I couldn't just respond with: *'sorry too late, back at my hotel now'* or something similar, no, I have to respond with: *Fuck I miss you baby, come and meet me, I'm at Stars & Bars xxx.*

My heart is pounding I need more alcohol. Well, clearly I don't, as I can barely stand up, but I hurry back to the bar and order champagne. What the fuck is wrong with me? Talk about a wasted drink when you're already pissed, but what the heck, I want champagne, so champagne is what I shall have.

We stay in Stars & Bars until four am, but rather than head off back to Cannes, (at this stage, I am still not quite sure how we are going to get there) we decide to have a nightcap at the Rascasse, which is a stones throw and staggering distance away, from Stars & Bars.

I find Claudette and promise to return very soon. Even better, she is planning a trip to the UK, so I will see her sooner than anticipated.

I head over to the bar to settle the bill, my head is whizzing, but I am not sure if it is because I have been handed the bill, or whether it's due to the amount of alcohol I've consumed.

We have amassed a bill of eight hundred and thirty Euros! Sweet Jesus! That is high by anyone's standards, especially as we have had masses, and I mean masses of free drinks too!

Mel is by my side, "Fucking hell Slapper! How did we manage to drink that much? I must be more pissed than I thought." she slurs.

"Listen, I'll settle it and then we'll sort it out tomorrow," I respond, hoping that I have my credit card in my wallet. Thankfully, God is looking down on me. I ask the barman to put nine hundred Euros on the card, so that it covers a tip.

What an expensive night. But forget the expense; we still need to figure out a way of getting back to Cannes tonight. Well, hardly tonight now, is it? How are we going to get back to Cannes, this morning? I bet the girls didn't think of that one, before they planned our trip to Monaco!

Next stop is the Rascasse, one of the trendy hangouts. We all pile to the bar and order beers for the boys, cokes for Belinda and Ellie; yep, they are definitely suffering, and gin and tonics for Mel and myself.

We dance without a care in the world and come to think of it, we drink without a care in the world, too.

The Rascasse is buzzing, but I am boiling hot, so I tell Mel that I am popping outside, for a cigarette.

Secretly though, I want to check my iphone, to see if either Howard or Alexandre, who is my preferred choice for this evening, have responded.

I light up a cigarette and pull out my iphone. Fuck! Can you believe that?! Neither of them has replied. That's a bummer. I'm not that bloody popular, after all!

I can hear a wicked song being played in the bar, 'I Need Your Loving' by Baby D, which prompts me to dance all by myself, outside. I am totally lost in the moment, but suddenly realise I am being watched rather attentively, by a couple of policemen who are sitting across the road from the Rascasse, in their police van. I wave and they eagerly wave back. Hey, this could just be the lucky break we need.

I head over to them, trying to walk as seductively as is humanly possible, when you're as pissed as I am. Also, my bloody feet are killing me, because I've been dancing on four inch killer heels for the past three hours!

"Bouna sera signorina, come stai? Ma, tu sei Italiana?" asks policeman number one.

"Si sono Italiano ma ora vivo in Inghliterra, I mio nome e Martha," I respond.

"Ah, so you speaka English, but you iz looking very much Italian. Beautiful. We iz both learning de English. My name is Franco and diz iz Marco. Are you, how you say now, 'aving a good time?" asks Franco.

"So you're both Italian but working in Monaco, very nice, the best of both worlds. Yes, I'm having a really great time. The night is still young and my girlfriends want to party more, but I'm a little worried, because we need to get back to Cannes, the Maritime Hotel. Tell me, are there any mini buses we can hire, or maybe the trains are running?" I enquire, tilting my head, akin to a child asking for chocolate, instead of vegetables!

"Marta iz 'ard to get a buz now, if you 'ave not booked. De trains to Cannes will not come until fifteen pass de seven hours. Why not, how you say ferme, ah yez, why not stay here in Monaco?" asks Marco.

"No. We definitely need to get back, as we are working in Cannes on a conference. Oh shit! What can I do?" I ask, leaning in close against the police van's open window, hoping all the while, that my breasts aren't sagging under the sheer weight of alcohol, pumping through me.

The two policemen turn to one another and start muttering, but I can't quite hear what they are saying. But deep down, I have an inkling that they might, just might, provide us with a lift! Eventually they turn to me. My fingers are crossed, as come on let's face it, this would be a perfect mode of transport, as it would easily fit the six of us in. Well, it might be a bit of a squeeze with Mel!

"Marta, we are to close our work at six clock, and we iz to return de police camio. Ah mamma mia, how you say polizia camio?" asks Franco.

"Polizia camio, si dice police van," I respond, a little too eagerly.

"Ah yes, de van to Nice, so perhaps we can take you from here at six clock, to Cannes. Would diz be good for you?" asks Franco.

"Boys that would be absolutely perfect for me. Are you able to fit six people in the van?" I ask, grinning like a Cheshire cat.

"Dio mio, there iz six?" exclaims Marco.

"Yes, is that OK?" I flutter my eyelashes, and adjust the top of my jumpsuit.

"Yes, six iz good," he replies, looking at my cleavage.

"That's great, so we will see you here at six o'clock then? Thanks boys, I definitely owe you one!" I smile, as I wiggle off, back towards the Rascasse.

I can just imagine what those two policemen are thinking now—a bit of rumpy pumpy, in return for a ride—ha, little do they know that we have Mickey and Dan with us!

Once back in the Rascasse, I find my drunken counterparts and divulge my scheming plan to get us back to Cannes. Now, how do you think they might respond? Maybe, a pat on the back or, a peck on the cheek? No, that would be too normal, wouldn't it? No, they go ahead and order more champagne. Fucking hell, this night, or, should I say, this morning, is out of control. The time is now five twenty am and we are due to be on site for breakfast, at seven thirty am. Not a fucking hope in hell!

We are all starting to feel a little tired, but, as if by magic, the DJ senses our fatigue and puts on 'Yeke Yeke' by Mory Kante. Well that's it; we all jump up and start dancing around, as if the night is still young!

At five forty five, we agree that we'll have one last drink, a shot each, to round off the evening.

Mickey proposes a toast: "To one an' all, you've made me night, good luck wiv re'earsals!" he giggles, unable to stand upright.

It's now six am. I suggest that we make our way over to our mode of transport, in an orderly manner. We settle the Rascasse bill, which thankfully only comes to three hundred and sixty Euros and I take the lead to the police van, followed by the young girls, (they will appeal to the policemen) then by Mel and then Mickey and Dan at the rear.

Much to my amusement, the police van is indeed waiting for us and has its lights flashing—ah, the shame of it!

"Marta, quick put de people in van, also you iz in de back, you can't sit wiz us," advises Marco.

"Ah, just a momento, who iz de two boys? I did not say for boys to come also," Marco looks taken aback, at the sight of Mickey and Dan.

"Oh Marco forgive me. We refer to Mickey and Dan as girls too, as they are, you know, gay, homosexual. So, is it OK for them to come, too?" I smile, stroking his hand.

"Yez, OK, but quick before any of de peoples sees," commands Franco.

We all pile into the back and within minutes we are off, laughing at each other—what a cool way to make it back to Cannes. Out of nowhere, Ellie pulls out a bottle of champagne, a gift apparently, from the barman at the Rascasse. Result! We swig in turn until it is empty, and slowly drift off, one by one, into deep slumbers.

"Marta, Marta, svegliarsi, come on, waking up please!" shouts Marco.

I am completely dazed. There is sunlight streaming in from somewhere, but I am totally confused because I don't know where the fuck I am! It takes a moment or two for me to realise that we are, of course, in the back of the police van, our taxi home from Monaco!

"Marta, we iz at de Maritime, pleaze all bodies out now!" he says.

"Oh Marco, sorry, I think we fell asleep, but thank you so much for bringing us back. What time is it please?" I say, squinting at the outline of a person standing at the rear of the van, but with the sun behind him, I can't see anything, other than a silhouette!

"Marta, de time iz now seven hours and ten minutes—we 'ad to go to Nice as dare was a small incidente, but everything iz OK and zen we come 'ere as quick as possible!" replies Marco.

I shake the bodies around me, one by one, trying to stir them from their slumber. Mel will need to exit the van first, as she seems to have fallen off her seat and onto the floor and is now blocking the door. Fuck! She is a sight for sore eyes! She resembles a beached whale; heaven only knows how we are going to move her!

Finally we are all awake. "Mel, come on will you, we need to get changed and over to the venue, come on girlie, move it!" I shout, shaking her violently.

"Keep your fucking hair on you dozy mare and pray tell me, what the fuck am I doing down here on the floor? And who the fuck is that, standing at the back door?" responds Mel, as she tries to shift herself, from the rather awkward position she finds herself in.

"Mel darling, I think you must have fallen off your seat during our journey back from Monaco. We are in the back of a police van. You do remember the police van don't you, and the very nice policemen who drove us back—Franco and Marco?" I respond, now being gentle with her. Mel is definitely in a horrible mood.

"Fucking hell Martha, I can't move! You'll have to roll me out of here, my fucking legs have gone to sleep!" yells Mel.

"Alright, come on, we're wasting bleedin' time here. Dan, you get one side and I'll take the other and after three we'll roll her out, gently though, we don't want to 'urt the old bird, otherwise we ain't gonna get to bloody rehearsals on time, are we?" instructs Mickey.

On the count of three, Mickey and Dan do, quite literally, roll Mel out of the van and supposedly into the arms of Marco and Franco, our dutiful policemen. Alas, they obviously did not take into account Mel's weight and as she is rolled out of the van they are not prepared and she drops to the ground, laughing like a hyena, legs akimbo!

We all start to laugh, belly trembling laughter. Ellie is crying with hysterics and Belinda is trying desperately to get out of the van to help Mel, but is unable to do so, as she too, is laughing so much.

Suddenly our laughter stops. Abruptly.

"And what exactly is the meaning of this street exhibition?"

We all look up, sunlight still streaming through the back doors of the police van and although we can't see who it is, we all instantly recognise that voice. Standing directly above Mel, is Ingrid. A stern and understandably, very unhappy, Ingrid.

"Boungiorno Signora, pleaze do not worry, for zay iz not arrested, zay 'ave difficulta in getting train, so we bring zem back. Diz is no, 'ow you say now, problema," interrupts Franco.

"On the contrary. I think there is a rather big problem here. Let me remind you all, that rehearsals commence at eight fifteen prompt. Please ensure you arrive in good time. And Mel, might I suggest you get up immediately, before our client sees you lying down in the road, making a complete exhibition of yourself!" responds Ingrid, sternly.

"Ingrid, it is not through choice that I find myself down here, these two clumsy dopes dropped me!" giggles Mel.

We are all holding our breath, even Marco and Franco. Ingrid's facial expression is full of anger and the whites of her eyes are gleaming with rage, as she sticks her head into the back of the police van, leaning awkwardly over Mel.

"Eight fifteen sharp. Washed, dressed and ready to go. Do you all hear? Believe me, this is not the end of this matter!" and with that, she turns and walks off towards the venue.

As soon as Ingrid has disappeared, we all start laughing even the policemen can't control themselves.

We each thank our new friends, Marco and Franco and exchange numbers, so that we can meet up next time we are in Monaco.

Hurriedly, we all go to our rooms to shower and change. If we are lucky, we might just have time to grab a croissant before rehearsals begin. Fuck me! It's going to be a long hard day and I have a cracking headache, that's just waiting to come out to play!

Chapter Ten

My God, it's been a long time since I've had such a major alcoholic blowout, but I have enjoyed every single minute, even though I am looking like a car crash—I am peering into the mirror and it is clearly obvious, that I am still blindingly drunk and if a mirror could laugh, it would be howling! Oh fuck! Shit! Bollocks! Today is going to be an utter disaster, I can feel it, in my drunken bones!

I strip off, jump in the shower and scrub myself sober. Well actually, I am imagining that I am scrubbing myself sober, but clearly as I stumble out of the shower and skid along the tiled floor, I know that I have yet to reach that sober point. I plaster Prada body lotion into my aching body and continue getting ready at breakneck speed. Finally, I am donning my rather attractive Angel Productions polyester polo shirt and throwing everything into my handbag—room key, perfume, mints, tissues, bottle of water and my iphone. Grabbing my laptop bag, I head for the door.

My iphone beeps, as I wait for the lift (I am far too pissed to take the stairs—we are talking instant body bash, if stairs were the only option. Christ alive, I couldn't even get out of the shower this morning, without stumbling, imagine what I would be like down a flight or two, of stairs!) I make a grab for my mobile, just as Mel comes out of her room. Jesus Christ! I think I look bad, but boy oh boy, Mel is looking totally shattered, although she does have a rosy glow to her cheeks, either caused by the fact that she is still very drunk, or, could it be due to all that effort in getting her out of the police van and up, off the road?

"Fucking hell Martha! That was some night, I am still buzzing, but bloody hell, don't we know how to party?" she puffs (yep, Mel is definitely suffering today). I note that she is wearing her polo shirt inside out and casually, point this fact out. "Oh fuck off, do I really care? I'll get it round the right way, when we arrive at the venue!" she smirks.

"Well, my darling, it's not often that we have a night off whilst working, which is probably not a bad thing, after all, we would certainly be attending AA classes, if we did it all the time. But, bloody hell we knocked it back last night, I am still feeling rather unsteady on my feet!" I giggle.

The lift arrives and we head down to main reception where we bump into Ellie and Belinda, who are looking totally wrecked. I can honestly say, I don't think I have ever seen two more beautiful girls, simultaneously looking different shades of green. I hope for their sakes, they can keep the content of their stomachs in-tact, otherwise, Ingrid will have a real hissy fit.

"Well, well, well, what's up girls, feeling a little delicate?" I ask.

"Delicate, are you kidding? I'm sure if I breathe too hard, I'll either breathe fire or I'll vomit. I don't think I've ever felt so bad and certainly not whilst I have been on a show. Ingrid is going to go absolutely ballistic, I just know it," whispers Belinda.

Ellie simply nods. I think she is in a slightly worse condition than Belinda and that really is saying something!

We all head off to the Palais du Roscoff, pulling on our overly large sunglasses, before we hit the sunlight, which is totally blinding today!

Arriving at the venue, we all bolt into the Fleur Suite for breakfast. First stop caffeine, copious amounts of it and Mel and I grab croissants too and then quickly head into the main auditorium, to set up.

"Morning Martha, and how are you this fine day?" asks Hugo, as I am taking out my laptop from its bag, croissant stuffed in mouth!

I do remove the croissant before I try to speak, as we girls all know, it's so rude to speak, when your mouth is full, isn't it? "If truth be told, we had a rather late night and Ingrid caught us sneaking back this morning, in fact, only an hour ago, in a police van of all things, can you believe it?" I giggle.

"I've heard. She is livid and on the warpath!" smiles Hugo.

"Are you mad with us? We didn't mean to get so drunk and we certainly didn't mean to stay out so late, but you know what it's like, you get caught up in the moment and the only mode of transport back to Cannes, really was the police van. Please tell me you're not mad with us." I look sheepishly, over my laptop.

"Of course I'm not mad, not with any of you; you're entitled to downtime, but it was rather unfortunate that Ingrid should witness your arrival this morning. I suppose it was a good thing, that client wasn't around too!" he replies, hugging me.

"Tell me, how did your secret date go with Eleanor? Did you have a good time?" I whisper.

"It went rather well, thank you," winks Hugo.

From nowhere, Ingrid appears backstage.

"Once again, good morning Martha. I trust you had an enjoyable evening and that you are all set up for rehearsals this morning?" asks Ingrid, a little sternly.

"Ingrid, I am so sorry about this morning, but we really did have transport problems getting back to Cannes, but thankfully, we are here now and yes, ready to go." I smile, in the hope that she might, just might, crack a smile.

"Well it was fortunate that it was only I, witnessing your return, rather than our clients. After all, I don't suppose Mr Johnson would think too highly of this, so called professional team, if he had witnessed Mel rolling around on the street this morning, having fallen out the back of a police van!" she responds, with pursed lips.

Ah, Howard Johnson, how could I have forgotten about Howard? But thankfully, he is back in my thoughts again, but only for a moment or two.

"Martha, Martha, oh for goodness sake, are you alright?" asks Ingrid anxiously.

"Sorry Ingrid, I was lost in my own thoughts for a moment. You were saying?" I respond. Fuck! I have got to pull myself together. Today is going to be long and I really do need to focus on getting through it.

"Here's the full running order for this morning's rehearsal. Our audience will be arriving within the next thirty minutes and I would like everyone and I mean everyone, to regard this as the real thing, even though we know it's a rehearsal. It's imperative that we get this right!" smiles Ingrid, with that look of 'get it wrong and you'll know about it and indeed your invoice won't be paid!'

Right then, so we've got Howard Johnson (the gorgeous one), Danny Mendosa (the Dickbrain), Bruce Shannon (the Australian laid back dude) and of course Marcus Driscoll (the Irish, cute, lovely gentleman). Am I ready for this? Yes, of course I am! Now, don't get me wrong, I'm not nervous, I don't get nervous. But today, well, let's just say, I am a little apprehensive and I think it's because I am simply nursing the hangover from hell, that I don't know if I can actually survive the morning.

I quickly rush off to grab another large coffee, a couple of croissants (yes I know, sometimes people call me 'Trotter!') and an additional bottle of water. Sitting down at my workstation, backstage, I pop a couple of headache tablets. I might as well nip the pain in the bud, before it fully kicks in.

Ingrid and various crew are busily finalising pre show preparations, including putting lapel mics on the speakers. I double-check that the scripts are in order, as per the presenters' lists and then quickly grab my iphone to check my messages, finally!

Wow wee, guess who is Miss Popular again today? Yes, you've guessed it, it's me. I have two missed calls and seven, yes indeed, seven, as in S-E-V-E-N text messages. Firstly the missed calls—both from Theo, with one at six forty am and then another at seven am. Both, when I was hauled up in the back of the police van!

Now then, let's check out these text messages for Miss Popular:

Text one is from Theo: *Ciao bella, I have tried calling you, but it would appear that you are having too good a time. Call me when you surface.xx.*

Text two is from Tom: *Good morning Martha, great to see. Give me a buzz when you get back. Have a great show. T*

Text three is from Claudette (Stars and Bars): *Brilliant to see you again, hurry back soon—my profits were amazing, thanks to you and your friends! Kiss xx.*

Text four is from Howard, gorgeous Howard Johnson III: *Miss Martha, I'm missing you and am wondering where in the world you might be—you're definitely not in your room... see you later. Hx.*

Text five is from Amelia, my darling sister: *Hi. Theo tells me you are having a wonderful time, wishing I was with you. Hugs and love xxx.*

Text six is from Alexandre, I'm too scared to open it up. Oh shit! Shit! Shit! Exactly what did I text him with last night? Oh well, only one way to find out: *Baby, I am sorry I missed your text, am getting older, so I need my sleep now, preferably with you. Let's meet up later today. Love you xx.*

Text seven is from Howard: *Well Martha, you have definitely disappeared off the face of the earth—I have been backstage, but alas, it was empty—where are you hiding? Hx.*

I am sitting here, with a huge smile on my face. Now, tell me, exactly why am I smiling? Is it because of Howard Johnson III? Or is it because of Alexandre? I have absolutely no idea who, or what, or why, I'm feeling so happy about!

I've no time to respond to the barrage of messages, but I will do later. Do I meet up with Alexandre, now that I am sober? I'll toss a coin later—best of three, will decide!

The make believe audience (now when I say make believe, you've got to understand that they are not imaginary, they are real people made up of KAYSO staff who are working whilst in Cannes) are now starting to arrive and are being seated in an orderly manner. Ellie has come to pay a visit. She is definitely not looking too good. In fact, she is looking pistachio green. Her head is in my lap, as she kneels on the floor. What the fuck am I supposed to do with her now?

"Sweetheart, are you OK? I think you need to go and have a large black coffee and here, take a couple of headache tablets with you," I say, passing Ellie a couple of pills, from the packet I have strategically placed on my workstation.

She takes the tablets from my hand and then I catch that look, you know, that look that clearly tells me that Ellie is about to vomit. She resembles a cat coughing up a fur ball. Oh fucking hell! Not now! I cannot cope with my own sick, let alone anyone else's sick.

Right then, keep calm, after all, we do have options. Option one—Ellie can be sick on the floor and I can sit here for the next few hours smelling it—not a good option. Option two—push Ellie from backstage, so that she vomits all over the stage itself, in front of an audience—nope, definitely not a good option. Option three—open up one of the flight cases, (you know, those large silver and black travel cases, used to transport equipment). Option three it is then, but only just in the nick of time.

Ellie still has her head in the flight case and who should appear? That's right Howard Johnson III. Oh fuck! This is not good. This is not good at all, but I suppose he has appeared alone, minus Ingrid, which is a blessing for Ellie, at least.

I'm blushing I can definitely feel my face reddening.

"Um, hi Howard, how are you? Gosh, it's been such a busy morning I haven't had a chance to catch up with you. Um of course, you know, just to make sure you don't have any changes to your script etc." I am trying, very hard, to shield Ellie, who is still retching and vomiting behind me.

Howard smiles and takes my arm, leading me away from my very sick colleague. Obviously her continuous vomiting is not appealing to him either.

"Well Miss Martha, you have finally reappeared in my life, I thought you had skipped town," he smiles.

"Howard what can I say? I definitely haven't skipped town, as there's someone rather special keeping me here at the moment." I smile seductively, (well as seductively as one can, after no sleep and several litres of alcohol). I desperately want to kiss him, but I am conscious that we have Ellie in the flight case and the possibility of any one of the crew coming backstage, after all, Hugo and Jerome are both due, very, very soon.

I blow Howard a kiss and he leans in to whisper, "meet me at lunchtime back at the hotel, you can have me for lunch." Holy shit! My heart is pounding and even though I am feeling sick beyond belief, due to tiredness and massive alcoholic consumption, I can't help but smile.

Howard disappears and I head back to Ellie, passing her a packet of tissues. I suggest she goes to the Ladies to freshen up, and I promptly lock the flight case and stick an A4 sheet to the lid, which reads, CAUTION—CONTAINS SICK!

The time is now eight forty five am and we are ready to commence rehearsals.

All crew are on cans (you know the ones—the silly, big, hair crushing headphones, which allow us to speak to one another without necessarily being heard by the audience). Hugo is positioned backstage too, as are Jerome and Dan, who has his head in his hands and I know instinctively that Hugo is sniffing—sniffing some disgusting smell, which is permeating from the flight case. I catch his eye, as he reads the A4 sheet of paper, which I have attached to the top. Hugo's look of horror is too much. I laugh out loud, but clearly Hugo does not find it amusing.

"Thankfully Hugo, it was not me," I whisper.

"We'd better remove the case from here, yours or not!" sighs Hugo, as he picks up the offending flight case and takes it away.

First up on stage to present, is Howard. Darling, gorgeous Howard. God, he makes me feeling utterly horny. I wonder what will happen after the show? Will he invite me to visit him in the States? Will he visit me in the UK? Will our sexual antics simply be confined to show time? All these questions are running through my mind. I can't help but think, that we have something special.

Immediately, I feel Hugo's presence beside me.

"Martha, we are going live, are you ready for Howard?" asks Hugo.

Jolting me back to reality, I am on standby. I can hear the audience applaud, as Howard takes to the stage. Oh my God, how I want him. Rein it in now girlie, come on, concentration is key to this job, so let's concentrate, I tell myself.

Howard is running through his presentation and although I have an overwhelming desire to close my eyes and sleep, I get through his script, professionally and without any hiccups.

Next up, is Danny Dickbrain Mendosa. Boy, I still loathe and despise this horrible creature, but hey, I am a professional and I will act professionally at all times, even with Danny!

Danny still has a relatively long script, but there is just no telling him, after all, who in God's name, wants to hear a man like Danny prattling on for around thirty minutes? Not many people, that's for sure. Approximately eight minutes into his script, we encounter a problem. Not just a little problem, either. No, we encounter a major, fuck off problem. And it's my problem. Oh fuck!

My prompt equipment has experienced a power surge, which has tripped the monitors, which means Dickbrain Mendosa doesn't have any words on the glass panels in front of him. Mel stops the rehearsal. Danny is on stage, standing around like a lemon in front of his colleagues, who are our make-believe audience and he's becoming ever so slightly impatient. I can hear him huffing and puffing.

"So what seems to be the problem here, is there anyone professional enough to rectify this situation? This isn't a joke, come on, let's take this seriously, let's kick this into action!" shouts Danny, from the stage.

I take off my cans, and make my way onto the stage. Danny is glaring at me he is seriously pissed off. I check the connections on the monitors, as well as the cables that run backstage and connect to the prompt computer. Everything is connected, but the power surge has locked everything out.

Danny is not impressed. Once again I walk onto the stage, but this time, I try to explain that we will need a few minutes to sort out this technical hitch.

Now here's the thing—picture this. OK. So seated in the auditorium are approximately one hundred people. And seated on stage, we have Howard Johnson III (who I've had sex with, just in case you needed reminding!) We have Bruce Shannon and Marcus Driscoll and stomping his fat, podgy foot, Danny Mendosa. Danny Mendosa is about to lose it big time and I think I am going to bear the brunt of his aggression.

"Right then, whatever your name is, remind me, what is it, Paula? Well, might I suggest that you pack your bags and leave right now, as we are a bloody large worldwide organisation and you, you clearly are in way over your pretty little head lady? You don't know what you are doing and you have had an attitude, since the first time I met you. Have you done this on purpose? Is this some kind of joke? Pack up and ship out. Now, someone find me another operator, someone who knows what they are doing!" shouts Danny, in front of the audience.

I am absolutely livid. Anger possesses me. Every vein in my body is pulsating, but I bite down hard on my tongue. I must not, I really must not, shout back at him. I taste blood. Fuck! It's my blood, perhaps I'm biting a little too hard!

Thankfully, both Mickey and Dan are now on stage, changing cables, trying to rectify this fucking fault. I catch Ingrid's eye. She is standing to the side of the stage. She is in a major state of panic. She is holding her hands up to her mouth. Holy fuck! I hope she doesn't start screaming or worse still, hyperventilating. All I really want to do is burst into tears, but thankfully, I hold them back. But only just. Never, have I been shouted at in front of so many people. In fact, I don't think I have ever been so humiliated in my life. Ever.

I catch Howard's eye and he winks. Getting up from his seat on stage, he heads over to me. I fight back the tears. Mendosa has really fucking upset me and it doesn't help that I am still probably drunk from the night before and so very tired. Yes, yes, I know. Being pissed and tired is self-inflicted, but a fucking power surge is not my fault!

Howard leans in close, "Martha, don't take it to heart, things happen, but please keep your cool." He squeezes my arm and goes over to Danny. I overhear him telling him to take it easy and it's not down to him to fire the crew. I suppose that's one saving grace, at least I am still on the job!

The problem has been rectified and prompt is now back up and running. Before returning backstage, I walk up to Danny, "Hopefully we'll have no further malfunctions, but please accept my apologies. Everything is working now," I say, in a very monotone voice, all the while staring directly into his piggy eyes. I think he's figured that I'm pissed as hell with him now.

Back at my workstation and on cans, Mel comes through:

Mel: Hang on in there Martha; the boys are gagging for justice

Sweet Jesus! She is definitely still pissed as she's slurring her words! Everyone is being so protective, as next on cans is Mickey:

Mickey: Don't worry kiddo, no one talks to crew like that and gets away with it—he'll 'ave his comeuppance!

Bloody helll! Mickey is sounding vengeful. Please Lord, let everything sort itself out. I don't want to cause any trouble!

The rest of the mornings' rehearsals run well. But, all the while in the back of my mind, I cannot forget how Danny spoke to me and in front of so many people. I am truly mortified.

Hugo has been a complete star, passing me a note; it simply reads 'A more professional prompt op I have yet to meet—fuck him!'.

Thankfully, the morning dress rehearsal is over. The audience is leaving, but all I want to do is cry. I am tired. I am pissed off. I am upset. I am angry, so angry. How fucking dare he be so rude to me?

But hey, it's lunchtime and therefore, that means only one thing, yep, I'm off for my pre-arranged lunch with the rather gorgeous Howard!

"Hey girl, you OK? Nicely handled, a true pro in action," smiles Mel, whilst hugging me.

"Not the best start to rehearsals and if I'm honest Mel, it's really upset me," I reply, hugging her back, resting my head on her ample breasts—hell, they are so comfortable!

"Pull yourself together. Dickbrain Mendosa has been a pain in the arse since the moment we met him and honey, he will continue to be a pain the arse, so get over it. OK?" replies Mel, totally unsympathetic.

"You're right. I'm over it and guess what? Well, between you and me, I am having a secret rendezvous with Howard over lunch," I chuckle.

"Well, no wonder, you've got a smile back on your face, good for you. Go have some fun, but be sure not to fall asleep on the job!" laughs Mel.

I head off back to the hotel, bumping into Mickey.

"Where you off to Mart, you not 'aving lunch with us?" asks Mickey.

"Mickey, I have the headache from hell, so I just want to freshen up back at the hotel, before this afternoon's session. I'll be back in a bit, promise." I kiss Mickey quickly on the cheek and rush out of the building.

My iphone vibrates; it's a text message from Howard: *Suite 444, lunch is waiting x.*

My heart is pounding. Arriving at the hotel, I come to a complete stop, for there in front of me, is Ingrid. Oh fuck! Shit, Bollocks! What is she doing back here? I wait for her to enter the building and then quickly dart into reception behind her and head for the stairs. Stairs, fucking stairs, I hate them!

I stop off at my room—a quick brush of my teeth, a swill of mouthwash, a lick of lip gloss, a squirt of Dolce & Gabbana and a ruffle of my hair and hey presto, I am feeling gorgeous again. I grab a copy of Howard's script from my laptop bag—I need something relevant to work, just in case I am spotted.

I call the lift (lets face it, there's no way that I can manage to walk up three flights of stairs, that would simply be far too exhausting, especially after my distressing morning). The lift doors open and to my utter horror, (Lord, why do you do this to me?) Danny Dickbrain Mendosa is standing there. Fucking hell! Now really, could my life get any worse?

I smile and step into the lift. Shit, what do I do now? Am I brazen enough to still go to Suite 444, or, should I take a detour? Fuck him! Of course I'm brazen enough.

"Where are you heading?" asks Mendosa, in an upbeat voice, as if nothing has happened. As if he didn't really humiliate me and compromise my professionalism, in front of so many people this morning!

"Fourth floor, please," I respond curtly. No further words are spoken between the two of us.

Ping! We arrive on the fourth floor. Stepping out of the lift, I am a little concerned that Mendosa is heading in the same direction as me. Oh fuck! Please tell me that he is not heading to Suite 444, to see Howard? We both continue, in silence, along the exquisite corridor, adorned with beautiful paintings and providing a soft breeze from the overhead air conditioning.

Well, of course, it just had to happen, didn't it? We both arrive at Suite 444. Oh my God, what if Howard is naked, awaiting my arrival? That would certainly shock this little prat.

Oh well, in for a penny, in for a pound.

"Hey honey, you know this is Howard Johnson's suite, right?" questions Mendosa, just as I am about to knock.

"Yes I believe I do. Apparently, he wants to run through some script amends and suggested that time could be saved, if this was done over lunch," I respond, curtly, once again.

"Oh well, in that case, if he's working over lunch, I'll see him later. Tell Howard I'll be by in about thirty minutes, I'll head off and grab some food," replies Mendosa, walking back to the lift.

I wait a few moments before knocking, just in case Mendosa changes his mind, but thankfully he seems to have gone, for the moment, at least.

I knock on the door and almost immediately, it opens and there is Howard, lovely gorgeous Howard (who at this point is still clothed).

"Come on in Martha." Howard smiles, and suddenly life is good again. Within moments, we are kissing like teenagers. His lips are soft against mine and his arms caress my back gently. I feel safe and I feel happy.

He steps back, moving my hair gently away from my cheek.

"Are you OK Martha? I am so sorry about this morning, but really there was only so much I could do to intervene, obviously I've told Danny to take it easy on you, but for sure, your job is safe here. After all, who else could we get to run the prompt at this late stage?" he says, in a rather serious manner.

"You know what Howard? I would rather not talk about Danny and his appalling behaviour and if I am really honest, I do think that you should have asserted your authority, just a little more this morning. Or, hold on a minute, do you think it's appropriate for your staff to act in such a manner?" I can feel my lips curling and my blood starting to boil. I'm angry again, but this time, rather worryingly, I am angry with Howard rather than Dickbrain Mendosa. Not a great career move, Martha DiPinto!

"Hey, now hang on just a minute Martha! What happens between you and I personally, outside of the conference is one thing, but I am not going to ball Danny out because of something that wasn't his fault. Surely, you can see my point of view here?" responds Howard. I can sense he's now getting a little angry, his cheeks are flushed and his face is kind of ugly, almost squinty.

"Howard, you have your opinion and I have mine. Manners are so important to me and to my mind, you are defending a man who possesses the manners of a pig! So, let's just leave it at that, shall we? I don't want to have an argument over precious Danny, he's certainly not worth it!" I reply, rather rudely.

"Martha, put your claws away, Danny may have a short fuse and lack finesse but he is definitely an asset to KAYSO and the management team," he responds, smiling now.

"OK. That was rude of me, but when all is said and done, he is definitely a prize prick!" I giggle.

I look around the suite hoping for some lunch. I help myself to a bagel. Howard comes closer, he seems a little unsure (does he think I am going to bite?) He starts kissing my neck, softly, gently, but all the while I keep on munching away at my bagel, boy I am starving.

The kissing of my neck has stopped and now I am having a shoulder massage. I can feel my body slowly losing control. Howard's touch is magical. His hands are now underneath my polo shirt. He's unclipping my bra and then halleluiah, his hands have found my breasts and I'm lost in a sea of desire. My bagel drops to the floor, as I turn around to kiss him. My polo shirt is off, as is my bra.

His lips and tongue are eagerly seeking my nipples. Arching my back, I encourage him. I'm panting. The desire is too great, as I feel my body coming in a wave of pleasure that is too overwhelming for words.

Suddenly there is a knock at the door. We pull away from one another.

"Oh fuck!" I mouth to Howard, "It's Danny. He did say he'd call by after lunch—I saw him in the lift earlier." Shit! Fuck! Bollocks! Why does this crap always happen to me? Surely half an hour hasn't passed?

I quickly pull on my bra and polo shirt and within moments, I have re-arranged my hair and grabbed the script from my bag. Howard opens the door.

"Hey there buddy, what's up?" asks Howard, inviting Danny into the Suite.

I look down and to my horror, my half eaten bagel is on the floor. Within a second, not dissimilar to a vengeful vulture, I make a grab for it and continue to nibble at it, in a very casual manner. Oh my God, how bloody disgusting am I? And it's been on the floor of a hotel suite, where millions of feet have trodden! YUK!

"Howard, I need to run through some figures with you. How about we do it now?" asks Danny, not even acknowledging me.

"Well, I was just getting things going with Martha here, can you give us a while, or, do we really need to do it now?" asks Howard, a little agitated.

"We need to get these figures sent over to the finance team at HQ. Rochelle is on standby, to get them emailed over. So, if you don't mind, Paula?" Danny turns to me, and I know that's my cue to leave.

"Not at all, that's absolutely fine, Mr Mendosa," I respond.

"Howard, if time allows, please give me a call and I will come back to make the amends to your script, as requested" I smile.

"Martha thanks. You're a star. Now, hey, we're on the yacht later, so if you and the crew want to call by for a drink or two, just let Rochelle know," responds Howard.

"Thank you, that's very kind." I head to the door. Hell, I think that was rather convincing. I am sure that Danny has absolutely no idea that I will be fucking his boss later. And furthermore, I am sure that he has no idea that moments before his arrival, his boss was caressing my breasts with his fabulous lips and tongue!

Two steps down the corridor and my second living nightmare ensues! (Danny Mendosa is undoubtedly my first living nightmare, of course!).

"Martha, is that you?" enquires Ingrid, in an agitated manner.

Oh fucking hell, Ingrid has seen me coming out of Howard's Suite.

I turn around and smile, "Hi there Ingrid. Yes, indeed it's me."

"Sorry, but um what are you doing coming out of Mr Johnson's Suite, if you don't mind me asking?" she asks, with a hint of sarcasm in her voice.

"Goodness me why ever would I mind? Howard, sorry, Mr Johnson had a few amends to his script and to save time, he suggested we run through them over lunch. Also, he wanted to apologise for Danny's behaviour this morning." I lie, because we all know that Howard no more apologised for Danny's fucking behaviour, than I've got three breasts (although I would be rather partial to three breasts, after all, I felt amazing when Howard was caressing just the two of them! Just imagine how I would feel, if he was caressing three!).

"Oh I see. Now Martha about this morning, I hope you are not too upset?" asks Ingrid, with genuine concern.

"All forgotten now, but thanks for your help," I snipe, walking down the corridor, heading for the lift and certainly not waiting for Ingrid.

I decide to call Theo. Thankfully he picks up immediately and we arrange to meet in the hotel bar in ten minutes. I need to tell him about Howard Johnson III and of course, all about the fucking living nightmare of a human being, namely Danny Dickbrain Mendosa.

Chapter Eleven

I rush to my room, to retouch my make up and partake, of yet another swill of mouthwash and then head down to the bar, to meet my brother.

The bar is busy, predominately with KAYSO personnel. I wave to Rochelle and Mary-Jo, who are seated in the corner.

There he is, darling Theo, sitting at the bar, sipping champagne. Tell me, just how cool, can one individual be? "Hi darling, oh I've missed you." I smile, giving Theo a big hug and sisterly kiss.

"Well, as gorgeous as you always are, just how late was your night, last night? I don't know how many times we tried your room, but you were clearly not there and by the size of those normally gorgeous eyes of yours, I suspect you were out until the small hours?" enquires Theo, brushing my hair away from my eyes.

"Theo, we had the most amazing night in Monaco. We drank, we partied and then we came back to the hotel in the back of a police van, as we couldn't find a taxi. Then the producer, Ingrid, have you met her yet? Well, she is quite horrible. Anyway, she caught us sneaking back this morning, at around seven am—my goodness me I have not felt this rough, for such a long time. But lovely Ellie, do you know Ellie? She's one of our production team. Well, she was sick in a flight case during rehearsals and then, oh my God, the worse thing ever happened. Danny Mendosa, God Theo I hate him! Well, he made me feel like a naughty schoolgirl. We had a power problem and prompt went down. He thought it was his God given right, to give me a bollocking in front of one hundred people who were sitting in the audience. You know, I just wanted to cry, bad enough that I felt like a car crash, due to too much alcohol and no sleep, but then to be blasted like that in front of everyone... Oh and I just need to quickly tell you something else too. Well, um I've slept with Howard." I take a deep breath and look at Theo, gauging his reaction.

"Well, tell it as it is why don't you! Did you draw breath once during that précis of events?" smiles Theo.

"Sorry, but I didn't want to miss anything out!" I chuckle.

"OK then, from the top and if my memory recalls correctly, you went to Monaco, stayed out all night, got drunk, came back to Cannes in the back of a police van, witnessed by horrible Ingrid. Ellie was sick, but hopefully not over you and then Danny had a massive fit, which upset you. Well, sounds like an eventful twenty-four hours. No wonder, you look the way you do!" smiles Theo, winking.

"Well, there was that one other thing that I mentioned," I say sheepishly.

Theo sighs, "I did hear one further thing from that rambling mouth of yours, but I kind of chose to ignore it, as I don't think it's my place to tell you what you should, or shouldn't, be doing!" responds Theo, looking a tad serious.

"Don't be angry. It's just fun. After all, what happens on site stays on site, you know that. It's nothing serious, but Howard is such a lovely guy, it would be hard not to fall for him!" I look at Theo wide-eyed, waiting for a favourable response.

"Just so long as you realise this is only fun, nothing will come of this. Howard is not the kind of guy to scoop you up into his arms and whisk you away to a new life. I've told you, he's going through a really shitty divorce at the moment and I can guarantee that his current wife, her divorce lawyers and his divorce lawyers, come to think of it, wouldn't take kindly to him showing off a new leading lady. I know that he doesn't need any complications in his life at the moment and of course, Jefferson has hinted that I should mention that to you. For Howard, this, well this fling, will be nothing more, than a short lived, event romp," says Theo, stroking my cheek, really rather tenderly.

For a split second, I don't know how to respond. Rather foolishly, I had thought that things would progress with Howard. We would somehow become a couple, even though, I live in the United Kingdom and he lives in the States.

I compose myself. "Theo, are you completely mental? Do you honestly think that I would view Howard as a long term commitment? Come on, who are you kidding? This is simply a little bit of fun, nothing more and nothing less. When this show comes to an end, that will be it Howard will go his way and I'll go mine. Simple as that!" I respond, kissing him lightly on his cheek, all the while my heart is beating way too quickly. I want to burst into tears, but I gain control.

I take a huge glug of my gin and tonic. I am not sure if the alcohol is helping, but I need something to calm my shaking hand!

"Is Jefferson annoyed with me for seeing Howard?" I ask, in a questioning tone.

"Not at all. He thinks you are great and also a great distraction for Howard, as he can relax around you and Jefferson hasn't seen his brother relaxing, in a long time," he smiles.

I am feeling totally deflated, but hey, I won't show that in front of Theo.

"So tell me, are you on the yacht later? I hear there is quite an exclusive party being set up. It would be good to see you there and I know that Jefferson would love to spend time with you too," he continues.

"Depending on how rehearsals run for the rest of the day, I think I might well be on board this evening. In fact, Howard invited the crew to attend, so I think Mel will come along and maybe Dan and Mickey. I am not sure about Belinda and Ellie—I don't think these youngsters can do two nights of debauchery, on the trot!" I smile.

There is a moment's silence. Where is Jefferson now? Is he resting, or, has he been summoned to the catwalk rehearsals, taking place this afternoon?" I ask, feeling a teeny bit awkward, but I'm not sure why I am feeling like this.

"When you called, he was on his way over to the venue, although I think he would much rather spend his afternoon with me on the beach. But, sometimes he needs to earn his crust!" laughs Theo.

"Cara mia, tell me, are you going to the rehearsals this afternoon? If so, I think I might join you, the beach can wait," asks Theo.

"Yes, yes I'll be there. After all, I am rather excited about getting a sneak preview of this next collection, especially if you have worked your magic into the garments!" I say, finishing my gin and tonic and hugging my darling brother.

"I just need to pop back to my room. Do you want to wait for me here? I'll be five minutes," I say.

"Sure thing, I'll see you in reception in five," he smiles.

I need to get back to my bedroom quickly, before I am caught, caught crying, crying tears for God knows who or what. Finally, I arrive in my room and I flop onto my bed. Oh shit! What is happening here? One minute, I'm on cloud nine and then I'm shot down to earth again. Surely, I know that this is going absolutely nowhere, with Howard? Did I honestly think that there was a chance that I would become the next, Mrs Howard Johnson III? Fuck me! I've been through enough short-lived romances, to know that they are easy come, easy go.

I'm exhausted; this must be why I'm acting in such a weird and irrational way. I have an overwhelming desire to see Howard. I text him*: Free to pick up from where we left off? Mxx.*

I wait five minutes for his response—nothing. Who am I kidding?

Oh well, Theo is waiting. I tidy myself up, swill another mouthful of mouth wash (obsessive) and then head for the door, donning my dark sunglasses.

Theo and I make our way over to the venue; his arm is round my shoulders, in a rather protective manner. I hope I haven't pissed him off by sleeping with Howard, but as baby brothers go, mine is at least kind enough to worry about my wellbeing,—he, no more wants to see me get hurt, than I do.

Arriving at the venue's foyer, Ingrid greets us with a hand wave and mouths 'just a moment,' Theo and I wait until she comes over, having finished her call.

"Hello Martha, just wanted to check that everything is OK?" she asks, all the while looking at Theo.

"Yes thanks, all is fine." She is still looking at Theo.

"Sorry, how rude of me. Allow me to introduce you to Theo DiPinto, my brother and consultant fashion director with KAYSO." I smile.

"Ingrid, I've heard a lot about you and I'm delighted to meet you, finally," responds Theo, kissing her on both cheeks.

"Well Theo, don't you believe a word of it!" she laughs, awkwardly.

'Martha certainly kept you quiet, I didn't realise her brother would be on this event too. Keeping it in the family!' she laughs again. "Will you be at the yacht party this evening? It promises to be a great event," enquires Theo.

"In fairness I'm not sure whether time allows for evenings on yachts, as much as I would indeed love to be there, but with the actual show less than a day away, I suspect I will have too much to do," responds Ingrid, full of self-importance.

"Well fingers crossed that everything runs smoothly," replies Theo. I watch Ingrid blush. Fucking hell! Don't tell me she's got the hots for Theo now, for she will be sorely disappointed!

We all make our way to the main auditorium. Ingrid heads towards Hugo. Theo goes off to find Jefferson and I look around and thankfully spot Mel.

"Hey slapper, how was lunch? Did you get all and more?" asks Mel, in an inquisitive tone.

"Well, we got as far as starters and then would you believe it, well, rather disappointingly, Mendosa appears. Honey, I don't think I've ever got dressed so quickly. I don't think he suspects anything, but nothing more happened. I met Theo for a quick drink afterwards and he's definitely trying to steer me away from Howard. I think, he thinks, that I'm going to get hurt. But, as I explained, this is just a bit of fun, nothing more." I gush.

"Right. Howard is a bit of fun and nothing more, pull the other one? So, tell me, why is it that every time you mention his name, your eyes light up, your body quivers and you turn to mush?" asks Mel, looking directly at me, waiting for a response.

"Oh don't be so bloody ridiculous! Do you honestly think I've fallen for him in a big way? Come on Mel, you're as bloody stupid as that brother of mine!" I laugh, all the while knowing deep down, that they are both right. Fucking hell! Just how stupid am I?

This afternoon it's the fashion show rehearsal. Let's hope that everything runs smoothly. After that, we will be rehearsing the awards ceremony—is there no end to this day? In fairness, I don't have a lot to do on the fashion show, so I decide to go to the Fleur Suite and grab a large coffee.

I spy a tray of rather delicious looking pastries. Needless to say, I cannot resist. I pick one and it just oozes cream and deliciousness and delicately, well, as delicately as I can, I take a bite. Pure heaven!

I cannot resist another. This time I opt for the horn shaped pastry. There's a surprise! One end is closed and the other is open and it's filled with tiny cubes of strawberries and cream. I take a bite and feel a shiver down my spine. Jeez, these are good! I take another bite and of course, it had to end in disaster. I now have strawberry syrup running down my chin and a dollop of fresh cream slopped all down the front of my, designer—not, Angel Productions polo shirt!

I search frantically for a tissue. I am startled, for there behind me is Howard. How long has he been standing there? What must he think? Oh Lord, please help me to grow up one day!

"Here, let me help you." He walks towards me, picking up a serviette and is poised to wipe away my gooey mess. He slowly starts wiping the syrup away from my chin. My heart is beating. Our eyes lock. I want so desperately to kiss him. No, I don't want, I need to kiss him. And I do. Our lips meet, passionately, tongues searching, probing. (Is he after those pastry crumbs in my mouth?) I am overcome with an uncontrollable desire to make love to him right here and right now!

What does Theo know? Would this not prove that Howard and I are not simply a fling, that there is something more to our, our what, our relationship? Our fling? Our being together?

But it's not Theo who is looking at us now. No, it's Mickey. I don't see him, but he definitely sees me. No, not me, he sees us, as in Howard and me together, in a passionate embrace. He steps away, quietly.

Howard and I finally pull apart and as he steps back, he smiles sweetly, longingly even.

"Martha, I am sorry about lunchtime and Danny's appearance. Will you make it to the yacht later?" he asks "I really would like to spend more time with you."

"OK skipper. I'll see you on board later!" I smile, grabbing my coffee and heading back to watch the rehearsal. My heart is pounding. My legs are shaking, as are my hands, fucking coffee everywhere! How elegant and chic!

Back in the auditorium, everyone is bustling around. Both Ellie and Belinda are still looking worse for wear and no doubt Ingrid is running them ragged because of their behaviour last night! The catwalk is in position and looks fabulous. It's made of clear Perspex and will eventually be filled with foliage, flowers and lights.

Pikey, whom I think was actually christened Patrick by his parents, but has always been known as Pikey in the industry, has the unenviable task of dressing the inside of the catwalk. Thankfully, he's of moderate height and really rather skinny, so will have no trouble in working his way through the structure.

Dan and Mickey are helping him bring in the foliage. There is definitely a bit of an atmosphere this afternoon. I think everyone has finally succumbed to exhaustion.

Ingrid is running around frantically, apparently three models have gone walkabout and Jefferson is anxious to finalise all the fittings, prior to the run through. Ingrid has now shifted a gear and gone into overdrive. Her voice comes through on our walkie talkies: "Ingrid to Ellie and Belinda. Your whereabouts please? Models missing. I repeat models missing. Over."

Silence. Oh no, what are they up to now? Oh well, I am sure they will materialise soon enough. I head off to my workstation; I need a few quiet moments to myself, as a wave of tiredness runs over me. Walking backstage, I am quite obviously disturbing the group hiding behind there.

"Well, what have we got going on here then?" I ask, very sternly. Almost sounding a bit like a sergeant major!

Belinda and Ellie simply stare at me and say nothing. One of the models continues doing, what she was doing, before I so rudely interrupted her. And what is she doing? Well, she's snorting a line of coke. Good God above! What is wrong with these girls? Not only are they fully emaciated, but they feel the need to shove drugs up their noses too. What is wrong with these people? Emotional, insecure wrecks, is my guess. It's actually, really rather, sad if you think about it.

I walk over to Ellie and Belinda and push them to one side. Neither speaks.

"And as for you three, fuck off out of here, before I call security!" I am so angry at what I've witnessed. I look down at the table I was using this morning and notice three lines of coke, already chalked up. Anger swims through me, as I sweep the white powder from the table, with only one hand movement, the heinous drug disappears.

All three models yelp simultaneously, but don't say a word. They don't move.

"I've told you once! Get out—right now!" and with that, they disappear.

"Martha, please, it's definitely not what you are thinking, honestly. I promise!" whispers Ellie.

"Ellie shut it. I cannot believe that you, you of all people and you Belinda, would be so fucking stupid, as to take drugs whilst on site. If you've got to do it, then do it in private, not where everyone can see you. For fuck sake, are you both stupid? In fact, no don't bother answering that, because I already know the answer." My fist is clenched, as I breathe deeply.

Mel appears behind the set.

"Hey there, what's up?" she asks, totally oblivious to what has just happened.

"Mel, have a word with these two. I just caught them snorting coke, with those fucking models, can you believe it?" I whisper, thankfully I am a little calmer now, but only a little.

"We weren't taking drugs! Honestly!" butts in Belinda.

"Do you honestly want me to believe that you were simply standing there, watching the models? Well, come on? Don't think I'm so bloody naïve!" I throw her a look—a look that would kill, if only I had such powers!

"Right, let's calm down here." Mel steps in. She walks over to Belinda and Ellie 'If you want to do that shit, then do it in your rooms. If you get caught, then you're off the job. If you're off the job, word will get round as to why and if that happens, you can kiss your careers goodbye. Understand?' Mel is furious.

Both girls respond simultaneously, "Yes."

"Martha, I'm really sorry. It's just that I am so tired and Precious said it would perk me up a bit," continues Ellie, in a very quiet voice.

"And who the fuck is Precious, when she's at home?" asks Mel.

"She's one of the models," continues Ellie.

"Oh for fuck sake! What is wrong with you?" responds Mel, shaking her head and walking off.

"Ingrid is on the warpath and it's you two she's after. Let's forget this whole sorry situation for now." The girls head out into the main auditorium.

Sweet Jesus! What is this world coming to? Snorting coke in public! Whatever next? Shooting up in the raked seating? I really thought they had more sense.

Pikey is doing a fantastic job with the catwalk. He has almost completed the installation of flowers and foliage and all that remains to be done is the lighting.

I catch Mickey staring at me and I wave, he seems distracted, but I'm not sure why. I walk over to him. "Hey you, what's up, you look as if you are miles away?" I laugh.

"Mart, what's with you and 'oward then?" he asks.

I am taken aback by his question. I look at him with a rather puzzled look. Has Mel said something to him? No, surely not. I have known Mel for years and I know she's not a gossip.

"What are you going on about? There's nothing going on between Howard and me," I respond, quizzically.

"Oh right. So you snoggin' the face off 'im earlier meant nothing then?" he responds, rather sarcastically.

Fuck! Fuck! Fuckity fuck! Come on think and very quickly, otherwise, I am going to get found out.

"You win, I lose. I will admit to kissing him, but only the one," I say, crossing my fingers discretely behind my back.

"Oh come on girl, pull the other one, that snog ain't a one off!" Mickey replies, not looking happy.

"I had a bet with Mel. One hundred Euros, to whoever kissed Howard Johnson III, but not just a kiss on the cheeks or a peck on the lips, no a proper kiss with tongues and guess what? I am up by one hundred Euros!" I giggle, feeling myself blush.

"Fuckin' hell Mart, what's wrong with you and Mel, you both off your fuckin' rockers?" laughs Mickey.

"We've got to get through this long week somehow, haven't we?" I laugh and then walk away to find Mel.

Once I find her, I suggest she takes a walk with me to the cloakroom, where I explain every lie I have just told Mickey.

Mel takes a step back and looks intently at my face.

"What the hell are you doing?" I ask, a little bemused by her actions.

"Nothing really, I was just seeing if your nose had grown. It appears that you, my dear friend, are a compulsive liar!" she smiles, tweaking the end of my nose.

"I feel so bad telling all these lies Mel, but I can hardly confess to Mickey that I am sleeping with the client now, can I? He just wouldn't get it," I say. 'But as they say here in France, 'C'est la vie!'

"You're right honey, keep it to yourself—it's better that way, otherwise it will spread, like wildfire" replies Mel, walking towards the door.

We head back to the auditorium and Pikey's catwalk masterpiece is complete.

The flowers look stunning, the foliage is delicate, but the lighting is, well simply amazing—he's a genius.

The models' choreographer, Mariella, together with Eleanor (Hugo's love interest), Ingrid, Ellie and Belinda together with Mickey, are going through the running order. Mickey is in seventh heaven, surrounded by beautiful women—that doesn't include Ingrid, of course.

I pop behind the catwalk, but don't get very far. I am blocked, by a big burly bouncer whose nationality I'm not quite sure of, but a big bugger, all the same. Apparently, get this—no pass, no entry. I only wanted to catch up with Theo and say "hi," to Jefferson. And as if by magic, Jefferson appears from behind the man mountain.

"Move out of the way and let this lovely lady through—this is Martha, she's VIP OK? Understand?" says Jefferson, very slowly and very loudly, to the bouncer. To which he responds "loud and clear mate." Nationality now known—British!

"Come here, how lovely to see you. Have you come to try on some of our collection?" asks Jefferson, placing his hand on my shoulder.

"Jefferson, as beautiful as your clothes are, I think we might have a slight problem; getting my body to fit into these model sized clothes!" I giggle.

"Well, let me know what you like and we will have them made to measure. Simple. Hang around, because I think we're going to kick off in just a few minutes." he responds, as he walks towards the models dressing area, arms waving in the air.

Theo is titivating some of the models' outfits; it's those 'cocaine snorting' models from backstage. I throw them a scowl, as I hug Theo. "My brother, don't you know?" I say out loud, to anyone who cares to listen.

"Ciao bella! So what do you think so far? Some of this collection is simply genius, even if I do say so myself!" he smiles.

Our walkie-talkies come live:

"Ingrid to crew, catwalk rehearsals due to commence in three minutes. Repeat three minutes. To your places and on cans please. Over."

There is a flurry of movement. Models are positioned, in order of appearance. Both Jefferson and Theo tweak the models' clothing and I have to admit, that some of their outfits, are quite simply sensational.

I have no official duty during the rehearsal, so settle down next to Mel, Mickey and Zak who are seated at their control desks. Mel is calling the shots to Eleanor backstage as well as to the rest of the crew. Zak is on lights and Mickey is on sound. Music been especially commissioned for this show, which by all accounts, is rather brilliant!

We are all on cans—(yes, those hair crushers) me, included. The lights are completely dimmed, but for one single spotlight, which points down to the entrance of the catwalk.

Voices come through, loud and clear, Mel is half-way through her cans check.

Mel: Cans check please. Eleanor?

Eleanor: "Yes Mel, models ready and waiting."

Mel: "Mickey, are your magical fingers poised?"

Mickey: "Good to go Mel."

Mel: "Zak, are you ready?"

Zak: "Sure am, Mel."

Mel: "Ok then, here we go. LX, Sound, Graphics, VT and Models, stand-by please."

All the crew acknowledge Mel's instruction.

Mel: "Lights, Sound, VT... go please."

Suddenly the auditorium is alive with upbeat music, loud and pulsating. I find my foot tapping almost immediately.

Mel: "Models, go please"

The models come out one by one, strutting their way down the catwalk, hips swaying from side to side, posing for three seconds at the end of the runway and twirling for their return walk.

Pikey comes through on cans:-

Pikey: "Mickey, I have got the best job in the world mate."

Mickey: "Why?"

Pikey: "Guess where I am?"

Mel: "I hope for your sake, you are not behind set with the models?"

Pikey: "No, but almost as good."

Mickey: "Where are you?"

Pikey: "On my back, with a perfect view!"

Ingrid: "Can I remind you all, that we are in the middle of rehearsals; is it absolutely necessary to have this constant and unnecessary banter?"

Silence. And then:-

Mickey: "On your back?"

Pikey: "In the catwalk amongst the plants. Fucking perfect."

Mickey: "You're 'aving a laugh mate!?"

Pikey: "The best."

Mel: "Pervert."

After about an hour, the rehearsal has finally come to an end and all in all, it wasn't a bad one. We only had two trips, same model, same shoes—and these are now being checked out. One dress malfunction—as the model swayed down the catwalk, the gorgeous midnight blue silk drape dress slipped and left the rather skinny model, fully exposed and when I say fully, I mean fully, zero underwear, not even nude coloured knickers! Sweet Jesus! I'm not sure when she last had a meal, but she definitely needs one. Her breasts resembled a couple of quails' eggs!

Both Jefferson and Theo are over the moon—the collection is outstanding.

I see Howard, talking to Eleanor. From what I can make out, he is praising the quality of her models. Fuck! I hope he's not into skinny birds otherwise I will definitely be off the Christmas card list!

Ingrid has assembled the crew together.

"Well done everybody. Let's hope the show runs as well as the rehearsal."

She runs through a few snagging issues and then turns towards Pikey.

"Pikey, could I have a word with you please?" she asks, pulling him to one side. Oh dear, he's in for a bollocking—he's pure magic!

The time is now four twenty pm. Most of the crew have been stood down, apart from Mickey and Dan, who now have to install two plasma screens on the KAYSO yacht, in readiness for this evening's party.

"Hey Martha, what do you reckon? Fancy giving Dan and me an 'and on the yacht?" asks Mickey.

"Are you leaving now?" I ask, all the while wanting to really say 'No, fuck off, deal with it yourself, as I'm tired and need a sleep'. But hey, I would never be that rude, even if I have turned into a walking zombie.

"Thanks Mart. There are only two screens to install, so it shouldn't take too long. There should be a van parked out front, waiting for us. Pucker!" says Mickey.

So, hi ho, hi ho, it's off to work we go. Again!

Chapter Twelve

The white van is indeed waiting outside, as we, all three, pile in. We pull away and start the short journey down to the harbour, where a small boat will, hopefully, be waiting for us. Is there no end to our combined talents?

"Have either of you ever rigged on a yacht before?" I ask, hoping desperately to hear the words 'yes, of course'.

"Nope, not that I can remember, but there is always a first time ain't there? After all, what's the worst that can 'appen?" responds Dan, smiling his happy, cheery smile.

"Lets face it girl, on land or sea, it's all the same thing, ain't it?" chips in Mickey.

As we drive towards the harbour, the three of us begin totty watching. The boys are in their element, as there are so many beautiful women walking about, in the late afternoon sun.

"If I 'ad my way, I would be happy to live 'ere. Can you imagine just looking at pretty girls all day long? Dan what d'ya say?" laughs Mickey.

"Mate, I'm with you!" he replies.

"What in God's name is wrong with you both? You're both married, yet you think it's OK to ogle the female form, not just a little bit, but constantly!"

"Mart, you know the rules, what happens on site, stays on site—never any 'arm done, is there?" smirks Mickey.

Arriving at the harbour, Mickey asks me to go and check out which boat we are using to get across to the yacht.

I jump out of the van and dutifully set off. I find the harbour master and he takes me to our little vessel, which is currently moored by the steps, leading down to the water's edge. We have a skipper, who is called Francois.

The boat is rather small, so I think it's unlikely that we will fit two plasma screens, stands, cabling, two technicians and me in, all at the same time—perhaps we are looking at two trips, which is no hardship, so long as we make it across safely, on both occasions.

I walk back to join the boys who have off-loaded the two screens which are still in their very big and extremely heavy flight cases.

"Guys, the boat is there, but it's small. I think the best thing to do, would be to take the plasmas out of their cases. What do you think?" I ask.

"Sounds like a plan to me Mart. Which boat are we going across in? Point 'er out and then, any chance you can go and park up, for us?" Mickey asks, tapping the side of the van.

"Sure, no worries!" I respond. I point out the boat and take the keys from Dan.

So, just where am I going to park a white van, in such a beautiful, parking restricted location? I jump in the vehicle, put her into gear and drive off to find a sufficiently large enough parking space. (And it needs to be big for me to fit this baby in, believe me!)

Now, I don't know about you, but when I have to park and I know that I am going to have difficulty in finding a space, I always call upon my Angel of Parking. I simply ask 'Parking Angel, please can you find me a space?' and I have to say, nine times out of ten, I do find one. Call it luck, or, call it divine intervention, the choice is yours, but most of the time it really does work! Try it.

I drive around for about five minutes and then, as if by magic, a van pulls out of a space, which is large enough for our van to get into. Yippee!

So, just how do you park one of these things? I indicate, well I get that bit right and then I try to find the reverse gear on this bloody enormous left hand drive van. Now, tell me, where exactly is reverse? Just my luck, there are no markings on the gear stick, just the black knob. You've probably guessed, I am usually pretty good with knobs, so I try pushing the gear stick over to the left and pull down. I look into the wing mirrors, to make sure I am not going to run over any unsuspecting pedestrians behind me and put my foot on the accelerator; to my absolute horror, the van lunges forward and just misses a rather elderly lady, pushing her shopping trolley, towards the pavement.

Well, if looks could kill, I would most certainly be dead now. I mouth apologies, as she pushes her trolley onto the pavement and struts off. Phew! That was a close call. Right, here we go again. Let's try neutral and over to the right and up this time. Here we go! Much to my relief, the van starts to move backwards and after a couple of attempts and a fight with the steering wheel, I manage to park perfectly.

As I get out of the van, as elegantly as one can, I hear applause coming from the pavement café opposite. To my total embarrassment, there is a group of men who, unbeknown to me, have been watching my parking endeavours. Only one thing for it then... I curtsy, smile and blow them a kiss, then make a quick exit.

With the van parked, I walk back to the harbour, to see how the transfer of our load is going.

Surprise, surprise. Did I think for one moment that perhaps, just perhaps, one of the plasma screens might be loaded onto the boat? Yes, I did think that, but it seems as if Mickey and Dan have been delayed!

"Hey boys, don't wish to interrupt here, but we have work to do and only a limited time to do it in!" I smile at the two bikini clad females, who seem to have interrupted their work.

"Girls, hopefully see you laters hey?" winks Dan, as he shoos them away.

"Sorry 'bout that, but you know what it's like? These young girls are like bees round an 'oney pot and me and the boy 'ere, are the best pots around!" winks Mickey.

Within ten minutes, both of the plasma screens are positioned near the steps, leading down to the boat, as are the cables and stands. We are all in agreement that the plasmas should go across, one at a time.

Francois is ready and waiting and he will get us across to the yacht, safely. Well, fingers crossed—that's the plan!

Dan steps into the boat with a slight wobble, as Francois steps out to help Mickey pass down the plasma screen, as it's a tad too heavy for me, to help with the lifting.

Thankfully, all seems to be going relatively well, perhaps I am worrying unnecessarily, after all, what is the worse that could happen? OK, yes I agree, there are lots of things that could happen: we could of course (a) fall into the water (b) sink the boat or, (c) drop the plasma screen. Well, thankfully none of these has occurred and neither will they. So fingers crossed.

"Dan, is there any merit in me being in the boat with you, when the plasma's handed down?" I ask.

"I think I can handle it as it's only a short drop from the steps, but you keep supervising!" responds Dan, with beads of sweat, slowly forming on his forehead. Yep, he's concerned. I know they both are, as they are quiet and it's not like the boys to be so quiet!

Dan is in position and Francois and Mickey are moving down the steps towards the boat, loaded down, with one heavy piece of equipment. So far, so good, all is well. Thank you Lord, thank you.

Within a matter of minutes, the first plasma screen has successfully been passed down to Dan. It was certainly a struggle; it's not the easiest of items to pass into a floating boat!

I wink at Mickey,

"Good job! Now, let's get you in the boat and I'll wait here, with the second one." I say, totally relieved that things are going relatively well.

Suddenly, out of the corner of my eye, I catch a police speedboat pulling out of the harbour. Are they on a drugs chase? Oh my God! Could you imagine—perhaps they are trying to catch up with those bloody models of ours? I laugh to myself and then, horror strikes.

My thoughts are interrupted, as I hear Dan scream out "Noooooooooo!!" in a really loud, booming voice.

Francois, Mickey and I, look down at Dan. The wash from the police boat, has hit the harbour wall and in doing so, has rocked our vessel in the wake, which has taken Dan by complete surprise and in that split second, he has lost his footing as well as his grip and the plasma screen has literally gone overboard, landing in the water with an almighty splash. It can no longer be seen; it has disappeared without a trace. Fucking hell! Bizarrely, it all appeared to happen in slow motion!

"Fuck no! Shit!" mutters Mickey, hands to his mouth.

I stand frozen to the spot. I am not sure what is going through my mind. I look down at Dan who is still on the floor of the boat, his head in his hands. I look at Francois and, oh my God, I don't believe it, he is definitely trying to suppress a laugh, as he turns away.

"Well at least we'll give Ingrid something to moan about now!" I say, starting to giggle and the more I look at Francois' laughing shoulders, the bigger my giggles become, until they morph into a total full-on belly laugh. I am laughing so much I have tears and mascara streaming down my face. Now we are all laughing, and a small crowd has gathered. Oh fuck! It really could only happen to us!

"Shit! Can you believe that? We were being so careful," says Dan.

"At least nobody is injured. Besides, I haven't laughed so much in a very long time. It's no-one's fault, shit happens and it happens for a reason—perhaps it was time for Tom Kremner to update his equipment anyway!" I giggle, tears still streaming down my face! Explain this one away to Tom boys, he will go ape!

Thankfully, we are a little more successful with the second screen and manage to get it over to the yacht in one piece. Eventually, we are all on board.

Rochelle is already there, so I pull her to one side and explain that we had a slight mishap but she seems unconcerned that we will only be using one plasma. Thank God for understanding clients!

We set up the equipment and then wander around the yacht—boy, she is a beauty. There are eight suites, together with dining area, sitting room, sun deck, jacuzzi and staff quarters. I absolutely love it.

Mickey is talking with Rochelle—they seem to be getting on a little too well, if you ask me. Dan is talking to one of the bar staff, laughing and joking, obviously recounting our earlier tale of misfortune.

The party is due to kick off at nine pm this evening and with the time fast approaching seven thirty pm, I suggest that we should head back and hook up with the rest of our crew.

Back on shore, we collect the van and return to Le Maritime Hotel, dropping the vehicle at the Palais du Roscoff on route. Mel, Hugo, Belinda and Ellie, are in the hotel bar. We immediately head over and recount the story of the lost plasma screen.

Thankfully, Hugo sees the funny side and we all roar with laughter and continue laughing until Ingrid appears. Oh fuck! We're busted.

"Hello everyone. What's so amusing? Can I be a party to this joke?" asks Ingrid, with a hint of sarcasm to her voice.

Hugo gets up and takes Ingrid to one side. I go to follow, but Hugo's hand immediately comes up, signalling for me to stay away, whilst he explains the situation.

Within a few minutes, Ingrid and Hugo return. Ingrid is definitely not a picture of happiness.

"Perhaps I could have a full written report of this incident, so that we can explain to Tom Kremner exactly what happened and why, we are now one plasma screen down?" demands Ingrid, scowling at the three of us.

"Not a problem. I mean obviously, we did not do it on purpose and if it wasn't for the wash from the police boat, then it wouldn't have happened," I respond, trying to defend our cause.

"Martha, I think we have had enough police intervention during this event, don't you?" replies Ingrid. "I am going to my room, to run through schedules for tomorrow. Belinda, Ellie, might I suggest you join me in approximately fifteen minutes?" she continues, as she walks off towards the lifts.

Both Ellie and Belinda roll their eyes simultaneously. "So, it looks as though we won't be on the yacht this evening then?" says Ellie, out loud.

"You're not going to miss much. It definitely won't be on a par with our Monaco night out and I am sure an early night wouldn't go amiss." I smile, feeling a twinge of sadness for them.

"You're right. We are both completely wrecked, so it's not a bad thing, that part of our night will be spent with Ingrid, rather than quaffing copious amounts of champagne and caviar!" laughs Belinda.

"Mickey, Dan, Hugo, are you guys coming on board the yacht later?" I ask.

"You know what girl? I think we might keep it local tonight, a couple of drinks in the bar and then forty winks; I'm fucked after last night," replies Mickey.

"I'm going to hit the sack soon, no more boats for me today, thanks girlie," smiles Dan.

"I'm otherwise engaged this evening and you don't need me there, it's only one plasma—but if there is a problem, then give me a shout," winks Hugo. Hey, we all know what he'll be up to later!

"Don't worry you old Slapper, I'll come aboard with you, but only for a short while. I need to get some beauty sleep before tomorrow's final rehearsal, after all, it's everything tomorrow, presenters, catwalk and awards ceremony. Jesus! It will destroy us all!" laughs Mel.

"Thanks Sweetie. Shall we aim to leave here, say around nine thirty?"

"Sounds good to me. Now get upstairs and get your glad rags on!" instructs Mel.

I leave Mel in the bar with the boys. She is already dressed and is looking particularly lovely this evening. Not that she doesn't always look lovely, after all, facially she is beautiful (the body needs a bit of attention), but the whole package really works well this evening. From her face down to her clothes, down to her whole persona, she seems, kind of alive. Have I missed something?

My iphone rings, just as I insert my room key into the lock and I answer it automatically, somehow thinking that it would be Mel, as I was just thinking about her, but it's not Mel. Oh my God! It is most definitely not Mel!

"Baby? hey you there?" comes a male voice, down the iphone.

I don't know whether to respond or not. I count to three and eventually find my voice "Hi yes, this is Martha," I say stupidly. Fuck! I am so stupid sometimes.

"Hi baby, I thought I might have heard from you earlier today, what have you been up to?" he asks. The 'he' I refer to, is Alexandre. The man I would dearly love to spend the rest of life with. He's on the phone now and I am making a complete tit of myself.

"Honey, can you give me just five minutes and I will call you right back, there's something I just need to sort out?" I stammer.

"No worries, speak to you in a minute," he responds, and with that he's gone.

The line is dead. Oh my God! I was not expecting him to call. It's thrown me. My heart is pounding. My mind is buzzing and my body is aching for him and only him. Who's Howard Johnson III again?

OK, I have to pull myself together. I need to call him back and I need to sound like me, rather than the complete wombat that answered the phone a few minutes previously.

What is wrong with me? I am physically shaking. He has really unnerved me. Right then, first off I need a shower. I enter the bathroom and plan what

I am going to say to him. Out of the shower and on with Prada, both body lotion and the most adorable Prada jumpsuit ever. I know, I know, it sounds so seventies, but hey, let me tell you, it looks absolutely bloody gorgeous. It's navy with a combination of silk and chiffon. I have the perfect shoes to match, which are ideal for yachts—flat, gladiator, strappy sandals in silver and navy. But before I go anywhere, I have to make that call.

My iphone beeps—another text message for Miss Popular. Subconsciously, I think it is going to be Alexandre. But I have three messages, not one. Boy, you see, I am Miss Popular again!

Text message one is from Howard: *Martha, this is your captain speaking. I am so looking forward to seeing you later Hx.*

Text message two is from Theo: *Ciao bella, Rochelle told me about the screen, what a bunch of maniacs you are. Only you Martha, only you. See you later xx.*

Text message three is from Mel: *Take your time. I've pulled a German!*

A German? I knew it. She looked too hot this evening, to go unnoticed. Best I get down there and suss him out! But first off, I really must call Alexandre.

I casually walk towards my mini bar and pull out a miniature whiskey bottle. And, in a terribly unladylike manner, I down it in one. Dutch courage—it is just what I need.

I scroll through the iphone and find Alexandre's number under 'Boo'—my nickname for him. So, I'm sure you're itching to ask—why Boo? Well, for the simple reason that he crept up on me one night, early on in our relationship and made me jump, just as I was just popping the cork on a bottle of champagne, but he made me jump so much, that I whacked him with it—it was simply my initial reaction.

I have the ringing tone. He picks up. "Hey baby, how are you? You were never good with timings, five minutes you said. It's been nearly twenty. Now you are making me late!" he laughs.

"Quit whinging, you are always late and yes, I'm fine and yes, I know I said five minutes, but hey I had to do this and that and before you know it... well finally, we speak!" I respond, trying to sound sexy.

"Have you got a cold? You sound strange?" he asks, in a concerned manner.

"No, no cold, but I do need to blow my nose." I sniff. I don't have a cold, do I? I was simply trying to sound sexy! Well that backfired!

"How's life? What you have been up to?" I ask in my normal voice.

"You know me, never stand still, for more than five minutes. I've been to New York for a film festival and then over to Switzerland. Spent a little time down at the villa in Puglia and of course, time with the girls," he replies.

"Wow—you have been busy." I swallow hard. "How are the girls? Growing up fast no doubt?" I say, as enthusiastically as is humanly possible, when talking about spoilt, horrible, little devil spawns.

"The girls are doing really well. Both of them are excelling at school. Both into music and of course boys, but they can forget all about them until they are much, much older. I'll kill the first boy who tries to kiss them!" he laughs, but I know he means it!

Kiss them? Fucking hell, the devil wouldn't even try to kiss them.

"Baby, are we going to meet up, whilst you are in Cannes?" he asks.

"That would be lovely, but my time is really limited. What with rehearsals and then of course the show, I'm not sure what time I have available." I stammer.

"I can't do this evening, I've got some drinks thing that I am going to. Tomorrow night, I am free. Are you able to meet up then?" he asks. Damn him! He whistles and I come running.

"I suppose we could meet up late, but you will need to come over to Cannes, as I won't have time to get to Monaco," I say.

"Hey, you're not trying to put me off are you? Come on, for old time sakes, let's at least have a drink together. I've missed you, baby!" replies Alexandre, making me go weak at the knees.

Fucking hell! Why does he do this to me? I HATE him.

"OK. Let's call it a date for tomorrow evening. I will call you when we are into the awards rehearsals, which should last no more than a couple of hours, so that will give you time to get over," I respond, hoping and praying that he says "yes."

"Sure thing. Which hotel?" he asks.

"Le Maritime," I respond.

"I'll see you tomorrow evening then. Have a good one tonight, whatever you get up to!" he responds.

"Thanks Boo and you," I say, very quietly.

"Big kiss baby!" are his final words and then he is gone. Oh my God! Just how much do I love that bastard? Way too much!

Bollocks! What am I doing with Howard, when I should be with Alexandre? Howard is a gentleman, Alexandre, is a player, a real bad boy. Howard is available. Alexandre is not. Oh God, why is my life so complicated? Tell me, what have I done to deserve all this shit in my life?

Well, it's not really shit, is it? I have a perfect life. Any complications are down to me and only me.

I finish reapplying my make up, fluff up my hair, a brush of my teeth, swill of mouthwash and a squirt of perfume and I am on my way back down to the bar, to meet Mel and her German!

Chapter Thirteen

Arriving in the hotel's bar, I spot Mel immediately, chatting away to a guy and yes, in fairness, he could easily pass for a German.

Everyone else has left, no Mickey, no Dan and no Hugo. Only Mel and her new suitor are left remaining. I am hesitant about approaching, after all, what if this is a crucial moment in a potential new romance? What if he is just about to ask her to spend the night with him? Oh my God! Perhaps I should text her? No, now I am just being silly, after all, if he wants to sleep with her, then whether I appear, or not, will have little bearing on the outcome.

"Hi Mel!" I say, hugging her.

"How lovely of you to finally join us. What happened, did you get lost or something? I thought we agreed nine thirty. By my watch we are fast approaching ten pm. Get held up, did we?" she asks, in a sarcastic but jokey manner.

"No, well yes. Everything happens at once. So who do we have here? I hope I'm not interrupting anything," I respond, smiling at Mel.

"No, definitely not interrupting. This is Hans, Hans Kleebauer. He's part of the KAYSO team; works in Europe, predominantly Germany, unsurprisingly!" responds Mel. She's definitely got the 'hots' for him.

"Hans, it's lovely to meet you and thank you, for keeping Mel company, I was indeed, slightly longer than expected." I smile, shaking his hand.

"Martha, I am very pleased to meet you, too. Mel has been recounting the tale of your Monaco adventure, it sounds as if you people have a perfectly good evening and morning!" laughs Hans.

"It was definitely a night to remember and that's for sure! Are you going to the party this evening?" I ask.

"Yes indeed and I understand that both yourself and Mel, are also planning to attend." he responds, in a rather official German manner. "I suggest we move now, so that we can enjoy ourselves on board the yacht. Is this a good idea, yes?" he asks.

We are all in agreement and head off to the harbour jetty, from where a series of small vessels are being used, to transfer guests to the yacht.

As we arrive, we can see the KAYSO yacht, shimmering under the moonlight. The music playing on board is loud, which can only mean that the party is now in full swing.

We transfer successfully from the harbour—thankfully, no mishaps or misdemeanours! Finally on board, Hans heads off to find Howard. There must be a good eighty people on here, some deep in conversation, others simply taking in the breathtaking moonlight and the remainder, dancing to their hearts content. What a brilliant setting.

Mel and I have grabbed a champagne flute each; we lean in close to one another, to make ourselves heard. "So, spill the beans. Are you and Hans an item this evening and I don't just mean here, either?" I giggle.

"Well, I think I am one hundred per cent right in assuming that he will indeed be spending the night with me at Le Maritime hotel. It was really weird, within minutes we were talking dirty to one another. Boy I know I'm fast, but that really was something else!" smiles Mel, looking completely besotted with the lovely Hans.

"Well good for you darling! It's good to get it whenever you can—there's never too much of a good thing!" I respond, hugging her lovingly.

"So, what kept you this evening? Was it just my text message, or, did Howard pay you a visit?" asks Mel.

"No, Howard definitely did not pay me a visit. But, I did get a call from Alexandre. Mel, it was so good to hear his voice and don't be angry with me, but I've arranged to meet up with him, tomorrow night, at our hotel. No funny business, just a drink and a catch up." I smile, waiting for her eruption.

"Right. So you want me to believe that when Alexandre arrives for drinks only, he will, under no circumstances, want to adjourn to your room, as in your bedroom? Are you completely fucking mad? Did we not agree, some time ago, that it was over, with you and him, that he is bad news, that he would continue to break your heart, until such time that you do not allow yourself to see him, ever again?" yells Mel, although I don't think she is really yelling for the sake of yelling, it's just that the yacht is really quite noisy with all these people and, of course, the really loud band.

"Keep your hair on. We are simply meeting for drinks and nothing more. Do you understand? After all, at the moment I find myself sleeping with Howard, so how would I explain that one away? 'Oh sorry Howard, can't possibly sleep with you tonight, as I am sleeping with Alexandre, an old boyfriend!' No, can't quite see that myself, can you?" I say, a tad agitated.

"Calm down! You see what happens when Alexandre is involved? For God's sake Martha, go find Howard and shag him senseless, hopefully, that will get the idiot out of your system. As for me, I am off to find Hans, as I don't have the advantage of two potential lovers!" And with that, she walks away to find her German.

Talk about feeling like a spare part. I do not recognise anyone on board and have visions, of me standing by myself all evening, but thankfully Theo and Jefferson, are about to rescue me.

"Hey pretty lady, now that is one beautiful outfit. Are you by any chance wearing Prada?" asks Jefferson.

"Well, what can I say? It was something I just happened to have lying around in the bottom of my suitcase, just waiting for an occasion; you know the sort, where you get invited aboard a beautiful yacht, with flowing champagne and fabulous people." I laugh.

"Seriously though, you look absolutely fabulous, no wonder that brother of mine is so taken with you, I'd be after you myself, if it wasn't for the fact that I'm with your brother!" laughs Jefferson, hugging me affectionately.

"Ciao carina, come here and give your baby brother a kiss!" says Theo, as he squeezes my hand.

"You are looking mighty hot, my darling, but I would have been inclined to wear a little less l'eau de sex!" laughs Theo, sarcastically.

"Button it Theo! After all, I am, who I am and tonight, I am delighted to be Martha DiPinto, dressed in Prada!" I giggle.

"Mel seems to be getting it on with Hans; have you met him yet?" asks Theo.

"Well, believe it or not, she met him in the Maritime bar, but you would think that they have known one another for years, they just seem to click, which is really lovely, because Mel is such a fabulous person," I respond.

"Yes, but she has such a huge derriere, perhaps that's why Hans has made a play for her?" continues Theo.

"Stop it! Just because you spend your days, surrounded by skeletal waifs, there is no need to be so fucking horrible and cruel!" I say, annoyed by his remark.

"If you were to make a play for Hans he wouldn't be the least bit interested. Hans likes his women big, the bigger the better. In fact, every one of his girlfriends, is one step close to huge and his wife hit the gigantic podium; honestly, he doesn't have any problems whatsoever, with curves." responds Jefferson.

"Oh no, do you think I should warn her, that Hans is a little perverted and bloody well married?" I ask.

"Don't be a spoil sport. Are you really going to ruin a night of sex for her?" responds Theo.

"No, you're right and after all, Mel really can take care of herself and if she is not happy with him, then I am sure she will have zero hesitation in throwing him out." I smile.

"Martha, can I get you another drink? Champagne, gin and tonic, what's your preference?" asks Jefferson.

"I would love a gin and tonic please and if you bump into a canapé waitress, please send her over in this direction, as I'm starving!" I smile.

Jefferson leaves, in search of alcohol and food. Theo is talking, but I can't hear him. He takes my hand and leads me down to the bedroom suites, indicating to Jefferson that we are disappearing for five minutes.

Boy, the difference in noise level is unbelievable. On deck, you cannot hear yourself think, but down here, it is almost tranquil.

"So, bro, what's on your mind?" I ask Theo, as let's face it, Theo would never leave a party, unless he had reason to.

"Cara mia, I just wanted to check that you were OK, you know, OK in the sense that obviously there are things happening between you and Howard, but, all too soon, the show will be over. Will you be alright when you have to say goodbye to him?" asks Theo, concerned.

"I think you are being a little too overprotective here. I've already told you that I am absolutely fine, with this set up. Howard is a really nice guy, but I know that he's not about to drop to one knee and declare his undying love for me. Why so much concern?" I respond, my heart now beating a little too quickly, at the mere thought of Howard and what we've been up to.

"You are my concern. I know that once Howard is back in the States, his mindset will be different. He'll focus one hundred percent on KAYSO and as importantly, he will focus on his divorce proceedings. This divorce is going to cost him dearly and he will more than likely dismiss everything else currently in his life, in order to sort out the mess. I just don't want you feeling despondent, rejected, or, used, once you've said your goodbyes," says Theo, caringly.

"Oh come off it, do you really think that I'm about to fall hook, line and sinker, for someone like Howard? This is fun, it makes my job enjoyable and more bearable and yes, he's a really nice guy and if I see him again, great and if I don't, then hey, no hardship!" I answer, knowing that deep down I will be absolutely devastated, if I don't see him again, after all, I don't want to feel used, do I?

"Anyway, you know me Theo, I play the field and yes, I know that it's not very ladylike, but I've also been in contact with Alexandre and he's paying a visit tomorrow evening, just for drinks mind, but who knows what will follow!" I smile, knowing full well, that I shouldn't have mentioned his name.

Theo's face turns to thunder.

"Are you completely mad? You have shed so many tears, no let me re-phrase, oceans, over that wanker. I cannot believe, for one moment, that you are going to see him again. Whatever is wrong with you?" he asks, slapping his forehead with the palm of his hand.

"Nothing is wrong with me! I am simply sleeping with Howard and having a drink with Alexandre. Tell me, where is the harm in that?" I respond, belligerently.

Thankfully, Jefferson has come to find us, "Hey, everything OK down here? Isn't this suite fantastic?"

"Yes, all is fine and dandy, I just think my brother is being a little over protective," I respond.

"Not always a bad thing, being over protective. I'm exactly the same with Howard. Anyone messes with Howard, then they mess with me too." smiles Jefferson, flexing his non-existent muscles.

"Come on, let's get upstairs and party. Jefferson, did you manage to find alcohol and food?" I enquire.

"Yes ma'm! Both are awaiting your arrival, upstairs!" he replies, taking my hand.

We return to the main deck. The party is now definitely in full swing. The majority of people are dancing. Not many speaking, as you can't hear yourself think, let alone speak and none are really taking in the moon's beauty anymore, as they are simply far too drunk!

The yacht is totally heaving. It's almost impossible to stand still, as you instantly get swept along in the dance wave that vibrates from one end of the deck to the other.

Looking around, I finally spot Mel and Hans, of course. I manage to get myself over to them, only to find that they are about to disembark. Apparently, they have a pressing engagement and I bet I know what that pressing engagement is. Should I tell Mel he's a pervert and a married one at that? No, she'll find out soon enough!

I hug them both and within moments, they are gone, just an outline of the happy couple remains, shimmering under the moonlight, as they head across to terra firma on the small transfer boat.

"So, this is where I find you. Are you trying to jump overboard, Martha?"

Even before turning around, I know that it's Howard standing behind me.

"Might I say, you look absolutely fantastic this evening?" continues Howard.

He is standing very close to me now. I still have my back to him, but he is delicately pushing into me. I can feel his cock brushing up against my silk covered bottom. Still with my back to him, I slide my hands behind my back and slowly reach for his throbbing cock. Slowly, very slowly, I unzip his trousers and work my hand into the opening of his underwear and start caressing his pulsating mass.

I don't turn around, but can imagine the expression of delight on his face. The pure ecstasy of having someone give him a hand job, in front of so many people, but keeping it so very discreet. No one can see us and no one will see us, unless they wish to leave or board the yacht.

Brushing my hair away from my ear, Howard moves in close.

"You are the sexiest tease I have ever met. I want to fuck you and lick you, until you ache. I have done nothing but think of you all day. Stay on board the yacht with me this evening."

Howard's breathing has intensified, he is about to come and I pray that he doesn't explode all over my beautiful jumpsuit. No, he's a man of experience. He quickly moves my hand and comes in his. What a gentleman!

Howard is swift with his handkerchief and without a word, disappears amongst the crowds; the crowds dancing on his yacht, drinking his champagne, enjoying his hospitality. I wonder if any of them could hazard a guess, that he's just had a hand job by the lady in the Prada jumpsuit! I use the word 'lady' loosely, you understand!

Rather bizarrely, I feel like a prostitute, don't ask me why. But wouldn't you? Was it because we did not exchange words after the deed? If I'm honest with myself, I rather enjoyed our moment of madness. Being with Howard made me forget all about Alexandre, which is a good thing of course, isn't it?

Back on deck, I drink and I dance, spending the majority of the evening with Theo and Jefferson. The yacht is so crowded that it's almost impossible to find anyone else I know, unless I bump into them by pure accident.

I am feeling decidedly drunk, so have taken myself away from the hustle and bustle of the crowds and I've managed to find a fantastic spot by the DJ. No one can see me, but I can see everyone. I text Theo to tell him, I've found a sneaky hiding place, just in case he gets concerned that I've gone overboard!

The waitresses are being particularly attentive to the DJ and as his new shipmate, I have a constant flow of alcohol and rather foolishly, I have reverted back to champagne, huge mistake, massive. I am drunk, but thankfully I am a happy drunk. I can feel my iphone vibrating. I have messages. Two messages. How exciting.

Text message one from Howard: *Where are you? I can't find you. That moment was fantastic xxx.*

Text message two from Alexandre. Oh shit! Alexandre. I had just about erased him from my mind*: I cannot wait to see you tomorrow evening. This yacht party is boring without you baby xx.*

Oh my God! What are the chances of Alexandre being on board a yacht, at the same time as me? How weird. How very weird. Hang on, just one moment... As quick as a flash, I seem to have sobered up. The shock of Alexandre being on board a yacht has sobered me up sufficiently to think, rather stupidly, that he might just be aboard the KAYSO yacht. No, he didn't say that he was coming to Cannes this evening. No, the chances of him being on board this particular yacht are practically non-existent.

I respond to the messages. Firstly Alexandre: *Which yacht are you on and where? Shall I come and join you? xx.*

Then I respond to Howard: *You bring out the naughtiness in me, you filthy shipmate. Am still on board. Cannot wait for later xx.*

I drink another flute of champagne and make idle conversation with myself.

My iphone vibrates. A text message from Alexandre: *Actually am in Cannes on board some fashion yacht—Kayso. Know them? xxx.*

Oh my God! I re-read the text message five times. My world has come to a stand still. Alexandre is on board THIS yacht.; somewhere, amongst the guests!

Shit! Fuck! Bollocks! Bollocks! Bollocks! I cannot let him know that I am in the same place. If he sees me, he will kiss me and if he kisses me, then maybe, just maybe, Howard might see him kissing me! Fuck me! It doesn't bear thinking about.

Shit! What do, I do? I need to get out of this floating mess. But, then what would Howard think, if I was to run out on him now? Fuck! Why is my life so fucking complex? What I wouldn't give to be married with two point four children (not quite sure how that is possible, but hey, who am I to argue?), living in suburbia and attending school fetes and coffee mornings! Did I really just think that? Well, if I did, it was only for a fleeting millisecond!

Our waitress reappears and brings reinforcements, in the guise of alcohol. I grab two glasses of champagne (greed I know!) and drink one quickly, which doesn't even touch the sides. I sip the other, in the hope that more alcohol will arrive quickly! I need to stay drunk to get through this evening, although in fairness, the party will be coming to an end soon. Well, at least I hope so.

Thankfully the DJ's booth is relatively dark, so it's difficult for people to see us, but thankfully we can see everyone. I peer into the crowd. I see Theo and Jefferson, dancing around. I see Howard. I see Rochelle and Mary-Jo and of course, I see Danny Mendosa, because let's face it, the bastard is taking up the space of four people and rather worryingly he's dancing. Boy, he definitely can't dance—he looks like Fred Flintstone, doing a rendition of YMCA!

I keep peering, hoping to spy Alexandre, but deep down, praying that he definitely does not, spy me. I don't need this complication in my life and especially, not this evening.

Suddenly, fear grips me. To my left, I see Howard and he is talking to a guy, who, from the back, looks identical to Alexandre. Oh God! Please no! Don't let these two know one another. I can't bear it. I gulp down another flute of champagne and out of the corner of my eye I can see the DJ watching me.

I throw him a glance and put my finger to my lips, to indicate that he should keep quiet. Poor chap, doesn't know me from Adam, but I've infiltrated his space and I am now, giving him orders!

I look out towards Howard and then slowly the realisation hits me. The guy he is talking to, is definitely Alexandre, who I am now looking at, full on. Sweet Jesus! Can you believe that my current lover and the man of my dreams actually know one another? Oh my God! How friendly are they? Shit! What if Howard tells Alexandre about me? What if he tells him about the hand job I administered earlier? I'm feeling faint. I am feeling sick. I need fresh air, but I can't leave my safe haven, because let's face it I am bloody well certain that I'll be spotted. I crouch down, low to the floor and give the DJ the finger, when he starts to question what I am doing.

After about forty minutes, or so, the party finally comes to an end. Slowly, the guests start to leave, the DJ starts packing up his booth, still giving me the eye, and not a good eye at that and then I watch Alexandre disembark. Hey, hang on just a minute; he doesn't seem to be leaving alone. Is he walking off with another guest? I struggle to my feet and head out to check out this situation. I am crouching after all, I don't want him to see me. Just how drunk am I? I delicately and gracefully fall to the floor.

Thankfully, Alexandre appears to be alone now; said female, is in the arms of another chap, thank God, otherwise I would have been forced to pounce! I don't want any females touching my man, not one...

As soon as the shuttle with Alexandre on board has disappeared, I stand tall; bloody thighs killing me. Aside from the yacht crew, there are only five of us remaining, Danny Mendosa included. I hope he's not staying the night—that would be just too much to bear. Oh God, he's walking towards me...

"Martha, are you coming on shore with me now?" he asks.

Excellent, he's leaving and of course I'm not going on shore, as I am spending the night with Howard. Aren't I?

"Hey Danny, I'm going to keep Martha for a while longer, it's been an age since we hooked up properly, so I'll send her ashore later!" quips in Jefferson.

"Sure thing, 'night all!" waves Danny, rather happily, as he boards the boat, taking him back to firmer shores.

"Jefferson, that was a close call. How was I going to explain myself away, if Danny was to stay on board tonight?" I giggle.

"Right then let's have a night cap and then to bed. Martha, you must be absolutely exhausted. Weren't you out on the razz last night in Monaco? And furthermore did I hear that you had a police escort back this morning?" Howard laughs.

"Shit! Did you hear about that? Listen, I really have no shame in jumping into a police van, if it means a lift back to my hotel, and yes, you're right about being totally exhausted. Gone are the days where I could party for days on end, that time has been and gone!" I smile and yawn simultaneously!

"Ah yes, the police escort. Funnily enough, I was talking to a film director from Monaco this evening and I mentioned to him, that some of our crew had been escorted home in the back of a police van, needless to say, he too, saw the funny side," added Howard.

My heart is beating so fast, I think it's about to burst, or, I'm about to faint, for I know that Howard is referring to Alexandre, Alexandre the film director from Monaco.

Oh well, in for a penny, in for a pound. "How is it that you know a film director from Monaco?" I laugh, "Do you know everyone?"

"Actually I met him in New York a few years back and every time, I'm over in the South of France, we hook up for a beer or two, nothing heavy, but he's a good guy to know," replies Howard. None the wiser, that I am actually madly in love, with said film director.

I catch Theo looking disapprovingly at me. This tangled web of a life is way too difficult sometimes. But, I only have myself to blame.

We toast our glasses and echo 'good health' and down our, forty year old cognac. Now, let me tell you, this is pure nectar. I kiss Theo and Jefferson and bid them sweet dreams, as they head off to bed and I wait for Howard, to lead me off to his boudoir.

We are now all alone. Finally. It's been a long time coming. The moonlight is shining, glistening on the still waters of the Mediterranean that surround us.

"So, now, it's just you and me. And of course, the full moon, which I just happened to organise for you this evening," he winks.

"Ah, so this beautiful moon light was your doing then, was it? Boy, there really is no end to your talents, is there?" I smile.

"Martha listen, I know what happened earlier, but it's OK, honestly," continues Howard.

I stop dead in my tracks. What the fuck is he on about? He is obviously referring to Alexandre. Shit! They have spoken about me. Howard has told Alexandre about this mad Italian girl he is shagging and Alexandre has responded that he knows of someone just like that and they have both, said my name, Martha DiPinto. I close my eyes, waiting for Howard's disappointment to ensue.

Eventually I open my eyes, but he's looking up at the moon, smiling. The suspense is killing, so, I ask the question.

"Howard, what are you talking about? What happened earlier?" I ask a little too anxiously, just waiting for him to say the word 'Alexandre'.

"You know," replies Howard.

"Nope honey, I have no idea what you are referring to." I reply, my breathing is a little heavier now and I think I am about to suffer a coronary.

"You know, when you were hiding," he smiles.

"Whatever are you going on about?" I walk over to him, wrapping my arms around his waist, from behind.

"When you were hiding from Danny. Why is it that you dislike him so much? OK, he can be a little opinionated sometimes, but give him a break!" replies Howard.

I let out a deep sigh. Thank God! He doesn't know about Alexandre and that suits me, just fine.

"Oh I know I was being silly, but I didn't want Danny starting on me again, you know, asking me what I was doing on the yacht blah, blah, blah. I simply don't like him," I respond, feeling quite at ease again.

Slowly, Howard turns around and kisses me passionately. I can feel his hand cupping my breasts and as I arch my back, I feel powerless, as I slowly slip backwards. Before I know it, I am flat on my back. Not in a sexy sort of way, no, basically I am far too drunk and have arched, just a little too far! Howard extends his hand to pull me up.

"Come on you, it's time for bed!" he says, leading me to his suite. I am so unbelievably tired. But, I suppose, I should really have a little session of jiggy jiggy, otherwise he might think me rude!

Arriving at his bedroom, I let Howard undress me, but ask him to hang my jumpsuit up, as I don't want it creasing. Fuck! I love that jumpsuit. I pull off my shoes. He unclips my bra and then eagerly sucks my nipples; slowly his hands work their way down my stomach and then very slowly, he takes off my knickers. He gently pushes me backwards, onto the bed and my legs part effortlessly. His tongue is so gentle and his fingers so strong.

Well, my tiredness has certainly disappeared. It's gone two am and I am ready for Howard, ready for him to make love to me for hours, which is exactly what he does. Tonight, we have zero inhibitions. We are so at ease with one another, it feels perfect. As my mother would say, 'it's meant to be'.

"Howard, that was amazing. Thank you." I smile, after our extended session of love-making. And love-making it was, not purely sex.

"No Martha, thank you. You know exactly, how to please." He leans over, to kiss me tenderly.

"Do you have an alarm clock? I need to be on site for eight am—we have a full day of rehearsals tomorrow, as I am sure you are aware." I say quietly, my eyes starting to feel heavy.

"Sure thing. What time do you need to leave?" he asks.

"Well, if I need to be on site by eight am, I need to be off the boat by seven am, which gives me time to get back to the hotel to change; so really, the alarm should be set for six thirty, which gives me a thirty minute window, to make love to you in the morning!" I smile, kissing him softly, before rolling onto my tummy for much needed sleep.

I fall into a deep sleep, but all too soon, I can hear alarm bells in the distance. My eyes open, surely it cannot be morning already? I am way too tired to move. Howard opens his eyes.

"Martha, is it really necessary for all this noise, so early in the morning?" he winks.

"Sorry my darling, but some of us have to work for a living and today, I am working for you," I respond, trying desperately to keep my eyes open.

We are both lying on the bed, naked. Suddenly, I am feeling horny again. I rush to the bathroom and swill my mouth with mouthwash, carefully bringing a capful through for Howard. I absolutely hate morning breath, doesn't matter who it belongs to, I simply hate it.

Jumping back on the bed, I make a grab for a condom and slowly place it over Howard's erect manhood. Jesus! This man is perfect. For the next thirty minutes or so, we have wild, rampant, wonderful sex.

Exhausted and panting I lie back. "I have so got to go; otherwise I'm going to be late. Ingrid will not be impressed, she'll throw a mammoth hissy fit," I say, kissing him tenderly.

"Up to you, it's your call. I can get rehearsals put back a couple of hours, if it helps?" he smiles.

"No, that's not fair; it simply means that the crew then have to work later into the evening. No, let's not do that," I say, hesitantly, as let's face it, I would love to stay in bed for a couple of hours, but that's purely selfish!

"OK, I get what you're saying, baby," he replies. Oh my God! He called me 'baby.' He's not allowed to do that! Only Alexandre calls me 'baby.'

Within minutes I am dressed, in my gorgeous jumpsuit and heading for the door. "See you later!" I smile and wave.

"Martha, I'll be late for rehearsals, but I definitely won't be late for you tonight," he winks, as he rolls over, snuggling underneath the duvet.

Tonight, is the night, that I am seeing Alexandre. Shit! This is not happening! I am too stressed and way too tired, to deal with this, at the moment.

Thankfully, the small boat is waiting for me and soon I am back at the harbour, still dressed in my Prada jumpsuit. Now, as much as I love my outfit, it's a give away that I am doing the walk of shame, i.e. the walk of shame, that suggests I've been out all night, because I have the same outfit on from the night before! Yes indeed, I am a slut!

I don't spot anybody, as I enter the Maritime Hotel, but someone spots me. And of course, it could only be one person, yes, indeed, the one and only, Danny Mendosa. I am totally unaware.

I rush to my room, calling Mel on her mobile, on route.

"Morning my darling, are you up?" I ask, a little too happily.

"What the fuck... what time is it?" she asks, sleepily.

"Oops, sorry, have I woken you up? Are you alone? Are you planning on meeting me in main reception, at precisely seven fifty?" I ask.

"Fucking hell Slapper! Too many questions! Yes, I will see you at precisely seven fifty. Now fuck off!" she laughs.

And with that, I arrive at my bedroom.

Chapter Fourteen

Shit! Yet another night with me getting very little sleep. I've no idea, how I'm going to get through rehearsals today. I am absolutely exhausted, but definitely on a high, so hopefully, that will see me through otherwise, I might have to tap the models up, for a bit of coke! Joking, only joking. I am too much of a wimp to take drugs, as for sure, they will have an adverse effect on me and that will be that, splashed across the papers for all the wrong reasons...

I jump in the shower and wish that Howard could be with me, right now. He is totally insatiable. Drying myself off, I catch my reflection in the mirror, thankfully the body is still in good shape, but the hair, well, that leaves an awful lot to be desired. Alas, I don't even have time to wash it. Today, it will need to be worn up—tousled look, just fallen out of bed, after a night of 'rampant sex' look.

My imagination starts to kick in. What is going to happen this evening? Will I meet with Howard, or, with Alexandre? My head is pulling me towards Howard, but my heart is definitely swinging towards Alexandre. Oh fuck! What am I to do? For starters, I can't meet Alexandre in the hotel bar, just in case Howard comes in for a drink. Far too many problems and there is not enough time to sort them out now. Obviously lacking concentration I rub too much Prada lotion onto my body and now I look like an infant on the beach with an over anxious mother, who has covered her child in factor sixty, sun lotion! I grab a towel and wipe it all off. How wasteful!

I apply my make up and the reflection staring back at me actually doesn't look too bad. Sex, and lots of it, obviously suits me. But, sex with which man later?

I dress quickly, shoes on, perfume squirted, hair up, huge sunglasses in hand.

Time now is seven forty six. Perfect.

Arriving in the hotel's reception, I spot Danny. Do I go over and be civil, as I am sure that will please Howard? No harm I suppose, especially as Mel has yet to arrive.

"Morning Danny, how are you today?" I ask, in an upbeat voice.

"Yeah, I'm good and you?" he asks.

"Thank you, yes, I'm fine. Great party last night and what a fabulous yacht," I continue.

"So, what time did you get back to shore?" he's looking directly into my eyes now.

"In fairness I couldn't tell you I kind of got swept up in the moment, so no, no idea what time I got back." I lie, fingers crossed behind my back.

I look around, still no Mel. Fucking hell! Move it girl! This man is asking too many questions. I wish I hadn't bloody spoken to him now.

"Well, I think you got back around seven fifteen this morning, quite a session you must have had. Now, you listen to me. Back off Howard, he's not interested in you. You're simply sex to him. Understand?" his lips are curled. Danny's really ugly when he's angry—correction, he's pug ugly, even when he's not!

Thankfully, I feel a hand on my shoulder. I turn to see who it is and thankfully, it's Mel.

"Morning darling, shall we go? I think Danny and I have finished our conversation, for now." I smile at Dickbrain and link arms with Mel, heading out of the hotel.

"What's up, your face is like thunder?" she asks.

"Danny knows about me and Howard, he caught me coming back to the hotel this morning, fucking arsehole," I say angrily. God he's pissed me off. Just who does he think he is?

"Don't worry about it. I'm sure Howard can make up his own mind, as to whom he sleeps with. Go with the flow, it all comes to an end eventually," smiles Mel.

"So, tell me all. Did you have a wonderful evening with Hans? Come on spill the beans and don't leave out any details!" I continue. "I want it all, lock, stock and barrel."

"Well, I think you need to be sitting down, to hear what happened, so I suggest coffee and a croissant, in the Fleur Suite first!" laughs Mel.

Even though she is looking tired today, she is definitely on a high. She looks different, all smiley and happy. See, sex is good for everyone!

Arriving at the Palais du Roscoff, Mel and I head up to catering, quickly—after all, we are both starving.

"So, how'd ya get on last night? Good time? Bloody hell Mel, did you get any sleep? You're eyes are like piss holes in the snow. I pity Howard's bar bill!" laughs Mickey.

"For your information, I had a restless night, as my bed was occupied by a gentleman, so up yours Mickey mate—were you alone last night?" retorts Mel, smiling, as she makes a grab for two croissants and a huge mug of coffee. Strong black coffee, with plenty of sugar.

We take a table, away from prying eyes and ears, and I snuggle in close, excited to hear all about her tales of the previous night. But rather annoyingly, our moment is ruined.

"Morning. And how are you both on this fine day?" asks Hugo, as he pulls up a seat. "Don't mind if I join you, do you?"

"No not at all, just catching up on life really," I smile.

"How was your evening? Did you get laid?" asks Mel, a little too crudely for Hugo's liking.

"A lady of your standing need not use such language, but for your information, yes I did and jolly good it was too!" he replies, with a huge smile spreading across his face.

"Good morning Martha, good morning Mel, how are you both today? I hope you had sufficient sleep last night, as I think we're in for a rather long day," smiles Ingrid, as she walks towards us.

"Hi Ingrid. Yes, no sleep deprivation for us, we were tucked up in bed before midnight, so bright-eyed and bushy-tailed today!" I lie, laughing. No fingers crossed this time!

"Hugo, can I please have a word with you in the auditorium? And ladies, I would like you at your workstations by eight thirty precisely, please," she continues.

Hugo and Ingrid walk away. Finally, it's just Mel and me.

"So, come on, spill the beans, I can't wait. I just know it's going to be filthy!" I laugh.

"Well in a nutshell, Hans is really into large women, the bigger, the better, as far as he is concerned. Walking back to the Maritime Hotel last night, he pulls me into a side street, pushes me against a wall, face forward, whips out his cock, lifts up my dress and fucks me, right there and then. I was, of course, slightly taken aback, but hey no-one saw. Back in the hotel we have a nightcap in the bar and whilst seated at the table, he starts playing with my fanny with his big toe. I can't begin to tell you what a turn on that was! The man just can't get enough," chuckles Mel.

"You dirty cow! I love it, go on tell me more!" I say, waiting in anticipation for more lurid details.

"Eventually we get to my bedroom, lights fully on and he starts to undress me, all the while kissing me all over my body. I can see he is so turned on, as his dick is poking through his unzipped trousers. Well, the rest is history. We did it on the bed, on the floor, in the shower, which in fairness was a little difficult as it was a tight squeeze and then he had me up against the window, looking down on the people below. But you know what? It was fucking fantastic! Hans made me feel alive again. Martha, I have not had sex like that in such a long time. What a turn on!" Mel is rolling her eyes. Shit! I hope she's not having another orgasm!

"Well, get you, 'dirty Gertie'. No wonder you look so fabulous today. Sex at the window no less? Oh, how I wish I had been walking by, at that precise moment," I laugh.

"So, I am assuming you guys have hit it off and that there will be a re-run this evening and perhaps in the future, too?" I continue.

"Well, I'm not so sure about the future, but I think there is a distinct possibility that this evening, we'll fuck like rabbits again!" she giggles.

"I am sure the future could be tackled. After all, he's only based in Germany, not too difficult to get to, is it?" I suggest.

"No hassle in getting to Germany, the problem is the wife when I get there! But, by all accounts she has lost a shed load of weight, which he's not happy about; he likes his women big and of course, he clapped sight of me and his dick spoke!" responds Mel.

What a tour this is turning out to be!

Mel and I grab more coffee and pastries and head off to our stations.

Ellie is backstage talking to Hugo, as I arrive.

"Morning my lovely, how are you today? Did you have a FAB time on the yacht last night?" asks Ellie, giving me a little hug.

"It was a great party! The music was brilliant, the champagne flowed and my headache has now kicked in!" I laugh.

"What are you like? What time did you get back? Please tell me you managed to get some sleep?" she smiles.

"Between these four walls, I actually snuck back at seven this morning, but I did get some sleep on the yacht. Thankfully, Theo was on board and so put me to bed, at a respectable hour," I giggle, all the while having my fingers crossed, yet again. I really do have to stop lying, as one day, all these lies will catch up with me—I just know they will.

"Martha, I have a copy of the rehearsal schedule, which is long, but hopefully we should be able to run through it without any problems. We have KAYSO's VPs this morning, followed by the catwalk run through and then the award ceremony rehearsal, which is pretty straightforward. My only concern is, that we get the videos lined up correctly and on time, as that seems to be our only issue at the moment. In fact, I think I'll go and have a word with Mel, just to reconfirm with her, so, if you'll excuse me..." and with that, Hugo is gone.

"Did you manage to catch up on your sleep last night, after your meeting with Ingrid? I ask Ellie.

"Well, sort of, but something happened and I'm not sure if I should tell you, or not," she replies whilst chewing her nails.

"It's entirely up to you, but if something happened that shouldn't have happened, I am more than happy to listen, but if you tell me you took drugs, I'll swing for you, so move now, if that's that case!" I respond, with authority.

"No! Definitely not drugs and I am sorry about yesterday. You know, Belinda and I never do things like that on site, but we were so tired. No, basically after the meeting with Ingrid, Belinda went to bed because she was really shattered, but I fancied a nightcap, so went to the bar and Dan was there, on his own. We had a drink and then, when I went to leave I asked him to walk me back to my room, just like a gentleman should and he obliged. We get to my room and he pecks me on the cheek and then I kiss him. It wasn't him it was definitely me, Martha. I start to kiss him, you know on the lips, tongues and everything," she stammers, her face reddening with guilt.

"Whatever possessed you? Please tell me that you didn't sleep with him. Well?" I ask, waiting for her response.

"No, I didn't. But yes, I did invite him in and he said 'no', I was too much of a temptation for him and he walked off. I am so embarrassed, why did I do it?" She starts crying.

"Stop those tears right now. Sometimes we all do things we shouldn't, but I have to say, respect to Dan. He has had the hots for you for a long time and I hate to say it, if he had spent the night with you, your friendship would never be the same again. So you know what? Count yourself lucky. Go and find him, give him a hug and thank him. It will all be forgotten." I smile, hugging her.

Rochelle appears backstage. "Hey, good morning! Good time last night and how's your head today?" she asks.

"Seriously? It's about to crack in two!" I laugh.

"Mary-Jo spoke to Howard earlier and something has come up, so he won't be at rehearsals this morning. OK?" she explains.

"That's absolutely fine. We'll start with Danny instead. Not a problem, I'll let Mel know." I smile. I am feeling deflated now. I was rather looking forward to seeing Howard. Oh well, he obviously needs his rest.

I send him a text message: *Hey sleepy head, enjoy your rest, but think of me! Ha Ha xxx*.

Within moments my iphone vibrates. Ah, a response from Howard, no doubt. I open up the text message, but it's not from Howard, it's from Alexandre. My hand starts to shake slightly, as I press the 'open' key: *Hey baby, can't wait to see you tonight, xx*.

Shit! What am I going to do? Do I see Alexandre? Do I see Howard? Can I engineer it so that I see both of them? Fucking hell!

My iphone vibrates again. This time it's a text message from Howard: *Sorry, major problems in the States, call you later xxx*.

Jesus! That sounds serious.

We commence our rehearsals and thankfully Danny Mendosa's presentation runs without a hitch. Bruce Shannon has made a few amends to his script, but presents well, as does Marcus Driscoll.

All three presenters are happy with their presentations and no further rehearsals are required. Thankfully. Marcus and Bruce come backstage to thank me for my help this morning—they are such lovely men. Then, Danny Dickbrain Mendosa appears.

"Hello Danny. Do you have any changes to make?" I ask.

"No, it's all fine. And no changes to Howard's script either, assuming he can make the presentation tomorrow morning. If not, I'll present it, so can you print out a copy for me?" he instructs.

"Yes, of course. So Howard might not be around then? Is he planning on going back to the States?" I ask, sounding a little too concerned.

"Maybe, maybe not, but it's nothing for you to worry about, OK?" he replies curtly.

I print out the script and hand it to him. He walks away, not even so much as a 'thank you.' That man is just so rude!

I phone Howard, but he does not respond and I don't leave him a message. Hopefully, he will call back when he sees my missed call.

We break for lunch and I go to find Ingrid, who is deep in conversation with Hugo.

"Hi Ingrid, sorry to interrupt, but I was just wondering if you have had any further updates, regarding Howard?"

"No nothing. But either way, I understand that Mr Mendosa will present Howard's script, if he is unable to do so himself," she responds, in a matter of fact kind of way.

No one seems to be letting on what's happening. I check my iphone, but no missed call and no text message. He'll call soon enough, I'm sure.

Lunch is delicious, coq au vin with the most wonderful array of vegetables. I eat like a king and like a queen, come to think of it and possibly like all the king's men too! I think three portions might just have been a little bit piggy but I am definitely craving food. I am feeling so much more alive. I grab an apple and go outside with Mel for a cigarette. Isn't it weird, I cannot remember the last time I had a cigarette, hey, maybe that means I'm a non-smoker now?

Outside I light up and thoroughly enjoy the sensation that my cigarette brings. No, I am definitely still a smoker!

"Mel, let me ask you something. If you had the choice between Howard and Alexandre for the night, which one would you choose?" I ask, inquisitively.

"Well, seeing that you and Alexandre are no longer together and he has a tendency of breaking your heart, I would opt for the sensible choice of Howard. After all, he's a safer bet. You've got him for a couple more days and then he's gone. Gone back to his world and you to yours," she replies, shaking her head.

"So, you don't think I should see Alexandre then?" I continue.

"No!" is her response. That one syllable says it all.

"What, not at all?" I smile.

"For fucks sake Martha! If you see Alexandre, he'll only break your heart and then whilst it's on the floor, stamp on it! What's the point? Tell me, just what is the point?" responds Mel, more than a little irritated.

"OK, keep your hair on, I was only asking." I reply sulkily.

"I actually know what will happen. You'll see Alexandre and then you'll sleep with him for old times sake and then when he leaves in the morning, you'll start crying, because he is going back to his wife and kids. It's not rocket science is it? He is a weak, selfish bastard who only thinks of himself!" she replies. Wish I hadn't asked now—especially as I know she's right.

"I know you're right. But chances are, that Howard might not even be around this evening," I say, rather dismissively.

"Might be a good opportunity for you to get some sleep then, don't you think? You must be absolutely knackered because I know I am," laughs Mel.

"Has Hans been in contact?" I enquire, changing the subject.

"Yes and he's texted me a picture of his dick. He really is a nob, but the guy is great fun! After all, what's to stop me circulating that picture around?" smiles Mel.

"Oh my God! You wouldn't would you?" I ask, mouth wide open.

"If he misbehaves this evening, then I might just forward it onto Howard and maybe Ingrid, can you imagine?" We are both laughing now. Exhaustion makes you think the weirdest things!

"Let's go back in. Next stop, catwalk rehearsal, so I suppose you'll be backstage having a snooze then?" smiles Mel.

"Sounds like a plan to me. But keep on eye on Pikey, I would hate to think of him in amongst the flowers and plants again, getting the perfect eyeful!" I giggle.

We return to the auditorium where the catwalk has been positioned. I go backstage and thankfully the big burly bouncer steps aside, he clearly remembers who I am.

I find Theo lurking amongst the models and rather limply, link his arm.

"Ciao bella, what's up, are you tired?" asks Theo.

"I am so tired I don't know what to do with myself." I smile, eyes shut.

"Great party last night. Have you heard from him?" asks Theo.

"Who do you mean, Howard? Yes, I had a text from him earlier, but I don't think things are too good in the States." I continue.

"I wasn't referring to Howard. Try again!" he responds.

I look at him blankly, all the while knowing full well, that he is referring to Alexandre.

"Well?" he asks, impatiently.

"Well what, who are you referring to?" I ask, rather stupidly.

"Shall I spell it out for you? Alexandre, that's who!" he replies, crossly.

"No I haven't. Well, no that's a lie. Yes, I've had a text message from him, but that's all, I promise," I reply, smiling.

"If you know what's good for you, you'll not see him whilst you are here. I can't be doing with the tears again, understand?" Theo is being authoritative now.

I simply smile, kiss him on the cheek and walk away. I don't want to get into an argument, far too many people around and I know, that whatever his argument, he will be right. After all, he always is.

I decide to put on my cans and listen to the banter amongst the crew.

Mel: "Martha, are you on cans?"

Me: "Yep, what's up?"

Mel: "Check your mobile and smile if you're jealous."

Ingrid: "Ladies, can we please limit conversation to that which is relative to the show only? There will be plenty of time later, for idle chatter."

Mel: "Thank you Ingrid."

Ingrid: "Mel, do you have Patrick (Pikey) in your sight? We don't want him amongst the undergrowth again, now, do we?"

Mel: "Pikey is with Dan, he's being supervised."

The catwalk rehearsal has commenced and the models come out, one by one.

I check my iphone. There's still nothing from Howard. Do I text him or, do I not? I decide not to, just in case the States business is really bad news. I do, however, have a text from Mel. On opening it up, I recoil in horror, for there on my screen is Hans' dick, erect and dressed with a bow. Boy, that man is seriously weird.

I text Mel: *Did that tiny thing really bring that much pleasure and enjoyment? Xx*

And then I text Amelia: *Hi darling, how are you? The week is nearly over. Just in rehearsals now, but nothing doing for me. Theo is on good form. Have slept with Howard! Hope you are well and so too, is Edd and the bambinos. See you very soon. Love you xx.*

Within seconds I receive a response from Mel: *His dick is plenty big enough and fits perfectly, thank you! xx.*

And then a response from Amelia: *For goodness sake Martha, does life revolve around you, on your back? Am totally jealous! Hope he is handsomely gorgeous too. Can't wait to hear the gossip! xxx.*

But, still nothing from Howard.

My mind starts to wander, as I think of Alexandre. I really do want to see him this evening. I mean, I don't necessarily want to sleep with him, but it would be good to see him again. I'd love him to be back in my life. I know he'll want sex—I just know it. But, I find myself in an impossible situation—I can't sleep with both men. So, which one should I choose?

I shut my eyes and I drift off into a very, deep sleep.

"Martha! Martha! Are you OK? Can you hear me? Martha, wake up."

For a split second, I have no idea where I am. I open my eyes, to see Belinda standing over me. "Martha, are you OK?" she asks. "I thought we had lost you then, hell, I couldn't wake you!"

"Sorry, gosh, I must have drifted off!" I laugh.

Every bone in my body seems to ache. I hope I'm not coming down with something. After all, it's the end of show party tomorrow night, can't miss that now can I?

In all honesty, I am not coming down with anything whatsoever. I am simply exhausted; in fact, so exhausted, that my body can't seem to function any more.

"We are going to take a short break after the catwalk rehearsal and then we have the run through for the awards ceremony, OK?" says Belinda.

"Yes, that's absolutely fine. Let me go and grab a coffee and then we'll get cracking." I respond, trying desperately to wake myself up.

I head off to the Fleur Suite. Dan is in there all alone. "Hey, how are you? Haven't seen much of you today, everything alright?" I ask, genuinely concerned.

"All's cool, ta." he responds.

"You sure, you seem a little distant, what's up?" I ask.

"Keep a secret for me Martha, will you? Ellie came onto me last night and it freaked me out, coz as much as I wanted to spend the night with her, I didn't.

But you know what the weird thing is? If it had been any other bird, I'd have jumped her bones, but because it was Ellie and she's just so bloody beautiful and lovely, I couldn't. Fuck Martha! I don't want to use her for sex, she's too good for that. She must really despise me. Why would I turn her down, hey?" he asks, rather forlorn.

"Listen, what you did last night was for the best. You and Ellie will continue to flirt until the day you both die, but, if either of you oversteps the mark your fabulous friendship is over. I say, 'well done you,' for not giving in to temptation. Ellie will certainly respect you more, because of your decision. Now go find her and sort it out." I give him a hug and a peck on his cheek and he dutifully goes off to mend bridges with Ellie.

I gulp my coffee and refill my cup. My iphone is vibrating. I quickly pull it from my bag. A text message from Howard: *I've got a lot to sort out with the States. Can we postpone our clandestine meeting until tomorrow, after the awards? Apologies xxx.*

Well, talk about being well and truly blown out. I don't know whether to be upset or happy. But of course, not seeing Howard this evening leaves the door wide open for me to meet with Alexandre. This is obviously fate.

I text Howard back: *The disappointment is too much for me to bear. I will surely die of a broken heart! Ha! Ha! Look forward to you making it up tomorrow night! xxx.*

And another text message from Howard: *You sexy tease x.*

I head back to the auditorium with my coffee. The awards are being presented by Howard (if he was here) and Bruce Shannon. In Howard's absence, Marcus Driscoll is stepping in. Between Bruce and Marcus, the presentation is bound to be full of laughs; even if it is only a rehearsal.

Rochelle, is taking on the role of stage dolly bird (you know, the one who smiles sweetly and hands out the awards to the winners) and boy, oh boy, she is in her element. I think she is taking the role a little too seriously, as she has changed into a long evening gown—God only knows, what she'll be like on the actual night.

We run through the ceremony. In all, there are ten individual awards and one group award.

The awards rehearsal runs without a glitch; in fact, Bruce and Marcus work together so well on stage, that we are pushing for them to do it on the night.

The time is now six thirty pm. The majority of crew have been stood down. All that remains now is for the auditorium to be cleaned. Ingrid has requested a meeting with Jerome, Ellie, Belinda, Mel, Dan, Mickey, Hugo and myself.

We all assemble in front of our esteemed leader.

"Right everybody, that was a very good rehearsal today, so thank you. Good is good, but tomorrow I want perfect please. At this stage, we are still not sure whether Howard will be joining us, but if he doesn't, then we'll work more closely with his immediate team. Any questions?" asks Ingrid.

We all shake our heads.

"In that case, thank you again and might I suggest that everyone gets an early night? No room for unnecessary errors tomorrow," smiles Ingrid.

We grab our bags, laptops etc and head for the exit.

"So, what's the plan tonight, anyone up for dinner, later?" asks Mickey.

"I, for one, am heading back to the hotel for a shower, room service and sleep," I smile; knowing full well, that I have alternative plans in place.

"I'm on a promise, so count me out!" laughs Mel.

"We've got a final catch up with Ingrid later, but then I think an early night is the right option," responds Ellie, answering for herself and Belinda.

"Hugo, what about you mate? You up for a bite to eat and couple of pints?" asks Dan.

"I'm afraid I am already booked, but do have a good evening," replies Hugo, giving Dan a wink.

"Well then, Mickey mate, it's just me and thee, bugger the rest of them," laughs Dan.

We all head off to Le Maritime and decide to stop off at the hotel bar for a quick drink. I take a look around, but there is definitely no sign of Howard.

I should have texted Alexandre to tell him rehearsals have finished, but I am still in two minds. To see him or, not to see him? I'll toss a coin. Heads for yes and tails for no!

My iphone vibrates, it's Theo: *Ciao bella, what are your plans for dinner this evening? Do you want to join Jefferson and me for a bite? xx.*

I know what he's up to. He's making sure that I don't get Alexandre over.

I respond quickly: *Thanks Theo, but am totally shattered. All of the crew are doing room service this evening, apart from Mel, who is being serviced by Hans!! xxx.*

No sooner do I put my iphone in my pocket, than it vibrates again. Another text message from Theo: *OK, behave. Sweet dreams. xxx.*

Grabbing a drink, we toast the show's success for tomorrow. There is no doubt that it will be a good one. We've rehearsed it enough times! But to tell you the truth that is actually when things do go wrong—too many rehearsals can sometimes equal rough show. However, we will have to wait and see!

I decide to text Amelia to ask her what I should do about Alexandre. If she says it's a good idea, then I'll get him over, but if she says it's a bad idea, then I won't. Here goes: *Tell me what to do—should I see Alexandre tonight or not? I am totally confused. xxx.*

Within seconds my iphone vibrates with Amelia's response: *Are you drunk? Did you really mean to text the word Alexandre? I thought you were into Howard? What the heck is going on and what does Theo say? xxx.*

I reply quickly: *Howard busy tonight, and I am really wanting to see Alexandre. xxx.*

Two minutes pass, Amelia is obviously thinking of a response... it arrives:

I think you're a slut and I would definitely see Alexandre this evening, if you can get away with it—however little brother will be fucking furious! Love you forever xxx.

I knew it. I knew Amelia would come back with a positive answer after all, she loves him, too.

Well, as is always the case, one drink leads to two and then to three. Before I know it, the time is nearly nine pm. So much for an early night and room service!

Enough is enough. We all head off to our rooms. Mel has sent a text to Hans, so she'll be entwined with him within minutes and I make my exit, in a rather sleepy state, still not having texted Alexandre. Am I chickening out of seeing him? My head is saying don't do it, but my heart and the butterflies in my stomach are saying yes, make that call!

My room is in darkness as I enter. Dumping all my bags on the floor, I flick on the light and am slightly startled, as there is someone on my bed. Well, not on the bed, but underneath the duvet. Oh my God! Has Howard come to pay me an unexpected visit?

Chapter Fifteen

There is absolutely no movement from the bed. Fuck! I hope it's not a dead body underneath that duvet! After all, how would I explain that one away?

I sneak into the bathroom, closing the door behind me very quietly, of course! (God, I am in desperate need of a pee!) I am one hundred percent certain that Howard, the lovely gorgeous Howard is lying in my bed. Thank heavens I didn't text Alexandre! Fuck! Can you imagine? Now, that would have been a difficult situation to get through.

Whilst peeing, I toy with the idea of having a quick shower, after all, I have been on the go all day and there's no harm in smelling gorgeous is there? So, for the next few minutes I lose myself in the massage setting of my shower. I am now feeling surprisingly awake.

I liberally rub Prada body lotion into my already soft skin and pull on my silk robe. I, for one, absolutely hate the towelling robes you find in hotels, because come on let's face it, someone else has already had it on and I can't think for one moment that they are laundered after each visitor has left; how utterly disgusting! I peer into the mirror and quickly touch up my blusher—not looking bad, for so few hours sleep, even though I say so, myself!

Suddenly, I am feeling desirable again and my nipples are erect. It really is amazing the effect Howard has on me. Coming out of the bathroom, I slip my robe off, so that it falls to the floor. As I walk over to my bed naked, naked that is, aside from my slippers of course, I crawl onto the bed, like a pouncing lioness.

Slowly, I start to pull back the duvet. No reaction? Fuck! Am I losing my touch? I slide off the bed, and yes, still in my slippers, decide on my next plan of action. After some contemplation, I decide to crawl underneath the duvet, softly stroking his legs as I slowly move up the bed.

At the midway point and you know exactly where I mean, so don't deny it! My hand reaches for his manhood. I hear a groan; well at least I know he's not dead now. Rather bizarrely I have to say, his cock feels different. Different, in the sense that it feels like someone else's cock. Is it because it's only semi erect? Well, it must be. Surely?

Suddenly, I stop dead in my tracks. Those legs, those male legs, which I have just caressed, I now know for sure, don't belong to Howard Johnson III. They are too fat! Oh fuck! Who the hell is in my bed? I scramble from beneath the duvet, (my heart is now beating as fast as a fomula one car racing around Silverstone) Who the fuck is it? I kneel rigid for a moment or two on the bed, time enough to compose myself. Right, here goes; one, two, three... I pull the duvet away from the body lying beneath it.

"Got you! You little tease, come here!" laughs Danny. Fuck me! It's Danny Mendosa. THE Danny Mendosa, the idiot who has made my life hell, he's butt naked and makes a grab for me.

I fling myself backwards and all I can hear is my scream. I land heavily on the floor. My legs are still up on the bed. I am still screaming, but now screaming words "What the fuck are you doing in my room, in my bed, you fucking creep. GET OUT?" My words echo around the room. They are loud and livid.

I can now see him standing above me. Naked. Oh my God! His bollocks are dangling above my head. Fuck! From this angle, his penis is actually very small. Sweet Jesus! He looks absolutely disgusting. He's so fucking sweaty and ugly!

"Hey come on Martha, I hear you put yourself around a bit. So you know, I'm your client too, so where's my portion?" he sniggers.

Thankfully, I have managed to get my legs off the bed and onto the floor and I am now standing up. I make a grab for my silk robe, which I try to put on before Danny is by my side. His hand reaches for my breast and I push him away violently, with both hands and with all the force I can muster; boy, I'm tough, when I need to be!

My robe is on. I start screaming "Fuck off! Go on! Fuck off out of here before I call security! No, no, not security, before I call the police. Go on fuck right off! You disgusting pervert. Who do you think you are, coming into my room, getting into my bed and expecting me to have sex with you? You absolutely disgust me. Now get the fuck out!"

"Martha cool down! Jesus I didn't expect this. You know it's good to keep the boss happy and right now, I am your boss!" he smiles, making his way back over to me.

"Oh really? Well, let me tell you something. If you don't disappear by the count of five, I am going to open the door and start screaming 'rape' and let me tell you right now, we'll finish this off at the police station!" I continue speaking slowly and then I lose it again. 'So, just fuck off! You filthy pig!' Still, the wanker just stands there. 'Right, on the count of five, one, two, three... .'

Suddenly, someone is banging on my door. I make a rush for it and Danny grabs me. I start screaming again. "Fuck off! Let me go! Help! Help me!" I scream.

Danny's face is close to mine now as he whispers "Shut the fuck up!"

Once again, I push him away, violently; he wasn't expecting it and tumbles to the floor. I make a rush for the door and pull it open.

Could life get any worse? For there, in front of me is Alexandre.

"What the fuck is going on? I can hear your screams from the lift. What's up?" asks Alexandre, pulling me close to him.

"Thank God you're here. That's what's up!" I scream, pointing to Danny who is still on the floor. "He came into my room, uninvited and oh, oh my God, Alexandre please just get rid of him!" I shout, stepping behind my hero.

Now, sometimes I like men for the wrong reasons. One of the reasons I like Alexandre, is quite simply because he is a bad boy. Bad, in the sense that he doesn't take any shit, absolutely none, from anyone and he is very, very protective.

I should have stopped him, but of course I didn't. I watch Alexandre casually walk over to Danny, without fear and pull him to his feet, which I think is very kind and then I watch him punch his face, followed by a kick to his bollocks. Now, I have no doubt that Alexandre would have zero hesitation in killing Danny, but, of course, I certainly don't want a dead body in my bedroom.

"Alexandre, stop it, that's enough!" I shout, running over to him. "Please, just get rid of him."

Not a word is spoken. Blood is spilling from Danny's nose. He's shaking, clearly shocked by what has happened. But thankfully, Alexandre has made a grab for Danny's clothes and is pushing him out of the door and into the corridor, butt naked. Finally, Alexandre slams the door so hard, I am sure that it will drop from its hinges. The room is silent.

Fuck, what do I say? For the first time ever, I think I'm at a loss for words.

Alexandre walks over to the bedroom phone. Dialling Reception he asks for Housekeeping to come and change the linen in Room 102.

"Martha, what the fuck was that all about?" he asks, in a normal tone, but underneath that calm exterior, I know that he is furious. I can sense his anger.

"Now listen, it is not what you are thinking. Danny is one of KAYSO's big chiefs and for whatever reason, he hasn't liked me from the start and then this evening, I come back from rehearsals and I find him butt naked, in my bed. I did not invite him here, he simply appeared. You've got to believe me, I've never suggested anything to him and I actually really hate the guy," I stammer.

"Enough! That scum works for KAYSO? KAYSO, as in Howard Johnson?" asks Alexandre.

Now I'm busted. Why didn't I just keep my big mouth shut?

"Yes," I reply quietly.

"Martha, get yourself dressed. We're going to pay Howard a visit and we'll get this sorted," instructs Alexandre.

Sweet Jesus! Now wouldn't that just be perfect? I rock up at Howard's Suite, whilst he has loads of shit happening in the States, with Alexandre on my arm, to tell him that Danny was butt naked in my bedroom, requesting a piece of the action. No! No! No! This is not happening to me! But, clearly, it is!

OK, I need to change tact here, but I am definitely not taking Alexandre upstairs to Suite 444.

I walk over to him. We're face to face now and my eyes are looking deeply into his. I kiss him tenderly on the lips and he pulls me close. He holds me tightly, a little too bloody tightly, if you ask me. My breathing is heavy, not because I am feeling aroused, no, because I am unable to get sufficient oxygen into my lungs. He is definitely holding me way too tightly. Is he being expressive?

I step back. Fuck! My ribs are aching and we're interrupted by a knock on the door. Alexandre opens it, Housekeeping has arrived. They are asked to change all the linen, together with the towels. Now, you see Alexandre knows me too well. He knows that I would definitely not sleep in my bed, knowing that Danny has been in there, butt naked. God, that vision repulses me!

Just how lovely is this bastard of mine? Too bloody lovely! We are now both peering into the mini bar. Alexandre makes a grab for the Jack Daniels and I pull out the half bottle of champagne. He pops the cork for me and we both drink out of our individual bottles, like a couple of desperate winos.

Finally, the linen and towels have been changed. Alexandre slips the cleaner a fifty Euro note and shows her out. Fuck! I'd change someone's linen and towels, for a salary and a fifty Euro tip!

He takes my hand and leads me to the bed. Has that little bit of violence aroused him? Is he going to make love to me, right here, right now?

No, in fact he's not. "Baby come sit with me, we need to talk about what just happened," he says. We both sit. I need to play this really cool, otherwise, I have absolutely no doubt, that he will be off to find Howard, to discuss this rather unfortunate situation, I find myself in.

"Boo listen to me. What's done is done. Danny's a wanker. But, really, I've been up against much worse and I don't want to cause friction with Howard Johnson, after all, the show is tomorrow and then I'll never see Danny Mendosa again. Please Boo, I really don't want to cause a scene, it's not worth it," I say quietly. I then give him a wink.

"Listen. I'm not going to kick off, but I want you to speak to Howard and tell him what an arse he employs, otherwise baby, I'm going to find that fucker and give him a proper kicking, as it's making me kind of mad here, alright?" he says.

"OK, OK, let me quickly get dressed and I'll go find Howard and explain the situation. But, I want you to stay here. Promise? I don't want you involved in this. Please, will you agree to stay here? Maybe order room service and some champagne and then when I get back, we can start from the beginning?" I say, well in actual fact, I plead.

"Sure, if that's how you want to play it. But I'm warning you if I see him again, I'll fucking kill him. Come to think of it, I think I saw him the other evening, he was dancing, you know at that party I went to, on the yacht. I should have fucking pushed him overboard!" laughs Alexandre.

My heart is beating so fast, I think it may well explode. Oh God! Please don't let him talk about the party on the yacht!

"Go and find Howard and I'll order room service. Anything in particular you want?" asks Alexandre.

"You know me, I'm easy," I reply, all the while knowing that I am indeed, just a little too easy sometimes, but for all the wrong reasons!

I quickly pull on a pair of jeans; no time to find matching underwear, so I pull on a vest with built in support, no knickers and a white shirt, together with a pair of flip flops.

Finally dressed, I walk over to my gorgeous man and kiss his forehead. Our eyes lock for a moment and I know, that we will sleep together this evening. Of that, I have absolutely, no doubt.

"I'll be back soon, just as soon as I've spoken to Howard." I smile and leave the room with my heart pounding so fast, I feel sure that it will burst.

I call the lift and press fourth floor. What the hell am I going to say to Howard? 'Oh hi Howard just to let you know that Danny let himself into my room, got undressed and decided I should shag him'. Fuck! That just sounds way too weird for words.

Perhaps, I should just check on Howard, not mention the Danny episode and then retire to my room for the night, with Alexandre? That's probably the easiest option.

I arrive at Suite 444 and feel a little hesitant, to say the least. I stand in front of his door, hand poised to knock, but somehow, I can't bring myself to do it.

Suddenly, I hear voices, and to my surprise, Howard and Ingrid are walking up the corridor towards me.

Howard spots me and smiles. Thankfully, he's a quick thinker and immediately launches into nonsense.

"Hey Martha, thanks for calling by, you got my message then? I've just got a couple of amends to my main speech, which I've scribbled down," he says.

He turns to Ingrid.

"Thanks for the drink. Suddenly life is not so bad and yes I'll see you in the morning. No fears about me skipping town, this conference is way too important," he smiles, as he leans in to kiss her on both cheeks.

"Well, er er Howard, would it be easier if you were to provide me with the amends and I can then get them to Martha?" stutters Ingrid, obviously taken aback by Howard's cheek kisses.

"Hell no, you've done more than enough and I'm sure that Martha won't mind me taking up five minutes of her time, will you now, Martha?" asks Howard, smiling at me.

"Not at all," I respond.

"Well in that case, may I wish you a 'good evening' and I look forward to seeing you in the morning. And Martha, thank you for your help this evening, in looking after Mr Johnson." Thankfully, she walks off towards her own suite.

"Come on in," says Howard, opening the door for me.

"You sexy little minx. What are you doing here? Did you get news through the grapevine that Ingrid had accosted me? Boy, she's full on, I think she wants a night of passion!" laughs Howard.

"Let's put this into context shall we. I don't see you all day. I get one lousy text. I've had a dreadful time. I arrive at your room on the off chance and then witness you flirting, outrageously, with Ingrid Lorne-Harris! Hell, I misread you. I thought you only had eyes for me, Mr Johnson," I say, a little too flirty, bearing in mind, that Alexandre is in my room, awaiting my return, so that we can eat food together and then make love, just like we used to.

"Well missy, what can I say? You've either got it, or, you haven't!" laughs Howard.

He walks over to me and suddenly his lips are on mine. We kiss passionately. His hand is holding the back of my head pulling me closer to his full lips. His tongue is eager. We stagger backwards towards the bedroom.

Shit! I've got to stop this, immediately. I can't possibly shag Howard and Alexandre, both in the same evening. Sweet Jesus! I might as well have fucked Danny too, I could have had a hat trick then!

We fall onto the bed and I pull away from him. He makes a grab for me, but I pull back. "I want you to lie there and do as you are told," I say, quietly.

I slowly unbutton his trousers and unzip his zipper. I can see the contour of his cock through his trousers. He is definitely aroused. I pull his trousers down and note that he's going commando this evening. I hope that wasn't for Ingrid's benefit. With his trousers down, I take his cock in my mouth. Within minutes, Howard has come. Now this bit always get me—to spit or to swallow? This is my reckoning—I think if you know someone quite intimately, then a swallow is fine, but if it is early days, then I think a spit is more appropriate, that is assuming you have somewhere to spit it, of course!

"Jesus Martha, you are just amazing. I could stay here, with you, forever," says Howard, looking at me.

I feel I need to tell him about the incident in room 102. Just in case Danny says something to him about me leading him on blah, blah, blah, which clearly I never have and never would! And then, could you imagine if Howard was to see Alexandre and Alexandre was to mention it? Shit! I have to tell him.

"Howard listen, I need to tell you something. I didn't come here this evening simply to satisfy your needs, although, it must be said, that was very pleasurable. But, I need to tell you something important," I say.

"Before you tell me what it is that you feel you need to tell me, I need to do something," replies Howard.

"Oh OK, but be quick because this is really important," I reply.

And quick he is. He is now straddling me, pulling my jeans over my hips. I try to stop him. No, really I do, by wriggling away, but he is so much stronger than me. I desperately want to shout 'stop' but the moment his tongue finds its way between my legs, I am rendered powerless. Howard knows exactly how to satisfy a woman and within minutes, I am writhing across the bed, amidst an explosion of pleasure.

"Fuck! Howard, that was amazing! What exactly am I going to do when you are back in the States and I'm in the UK?" I laugh.

I get up and pull on my jeans quickly, before he can stop me.

"Where are you going? Are you not staying with me this evening? I think I've done just about all I can with the States for today, so please stay."

Come on girl! Think of a bloody good excuse why you can't stay in Suite 444 all night with a man as gorgeous and powerful as Howard Johnson III. Easy! I know, I could just tell him that Alexandre is waiting for me in Room 102, I am sure that would go down well.

"Howard, as much as I would love to lie here beside you for the rest of the night, I need to sleep. I've not slept for forty-eight hours and it's show day tomorrow, so I want to be on the ball. And come on let's face it, if I was to stay here this evening, I suspect we wouldn't be getting much sleep, especially after a performance like that!" I respond, with a wink.

"Doesn't the client always get, what the client wants?" he smiles.

"Not all of the time, no!" I respond smiling.

"OK I hear where you're coming from, but I'll only let you go if you agree to be my date tomorrow evening. I want my final night in Cannes to go with a bang. So, do we have a deal?" asks Howard.

"Most definitely, you're on!" I say, edging my way towards the door.

"Hey, you didn't tell me why you came here in the first place, what was it that you wanted to tell me?" he asks inquisitively.

After that little performance, I don't feel comfortable in telling him that his number one was butt naked in my bed, less than one hour ago and I actually touched his dick. No, I think under the circumstances, I'll not divulge Dickbrain's naughty episode and just hope for the best.

"You know what, it really doesn't matter. I'll see you tomorrow morning. Sweet dreams!" And with that, I leave Suite 444 and head down the corridor towards the lift.

I call the elevator and eventually it arrives. But, of course, it couldn't arrive empty; no, it has to arrive on the fourth floor with a guest. A guest by the name of Mr. Danny Mendosa. Fuck! Is this man going to plague me forever?

He steps out of the lift and grabs my arm, pushing me against the wall. You can definitely tell he's been punched in the face. His eye is slightly puffy and there's a cut above his lip. Ooops, naughty boy Alexandre!

"Have you told Howard about our little game earlier?" he asks, his mouth so close to my face, I can smell his alcoholic breath.

"Fuck off and leave me alone. Why would I burden Howard with your silly antics? Let's face it, he's all man but you, you've got a dick the size of a child's and the fucking body of a rhino. Don't you ever fucking touch me again!" I respond, pulling my arm away from him.

I call the lift again and thankfully, the doors open immediately. I get in and shakily, press the button and once on the first floor, I compose myself. After all, Alexandre is waiting for me. But first, I think I need to take a shower!

Entering my room, Alexandre is flicking through the TV channels.

"Hey baby, you took your time," he says looking over at me. "Are you OK, you look, I don't know, kind of messed up?" he continues.

"Boo, I'm fine honestly, so can we now lay this horrible episode to rest please?" I ask.

"Fine by me, but don't let me bump into that prick, because he'll be as good as dead, if I see him again!" mumbles Alexandre.

"Have you ordered room service?" I ask, desperately wanting to change the subject now.

"Yep! Should be here within the next ten, to fifteen minutes. Are you hungry?" he asks.

"You know me Boo, I'm always hungry. But for now, I need a quick shower. Give me five minutes," I say, heading off towards the bathroom, picking up my slippers on route.

I shut the door behind me and let out a long, painful sigh. How do I manage to fuck up my life, time and again? Well, at least Danny won't be paying another visit this evening. And, at least Howard is not going to wander down either so hopefully, it's just me and Boo for the rest of the night. Although, I am so bloody tired, I just want to get into bed and sleep for a week!

I run the shower and step in, fighting hard to keep my hair dry. Up it goes, into a big clip. My thoughts start to wander, whilst the water droplets splash against my skin, the tingling sensation is wonderful.

Suddenly, I realise that I am not alone. I catch sight of Alexandre standing at the bathroom door, watching me. I smile and indicate for him to join me.

My emotions are all over the place, but, one thing I know for sure, is that I simply love him, always have and always will.

Alexandre undresses and joins me in the shower. "You look so sexy, God baby I miss you." he says, pulling me close to him. He holds me tightly and I shift slightly. Fuck! Doesn't he realise that I am trying to keep my hair dry? He pulls me forward again and once again I shift; this, we repeat three or four times, before I say: "Boo, listen. I have a big show tomorrow, can we at least try to keep my hair dry, I don't have the energy to spend hours bent over drying it tonight?"

He steps out of the shower. Oh shit. Have I offended him now? I watch him walk over to the bathroom cabinet. What the heck is he looking for now? Perhaps he's planted a gun in the bathroom and is going to shoot me? Or, perhaps he has a syringe filled with a fatal potion, with which he will kill me instantly? Or perhaps, just perhaps... I am so bloody tired; I just need sleep, as my mind seems slightly out of kilter with reality, at the moment!

Alexandre finally returns to the shower, neither with a gun, nor a syringe, but with a plastic shower cap. Caring, it is. Romantic, it's not. Well, let's face it, a plastic bag stuck on your head, whilst you're in the midst of passion is not the ideal look, is it? But hey, it will do the job.

He starts to slowly lather my body. His touch is sensual, slow and inquisitive. I am totally transfixed on his face. My heart is racing and every sense in my body is about to explode. We finally leave the shower and head back to the bedroom. Thankfully, I remember to take off my headgear and let my hair down. Hey, come on, I'm trying to be seductive here! And of course, I put on my slippers on route to the bedroom—now that's class, well it's not really, but there's no way that I'm walking on that carpet, as lovely as it is!

Once into the bedroom, we bounce onto the bed, like naughty children. Me butt naked and my gorgeous man wearing only a towel. We kiss passionately and his hands start to explore my body, just like they always used to. He starts to work his way down, stopping to kiss my breasts and then my stomach (Fuck! I wish I hadn't eaten so much at lunchtime!) and then just when my body can take it no more, there is a fucking knock at the door. Can you bloody well believe it?

Alexandre looks up from his position, in between my inner thighs. "Shall we leave it?" he asks. "Are you crazy? I'm starving. Go on, open the door, let me suffer no more, bring me the food." I giggle.

He jumps up and re-wraps the towel around his waist.

"Just a moment!" he shouts, throwing me my robe. "Cover yourself up, I don't want the world knowing just how sexy you are," he laughs.

"What the fuck are you doing here?" Are the words I hear immediately, which throw me slightly, as I don't recall room service being quite so aggressive. I scramble to the end of the bed, trying to see who he's talking to, but before I have time to get there, Theo is standing in front of me. Thank God, I have my robe on.

"So, cara mia, this is your idea of room service is it? I was concerned that everything has been a little bit well shall we say, chaotic, over the past forty eight hours? So, here I am, checking up on you. But it would appear that I need not have bothered. You promised not to see him again. So, was it too hard for you to keep your promise?" says Theo, wagging his finger at me.

"Hey listen Theo I think Martha is old enough to make her own decisions. I don't think she needs you, to tell her what to do," interrupts Alexandre.

Theo turns around so quickly, that for a moment, I think he's going to lose his balance, but he somehow manages to regain his composure.

"You think Martha is old enough to make her own decisions then? I quite agree with you, but the moment you return to your wife and children, who exactly are the people left behind to mop up the fucking mess? You should be ashamed of yourself. Is your wife not enough for you? Obviously not! You prey on Martha. Do you not realise that each and every time she sees you, you destroy her? She loves you, you fucking fool and this is how you treat her!" spits Theo.

Oh my God! I cannot believe that Theo is being so aggressive.

I'm on my feet now. "That's enough. I am sorry I lied to you, but you know what? This my life and I will make up my own mind, as to who I do and don't see. Now you've seen me and I'm fine, so please can I ask you to leave us alone?" I say quietly, tears welling up in my eyes.

We are all startled by a knock on the open door. "Good evening, room service," says the waiter.

Alexandre signs the chitty and all too soon, it is just the three of us again.

"Cara mia, you obviously know what you are doing, you are hitting that self-destruct button again!" says Theo, kissing me on the forehead and heading out of the bedroom, but not before lifting his finger to Alexandre's face with the words "Hurt her again and I will fucking destroy you. Do you understand me?"

With that, Theo is gone.

There is now a trolley loaded with food in my room, but not surprisingly, my appetite has disappeared, although I am rather fancying a glass, no not a glass, a bottle of champagne, to calm my nerves.

"Boo, listen, I am sorry about Theo's outburst, he had no right," I say.

"Baby listen. He has every right to think I'm an arsehole, because I am. He's right. I do have a wife. And yes, he's right again, in that she isn't enough for me, not any more. I should be more of a man and less of a coward and let her go and get on with the rest of her life." he says, looking across at me in a rather sad way.

"Will you crack open the champagne, I think we both need a drink?" I smile.

We sit on the bed and quaff champagne. Alexandre feeds me morsels of food from the trolley and soon we laugh and joke and Theo's outburst is soon forgotten—well for now, at least.

The time is now fast approaching midnight and I have a call time of seven am. What I wouldn't give, for a weekend in bed with Alexandre. Just the two of us, no mobile phone interruptions, no knocks at the door, other than of course, trolleys of food and alcoholic refreshment and clean towels and linen.

It just feels so right between the two of us. Suddenly, I think of Theo and am riddled with guilt. I did promise that I wouldn't see Alexandre, but it was a promise I knew I would break.

I feel the need to text him. Scrambling out of bed I hunt down my iphone. *I am so sorry to have lied to you. I promise I know what I'm doing. I love you. xxx.*

"Who are you texting?" asks Alexandre.

"I'm just sending a text to my brother I'm feeling a little bad about earlier. It's not like us to fight," I respond. Theo is probably recounting what's just happened to Jefferson.

Shit! Fuck! Bollocks! I clean forgot about Jefferson! Fucking hell! I feel sure that Theo will tell him that Alexandre is in my room and of course Jefferson knows about me sleeping with his brother, Howard and there is no reason whatsoever, why Jefferson won't tell Howard of my indiscretion. Why, oh fucking why, is my life so fucking, fucked up?

"Baby, leave it now. He's a big boy he'll be fine in the morning. Now come here and show me how much you love me," says Alexandre, throwing me a wink.

With my iphone on the bedside table, I clamber onto the bed and straddle the man I love. The true love of my life. He unties my robe and slips it off my shoulders. Our lips lock and all too soon, passion overwhelms me from the top of my head, to the tips of my toes. Slowly, our passion becomes all too consuming and we make love, with utter disrespect for anyone who can hear us.

Suddenly, I am aware that my iphone is vibrating—I have a text. I desperately want to read it, as for sure it's from Theo. But it's a little too rude to stop our love making so I continue, at a ferocious pace and then silence looms, aside from heavy breathing, our heavy breathing.

"Jesus, Baby, that was sensational. You're fucking amazing!" says Alexandre, through his short breaths. Kissing me tenderly, on my shoulder.

"Always a pleasure my darling, always a pleasure," I respond, leaning over to pick up my iphone.

"Baby, put that bloody phone down! You're obsessed with it!" he says really annoyed.

"I am not obsessed, I just want to see what Theo has to say," I respond, turning my back to him.

But it's not from Theo. No, that would be too obvious. It's from Howard: *With my hand on my cock, you are in my heart. Sweet dreams my darling Martha xxx.*

I feel myself blush.

"So, what does he have to say then?" asks Alexandre.

"Nothing, other than 'sorry' and 'sweet dreams.' You see, he is still my lovely brother," I respond, fingers crossed whilst the lying words come tumbling out of my mouth.

I don't respond to Howard, it seems inappropriate to do so.

I set my alarm for five thirty am. Early, yes, but I just know, with Alexandre by my side, I will want to make love to him before I leave for work, so you see, there is method in my madness with early alarm calls.

We dim the lights and Alexandre wraps his arms around my body, kissing me tenderly, as we both drift off into a very, deep sleep.

Chapter Sixteen

As tired as I am, I actually wake up very early, way too early. It's now four am and all around me is quiet, except for the faint snore coming from Alexandre's direction. I slip out of bed without disturbing him, after all, I know what it takes to wake him and me getting up definitely won't do it. I head for the bathroom and take a peek in the mirror. Oh my God! (And that's the mirror's expression, not mine!) In all the excitement of last night, I forgot to take my make up off in the shower and now look like bride of Dracula!

I run the tap and dampen my facial wipe, so that I can rid myself of these 'panda eyes' that are staring back at me. I am mesmerised by my own reflection, but I'm not quite sure why? I continue looking at myself and the only question that keeps popping into my mind is 'what have you done?'—I haven't done anything. I've done nothing wrong, but why am I questioning myself? Why has this woken me up? Am I thinking about what happened with Danny last night? No, I don't think it really bothered me, that much. Am I thinking about Howard and that we are soon to be parted? I honestly don't think that is bothering me either, as in all fairness, if I want to see Howard again, I can and I will. Am I bothered about Theo's outburst? Quite possibly. It's not like Theo to throw a hissy fit and yes, I know that he is only looking out for me, but sweet Jesus his reaction was totally uncalled for and he didn't even bother responding to my text.

I think I know the real answer to the 'what have you done?' question. The answer is lying in my bed, snoring softly. What have I done? I am still staring at the reflection in the mirror and from nowhere, tears of sadness spring to my eyes. At this moment in time, I am so sad, I don't think I can hold back the tears that threaten to cascade down my face. I am in love with Alexandre so much, that it hurts my heart. Yet I know, that once I leave for the Palais du Roscoff this morning, then he'll simply get up when he's ready and he'll return to his 'normal' life; whereas, I will think about him non stop, wanting him with me, wanting him by my side, wanting him to love me for who I am.

Oh fuck! Why did I ever agree to see him again? Why couldn't I simply listen to Theo?

The tears have started and try as I might to hold them back, I can't. The fear of big puffy eyes doesn't do a lot to quash the tears either. Head in hands, I cry softly for about fifteen minutes and then I eventually pull myself together.

I splash cold water onto my face, in the hope that it will reduce the puffiness and then hunt for my most precious of eye creams, which only ever comes out in a massive emergency, as it costs over one hundred and forty pounds per tiny pot.

I apply the cream and know that I will not allow myself to cry again, after all let's face it, I can ill afford to apply the cream twice!

I head back into the bedroom and turn the dimmer switch, so that I have a little light in which to watch Alexandre, my darling 'Boo' sleeping. Lying beside him I stroke his cheek delicately and then I trace the contour of his mouth with my finger. I never want this moment to end, but the sadness is too great for me and slowly, I feel the trickle of my tears reach the pillow.

I continue staring at him, wishing the minutes to be longer, but before I know it, the time is fast approaching five thirty am and I know, that very soon my alarm will buzz. Should I turn it off now and allow him to continue sleeping and then simply slip out of the room? Or, should I wake him, so that I can make love with him one more time, before he is out of my life again?

Was there ever going to be any competition? No. So, sure enough, I decide to wake him. He can always go back to sleep afterwards! I rush off to the bathroom to brush my teeth and bring through a capful of mouthwash for Alexandre. He is still completely out of it, not even a slight movement. I nudge him softly. Nothing! I tweak his nipples gently, still nothing so I tweak a little harder. Still nothing! I nuzzle his ear and God damn it, he pushes me away. So, as a last resort, I start to stroke his cock. I can hear his breathing getting deeper now and then slowly he rolls onto his back, spreading his legs.

I tease his nipple with my tongue and finally, he opens one eye followed by a half smile. "Baby, what time is it?" he asks, barely able to get his words out.

"It's just gone five thirty am and I need to be up soon, so I just thought I might have my wicked way with you before I go!" I smile, kissing him tenderly on the lips.

Oh my God, 'morning breath' alert. Fuck! How I hate 'morning breath.'

"Baby, don't stop playing with my cock," says Alexandre, tweaking my nipple between his fingers.

"OK, but first you've got to swill with mouthwash," I say giggling.

"Fucking hell! Are you just the weirdest creature around? Is this what I risk everything for, just so I can swill mouthwash in the morning?" he asks, a tad irritated.

"That's exactly why you risk everything. The mouthwash is on your bedside table," I respond, and like the good puppy dog that he is, he swills out his mouth.

"Now, I'll willingly continue playing with your cock," I say, seductively.

Immediately, we are in the throes of passion once again. He is absolutely the best lover I have ever had and by six fifteen, we are both so exhausted, we can hardly speak.

We lay there in silence. I don't know what to say to him now. Knowing that very soon, I will be leaving this room and I don't know when we will see each other again, if ever.

I sit up. I can feel the emotions starting to overwhelm me. I turn to Alexandre and simply mouth the words 'I Love You'. I don't wait for a response, I get up and head to the bathroom and quickly jump in the shower, all the while trying not to get my hair wet and more importantly, trying not to cry. I tell myself that I will see him again, tonight after the party, or, tomorrow morning, before I leave for the airport. I desperately want it to be true. I need to see him again, I can't simply walk away. My love for this man is far too deep.

Stepping out of the shower, I feel slightly more composed. I have reassured myself that I will see him again, definitely, most definitely, over the next twenty-four hours.

I rub my body with Prada body lotion and I apply my make up. Finally, I am ready to head back into the bedroom to get dressed and say my 'goodbye,' for now, to the love of my life. My darling 'Boo.'

So can you believe this? I'm in the bathroom crying like a baby because I can't bear to say goodbye to Alexandre and he is in a fucking deep sleep, yet again! So deep, that he is snoring like a pig. Fuck! Can you believe this? Well, of course you can, they are all the same aren't they? And be honest in your answer to that question!

I get dressed, noisily. Crashing and banging about. I get all my gear together—my handbag, my laptop bags and my big sunglasses (yes, the eyes are definitely puffy—damned if I'm buying that cream again, it definitely doesn't work). The time is now six thirty eight and I am meeting Mel, in the hotel lobby at six forty five. I have precisely seven minutes, seven lousy minutes, to wake him up and tell him that I love him.

I walk over to his side of the bed and shake him gently. Nothing. I thump his arm, not hard, but enough to gauge a reaction. Still nothing. I put my lips close to his ear and call out his name. And still nothing.

One final shake and he simply rolls over. What a fucking arse he is! Perhaps it's for the best. At least he won't see me burst into tears, as I am sure I will, when we say our 'goodbyes.'

Fuck this man! I quickly write him a note: "Boo, tried waking you, are you dead? Fantastic to see you. Are you free later? I love you xx."

Now hang on a minute. Should I really ask him if he's free later? Shouldn't he take the lead and be begging to see me? Oh well, too late now, time is six forty three am and I'm out of here. I kiss his forehead, his beautiful forehead and grab all my gear, heading for the door.

I look back and yes those tears have sprung again and I say out loudly, "I love you Boo, I've always loved you." And with that, I am out in the corridor, taking in deep breaths, so that I don't cry proper girlie tears! Right on cue, Mel comes out of her room. Oh my God, she is looking like death.

"Fucking hell Mel, what's up with you? You look like you've gone a few rounds with Mike Tyson. Are you OK?" I ask, giggling.

"Slapper, I don't think I've ever had quite so much sex in one night. He just goes on and on and on. I am a physical wreck, he has destroyed me! But what a fucking way to be destroyed!" she laughs out loud. "And what about you honey, who managed to bag you for the night and, hey hang on a minute no need to answer that one, have you been crying? Oh for fuck sake Martha, tell me that dick's not in your bedroom. And by dick of course, I mean Alexandre."

"I cannot begin to tell you what happened last night. It was the most bizarre evening ever. Let's get out of here. I need coffee and then I will tell you the most incredible story." I smile, pushing the lift button with my elbow.

Arriving at the Palais du Roscoff, Ellie and Belinda are already running around like absolute lunatics in the foyer. "Hey girls, you want to slow down, otherwise you'll be exhausted for this evening's party!" shouts Mel.

Mickey and Dan are already in the Fleur Suite having breakfast, as we walk in. "Well hello boys! And how are you both today? Mickey, were you out on the piss last night? You are looking slightly worse for wear, my friend," asks Mel.

"I 'ate to disappoint you, but you don't look so bleedin' 'ot yourself girl. Was he worth it?" asks Mickey, laughing out loud.

"I am a new woman and yes, in answer to your question, he was definitely worth it!" smiles Mel.

"And what about you Mart, were you out on the razz? I thought you were having a quiet night in, with room service?" asks Dan.

"Thankfully I did not leave the hotel once last night, but I still managed to have a fight with Theo, hence the puffy eyes. It still hurts when my baby brother gets it right all the time," I respond, all the while wanting to burst into tears and tell the world that I am so desperately in love with Alexandre. However, I gain control because I have more dignity that that and after all, they all hate him, for what he puts me through.

"Now boys, if you'll excuse us, we need a girlie talk before we get this show on the road, so both of you, eat up and fuck off!" laughs Mel.

Mel takes me by my arm and leads me to the far table. She sits me down and rushes off to grab a couple of coffees. Large coffees and croissants.

I push my croissant away. I can't possibly eat. I am heartbroken. Hey, this might not be a bad thing; after all, I can always do with losing a few pounds!

"So, what the fuck happened?" asks Mel.

"In a nutshell, after we left the bar, I went straight to my room, opened the door and there was a body lying in my bed..." I start.

Mel interrupts. "Fucking hell! Was it dead?"

I throw her a look that means 'hush.' "Let me finish. Whoever it is, is under the duvet, so all the while I'm thinking it's Howard. I go to the bathroom, take a shower and seductively crawl under the duvet and latch on to a penis. Thankfully with my hand, rather than my mouth. Immediately, I know it's not Howard. No, definitely not Howard's, but shit alive, wait for it... Are you ready? Well, it was Danny Dickbrain Mendosa in my bed, butt naked."

"Oh my God, no way!" shrieks Mel.

"But that's not all... I too, am butt naked. I make a grab for my robe and tell him to fuck off. We fight, he says he's the client, so I should give him a bit too. We fight more and then thankfully someone is banging on my door. Guess who? Well it was Alexandre. But don't say anything bad, because he was my hero. He punches Mendosa and kicks his bollocks and then throws him out into the corridor, stark naked, followed by his clothes."

"Oh my God! No way!" shrieks Mel again.

"Then, Alexandre tells me that we should go and find Howard and explain what has happened. Of course, that is not going to happen, is it? So, I go alone to Howard's room to explain, but before I know it, I'm sucking his cock and then I leave. I definitely did not make love with Howard last night; you've got to believe me," I gush, exhausted through lack of breath!

"Oh my God! No fucking way!" Mel shrieks, yet again.

"So then, on the way back to my room, after seeing Howard, I bump into Danny. I am shit scared and he is so fucking angry and he grabs my arm. We exchange words, but finally I get to my room and before I know it, I've told Alexandre that I've told Howard what happened and next thing, we are making love. God it was total madness." I gush.

"Danny Mendosa was in your bed? Naked in your bed?" questions Mel.

"Yes Mel, he was naked in my bed. But thankfully, Alexandre called house keeping and got the linen and towels changed. See, he is good to me," I smile.

"I don't fucking believe it. Danny Mendosa in your bed, naked. Fucking hell! Now, that would have been bad enough, but then you grab his dick. What the fuck possessed you?" she asks, questioningly.

"I didn't mean to grab his dick, stupid; I thought it was Howard in my bed. Not for one minute, did I think it would be a stark bollock naked Dickbrain Mendosa," I laugh.

We both laugh. We laugh so much that tears are rolling down our faces and Ingrid, who has wandered into the Fleur Suite, is intrigued to know exactly what we are laughing about, as she sits down at our table.

"Ingrid if I told you, you wouldn't believe me. So I'm not going to even bother," I respond, leaving Mel to wipe her face.

Ingrid looks intrigued by my comments but carries on, tucking into her croissant. Mel and I look at each other and whilst our illustrious producer is chomping her way through her second croissant, we seize the opportunity to make our excuses and head towards the auditorium, in readiness for the show.

There is definitely a buzz this morning. The adrenalin is kicking in and crew are scurrying around making final adjustments. Backstage, I find Hugo tapping into his phone.

"Morning Hugo, how are you my darling?" I ask, planting a big kiss on his cheek.

"Well that's a lovely greeting, thank you and in answer to your question, I am fine, very fine actually," he smiles.

"And pray tell, why is everything so very fine?" I ask, smiling as if I didn't already know the answer.

"If truth be told, I had a rather enjoyable evening with Eleanor and things seem to be progressing at a very comfortable pace and indeed, rumour has it, that she may be transferring to the UK office for six months, which of course, would suit us both down to the ground," replies Hugo, grinning from ear to ear.

"Oh my goodness Hugo, should I start looking for a hat? Better still, will you require the services of Mel and myself to act as bridesmaids?" I giggle.

"Behave yourself, Martha. It's early days, but I do think she is utterly adorable and I must say, I am hesitant at the thought of you and Mel acting as bridesmaids," he responds, laughing.

"So how about you, it seems as if I haven't seen an awful lot of you over the past couple of days, is everything OK?" he asks, with a little concern.

"Thankfully my complicated life never fails to disappoint. Lots has indeed happened over the past couple of days, including a fight with Theo, who of course, I never ever fight with and a clandestine meeting with Alexandre, which was perfect..."

Hugo interrupts before I can finish my words. "You've seen Alexandre? Was that wise? Is he not a heart breaking wanker, Martha?"

"Oh Hugo, it was just a bit of fun. He called by, we had dinner and that was about it. He's not going to break my heart again, because I simply won't let him. I promise," I smile; all the while knowing full well that I could quite easily burst into tears right here, right now. I breathe in deeply, in the hope that Hugo doesn't persist in his questioning, which will bring me to tears.

"You know best, but please don't fall for his charmed silver tongue again. The man is a waste of space, a 'cad', for want of a better word," replies Hugo, as he hugs me, rubbing my back, which is a little strange, but at least it has distracted me from my soon to appear tears.

"Morning Hugo, morning Martha. How are you both?" asks Ellie, as she comes bounding backstage.

"Morning Ellie! I'm absolutely fine and dandy thank you. You seem bright and breezy this morning you obviously got a good night's sleep then? You and Belinda are buzzing," I say, looking at her inquisitively.

"I slept solidly for seven hours; it was absolute heaven, nirvana in fact. Right then Hugo, a copy for you, Martha a copy for you and have either of you seen Jerome or Dan this morning?" asks Ellie, putting their running orders down at their workstations.

"Yes, both were at breakfast earlier, so they are definitely on site, fear not," responds Hugo, as he wanders off to locate Ingrid, linking arms with Ellie and taking her with him.

I take a look at the running order, which thankfully has not changed from yesterday. First up, we have Howard Johnson III. I suddenly feel guilty at the way I've treated him, but is he really going to care if he doesn't see me again after tomorrow? Probably not, but I know deep down that I will miss him. He makes me feel special. He is a real gentleman, who knows exactly how to treat a lady. I know he's not like Alexandre; he's a totally different kettle of fish. Alexandre is a 'bad boy' through and through. Why do women always go for 'bad boys'?

My mind seems to be wandering, 'So darling Martha,' I say to myself, 'I suggest we get back on course here.' Right then. After the lovely Howard we have Dickbrain Mendosa. Oh, how I'm dreading seeing him this morning. I cannot bear the thought. He repulses me and I am absolutely sure he will have no hesitation in belittling me, if an opportunity arises today. Oh shit! I wonder what his face looks like this morning and more importantly how his bollocks are feeling! But do I really care? I don't think so!

After Dickbrain, we have the lovely Bruce Shannon, swiftly followed by the even lovelier, Marcus Driscoll. And finally, the close of the morning session will be made by Howard. That all seems pretty straightforward, nothing has changed other than Dickbrain Mendosa's attitude towards me. I am sure it's gone from a lowly hatred to a rather highly despised.

"Morning Martha, how goes it?" asks Jerome.

"Hey sweetheart, all's good, thank you. I had a night of trauma, so you are lucky to have me here this morning. The transformation behind set is amazing; the stylists must have been working late into the night, to get all these clothing rails set up in such an orderly manner. Hell, I wish my wardrobes at home were so bloody neat and tidy!" I smile, as I wander over to them. "J, check out these names, we have Starlight, Sunflower and Jane. Do you think Jane feels hard done by being christened with such a simple name?" I giggle.

The stylists must indeed have worked throughout the night to transform the rear of the set, into this 'behind the scenes' fashion parlour. There is a section for makeup, a section for hairdressers, a section for accessories and then the biggest section of all, for the dressers and stylists. Amazing.

"Hello? Hey, are you guys behind here?" calls out Rochelle, the lovely Rochelle Schneider.

"Yep, back here!" I call out.

"Ah, just the girl I was looking for. Just so you know, there are a few rumours flying around this morning, that Danny got into a fight last night and came off a little worse, if you know what I mean," smiles Rochelle.

Oh fuck! I've stopped breathing.

"He looks like shit, but you gotta blame his tumble in the restroom, rather than a fist. Although I was kind of wondering whether you had finally lost it with him and punched him," laughs Rochelle.

"Oh my God! How terrible! Is he OK? Will he be able to present this morning?" I ask, praying and I mean absolutely praying, that he won't show his face. But alas, God's not listening to me this morning. Again!

"Oh yeah, he'll be here soon. I think Mary-Jo was trying to hide his bruise with some make up. He'll look like a fucking tranny," giggles Rochelle, as she walks off.

I throw Jerome a glance, as I catch him staring at me. "What? Oh come on, you don't think for one moment I hit him, do you? Jesus Jerome, I would have at least hurt him enough to ensure that he couldn't make it here this morning, if I was going to do that, which of course I didn't. So stop looking at me like that." I giggle.

"I believe you; thousands wouldn't! However, I would just like to remind you, that you did mention trauma last night. Your words, not mine," laughs Jerome.

"Oh piss off and do me a favour will you? I'm in desperate need of a large injection of caffeine. Would you be kind enough to get me a coffee, or, do I have to be rough with you?" I snarl.

"OK tiger, so long as you promise not to hurt me, I'll get you what ever you want," replies Jerome smiling, as he heads off to fetch my coffee.

Peace and quiet reigns over backstage once again. This is pure bliss prior to a show getting underway. I focus on the screen of my laptop, all presentations are in the correct order, as if they wouldn't be; after all, I've checked the running order about a dozen times already.

Suddenly, I'm startled as I look up to see Danny Dickbrain standing in front of me. How the fuck did he manage to get in front of me so quietly? After all, he's the size of an elephant. Hell, this wanker gives me the creeps. I ignore him. I wait for him to say something, which eventually he does, in a rather aggressive, angry manner.

"You think you're smart don't you? You think because you got your arsehole of a guy to hit me, that you've won. Well it ain't over yet. You wait until Howard hears that you invited me to your room and then got scared at the last minute. You wait till Howard hears that your boyfriend has been here and that you've been screwing everything that moves and just you wait until we're on our own. Just you and me," he hisses, now so close to my face, that I can feel specks of spittle landing on my cheek.

I stand up quickly and pull myself away from him and his disgusting body. "You know what Mendosa, you don't scare me. You can tell Howard whatever you want, because at the end of the day he's not going to believe you. Do you honestly think for one moment, that I would ever entertain the idea of sleeping with you? Not in a million years. And if you want to play dirty, can you deal with a rape accusation?" I say, calmly. Very calmly.

"So, why don't you simply go away and leave me alone? You are nothing more, than a frightful little man. Now piss off!" I say, a little too loudly.

"Hey Mart, is everything OK back 'ere?" calls Mickey.

"Hi Mickey! Yes, um everything is just fine. I think Mr. Mendosa was just leaving, weren't you?" I respond, whilst smiling sweetly at Danny.

He walks off and it's now Mickey's turn to be by my side. "So, you wanna tell me what that was all about then, eh?"

"Oh it was nothing. We just don't get on and I think he's still pissed about the equipment going down during rehearsals the other day. He'll get over it eventually, but I think it will be a long time coming," I giggle.

Mickey plants a kiss on my cheek. "Well don't you worry 'bout a thing Mart. He'll get what's coming to 'im and looks as if he's already 'ad a good beating. Hey, it wasn't you was it girl?" laughs Mickey, as he walks away.

"Would I do such a nasty thing? No, of course it wasn't me!" I laugh.

Thankfully, Jerome has returned with my coffee and suddenly I am feeling peckish. "Jerome, you know that you are my absolute favourite graphics chap in the whole wide world, don't you?" I smile. "And because you are my absolute favourite, I was wondering if you would go and get me a couple of almond croissants; you know, the really big ones. I've got a major starve on now and you don't want me grumpy during the morning session, do you?" I say, tilting my head.

"Jesus Martha, what am I? Your bitch?" asks Jerome, as he wanders off, shaking his head.

"Jerome, I love you, thank you!" I shout after him.

"I thought it was only me you loved, but obviously I was mistaken." I look up and spy Howard behind the stage panels.

"Good morning Mr. Johnson and how are you this fine day?" I ask.

"Very well thank you, Martha. So, are you going to answer my question, or not? Are you in love with more than one person, or, are you simply using him in return for croissants?" he laughs.

"OK you caught me out. I'm a user and Jerome has his uses," I giggle.

"Miss Martha, would it be inappropriate for me to kiss you, as I have an overwhelming desire to?" asks Howard.

"Well Sir, I think that would be highly irregular, especially as there are so many crew members wandering around. I don't think for one moment, that privacy is on our side," I smile.

"Well, in that case, could I suggest that you come to my room at lunchtime, so that we can rectify this matter?" he suggests, oh so coolly as he walks off slowly, waving his hand in the air.

"Most certainly Sir, have a good show," I respond, as I blow him a kiss.

Now believe me, or, believe me not, but I was feeling massively guilty during that conversation, as all the while I was thinking of Alexandre and not Howard. Oh my God, how can I possibly meet him at lunchtime? What if Alexandre is still in the hotel? I should be with him, not Howard. Howard will leave me soon enough, but Alexandre and me? Well, we'll always be together, in one way or another. Fuck! Shit! Bollocks! This pissing, awful, complex life of mine.

The presenters are being mic'd up. The show will go live in approximately twenty minutes. No last minute hitches, which is good. Videos are cued. Crew are on standby. I have a large coffee and two croissants and the lovely Jerome, Dan and Hugo are backstage. So, almost ready, all I need now is a comfort break.

As I head off to the Ladies, I spot Dickbrain Mendosa deep in conversation with Howard. I hope for my sake, that Danny's not telling him about what happened last night. Oh shit! Please God no! Please don't let him tell on me.

Arriving at the Ladies I head into the last cubicle and hum to myself as I take a pee.

"Hey slapper is that you?" calls out Mel.

"Hello darling, how are you feeling?" I ask.

"How the fuck do you think I'm feeling? I haven't slept and my fanny is on fire. Jesus, how the fuck am I going to get through today? God help us all!" replies Mel.

"Well, that'll teach you for being so bloody rampant won't it? So tell me, have you got a repeat performance booked for this evening?" I giggle.

"Too bloody right, yep too bloody right girlie," responds Mel.

Peering into the mirror, I don't think I actually look too bad. Mel, on the other hand, is definitely looking worse for wear. It's fair to say that her skin tone is grey, her eyes are like piss holes in the snow and her hair is a complete and utter mess. All in all, not the best look.

"You know what Slapper? And I can officially call you Slapper now, after your antics this week, I am wishing that the models were around this morning as I might try to steal some of their marching powder. That will definitely get me through the show," laughs Mel, applying lip gloss, for what it's worth!

On route back to the auditorium, I call Theo. Yes, I know it's early, but I really do need to speak to him. It's ringing, but I bet you a million dollars he doesn't pick up and sure enough, it switches to voicemail. I don't want to leave a message I want to speak to him. I'm upset about our tiff last night and I need to make amends, but I suppose if he's not ready to talk to me, then there's nothing much I can really do.

Suddenly my iphone vibrates. For a split second, I think it might be Alexandre, phoning to tell me he loves me, phoning to tell me that he won't ever leave me again, phoning to say 'break a leg' before the show. I look at the iphone and see Theo's name flashing. Thank the Lord! I think my little brother still loves me.

I click answer. "Theo listen, I am sorry for being such a prick last night I really, really didn't mean it and oh my God I can't believe that we fell out over Alexandre. You know that I would never ordinarily tell you fibs, honestly, I wouldn't and if I am totally honest, I didn't know for sure that he would come over and just imagine if he hadn't been there, oh my God, Danny might have given me a real beating. And honestly I haven't hurt Howard. Oh Theo, please tell me you forgive me." I stammer all too quickly, taking a deep breath at the end of it all.

Silence. More silence.

"Hello? Hey, Theo can you hear me? Theo, speak to me," I say loudly.

"Hey Martha, it's Jefferson here. I tried to get to the phone as Theo was in the shower, but I just missed it, so I called you back. But look, you know what, I'll get Theo to give you a call when he's finished. OK?" responds Jefferson.

FUCK! No! No! No! Oh sweet Jesus! So, let's go over this very slowly. I tell Jefferson about Alexandre. I tell Jefferson about Danny. Is there anything I haven't told Jefferson? I have to phone him back and explain.

I press Theo's number and it rings and keeps ringing and then eventually clicks into voicemail. So, this time, I leave a message "Theo honey, I think I have seriously fucked up. Please tell Jefferson I'm sorry. Love you."

Martha DiPinto fucks up big time, once again. Will there be a way back from this holy mess? I fucking hope so!

Chapter Seventeen

Arriving backstage, I feel decidedly unsettled, because, let's face it, in the past few hours; I've had a fall out with Theo, I've had a major fall out with Dickbrain Mendosa, I've probably angered Jefferson and I'll probably have a fall out with Howard, once Jefferson has caught up with him. You know what? Perhaps, I am just not supposed to have relationships. Perhaps, I should just stick with one-night stands and leave it at that. Perhaps, I wasn't put on this earth to meet a man and stay with that man for the rest of my life. Perhaps, just perhaps, I am to remain single forever, which I find very sad, as I would ultimately love children. Scary thought I know, but I actually think I would make a rather good mother. Quit sniggering—I can hear you!

"You OK?" asks Dan, bringing me back into the real world.

"Of course I'm OK. Why wouldn't I be? My life is a nightmare, my tongue is wearing a fur coat, I have panda eyes and I feel one hundred and forty years old, so yes, I'm good thanks" I respond cynically.

"Just checking, just checking. Keep your hair on. After all, it's not everyday I get to sit backstage with you and manage to get a word in. Normally, I can't shut you up, so this makes a welcome change." giggles Dan.

"Piss off and cue your videos. How many do you have?" I ask, abruptly.

"Surprisingly, the same number as I had during rehearsals, which is not many, certainly not many for such a long show. We've got the opening montage, followed by two for Howard, then the opening again, after their coffee break and then one each for the other two presenters. Life couldn't be sweeter for me," smiles Dan.

"Well, just so long as you hit your cues Dan my man that is all we ask of you," interrupts Hugo, who is an absolute stickler for shows running perfectly, which is of course, what makes him the best production manager in the business.

"Hugo mate, don't you worry, everything will run like clockwork, no worries," replies Dan.

"Jerome, no need to ask if you're happy and that the backup laptop is up and running?" asks Hugo.

"All shipshape Hugo, I am looking forward to this show, it's been a long time in the planning and even longer in the rehearsing," laughs Jerome.

"Martha, if at any point you feel the desire to sleep, you will let us know won't you?" asks Hugo sarcastically, looking at my overly tired face.

"Touch wood, I've never missed a show through exhaustion yet, so fingers crossed, this isn't going to be the first," I smile, all the while thinking about Theo and how I desperately want to find him and make amends. I also want to find Jefferson and make amends and I want to find Alexandre and, and, and... make babies! Only joking, well not really, as I would definitely have babies with Alexandre, if it was just me and him and they would, of course, be beautiful babies! Our babies. Such perfect babies.

I lean across and pinch Dan under his arm, the tender fleshy bit. He leaps out of his chair and has zero hesitation in pinching me right back. "Ow, you bastard!" I whisper.

"Serves you bloody well right, you little madam. Piss off and stay on your side of the table," Dan replies, throwing me a wink.

I turn my back to him slightly. I love working with Dan, he is just one of the funniest guys I know. He also provides the majority of the movies we watch whilst rigging. In fairness, they are not all to my liking, but somehow Dan manages to get hold of the sort of movies crew just love to watch! And believe it or not, The Sound of Music is one of them—well, one scene in particular. The one where Maria is agonising over her feelings for Captain Von Trapp and confiding in Mother Superior. If you listen carefully to the scene, you will hear the question 'what is it, you can't face... ?' and if you say the last two words very quickly, it really is not something you would expect to hear from a nun! That just about sums up the level of crew humour!

We all have our headsets on and we look like wise monkeys sitting in a row.

Over the airwaves comes our illustrious leader, Mel.

Mel: OK everyone. Less of the banter. Cans check please. Martha, you ready?

Martha: Prompt standing by and just raring to go!

Mel: Glad to hear it! Jerome?

Jerome: All good with me.

Mel: Dan, have you got the videos in the right order?

Dan: Of course! How are you Mel? I hear your world rocked last night.

Mel: Jealously young man, will get you nowhere. Mickey, are you ready with walk-in music?

Mickey: Sound standing by, Ms Arethusa.

Mel continues with her checks and makes sure that all the show crew are in position and ready to start the morning session.

Hugo: Mel, we've had the nod from Mary-Jo and we're ready to let delegates in.

Mel: Thank you Hugo—lighting, sound and graphics can I have walk-in state please?

As Mickey pushes up the faders on the sound desk, the sound of Heather Small oozes from the speakers. The doors open and the delegates start to make their way into the auditorium. It's a relatively large show in respect of delegate numbers, there are over nine hundred from all continents and as they enter the room, you can hear the excitement in their voices, their excitement at the prospect of what the day holds for them.

With all the delegates seated and the auditorium doors closed, we are ready to run the show. Ingrid has now joined us on cans.

Ingrid: Ingrid here. Good luck everybody and let's make this a show to remember. After all, these are Angel's best clients, so let's impress.

Hugo: We'll do our best, I'm sure.

I throw Hugo a look, a look of bewilderment at his comment and he simply shrugs his shoulders and smiles, his lovely 'lets be nice to Ingrid' smile. She has just put the kiss of death on the show by wishing everybody good luck. Why she couldn't say 'break a leg' or, 'see you on the other side,' I don't know—oh well, it's her show and on her head be it!

Mel: Not that I need to remind you all, but phones off. I repeat off. Not silent. If I hear any interference on cans or indeed a noise from a mobile during this show, it's drinks for the entire crew, at the culprit's expense! Understand?

Mel is sitting behind the control desk at the back of the auditorium with the sound and lighting guys, from where she has a clear view of the stage and audience. She is God during the running of the show. Nothing happens, unless Mel instructs it. And what she says goes—no question.

Talking of the fashion show, my thoughts turn to Theo. I reach into my handbag and pull out my iphone and switch it back on. Jerome glances across, so I stick two fingers up and pull a gurney face.

I click into text messages and yes, thank the Lord; there is a text from Theo.

Mel: Ladies and Gents, our auditorium is filling up nicely, in precisely three minutes we will go live.

I open the text message: *Cara mia. Only you could sleep with another man and then confess as much to your lover's brother. Stupida! We are both still laughing. Have a great show. Love you. PS Still would like to decapitate Alexandre though! xxx*.

I quickly text back: *Love you too. See you both later xxx*.

I switch my iphone off. I am now going to concentrate for the next few hours. I am a professional and therefore I must act like a professional, at all times—well that's the theory!

Mel: Stand by lights...

Belinda: Mel, hold just a moment, we've got a couple of late-comers, just registering and then we are all in.

Mel: Thanks Belinda. You got them in and seated rather quickly—did you use your cattle prod?

Belinda: I wish I had one; we'd have them seated in minutes.

Mel: OK everybody, here we go. Standby please lights, sound, VT.

We all hold our breath, waiting for Mel's cue to start the conference.

Mel: Lights, sound and VT—go please.

The opening video appears on the screen in front of us. The accompanying music is loud and vibrant. Images of beautiful women wearing KAYSO's new collection appear on screen, but the images move so quickly that it's difficult to make out the style of clothing, which is altogether intentional. Imagines of KAYSO staff, offices, factories and cities of the world also appear, bringing together two minutes of this video montage.

Once the opening VT has run, we have lights up and Howard, the lovely gorgeous, oh so handsome, Howard Johnson III, steps up to the lectern, to start his presentation. He really is quite something.

"Well, good morning KAYSO!" he shouts out to the audience. It's a good start—as those words are actually on his script!

Thankfully, when Howard goes off at a tangent and ad libs, he always comes back to the words on the script, so I am not left wondering where in his presentation I should be. He is such a professional presenter, more than can be said for Dickbrain Mendosa. Howard has real presence; you can tell he enjoys being in front of an audience, so much so, that he is running over his allotted time.

Mel's voice comes over cans.

Mel: It looks as though Mr Johnson is going to over run; he's still got a page to go. Martha next time he goes off script, can you flash a warning up that he is already ten minutes over his allocated time?

Martha: Certainly can. Here we go...

Just at that moment, Howard decides to expand on the details of the new KAYSO factory opening in Moscow. I seize the opportunity and quickly type in a message: *10 minutes over running time. Fancy a shag? X*

It's so naughty to send messages during a presenter's speech unless of course it's urgent or they are over-running on time and there is only a very small percentage of speakers I would dare send them to, as I do want to keep working in the industry—well, for now anyway. But I guess, or rather hope, that Howard will see the funny side!

Thankfully, Howard sees the message and then shares it with the audience. (The fact that he has been told he is out of time, not the offer of a shag! Thank the Lord! Can you imagine Ingrid's reaction if he'd done that? Yes, quite...).

Howard's presentation runs without a hitch. His video is right on cue and it's a thumbs up effort, all round.

Mel: Martha, give it your best and then some, you know who we have next.

Martha: I'm a professional.

Mel: Always.

Mickey: Have you organised another power surge, Martha?

Martha: I'm waiting to hear back from the Electricity board to see if it is possible to arrange for one to take place during the next twenty five minutes.

Mel: Thank you, you two. Now let's get back to Mendosa.

My heart is pounding and when I say pounding, I mean pounding. I don't think I have ever been as nervous as I am, at this precise moment. Danny Mendosa has reduced me to a quivering wreck. Hugo leans over to me. "You'll be absolutely fine." he whispers, squeezing my arm.

Dickbrain Mendosa is at the lectern. His words are on the prompt screen and they read "Good morning Ladies and Gentlemen and how are we all today? Well you've heard from Howard and now it's my turn..." But no, he immediately starts ad libbing. Is he trying to destroy me on purpose? Because, if he continues, he will surely succeed. Danny's actual opening words are, "I woke up this morning and I knew it was going to be a fabulous day. We've heard from Howard and now you're going to hear from me. Straight talking, as I am, I'm going to tell it as it is."

I am poised at the beginning of Danny's presentation, as I am assuming this is where he will begin.

"Sorry everybody we seem to have a technical hitch; just a moment..." says Danny to the crowd and I know, just know, what his next words are going to be!

"Paula, wakey, wakey, do you think you can keep up? We're on to the next paragraph, get with it honey!" says Danny slowly. There is laughter and sarcasm in his voice.

I move onto the next paragraph, in the hope that he will run to this presentation now. I am visibly shaking. All I want to do is go to the front of the stage and punch the wanker's face. But no. I am a professional and I will act like a professional, at all times.

Mel: Hang on in there Paula, oops sorry Martha.

Martha: Still smiling.

Mickey: Don't worry Martha; a lot can happen in a day. To him that is, not you!

We are a third of the way into Danny's presentation and thankfully, all is running smoothly now. Occasionally, he veers off, so I simply stop and wait for him to come back to where he is, within his script.

Finally, we are nearing the end of his presentation. I only have about another three minutes of Mendosa and then I am done, well and truly done with him, forever.

We are now on his final paragraph and he decides to ad lib again "... and before I go, I just want to say a big thank you to Howard for arranging this conference in such a fantastic location and a special thank you employees of KAYSO for attending. Without you, we are pretty much nothing and a final thank you to the team from Angel Productions, in pulling this great event together, especially Mel, Jerome, Ingrid, Ellie, Belinda and Hugo, without them, it wouldn't have been possible, so thank you all. Now please make your way out to the foyer for refreshments." he finishes.

Mel: House lights and music. Go please.

Thank God, Dickbrain Mendosa is over. I can now relax again.

Mel: Martha? Dickbrain forgot to mention you, so a big thank you from us and well done, I know that wasn't easy. Now let's go grab a smoke and some coffee.

All back on cans by ten fifty five please.

I lean down to grab my bag and as I come up, Dickbrain Mendosa is standing in front of me. Thankfully, Hugo is still backstage and makes his way towards me, to see what the bastard has to say.

"You had to mess it up, didn't you?" says Danny.

"Um, just a minute Mr Mendosa, I don't think it's fair to accuse Martha of 'messing up' as you put it," butts in Hugo.

"Yeah, whatever," responds Dickbrain, as he walks back out into the auditorium.

"God that man is such a bastard. I hate him!" I spit, not literally of course, as that would be totally unladylike!

"Martha, take no notice. It's over now. The chap really is quite awful," replies Hugo.

I grab my bag and make my way front of stage to find Mel. Dickbrain is speaking with Howard. Howard looks over and waves for me to join them. I totally ignore him and thankfully, find Mel walking towards the door.

"Come on Mel, let's get out of here, before I say, or, do something I shouldn't, God he's such a fucking prick!" I say.

Outside, I tell Mel and Mickey about Dickbrain coming backstage and having a go. He has upset me so much that I am beginning to doubt my own prompting ability.

"Girlie don't you worry, what goes around, comes around," smiles Mickey.

"Mickey. Now hang on a sec, what are you up to?" asks Mel.

"Nothin' Mel, nothin'," he replies, walking off back into the building.

"Oh fuck! What is he up to? I know him too well and I can smell a plot a mile off," laughs Mel.

"Oh well, whatever it is, I hope it involves Dickbrain," I respond, rather despondently.

We manage to smoke a couple of cigarettes, before we head back to the auditorium. I feel slightly more awake now, which is great, but I can't get Dickbrain out of my head. He really is such a bastard.

Heading backstage, it would appear that Dan, who is alone at this point, is up to no good too, as he seems startled as I walk in. "What are you doing?" I ask

"Nothing, just making sure all the VTs are ready for this second session. OK with you madam?" responds Dan.

"Fine, but you've definitely got a guilty look on that face of yours. You're up to no good. No doubt about it!" I laugh.

"Piss off you bleedin fruitcake, what mischief can I get up to behind here? Now, if I had a couple of them models with me, then that would be a different matter, wouldn't it?" responds Dan, with a wry smile.

The time is now approaching ten fifty five am; the show will start again in approximately five minutes. Hugo and Jerome have joined us backstage and once again, we are all sitting in a row, awaiting instruction from Mel.

Mel: Is everyone good to go?

Hugo: Present and correct backstage, Mel.

Mickey: Martha, just remember, what goes around, comes around.

Mel: What have you done?

Mickey: Nothin'. Honest.

Martha: Liar.

Mel: Calm yourselves you two, we'll go live in one minute.

Everybody is silent. We are all thinking about what might occur. What has Mickey done? Something and that's for sure!

Mel: Standby please lights, sound, VT.

The boys acknowledge they are on standby, and with that, Mel gives the go ahead.

Mel:... and run VT please.

Dan presses the button to run the video and then our world is momentarily suspended. There is a sense of fear. You can audibly hear the sharp intake of breath from backstage and from within the auditorium. For there, on screen, is not the opening montage with KAYSO's beautiful clothing, gorgeous models and happy employees, but a naked woman lying on her back on a sun lounger, her over-sized breasts wobbling in time with the naked sun-tanned man who is astride her, fucking her like a train.

Dan is motionless. He doesn't even make an attempt to switch the video off. It surely must have been running for some ten to twelve seconds, before Hugo lunges over Jerome and finally gets to Dan's workstation and manages to switches the data switcher over to graphics, so that the KAYSO logo is static on the big screen.

Dan: OH FUCK! FUCK FUCK! I am so sorry.
Mel: Idiot. Have you got the opening montage cued up?
Dan: Yes. Yes, I think so.
Mel: Run it. Run it now.
Ingrid: Mel, whaaaaaaat the...
Mel: A mistake. We'll get it sorted.

The opening montage is now on screen. The correct version. The version without naked bodies, without grunting and groaning and without breasts wobbling in time to the man pumping his bitch, for all she's worth.

I start to laugh uncontrollably. Immediately I feel guilty, so I try to stop. I look across to Hugo and his face is still startled, akin to a rabbit in the headlights. He is trying to suppress his laughter too. I lean over. "Are you OK Hugo? Did you hurt yourself when you lunged? That was some move." I giggle.

Hugo can hardly speak. "Not fucking funny Martha. I cannot quite believe that we have just shown porn to an audience of nine hundred people! Just how the hell do I explain this to Ingrid?"

I lean into Dan. "Hey you OK?" I ask.

"Are you taking the piss? I'm for the chop after this. Fucking hell! I can't believe I just did that. It's your fault. You startled me earlier after the break and I must have forgotten to switch channels. Fucking hell!" replies Dan, in a whisper, with his head in his hands.

"Don't worry, at least you've woken up the audience," I laugh, knowing full well that he is going to be in so much shit.

As the opening montage comes to an end, Bruce Shannon, KAYSO Australia's Vice President, is at the lectern. "Well, Ladies and Gents, not quite what we were expecting, but hey, it just goes to show how ugly things can look without our clothing." The audience erupts into laughter and from their reactions we know that all is going to be good again.

We run through Bruce's presentation without a hitch and even his video is cued correctly. His presentation runs exactly to time. Perfect.

Next up, we have Marcus Driscoll, KAYSO Europe's Vice President. "Well, Ladies and Gentlemen, as openings go, I think young Bruce wins the prize." Once again, the audience erupts into laughter. Thank fuck!

At the end of Marcus's presentation, he announces that there is now time for a question and answer session from the audience and he asks the other presenters to join him, on stage.

Part of the set comprises directors' chairs, you know, the sort that are used on film sets. And each one has the KAYSO VP's surname printed on the backrest. It's easy to see which one is Dickbrain Mendosa's, as his is twice the width of the others.

The presenters make their way onto the stage and take their seats. As Dickbrain Mendosa sits down, backstage we hear an almighty thud, the sharp intakes of breath from nine hundred delegates in the audience and Dickbrain's never-ending cry of 'oooooooowwwwwwwwww'.

Hugo takes off his cans quickly and rushes from backstage, to the aid of Dickbrain, who now finds himself sprawled on the floor, red-faced in front of the audience. Hugo and Howard help him to his feet, or, rather haul him onto his fat feet. Bruce and Marcus are trying to keep straight faces, but don't succeed!

With Dickbrain now in an upright position, Hugo rushes to the side of the stage, where he grabs a spare auditorium chair and takes it for Mendosa to sit on. Thankfully, he grabs one without arms, as let's face it, Dickbrain wouldn't fit into a normal sized chair with arms, would he?

After all the hysteria, Marcus carries on with the Q&A session. "Well Ladies and Gentlemen, this morning is nothing short of surprises for you." he laughs, and carries on. "Now can we take the first question please?"

After the furore of the collapsing chair, all show crew are now back on cans, apart from Ingrid, who has disappeared into the Ladies cloakroom, to be sick.

Mel can hardly speak through her tears of laughter.

Mel: Mickey, Dan, did that have anything to do with you two?

They reply in unison.

Mickey & Dan: No way.

Mel: Tell me the truth.

Mickey: OK. Dickbrain Mendosa has been a real prick during this show and he's given Martha such a fucking hard time, so me and Dan thought we'd give him a taste of his own medicine. No-one fucks with crew Mel, no-one!

Unbeknown to the rest of us, Mickey and Dan had taken a Stanley knife to Dickbrain's chair and cut away some of the stitching, so it was only a matter of time, under such a huge strain, that the chair was to collapse and collapse it did!

Mel: OK. Let's try and hold it together, we're nearly at the end of this farce and possibly our careers. Ingrid isn't back on cans yet, but I suggest we all keep a low profile, very low profile, when she returns.

The questions and answers session has come to an end and Howard makes his way back over to the lectern, for the closing speech of the morning.

"Ladies and Gentlemen. You've heard our plans and ambitions, our desires and needs. We want you all to be part of this ongoing transformation of making KAYSO a force to be reckoned with. Worldwide. After lunch, we have a superb fashion show and then this evening, we have our awards ceremony and closing party. A great day and night ahead of us. The fashion show will commence at three thirty pm, but for now, please make your way out to the foyer for lunch and we'll see you later. Thank you."

Mel: Lights, music and graphics go please.

Mel: Well done everybody.

Mel: Dan, are you trying to fucking kill me?

Dan: No, honest, genuine mistake. Forgive me?

There is a huge sigh of relief, as we all remove our cans backstage. We are just about to start discussing the disasters of the wrong VT, as well as the demise of Danny, when the calling lights flash on the control boxes of our headsets. Dutifully, we all go back on cans. Oh my God! It's Ingrid!

Ingrid: Dan, I would like to see you immediately. Hugo, I want both you and Mel, backstage NOW. Everyone else, please leave the auditorium.

I, for one am out of here. Ingrid is about to blow a gasket. I power down my machines, as they are not needed until the awards ceremony later. I grab my iphone and switch it on. I have two text messages and one missed call.

Text message one from Theo: *Rumour has it I've missed a porn show rather than a conference? What the fuck happened? Ciao bella xxx.*

Text message two from Alexandre: *Hey baby, you left without saying goodbye. Call me. Am still at the hotel xx.*

Voice message from Tom: *Hi Martha, can you give me a call when the show is over, I have some dates for you for a potential road show next month. Speak later.*

Ingrid has now arrived backstage, with Mel. This is my cue to leave, together with Jerome. Ingrid is spitting feathers and her facial expression is pernicious and tight. I'm glad I'm not on the end of this reprimand!

I head off to the front of the auditorium and see Dickbrain and Howard. Howard comes rushing over. "Hey you minx. Thank you for your message and the answer is yes!"

From the corner of my eye, I see Dickbrain looking across at me, giving me the evil eye, so I turn my body sideways, so that I can't see the prick.

I smile at Howard, but I am not particularly forthcoming, with either words or expression.

"What's up? Have I offended you? You ignored me earlier. Any reason?" he asks.

"It wasn't you, I was ignoring, it was Mendosa. That guy is such a prick. Sorry, but it's true. He's like a fucking dog with a bone and just won't let it go," I respond.

"Hey come on. He's just had his nose knocked out of joint by falling on his butt in front of nine hundred KAYSO employees. He has his good points and yes, he has his bad points, but it's not my place to bitch about him, so let's drop it. OK?" replies Howard, sticking up for him.

"Whatever," I smile, sarcastically.

"Now, I think we were scheduled for a hot date over lunch and after that burst of porn earlier, its got me feeling quite horny. But don't shoot me, something has come up and I need to spend time with the team before the fashion show, so perhaps we could reschedule to this evening?" asks Howard.

"If porn can't even get you excited enough, then I know my place, Mr. Johnson. If your team come before me, then so be it," I reply, still a little rattled that he is standing me up for Mendosa.

"Martha, you will always come first, in every sense," he replies, leaning down to kiss my cheek and cleverly brushing my breast without the world noticing. "I'll see you later and I'm looking forward to it."

"OK, see you later. Shall we watch a porn movie? I am sure there must be something suitable to watch, if not, I'll ask Dan to lend us his!" I suggest, blowing him a kiss.

I text Mel to tell her that I am heading back to the hotel for a lie down.

Our rig crew are setting out the stage and Pikey is on hand to ensure the floral display and lights work perfectly. He has strict instructions not to stay amongst the foliage within the catwalk, once the show has started.

The models are arriving for hair and make up. I look out for Theo and spot him talking with Jefferson in the foyer. Fuck! Might as well strike whilst the iron's hot. After all I've got to speak to Jefferson sooner or later.

I head over to them and immediately Jefferson embraces me. "Martha, tell me how good was the porn show we missed earlier? I didn't think for one moment Howard would have had porn scheduled into the show, but good on him." he gushes.

"Oh my God Jefferson, it was heart stopping. We were all gripped by fear and sat there motionless. It was unbelievable." I giggle.

"Oh and Jefferson listen, about our little conversation earlier. I am not out to hurt Howard, far from it. An old boyfriend turned up and oh I don't know, you know what it's like, I just wanted to see him. Are you angry with me?" I ask.

"Angry? Are you completely mad? Why would I be angry? Come on Martha, what's the likelihood of you and Howard keeping in touch? After all, you live on different continents, so it's not as if you are going to bump into each other, is it? Enjoy life, that's what it's for." he says, giving me a hug.

"Ciao bella. I hear all was good this morning, aside from the porn show and Danny's chair collapsing. I hope that had nothing to do with you?" chips in Theo.

"As if I would do such a thing. It had absolutely nothing to do with me and neither did the porn. That was down to Dan. God, he was shitting himself, he's with Ingrid as we speak." I respond, kissing my baby brother on the cheek.

"Martha listen, when you've had lunch, why don't you join us backstage whilst we are dressing the models, it's exciting, really it is, and I am sure you would love to see us in action." suggests Theo.

"Sounds like a plan to me," I smile, waving goodbye.

I head off to the hotel, calling Alexandre on route. No answer. Suddenly I feel down trodden. According to Jefferson, Howard is not interested in seeing me again after Cannes and now Alexandre has left me too. Shit! I am feeling just a little sad. But hey, I can feel the sun on my body and the sea breeze blowing gently through my hair, so it's not all bad.

I head up to my room, taking the lift, which is so bloody lazy after all, I am on the first floor! When I get back to England I am going to get myself into a healthy regime. No more excessive drinking and definitely more exercise, hey I might even renew my gym membership!

I arrive at my bedroom and notice that the bed has not been made. Obviously Alexandre was still in the room, when room service were on their rounds. I head over to the bed and grab a pillow and stupidly sniff it, in the hope that I might, just might, smell Alexandre on it. I can feel myself rocking slightly, boy I'm dysfunctional.

Suddenly, I am shaken from my thoughts. I hear a noise in the bathroom. Perhaps it's room service? I pop the pillow down and head over to the bathroom door. I open it slightly and call out 'hello'.

No answer. I push it fully open and to my utter surprise Alexandre is taking a shower. He looks over, and smiles. He motions for me to join him. I shake my head. I simply cannot get my hair wet, not if I am to make the fashion show. Jesus, I'm just so shallow.

I head over to the shower cubicle with a towel, as he comes out to greet me. His body is glistening with droplets of water on his hairy chest, on his beautiful arms and on his gorgeous face. I hand him the towel and he wipes his face dry. And then he kisses me. Tenderly. He pulls me towards him; I can feel the wetness of his body through my clothes. Our kisses become more eager. We stagger out of the bathroom, kissing all the while. I kick off my shoes and in one movement, my polo shirt is off. Eagerly he unclips my bra and within seconds, his tongue is licking at my breasts. Passion overwhelms me. We fall onto the bed. My hand finds his cock, hard and erect and slowly I massage it, until his breathing deepens and I move my hand faster until I hear his groan of ecstasy.

"Baby, you are unbelievable. Fuck! Just the touch of your hand makes me come. I wasn't sure if you would come back here. Why didn't you wake me this morning, before you left?" he asks.

"Boo, I did try waking you. Several times. You simply rolled over, nothing was going to shift you," I giggle.

As I speak, I kneel on the bed to unbutton my trousers. Alexandre watches me intensely. I slowly push my trousers down and then fall back on the bed waiting for him to pull them off, which he does with such ease. We look at each other, for what seems an age and then he starts to trace his finger up the inside of my leg. I watch him, his cock becoming erect again. I raise my bum, as he slips off my knickers and within moments, his head is buried between my legs. His hands are on my breasts and my entire body quivers, as I reach the most amazing climax that I only ever reach with him.

Still quivering, he enters me quickly, roughly and thrusts intensely and then he comes. I scream out, unable to contain myself. Pleasure, like I have never known before.

He takes me in his arms and holds me close. I have no doubt that he loves me. This is his way of showing it. We lie still for a few moments, as our heavy breathing subsides. "Baby, when am I going to see you again? What are your plans for later?" he asks.

"We've got the fashion show this afternoon, followed by the awards ceremony. Then we'll have our end of show party. Will you be here this evening?" I ask a little too eagerly, completely forgetting I have a date with Howard later!

"No, I've got plans this evening and they can't be changed before you ask, but why don't I come by tomorrow morning—what time are you leaving?" he asks, stroking my cheek, tenderly.

"The coach is picking us up around one pm, so tomorrow morning would be good, but come early, I want to spend as much time with you as possible," I smile, in a desperate kind of way.

Kissing him seductively and slowly stroking his cock again. He rolls onto his back, an open invitation for me to give him a blow job. The chemistry between us is amazing. He comes in my mouth and I taste the sweet juices of the man I love. We make love again, but this time, it's slow and intense. So intense, that I never want this moment to end.

It's two pm, as I get up out of bed and head to the shower. I put on the ridiculous shower cap to protect my hair, as I really don't want to get it wet and besides, I don't want to wash the smell of my man off in totality. Note to self—talk to Jefferson and that brother of mine, about coming up with a new design for a more attractive hotel shower cap!

Once clean and Prada'd I get dressed. I really don't want to leave the love of my life, but after all, I promised Theo and Jefferson I would go to the fashion show and a promise is a promise. And let's face it, Theo would go mad if he knew that I was with Alexandre, rather than being with him and Jefferson! I lean in to kiss Alexandre and as I do so, he speaks the words that I long to hear, "I love you babe."

I feel the tears springing to my eyes and know that's my cue to leave. I kiss him again. "I love you too Boo, always have and always will."

Chapter Eighteen

As I make my way back to the Palais du Roscoff, I keep repeating the words Alexandre said, 'I love you'. Just how can I be with him forever? I really would do anything, within moderation, to live the rest of my life with him, but I can't bear to be around his spoilt, utterly bratish children; they would drive too much of a wedge between us.

Arriving at the venue, I find Mel deep in conversation with Mickey and Dan. I sneak up behind her and kick the back of her knee, so that she loses balance and tumbles towards Mickey.

"Ah fucking hell! Do me a favour, I can barely stand at the best of times!" she shrieks, pulling herself upright again. "Could only be you Martha. Anyway what's all this sneaking back to the hotel for a lie down, light weight?" winks Mel.

"Fucking 'ell bird, I thought we was going for wipe out then. Close call," laughs Mickey. "You'd 'ave crushed me."

"If truth be told, I didn't actually manage to have a lie down, well not in the sense of lie down per se, but well, Alexandre was there, so we had a little kiss and cuddle" I giggle.

"Oh shit! Don't tell me you're hooked on him again. It'll end in tears girl," says Mickey, with a concerned tilt of his head and a raised eyebrow.

"No it won't. What harm is there in a kiss and a cuddle?" I ask.

"Well, you know where kisses and cuddles lead to. Straight to heart break, that's where!" chips in Dan.

Wanting to avoid this conversation altogether, prior to Mel throwing in her 'two penneth,' I change the subject, quickly.

"So, tell me Mickey, I don't suppose Mendosa's chair collapsing had anything to do with you did it?" I ask.

"Nowt to do with me. Nor Dan. Nah, it must 'ave been down to his weight. But it's true ain't it, don't fuck with crew, coz see what happens?" laughs Mickey, as he does a one two boxing punch with Dan.

"Well, whatever you didn't do, was bloody brilliant, well done to you both," I smile, knowing full well that the instigators were without a shadow of a doubt, Dan and Mickey.

"Mel, how's the prep for the fashion show going?" I ask.

"All good. Ingrid has gone for a lie down. The porn show was too much for her. She went like a train behind set didn't she Dan? And then, burst into tears before storming off. Hugo, our hero, went after her and escorted her back to the hotel. Dan has duly been chastised and has promised me a copy for this evening, when I get it on with Hans, haven't you Dan? So, all in all, life is good," responds Mel laughing.

Dan and Mickey wander off. I think they've spotted models in the distance!

"But enough about me, after all, it's all about me, me, me. Tell me about you. Are you OK after this morning's outburst from Dickbrain? And more importantly, what the fuck is going on with you and Alexandre and more importantly, you and Howard? All these questions, give me answers now," requests Mel looking at me, waiting for me to respond.

"Yes, well now I am fine about Mendosa. It's all over. I need have nothing more to do with him. He's such a fucking loser. As for Alexandre, what can I say? I can confirm one hundred percent that I, Martha DiPinto, am absolutely in love with him. More now than ever before. What am I going to do about it? Haven't got a fucking clue! As for Howard? Well he's adorable and really, really sexy and lovely, but come on, lets face it, when he's back in the States, is he really going to be thinking about me? I think not. He's probably got loads of women, socialites after him. I don't think for one minute a prompt operator such as me is going to bag the likes of Howard on a full time basis. This is nothing more than a fling. Yes, I would like more, but I think I'm dreaming if I hope for more," I respond, a little forlornly.

"Well girl, you never know. It may come good with Howard. He might be falling in love with you. But, I've said it once and I'll say it again, steer clear of Alexandre, he'll break your heart into a million pieces and then stamp on those pieces and that's not fair, not again," says Mel, as she pulls me close to her and hugs me with one of her lovely, all embracing hugs.

"I know, I know, but you know whatever happens, I've had a fucking brilliant time on this show. The best ever." I smile, but really wanting to burst into tears, as the show is now coming to an end and my love life is spiralling out of control.

"Quite agree girl, this show has been bloody brilliant!" smiles Mel.

"Right then, I'm off backstage I told Theo and Jefferson that I would hang out with them during the show—I think they are eager to show me what they do for a living!" I giggle.

"Good on you girl. As for me, I'm off for a pee. See you later!" smiles Mel, as she walks off. I really do love Ms Arethusa; she is definitely one of a kind.

Heading backstage there is an air of calm, which surprises me. The models are either with hairdressers or having their make up done. Jefferson is deep in conversation with Eleanor, who is in charge of the models and Theo is looking over the clothing rails, for the millionth time.

Now unsurprisingly, Dan and Mickey are also behind set. Thankfully not spying on the models, but setting up a couple of monitors, so that Eleanor and her assistants can see the runway and will know when to send the next models out.

I creep up behind them to listen to their conversation and although they are speaking in whispers, I just about hear Mickey say to Dan "Fuck, yeah they're right pretty, but come off it mate, it would be like having a skeleton lying on you. No way, give me a proper girl any day. Now take Mart, she's pucker. She's got hips and tits, just the way I like 'em."

I sneak away after all, I don't want to embarrass Mickey by letting him know that I have overheard his comments.

I loiter and then I make my entrance. "Hello boys, how surprising to find you backstage with all those lovely models. Now what brings you here?" I ask.

"We've got to rig another couple of monitors, so we're legit," laughs Mickey, tipping his imaginary cap.

"As legit as you'll ever be, I suppose. So, is everything ship shape?" I ask.

"As good as it's gonna get," replies Dan. "Hey, talking of shipshape, what happened to the plasma on board the yacht?"

"Ah, thankfully the crew loaded it up and got it safely across the waters and it is now on terra firma," I respond, with a smile.

"The catwalk looks fantastic. Pikey has done a really good job. Pray tell me though, who is keeping an eye on him later, so he doesn't make it inside the catwalk structure again?" I giggle.

"He'll be handcuffed to me," laughs Dan, "And he definitely won't be looking up no skirts, that's for sure!" he adds.

"Well done boys, keep out of trouble," I say, leaning in to kiss them both on the cheek. "And thank you for earlier. I know it was down to you two, but it rather made my day when Dickbrain fell to the floor. A perfect ending for the little prick," I wink, as I head off to find Theo.

"Ciao bella, look at you, you look radiant. So much better than earlier. Did you have forty winks?" asks Theo, as he embraces me.

"I'm not going to lie to you. Alexandre was at the hotel and we talked and well it made me feel good again, so don't kick off please, as I'm in a happy mood, so let's keep it that way, OK?" I say, kissing him tenderly on the cheek.

"Don't mention him. But rest assured bella mia, if he hurts you again, I swear I will kill him, do you understand me?" replies Theo, a little too seriously. Shit! Does he now have access to 'bad boys'? As let's face it, Theo could no more kill Alexandre than I could live in a convent!

"Don't get yourself worked up. No point as (a) he won't hurt me again and (b) you are far too meek and mild to fight Alexandre, he would tear you limb from limb, but of course I wouldn't let him, so you're safe!" I say, smiling all the while, knowing that Theo would mentally give it a good shot at trying to kill Alexandre, of this I have absolutely no doubt. But then Alexandre is a naughty, tough boy. He can fight if he needs to, whereas Theo can definitely not fight, never has done and never will.

"Anyway honey, what time is it? I've just remembered I haven't had any lunch and I'm bloody starving!" I smile.

"It's two pm, go grab yourself some lunch and come back, so that you can help dress the models," suggests Theo.

I head off to the Fleur Suite in the hope that there is still crew food available and en route, I bump into Belinda, who looks a little anxious. "Hey Belinda, are you OK?" I ask.

"Oh my God Martha, you're not going to believe this. I just went into the Ladies for a pee..." starts Belinda.

"Oh my God no! Not a pee!" I say in an alarmed tone.

"Stop it, let me finish..." responds Belinda quickly.

"Sorry!" I say, suitably reprimanded.

"Well, I walk into the Ladies and I hear groaning and heavy breathing and someone calling out 'yes, oh yes harder' then it goes quiet. So, then I don't know whether to rush into a cubicle for a pee or rush out of the

Ladies. Well I am desperate, so I turn on the tap and hurry into the cubicle," continues Belinda.

"Right and you turned on the tap for what reason?" I ask.

"Well, just in case they started up again, I didn't want to hear them, did I? So, then after I peed, I quickly wash my hands and grab a towel to dry them, but, oh I can't believe I am going to confess to this, but curiosity got the better of me and I bent down to see who was in the cubicle and oh my God, you'll never guess who it was? It was Mel, in fact I think I already knew it was Mel, as I could tell by her voice, so I quickly rushed out," gabbles Belinda, with her head in her hands.

"Belinda, what exactly is the problem here? If Mel wants a little naughty sex then so be it. I don't think it's anything to get worked up about is it? Not really. Come off it, she's been with Hans for the past forty eight hours, so we shouldn't be too shocked, should we? What baffles me though, is how the hell did she and Hans get into a cubicle together and manage to do the business? Bloody hell, those cubicles are so small," I reply, giggling whilst looking at Belinda.

"No, no, no, no, she wasn't in the normal cubicle, but in the disabled one, so of course they're much bigger aren't they? But the thing is, what if it had been a client who walked in rather than me? Don't you think they're taking risks?" responds Belinda, once again, with her head in her hands.

"We don't have very many female clients on site, only Rochelle and Mary-Jo and to be perfectly honest, I don't really think that either of them would be too concerned and let's face it, I am sure they've both had sex in interesting places, haven't we all?" I reply, laughing.

"Oh my God! Do you think I should tell Mel it was me who walked in on her? Oh, what should I do?" asks Belinda, pleadingly.

"Sweet Jesus girl! Pull yourself together. Does it really matter if Mel is copping off with Hans over lunch? Good on her and no, don't you dare say a word. This stays strictly between us, unless Mel chooses to say something. Understand?" I say, in my grown up voice.

"Goes without saying—I won't say a word! It was just such a shock. But you're right, what does it really matter that I hear Mel getting it on with Hans? I'm just jealous. Not of Hans but..."giggles Belinda, blushing somewhat.

"Each to there own. Now go on be off with you, go do what you need to do." I say, grinning. Well, would you believe it, Mel is such a dirty dog! Can you imagine Dan and Mickey if they found out, how jealous would they be? Totally!

I head off to the Fleur Suite to grab a coffee and much to my horror as I enter the room, I spot Dickbrain talking to Rochelle, but before I can turn on my heels, Rochelle spots me. "Hey Martha, come on in, we're done here. How's it all going?" she asks, in her upbeat tone.

"Everything is going really well, thank you. The fashion show is going to be brilliant, I've no doubt about that," I respond, all the while wanting to run over to Dickbrain and punch his pug-like face. Wanker!

"Great, well listen, if you'll excuse me M'am, I've got work to do. See you later!" says Rochelle, as she heads out of the Suite.

So now, it's just him and me. I walk over to the coffee station and grab a cup and saucer. These are my weapons if he should start on me, but he doesn't say a word, not a single word. I decide to eat something as the food that the venue has provided looks too good not to sample. I put down my cup and saucer and pick up a plate. I turn round to look at him and he is simply staring at me.

"So what's up, lost for words are you?" I ask.

"Nope!" comes his response.

I put salami, mortadella and bread on my plate and head over to the table where I have placed my coffee, grabbing a bottle of mineral water on route.

Still, he sits there—just staring.

I start eating, but feel totally intimidated. I quickly text Mel: *Pls come to Fleur, urgent xx.*

I carry on eating. Nothing is said, but all the while I just know that he is building up to something. He starts tapping his fingers on the table. An over-whelming urge washes over me; I really want to take my knife and stab it through his hand so that it is impaled on the table—I refrain, of course, but only just.

Thankfully, within a couple of minutes Mel appears at the door, huffing and puffing. "Hey girl, so this is where I find you. Hi Danny, how are you?" asks Mel, confidently.

"Fine, just leaving," he responds, and with that, he gets up and walks out of the suite.

"I'm sorry to text you, but I didn't know what else to do. I could sense things brewing and didn't want to get into another fight with him. Fuck! Not just the two of us, he'd kill me," I whisper.

"Mel, are you alright you look flushed?" I ask, knowing full well why she's flushed. I carry on eating my food, boy, I didn't realise just how hungry I am.

"Yeah fine, just had to get here pretty pronto didn't I? Thought it was an emergency. Well, I suppose it was an emergency of a kind, what with you the two of you alone, Jesus that's not good!" responds Mel.

"Thanks for rushing, I do appreciate it." I say, desperately wanting to ask what went on earlier in the Ladies. But I refrain. I'm biting down on my tongue. I must not ask. I must not ask.

"Slapper, you are not going to believe what happened to me earlier..." starts Mel.

I look at her with wide eyes. "What happened? Are you OK?" I ask, knowing exactly what's coming next.

"There I was, heading off to the Ladies and I just happen to bump into Hans. Nothing odd in that, you might think, but then he follows me into the Ladies and before I know it, he's got me into a cubicle and we're having sex. I didn't want it to stop, it was amazing, but then someone came in, haven't a clue who it was. Can you believe it, sex in the Ladies toilets, whatever next?" says Mel incredulously.

"How the fuck did two of you get into a cubicle?" I ask.

"Oh Jesus, is that all you can ask? We were in the disabled cubicle, more space isn't there? So, what do you make of that?" asks Mel, giggling like a school girl.

"I think I'm rather jealous! But, I must say it sounds kind of horny," I laugh.

"Behave! I don't know what came over me!" replies Mel, shaking her head. 'I don't have such behaviour on my shows!'

"But, at the end of the day, it was enjoyable and there's no harm done is there?" I say, smiling.

"Fuck it, you're right. No harm done. Come on, let's go and enjoy this show. By the way, who is babysitting Pikey? Is he under control?" asks Mel, linking her arm through mine. Clearly, she thinks I've had sufficient to eat!

"Dan is on 'Pikey sitting' duties. Can you just imagine if he manages to make it into the catwalk again?" I laugh. "It will finally kill off Ingrid!"

With only forty five minutes until the show starts, tempers are starting to fray backstage. Eleanor is in the middle of an outburst with two of her models. One model, whose name is India is screaming, because she does not like her hair and make up and the other, called Summer, seems to be having a fit because she's having a 'fat day'. Now, let me put into perspective what fat means to this stick insect—she stands around six foot tall, I can see every one of her ribs (she's in her bra and knickers) and I can easily encase her waist with both my of hands. Summer is so tiny in width and depth that really, if she turned sideways, we would lose her. Eleanor is now getting a little hissy.

Eleanor turns around and I see her take a very deep breath, I can see her European temperament is about to explode. She counts to five, all the while India and Summer still yapping behind her and then she turns around and gives an almighty shout. "If you don't like being here then go. Go now, because I will not tolerate such insolence. You are nothing in the eyes of fashion, other than a clothes-horse and there are many of those around, so you decide. Either shut up and get on with it, or, leave. NOW!"

Blimey, who would have thought it possible? Eleanor so meek and lovely on the surface, but boy she's really quite gusty underneath that lovely exterior. No wonder Hugo is struck on her.

I move towards Theo, who is talking to Jefferson. They are holding the most divine necklace. "Hi boys! Wow Wee! Take a look at that necklace, it is simply fantastic. Where did you find a piece of jewellery so gorgeous?" I ask, desperately wanting to get my hands on it.

"Ah cara mia, this piece was especially commissioned to be worn with the cream evening gown," responds Theo.

"Evening gowns? Since when have KAYSO ventured into evening gowns?" I ask.

"It's a new line we are trialling. This will be our first season, and so we want to make it extra special. Every lady, let's face it, needs a special gown at some point in her life and we just hope she chooses a KAYSO one. There are eight in this season's collection and the piece de resistance is the cream evening gown, which is so simplistic, it is beautiful, truly beautiful. And this necklace works so well with the design, but by all accounts, Summer, the model who is down to show the dress, is having a fat day," replies Jefferson.

"Ah yes, the fat model. All of a size 2 or 0. I saw Eleanor have a little word with her earlier. How in God's name she can call herself fat is questionable. I don't think I've ever seen anyone as bony as her. I would of course offer you my services, but I don't suspect for one moment that I will fit into the gown you speak of. But if you want to give it a shot, just let me know, but only if I get to keep the necklace afterwards," I chuckle.

"Yes, it is truly beautiful in its design. If truth be told, I'm not sure what will happen to the necklace after the show. After all, KAYSO aren't into selling jewellery, so who knows?" smiles Jefferson.

"Anyway cara mia, I am off to find Summer to discuss her fatness and another model with hair and make up issues. I can't event think of her name they all have the strangest names you know. Pretty but strange," says Theo

"Is it India?" I ask.

"Oh my God, yes that's her name, but how do you know?" asks Theo.

"Ah well, once again I spotted Eleanor having a go at her too—good luck!" I smile.

"I mean for goodness sake, since when has a model the right to question the look for God's sake. This is a different breed of model nowadays, not like the true professionals of before. OK, so they wouldn't get out of bed for less than ten thousand dollars, but when they did, they knew how to behave, how to be a professional and how to endear themselves to the designer, so that they get used time and time again. But no, nowadays, well what can I say, times have changed!" replies Theo, shaking his head, slowly, from side to side.

Jefferson rolls his eyes.

"Jefferson, is there anything I can do to help?" I ask.

"Well funny you should say that, but is there any chance you can give Lucy a hand with accessories when we start to get the models dressed please? Her side-kick, I can't remember her name, has gone down with a sickness bug, so any help would be totally welcome," replies Jefferson.

"Sure, I would love to help." I respond, smiling.

"Let me show you what you will need to do. On each of the outfits is a Polaroid, this Polaroid shows the finished look—what the outfit comprises and also the accessories. You will see they are all set out in order of appearance and there is an individual box per look. Lucy will be on hand and if you get stuck, simply shout. In most cases it's a necklace, a flower, a ring and bracelet or possibly a belt," responds Jefferson, full of passion.

"OK, sounds straightforward enough to me. So, can you introduce me to Lucy now?" I ask.

"Of course. Lucy, Lucy where are you?" shouts Jefferson.

Lucy appears, as if by magic. In my mind I pictured Lucy as a petit blonde, but I am wrong, so very wrong. Lucy has bright blue hair and the most amazing green eyes.

"Hi, I'm Lucy!" she says, extending her hand.

"Hi, pleased to meet you, I'm Martha," I reply.

"Ah, so you're Martha. I have heard some stories about you. Theo raves on about you constantly. He is such a darling!" gushes Lucy.

"Whatever Theo has said about me, take it all with a pinch of salt. I'm a nice girl really," I smile.

"Yeah, I'll believe you, millions wouldn't!" laughs Lucy.

In total we have twenty two models. Each and every one of them looks the same in size and height. The only difference is their hair colour and styles. Some are up-do's, some are bobs, some are wearing extensions, but other than that, I have to say, they are all very similar.

Dressing has started. Models are lined up beside their dresses and they are slowly ridding themselves of their robes and towels. None of them are wearing bras, well let's face it, they don't need them; but they are all wearing nude thongs, obviously a regulation down on the catwalk.

Once a model is dressed, they come over to Lucy and me, for accessories. We are working at quite a pace, to ensure that all models are one hundred percent ready for inspection by Jefferson and Theo, before being paraded out down the catwalk.

I spot Summer, the supposed fat model who is looking absolutely gorgeous in a multi coloured maxi dress. She is wearing gold gladiator sandals and we are accessorising her with a chunky gold necklace and gold bangle. She looks amazing.

Most of the models are now ready for inspection. I then spot India, who was having a big fit about her hair and make up. I can't take my eyes off of her. She looks stunning. She is wearing a pair of camel coloured city shorts, together with a very chic, navy blue blazer. Her legs are so very long, despite being a bit on the thin side. I am totally mesmerised by her. She is wearing nothing underneath her blazer, but we have accessorised with a man's tie. She looks a million dollars.

Hugo has made an appearance and I spot him kissing Eleanor on the cheek, wishing her the best of luck. I dart over to him. "Hi Hugo, don't they look amazing? I think I'm in awe." I smile.

"I quite agree and I hear you have been invaluable, so well done and thank you for stepping in and helping out," smiles Hugo.

A quick squeeze of my arm and he rushes off. I think he's embarrassed at the thought of seeing a semi naked model, but in fairness, these models really don't care who sees them, semi naked, or fully naked, for that matter.

Jefferson and Theo have started their inspection of the girls. Collars are tweaked, hair is fluffed, buttons done up and buttons undone and a quick shout and shoes are changed. With three minutes to spare before the catwalk show officially starts, there is a wonderful calm.

I wander over to Theo and link my arm through his. "What can I say? These women look absolutely fantastic. Who'd have thought I have such a talented brother? I am so very proud of you." I whisper, tears springing to my eyes as I kiss him on the cheek.

I have an overwhelming desire to cry, but I push back those tears. Theo looks the happiest I have ever seen him. His collection is amazing and he seems to have the love of a good man. Now all we need to do is convince our lovely Pops that being gay is not an issue and his life will be perfect. But hey, come on; enough of that, let's get back to the show.

Mel has come to pay a visit and is having a quick conversation with Eleanor. She spots me and hurries over. "What the fuck... have you changed your profession now?" she asks laughing.

"Not quite. But I am sure I could master the world of fashion with teachers like Theo and Jefferson." I giggle.

"Don't even think about it!" smiles Mel, walking off, hand waving in the air.

The 'behind the scenes' crew put on their headphones, the models pucker their lips and silence sweeps backstage, an eerie silence. The models look anxious, awaiting their moment of fame.

They will walk from backstage, up four steps, walk the length of the catwalk, do a twirl, walk back down the catwalk, give another twirl and walk down the four steps on the opposite side before moving backstage, to quickly change and do it all again, with a different outfit.

Jefferson and Theo are tweaking. Eleanor is holding back the first model, who seems a little anxious to get out and strut her stuff!

"Thirty seconds..." commands Eleanor.

Oh my Lord, they were like the longest thirty seconds of my life. I even tried holding my breath, but exhaled after seventeen seconds!

Suddenly the lights dim. Total darkness, aside from our minimal lighting backstage. A roar of music and the show begins. Model one moves out, the lights begin their display, the music is loud, the audience is cheering and the men don't hold back with their woof whistles.

Models two, three, four, five and six move quickly. They strut their stuff down the catwalk, twirl and then strut back. The adrenalin rush is amazing. I don't know whether to laugh or cry.

Once backstage, they quickly strip themselves of their garments and change into their next outfit. Jefferson and Theo are helping the dressers and Lucy and I are making sure the right accessories match the right outfits. Eleanor moves the models swiftly; it is like a well oiled machine backstage.

The audience are going crazy. My body is absolutely covered, quite literally, in goose bumps and I cannot begin to imagine how Jefferson and Theo are feeling at this precise moment. I look across to the boys and catch Jefferson high fiving Theo. Boy, they look great together.

The show is running fantastically well. Four of the five sections have now been shown and the final section is evening gowns. Eight of the models are dressed in their finery and the cream dress will feature as the finale. The gown looks amazing on Summer. And let me tell you, there is absolutely no hint of fatness. She looks a million dollars, especially with the beautiful necklace, I was admiring earlier.

Suddenly the music changes tempo. And the models filter out slowly, one by one. The audience are hushed. There is not a sound to be heard. They are all completely mesmerised. Such beauty, such elegance, everyone is haunted by the visions before them. And then finally, Summer takes to the stage and there is an almighty roar. The audience are standing up cheering and clapping. The evening wear models together with Jefferson and Theo are now out on catwalk. The adulation continues. I can see my brother on the monitor, with Jefferson standing by his side. They hug each other and then I catch Jefferson gently, ever so gently, wiping a tear away from Theo's eye. The moment is too much for me and I feel tears roll down my cheeks. Are these tears of happiness for Theo, or, tears of sadness for me?

I rush off quickly, hiding behind a rail, to pull myself together. Within moments, champagne bottles appear, corks are popping and Theo is kissing the models and thanking the crew. He spies me watching him and blows me a kiss. So much for me trying to make myself invisible! My tears start again and I make a quick exit; away from the emotional scene around me.

Chapter Nineteen

I hide outside, away from all the hustle and bustle of the aftermath of the fashion show. My body is still tingling, I feel a rush of adrenalin every time I think about Theo, Jefferson and the models and the wonderful, gorgeous clothes.

I suddenly have the urge to text Alexandre. I shouldn't really, as no doubt by now, he is back fully ensconced in the arms of his family, but what the heck: *Great to see you. The fashion show was brilliant. See you in the morning xx.*

I close my eyes for a moment, leaning back against the brick of the building. My mind is all over the place. Will I see Howard again after this event? Who knows? The question is of course, do I want to? And I think the answer is 'yes'. We seem to have a connection. A bond. Whether it's because we are in Cannes, away from normal everyday life, who knows? But one thing is for sure, if he suggests meeting up then I will say 'yes', so long as it doesn't clash with any meetings scheduled with Alexandre of course!

My thoughts are interrupted by my vibrating iphone. As if cyberspace has caught up with itself, I have a flurry of text messages, five in total. Yes indeed, I am still Miss Popular.

Text message one is from Howard: *Where are you my scarlet woman? I seek you here, I seek you there but still I find you nowhere! Hxxx.*

Text message two is from Amelia: *Hope the fashion show went well! Count me in for the next one. Edd will babysit! Love you xx.*

Text message three is from Tom: *Hi Martha! How did the show go? Speak soon. Tom.*

Text message four is another one from Howard: *I have a beautiful gift for a beautiful woman. Hxxx.*

Finally I come to text message five and yes, it's from my darling Alexandre: *Baby fantastic to see you. If my plans change for the morning I will let you know. Boo xx.*

I look at my iphone, as if it's trying to mesmerise me. Just hang on a minute. I re-read his text message again, very slowly. *If my plans change for the morning I will let you know.* What the fuck... ? I thought we had made firm plans. Alexandre cannot see me this evening, so we are meeting in the morning. Well you know what? He can well and truly piss off now. Who the fuck does he think he is? I'm angry, really angry.

"Hey what's up slapper? You've got a face like thunder." I look up and see Mel approaching.

"Nothing, other than a possible change of plan with Alexandre. We had made arrangements to meet up tomorrow morning, before I leave for the UK, but can you believe it, he's just sent me this text message," I say, passing her the handset, so that she can read it for herself.

"He's an arsehole and you know it! When will you learn? The only thing that snake loves is himself," replies Mel, a little angrily.

"He's an out and out bastard but I'm not going to let it upset me. There's no point. So tell me, is everyone happy with the fashion show? Isn't the collection just fabulous?" I say smiling, once again thinking of Theo.

"Listen to you referring to clothes as collections now. You see, it was only a matter of time before fashion went to your head, especially now that you are 'Accessories Queen.' Collection indeed!" smiles Mel, hugging me lovingly.

"So?" I ask.

"So what?" questions Mel.

"I just asked if everyone is happy with the fashion show," I repeat.

"Everyone is air kissing and being very darling this and darling that. Can you believe it? Boy, I will never fully understand fashion!" responds Mel, lighting up her second cigarette.

"Well that's brilliant! So all we have now is the awards ceremony and KAYSO's after show party," I giggle.

"The lads are already stripping the catwalk out and you will be pleased to hear that Pikey was on his best behaviour. He promised Dan faithfully that he would not be anywhere near the catwalk and he kept his promise. Which you might think was admirable. But no, Dan found him after the show, hidden away behind one of the packing cases backstage. He had a perfect view of the models dressing and more importantly undressing. He is such a prat!" laughs Mel.

Cigarettes finished, we both go back into the auditorium. The crew are hard at it. The catwalk is now in sections and the venue staff are re-arranging the seating area in preparation for the awards ceremony.

Once the formal part of the evening is over, the guests will be moved into another suite for a sit down dinner, followed by dancing with a live band. By all accounts the cover band booked for this evening is particularly good. They are called 'Blah' and perform widely in the South of France.

I head backstage and immediately spot Theo, Jefferson and Howard, hugging and congratulating each other. I don't interrupt, but simply look on, hoping that this moment will never end for Theo, but end it will until his next, bigger and better show, that is. Although, how he can possibly top this collection is quite beyond me.

Jefferson spots me. "Hey Martha, get yourself over here!" he shouts.

I walk towards the boys and give Theo and Jefferson the biggest hug. I quickly kiss Howard on the cheek. "Well, I am lost for words, which believe you me rarely happens, but that collection was something else. Absolutely perfect!" I smile, but immediately feel my eyes becoming watery.

"Cara mia, whatever is the matter?" asks Theo, hugging me.

I sniff, not particularly ladylike, but so what! "Nothing is wrong, honestly. It's just that I am so very proud of you. My baby brother, all grown up and designing the most stunning outfits. It's all too much for me," I say, pursing my lips together to try to suppress more tears.

I feel Howard's arm around me, as he passes me a handkerchief. "Thank you. I don't know why I am being so silly." I smile. "And as for you Theo, Pops would love this and guess what, Amelia and I will be attending your next showing together. So front row seats please." I continue.

"Consider those seats booked. And hey why not bring the family?" suggests Jefferson.

"Sounds like a plan!" chips in Howard.

Fucking hell! Can you imagine Pops here, in the midst of a fashion show with Theo and his partner? Never in a million years!

Jefferson and Theo then make their exit as they have to attend a press meeting. Howard and I are now alone.

"Are you sure you're OK?" asks Howard.

"Absolutely fine. You know what it's like. Little brother suddenly excels and wow it makes me feel amazing. I can't put it into words," I say quietly.

"If I were to invite you to join me at my table this evening for dinner, what would your answer be?" asks Howard.

"No, but thank you," I respond, without a moment's hesitation.

"No? You dare to say no to me? Me, Howard Johnson III." he replies, in a deep Russian voice (not quite sure why Russian, but there you go).

"That's right, you heard correctly. Thank you for the invite, but no." I respond.

"But why ever not?" he asks in his normal voice, slightly taken aback.

"If truth be told, your staff, especially Danny would certainly not appreciate me sitting at your table. I am crew. I am nothing to do with KAYSO and well, I just wouldn't be comfortable. Don't get me wrong, I love being with you, but that's just it, I love being with you and not your entire workforce." I respond. 'also Belinda and Ellie have organised a crew dinner this evening.' I add.

"I think I understand what you're saying. Basically, your crew are more important than me." he responds, with a hint of wit.

"That's right, you've got it in one. Well done" I laugh.

"No seriously, I understand where you're coming from. But promise me, you and the crew will join us for the party later? You have all been so brilliant that it wouldn't be quite right without you all there. And then of course, I had rather hoped that you and I might spend a little time together after the celebration. No pressure," replies Howard, throwing me a wink.

"How could I possibly say 'no' to a party and furthermore, how could I possibly say 'no' to further entertainment late into the night with a certain gentleman who quite possibly, has a gift for me. Any chance I could have the gift now?" I ask, cheekily.

"You'll get your gift later and I'll see you at the awards ceremony," responds Howard, kissing me lightly on my cheek and holding my gaze just a little too long, before walking away. I melt, immediately.

Suddenly, a voice rings out behind me. "Mart what was that then, another bet?" asks Mickey, sarcastically.

"Fuck! You scared me. I didn't see you. What are you on about, another bet? We were only talking and he was kind enough to invite the entire crew to their party this evening. The kiss on my cheek was merely a 'thank you' for all the shit I've had to put up with, in the guise of the wanker who goes by the name of Mendosa," I respond, with a smile.

"From where I was standing it looks as if he's got other ideas, just watch yourself, yeah?" replies Mickey.

"If I didn't know better I would think that right here and right now you are positively jealous. Mickey, have you got the hots for me?" I ask, giggling.

"Now why would I 'ave the hots for you? What you got going for you? Not a lot, other than your looks, your personality, you're a bloody good laugh and you're a right special bird. So no, I ain't got the hots for you! But don't be letting the likes of Howard bleeding Johnson the fucking third get the better of you neither and take advantage. Get what I'm saying?" responds Mickey, with genuine concern.

Mickey is standing very close to me. For a split second, I don't know whether he's going to kiss me, or, punch me, but he simply pulls me close and hugs me. "Mart, I wouldn't let anybody ever 'urt you, not even for a million quid, although come to think of it, it would be a close call," he laughs as he kisses me tenderly on the cheek.

"Jesus! If someone was offering a million, I'd say hurt me and then we could split the money!" I laugh.

"Sounds good to me girl! What's going on with that other idiot, what's 'is name, 'im Alexandre. You given 'im the boot yet?" asks Mickey.

"There's really nothing going on between us. I know he's hurt me in the past, but that was then and this is now." I respond, suddenly angered, as I recall the text message he sent through earlier.

"As long as you know what you're doing and I mean it Mart, don't go getting 'urt by no-one, you're too good for that and don't you forget it!" he says as he picks up a flight case and heads for the door.

I get out my iphone and re-read Alexandre's text and sure enough, it says exactly what I remember it saying: *If my plans change for the morning I will let you know*. How can he possibly think that it's OK to send me a message like that and not upset me? As I understand it, we had made plans. Plans to see one another before I return to the UK. Why am I so bloody gullible?

I really did think that things would be different this time, but clearly they are not.

I decide to text him back and before I know it, I've pressed the SEND button with the following message: *Good times come and go—a bit like you!*

I head out into the auditorium. The catwalk has gone completely and the lighting crew are way up high (on proper rigs of course, not flying around like batman, robin, or, spider man, you understand) adjusting the lighting for the party this evening.

"Martha, how are you? I must say Jefferson and your brother are quite the formidable pair. The outfits were absolutely superb," says Ingrid, rather awkwardly. I am just about to respond when she continues.

'I bumped into Mr Johnson a few moments ago and he has invited the entire crew to join his party this evening. Isn't that wonderful? I've already asked Belinda and Ellie to let everyone know. How splendid!' she gushes, a little too excited.

"Great!" I smile. "Ingrid, a quick question regarding the awards ceremony. Do we know yet who will be presenting this evening? Are we having Howard and Danny, or, is it the witty duo, Bruce and Marcus?"

"Danny Mendosa will be reading out the award categories, nominees and winner and Howard will be handing over the award itself. The recipient will of course, have their photograph taken with Mr Johnson. Also on stage will be Rochelle, who will be handing the awards over to Howard. All in all, I think we are in for a good evening. We are scheduled for a run through at six thirty pm. And before I forget, I know that this hasn't been the easiest of shows, but very well done for all your hard work and commitment." And with that, she picks up her papers and briefcase and leaves.

I've got an hour before rehearsals and I'm at a loss as what to do! Shall I go back to the hotel for a rest? No, bad move. If I fall asleep now, I'll never wake up. Shall I call Alexandre and have it out with him? No, bad move. We'll end up fighting and then I'll start crying. Shall I find Mel and tempt her away for a quick drink? Brilliant move. I look around and spot her deep in conversation with Ellie.

"How are you both?" I ask.

"Absolutely fine" answers Ellie. "I'm going to start putting the awards out, but Mel and I seem to have conflicting award winners, which is a worry, so I'm off to find Jerome to sort it out with him as he, by all accounts, has the definitive list. Once I've got the correct version, I'll let you have a copy, as we don't want Mendosa screwing up by reading out incorrect names do we?" laughs Ellie.

"Most definitely not!" I respond, sarcastically.

"Mel, what do you reckon, have we got time for a quick drink?" I ask, eagerly?

"You're a bloody alcoholic. What's up with you drinking in the middle of the afternoon, do you have no shame woman?" responds Mel.

"Zero shame and anyway it's gone five pm, so therefore, its official gin & tonic time, or, quite possibly, champagne time!" I laugh.

"Just give me five minutes to chat to Hugo and then we'll sneak off for a quickie, but it will have to be a quickie, as I need to get this fucked up running order sorted out," replies Mel.

Mel goes off to find Hugo. I look around, everyone is deep in activity. I feel like a spare part. My computer is already backstage. The monitors are already set up for prompt and there is honestly very little for me to do, other than have a sneaky drink!

I feel my iphone vibrating. I have a text message. It's Alexandre: *Baby, what's with the text? xx.*

Well would you believe it? He still doesn't get the fact that I am ever so slightly pissed with him. Unbelievable! I text back. *Let me know this evening if you can make the morning, as I can then make alternative plans.*

Yes, I am definitely pissed with him!

"OK slapper, let's head for that drink now. I've got twenty minutes before my next briefing. Plenty of time for a couple," says Mel, bounding towards me.

We go to a bar adjacent to the venue. The streets are busy, but we manage to find a table outside and promptly order two gin & tonics and two glasses of champagne, together with olives.

"Mel, hang fire just a moment. You accuse me of being the alcoholic, but I'm not the one ordering my drinks two at a time!" I laugh.

"I know, I know, but it saves time this way. See where I'm coming from?" asks Mel.

"Totally. So are you feeling a little sad that this wonderful show is coming to an end?" I ask.

"Sad. That is such a non-descript word. I am fucking gutted. I don't think I've had so much fun on a show in well, I don't know, bloody ages. It's just been a scream from start to finish and I still chuckle, whenever I think about our night in Monaco, that for me, was simply the best evening of my life and boy, I've had a few!" replies Mel.

"It was something else, wasn't it? But the best bit of course was the journey back to Cannes in the back of that police van and then you falling out. Jesus I don't think I've laughed so much, ever. It could only happen to you." I laugh.

Mel is looking at me curiously. "Slapper, are you going to tell me what's wrong? I don't know what it is, but I know something ain't right, so spill the beans."

"Whatever are you going on about? There is absolutely nothing wrong with me. Aside from needing a week in bed to get over exhaustion. I can't even remember the last time I had a proper nights sleep, in fact, come to think of it, I don't think we've really slept since the first night we arrived here. Sweet Jesus! I'm getting too old for this shit." I laugh.

"OK, so you're not going to spill the beans. Fine by me. I'm always here when you need me. Be it in Cannes or the UK. Understand?" she says.

Right on cue our drinks arrive. We clink glasses and down our champagne in one. This sweet nectar is simply perfect.

"I suppose there is something playing on my mind..." "It's... well... it's just that I don't know how to play it with Howard after tonight. I mean, do we simply say our goodbyes and leave it at that, or, should I push for more?" I ask.

"What do you mean, push for more? Are you planning on moving in with him now?" asks Mel, in disbelief?

"No, of course not stupid! It's just that I do like him and I think he is rather keen on me. He's been so lovely and well I, oh I don't know, I suppose I just don't want to say goodbye. There, I've said it." I say.

"So, that's the only reason you're feeling sad then, is it?" she enquires, spilling her drink over the table in order to get to the olives!

"Yes, why, what else would make me sad?" I ask.

"Could it have something to do with that fucking idiot Alexandre? The one who breaks your heart every time you see him? The one that uses and abuses? The one who has a wife and children and is completely spineless and selfish?" asks Mel, sternly.

"Nothing at all," I quip.

"Yeah right. Anyway drink up and let's get back to the venue. After all we have rehearsals to get to," says Mel.

We settle the bill. Can you believe forty eight Euros for four drinks? Bloody hell! I've spent a fortune on this event and I still haven't gotten round to splitting the bill from Stars and Bars; which if my memory serves me correctly, was fast approaching one thousand Euros!

Arriving back in the auditorium, we join some of the others who are standing by the control desk front of house.

"Hugo, you have that look of concern. What's up?" asks Mel.

"We still haven't managed to finalise the winners! Our list is slightly different to Rochelle's, which in turn, differs to the names Jerome has.

Mary-Jo is waiting for an email from HQ, to confirm exactly who tonight's winners are," responds Hugo.

Right on cue, Mary-Jo walks into the auditorium. "At last! Here in my sticky hand is the correct list of winners. I am going to give this to Belinda, who will then circulate it to you all. This is the definitive order," She explains.

Belinda quickly rushes off to photocopy the all important piece of paper. Once back, she distributes it. I nip backstage with Jerome. I amend the names, as does Jerome. We quickly run through the detail, just to make sure that they are both the same, which thankfully they are.

Rehearsals are due to commence in approximately ten minutes. Rochelle has already positioned herself on stage. Dickbrain Mendosa is having his lapel mic positioned, but no sign of Howard. Perhaps he's not going to do rehearsals, not that he really needs them, after all, just how difficult is it, to hand over an award and smile? Not difficult at all.

All crew are on cans and awaiting instruction from Mel.

Mel: OK guys and gals. Shall we take this from the top? Jerome are you happy with the running order of your slides? Are you up to speed with Martha?

Jerome: All checked boss.

Mel: Dan, no Freudian slip ups please!

Dan: As if. Once was unlucky. Twice would be foolish.

Mel: Mickey, you set?

Mickey: Yep. I am cued up with 'The birdie song'

Mel: You better fucking hadn't be Mickey! I'll have your balls attached to your sound desk if you are!

Mickey: Keep yer 'air on Mel. I'm cued up with the right track... well I think it is...

Mel: Good job I trust you Mr Prowse! Right everybody here we go. Standby please LX, Sound, VT...

The lighting, sound and VT boys all acknowledge that they are standing by and ready to start the show.

Mel: LX, Sound, VT go please...

The lights are dimmed and on the big screen is video footage of the weeks' events. The music is once again loud and vibrant and I feel goose bumps running down my spine simply watching the video. The video crew have done a fantastic job of putting all the footage together.

As the video comes to an end, Dickbrain Mendosa starts his blurb. Thank fuck, he's sticking to his script, for a change!

The rehearsal runs without a hitch. Dickbrain is pleased, as is Ingrid. Now, we just need to make sure that the show is a success too. Well, we'll soon see. Only forty-five minutes until we go live.

Chapter Twenty

Dan lines up the opening montage again. No mistakes this time round. Can you imagine how porn would go down a second time? No, I quite agree with you. It definitely wouldn't go down well!

"Martha, hey Martha, are you OK?" asks Dan, shaking me by the arm.

"Oh Dan, I'm sorry. I was miles way. Just thinking about getting back to the UK and normal life. I find it so hard to re-adjust to everyday life, after being away for more than a few days. It takes a long time to get used to mundane chores and functions, such as making your own bed and feeding yourself. Conference blues you know. Anyway what's your next job when you get back to Blighty?" I ask.

"I've got a couple of days at home with the missus and then I'm off to Edinburgh for the Silhouette conference. Are you working on that one?" asks Dan.

"I was asked but said I wasn't available because it was so soon after this job and the crew are all youngsters. I was thinking I could have a few days at home. Catch up with family stuff. Had I known you were on it, I would have said yes. But well, too late now," I respond.

My iphone vibrates and I have a text from Mel which simply reads: *Fag Slag?*

I head off into the Auditorium and find Mel and we pop outside. The night air is still wonderfully warm with a slight breeze. "I've just received a text from Hans. He wants to know if I'm up for naughty sex this evening. Well you know me, I'm partial to most things in life, so I text back as affirmative. Apparently, he has been out to buy an assortment of toys. Now, I'm not quite sure how to take this. Is it because I, as in me only, minus any toys, is not enough for him, or, do you reckon or is it because I'm so good he wants to have more fun?" laughs Mel.

"Definitely the latter. Bloody hell! It seems that he can't get enough of you. It wouldn't surprise me if he didn't come over the UK to pay you a visit from time to time. Would you let him?" I ask Mel.

"You know what? What happens on tour, stays on tour. I don't know if having him visit me would be the same if you know what I mean. A bit like if Howard came to the UK to visit you. Would it be the same as your time in Cannes? I don't know that it would and if it wasn't, would it dilute your fabulous memories of this shows?" responds Mel, philosophically.

"I get where you're coming from, but I must admit if Howard was to pay me a visit, I wouldn't turn him away. After all, let's face it, I don't have a string of men waiting for me when I return home to the UK do I?" I giggle.

"Maybe not, but then perhaps you shouldn't be so fucking fussy!" laughs Mel.

"Come on. Let's get back inside and get this show on the road," says Mel, beaming.

With only fifteen minutes to go, until the start of the awards ceremony, the auditorium is starting to fill up, with KAYSO employees dressed in their finery. The ladies have really gone to town; some of the dresses are absolutely gorgeous, but then in fairness there are a few dresses that leave a lot (and when I say a lot, I really do mean a lot) to be desired.

Backstage Rochelle has appeared. "Holy Malony! Have you seen some of those dresses in the audience? How do they get away with it?" she giggles. I think she may have had a drink, or, two, to steady her nerves!

"You look absolutely amazing, your dress is beautiful," I say, with all honesty. She is wearing the most amazing long, red halter neck evening dress. It is beaded in diamante detail around the hem, so simple and so very elegant.

"It took an age to find, but you know what? The moment it was on, I knew it was the one," She says, almost preening herself.

"Is everything OK back here? Jeez, I'm starting to get jittery. What if I drop one of those damned awards, no laughing OK" smiles Rochelle.

"No need for jitters. Simply go out there and be yourself," adds Hugo.

There are eleven awards to be handed out this evening, which is a fair few. We reckon the ceremony will run for approximately one hour and then of course its party time.

Mel is on cans:

Mel: Dan, are we watching any particular genre of film this evening, or, can we run with the correct opening montage please?

Dan: Mel, we can watch whatever you want to, but for now we're running with KAYSO's opening awards montage

Mel: Thank you. That is good to hear

Mel: We will go live in three minutes. Belinda and Ellie are just getting the stragglers in.

We wait in anticipation backstage. I notice my phone vibrating and make a grab for it before Hugo notices. It's a text from Alexandre: *See you in the morning baby x.*

Oh my God, he loves me, he really loves me. Yippedy doo-dah. Why else would he come all the way to Cannes from Monaco, if he didn't? Suddenly, I am happy again. Very happy.

Mel is on cans again:

Mel: Mobiles switched off please, I'm picking up interference. And you know how I don't like interference

Oops that must be me then! I switch my phone off quickly.

Dan leans in close to me. "What's with the smile, you won the lottery or what?" he asks.

"Nothing, some plans I have been working on, have just been finalised, so I'm happy," I smile.

"What time's your flight out of here tomorrow?" he continues.

"I think I'm on the three thirty. Coach is picking us up at one o'clock for the airport transfer. Why do you ask?" I respond.

"I know that we are supposed to be on site from ten, with the de-rig tomorrow morning, but I was thinking we could all go for breakfast, you know just the old crowd. It's kinda sad that the shows over," continues Dan, forlornly.

"Nice thought, but come on let's face it, if it's the difference between breakfast and a lie in, I'm opting for the lie in. After all, I see you too often as it is!" I respond, with a wink.

It would have been nice for us all to meet up, but I already have prior arrangements. Arrangements in the guise of Alexandre paying me a visit. My heart suddenly beats faster. I am not sure that it is beating faster for the right reason, namely that the love of my life is paying a visit or it's beating faster because I've just remembered that I have a 'date', a 'date' with Howard this evening after their party. A 'date' that might just lead to bedroom activities. Oh sweet Jesus! Am I a slut? No. Yes. No. Fuck, I don't know, but I don't want to sleep with Howard. Well I do, but it's wrong to then sleep with Alexandre a few hours later. Oh God, please, please help me.

I catch Hugo looking at me. "What's the matter?" I ask.

"We are about to go live. Are you ready?" he replies, rather sternly.

"Sorry, yes I'm ready," Now my heart is really beating. I don't want to fuck up prompt for Dickbrain Mendosa this evening, as I am sure he'll have no hesitation in coming down on me, like a ton of bricks once again, if I do.

Mel: OK everybody here we go. Standby please lights, sound, VT

Once again, we hold our breath, waiting for Mel's cue to start the show.

Mel: Lights, sound and VT—go please

The screen comes alive with images of happy smiling KAYSO employees from America, Australasia and Europe. The beat of the music is loud and the audience are totally hushed.

I am now totally focused and as soon as the video comes to an end, we go live with prompt and graphics. Dickbrain Mendosa is reading the words on the glass and so far, has not ad-libbed once. I will not give him any excuse to chastise me, either during, or, after this awards ceremony. I am a professional and will act like a professional, at all times.

We come to the first award for Most Innovative Design Concept. The winner is from Ireland and I can hear Marcus, even though he is surrounded by so many people, whooping like a madman that one of his team is picking up this award. The winner is Marianne O'Leary. She duly comes to the stage, takes her trophy, has her photograph taken with gorgeous Howard and then walks off stage again. Simple.

Awards two and three run without a hitch. It's all pretty straight forward and, after all, there's very little margin for error. Thank the Lord. Chances are, we might still all have jobs at the end of this event!

Award four is for highest grossing design concept. The award winner according to my prompt presentation is Shane Symonds from Australia.

The audience start to applaud and whistle, as Shane takes to the stage. I glance across to Jerome's screen, of course expecting to see the words 'WINNER—SHANE SYMONDS, but I don't. I see the words: WINNER—LAURA STEVENSON. I look up at the main presentation screen and sure enough, I can see the name, LAURA STEVENSON.

Martha: Fuck! Mel the names don't match. We've just called Shane Symonds and Laura Stevenson's name has appeared.

Mel: Jerome—are you on the correct slide. Can you see Shane Symond's name?

Ingrid: Please not again.

Mel: Jerome switch to KAYSO holding slide.

Mel: Martha type Mendosa a message that we have a technical hitch.

I quickly type a message to Mendosa: Technical hitch, awards ceremony will be resumed very shortly.

Mel: Jerome, Martha what the fuck is happening. Are you two out of sync?

Mel: Hugo—take a look for me please?

I hear Dickbrain Mendosa speak out to the audience and fear the worse. "Well Ladies and Gentlemen it would appear that we have a slight technical hitch. Everything seems to be OK my end, so I suspect it can only have been caused by the production company. Hey Teleprompter, you want to let me know what's going on perhaps?" he calls out.

I type him another note: Technical hitch with slides. We will be live again shortly.

Hugo: Martha are you sure you have loaded the correct version?

Martha: Yes, version two—final awards ceremony presentation.

Hugo: Jerome, why are the names not matching up. Which version are you running?

Jerome: Oh shit! I've loaded version one. I should have loaded version two. Let me quickly load version two. I'm sorry everyone.

Hugo: Mel, I think we've sorted the problem. Jerome, does award four read Shane Symonds?

Jerome: Yes, I've got Shane Symonds on award four.

Mel: Thank fuck. Can we get going again now please.

I quickly type a message to Dickbrain Mendosa: Presentation reloaded, good to go.

On the main screen appears the name Shane Symonds, who is indeed, the official winner of this award. Fuck! At this rate none of us will have jobs come tomorrow.

By the grace of God, we manage to get to the end of the ceremony without further error. Everybody is on tender hooks. Ingrid has gone into total melt down and Jerome is displaying fear, fear for his life, once Ingrid and Mel, come to think of it, catch up with him.

As shows go, this one has been eventful to say the least!

The awards ceremony has come to an end and the KAYSO delegates are moving into another suite for dinner.

Ingrid: Jerome, I would like to see you backstage NOW. Once again Mel and Hugo, please meet me there.

Mel: On my way.

Ingrid: All other crew please move into the auditorium.

Fucking hell! Sounds serious! Ingrid has had a royal week of fuck ups, which in fairness don't ordinarily occur. I mean, what's the likelihood of porn being shown instead of a corporate video? Very low. One of our main clients breaking a chair and collapsing on stage? Very low (unless of course he's a seriously obese and is diabolical to the crew). And what's the likelihood of showing the wrong name at an awards ceremony? Well in this case, very high, because it happened! Just like everything else happened.

The band for the party has arrived and are setting up their gear on stage. The lighting is being checked and I am busy dismantling the prompt screens and cabling, as these are no longer required.

Mickey is giving me a hand front of stage. "Fuck! You know what Mart, I don't think we could 'ave fucked up more if we tried on this show," laughs Mickey.

"What's the likelihood of us all working for KAYSO again? Would you risk your life's savings on the outcome being a positive one?" I ask.

"It will be a fucking miracle if we ever work again! Never mind KAYSO!" replies Mickey.

There are raised voices backstage. We both try to ignore them, but secretly we are both listening intently.

Moments later, Ingrid scurries into the auditorium, mumbling away to herself 'I just can't take this anymore. No more. Enough!' And with that she is gone. Gone where, I am not quite sure. I spot Ellie and Belinda and motion them over. "Girls, I think it might be a good idea if you follow Ingrid, just to make sure she's OK. Don't give her any added hassle or shit, just make sure she's OK." I suggest.

"Sure thing. We'll see you all, over at the hotel shortly. Dinner is booked from eight thirty pm. We are eating in the Terrace Restaurant. Can you please let everyone know?" responds Ellie.

There is definitely an air of unhappiness, which of course could be because the show is over and we will be leaving Cannes tomorrow. Or, perhaps the unhappiness stems from the fuck ups that have occurred and have left the crew, feeling a little on edge.

I find Mel and head back to the hotel with her. Thankfully, she is relaxed and certainly doesn't seem upset by the minor (well major) mishap this evening and in her words, 'shit happens.' By all accounts, Ingrid has gone into melt down and is in dire need of a very large vodka, minus tonic, ice and lemon—she must be in a real state!

I arrange to meet Mel in the bar in twenty minutes. I hurry to my room, after all, I only have twenty minutes to make myself look respectable. Entering my bedroom, I am transfixed at the sight before me. Two dozen, long stemmed, blood red roses have been delivered. The fragrant smell is overwhelmingly beautiful and I don't know whether to laugh, or, cry. Who on earth has sent these?

I spot a calling card and with trembling fingers, I am not quite sure why I'm trembling at this point, but I am, I open the envelope. The words simply read, 'thank you for a perfect time'.

I re-read the words several times, but I am still none the wiser as to who has sent them. Was it Alexandre or Howard? I call the concierge to determine whether he can help me in my plight, but alas, the flowers were not ordered through the hotel and therefore he cannot assist.

Well, now what do I do? I think the best thing would be to simply say nothing. Say nothing, until either Alexandre or Howard (surely it's one of those two who sent them?) asks about the roses because then I'll know and won't thank the wrong lover...

I have an ultra quick shower, moisturise with Prada and then apply my make-up. A squirt of D&G and a ruffle of my hair and I am practically ready, aside from being dressed of course! Now what to wear? Should I go rock chick, as I rather like that look, but bearing in mind, so many of the women are dressed in cocktail dresses and full length gowns, it's probably not appropriate. Shall I wear my gorgeous black jumpsuit? No, that's already had an outing and besides which, it hasn't been laundered since our journey in the back of a police van. Eventually, I opt for a black halter neck cocktail dress that shimmers with tiny crystals. I put on a pair of black strappy sandals, with five inches high, huge mistake, but I won't be told and accessorize with a silver and crystal cuff and diamond earrings. I actually look quite glam, even though I do say so myself.

After another coat of lip gloss, I find my clutch bag; fill it with iphone, cash, credit card, lip gloss, tissues and cigarettes. It's bulging and looks distorted now, but needs must—I can't leave anything out!

I head out of the door at the same time as Mel, who I must say, is looking fabulous. "Wow wee, check you out. You look amazing. Where on God's earth did you find such a fantastic dress? That colour is perfect!" I say. Mel is wearing an emerald green calf length dress with sweetheart neckline, which is totally flattering.

"Every once in a while, one needs to make an effort and tonight is the night for effort." she smiles. "Anyway, you seem to be pulling out all the stops this evening, you look a million dollars. Howard is a very lucky man!" says Mel, hugging me.

"Watch the hair though it could flop at any time! Now let's get down in the bar and start this party off!" I respond, taking Mel's arm, leading her to the lifts. Can't take the stairs, these shoes are way too high!

Arriving in the bar, most of the boys are already downing their drinks. Tonight, is undoubtedly going to be a boozy affair. Mickey and Dan are deep in conversation with Hugo and Ingrid and I have to say that Ingrid is looking surprisingly relaxed. Although relaxed, could be translated as drunk. She is definitely swaying a little.

Tonight is for merriment. All the tiny mishaps, (aka major fuck ups) which have occurred, over the past forty eight hours, will be forgotten, well certainly forgotten by Ingrid, because I don't think she'll be able to remember her name at this rate, with the amount of vodka she is consuming.

Champagne arrives and Mel and I toast each other. I look across at Mickey, who I must say is looking so smart this evening. Our eyes lock for a moment and he blows me a kiss. Who knows what would have been if we had continued our short lived relationship? But, what would I rather have; a dear, trusted friend or a no-good lover? Yep, friend definitely wins!

After a few drinks in the bar, we head into dinner. A table has been laid for the entire crew and we jostle for places, next to our favoured friends. To one side, I have Mel and to the other, I have Mickey. Dan is sitting next to Mickey and Hugo is sitting next to Mel. Ingrid is giggling like a child, if she makes it through dinner, it will be a miracle.

There is lots of wine on the table, together with jugs of cocktails—life is perfect. For the next ninety minutes we eat, we drink, we joke, we laugh, a couple cry and one passes out. No guessing as to who passes out. That's right, Ingrid has had one too many vodkas and before Hugo can make a grab for her, her head flops down into her buttered sole, served on a bed of sautéed vegetables and crab mousse. Not a pretty sight. Hugo is a gentleman and escorts (well drags) Ingrid to her room with the help of Mickey and Dan.

When the boys return, we toast Ingrid and continue with the feeding of our faces, followed by the downing of cocktails and wine.

Finally, dessert arrives. Now I say finally, not because I am a dessert fiend, in fact, I don't particularly like eating dessert, although I love making them, but its arrival simply means that shortly, we will be back over at the Palais du Roscoff for the party and of course, at the party we have the gorgeous Howard Johnson III, who I am sure will be eagerly awaiting my arrival.

I lose myself in thoughts of Howard. Does he secretly want to see me after Cannes? I suspect so, especially as he has a gift for me. And, no doubt this gift will be special. Howard is not the type of man to simply give cheap, ineffective gifts, I'm sure.

"Hey Mart! You with us girl?" nudges Mickey.

"Sorry, I drifted off," I respond, making a grab for my glass, as we all toast the success (well, sort of success) of the KAYSO Cannes show. The clinking of glasses carries on for several seconds, with spillages all over the table. The majority of the crew are pretty drunk, it's fair to say, as we all get up from our table and walk, or, rather, stagger, towards the hotel foyer.

I feel my phone vibrating. I have a text message. It's from Alexandre and simply reads: *Love you xx*.

Oh my God! He loves me! It says so. And I love him, but then why is it that I am eager to see Howard? Is it the thrill of getting a man like Howard, after all, we are leagues apart. Or, is it, that deep down, I know Alexandre will never truly be mine and therefore I am searching for someone else? Oh fuck knows! And in fairness, who the fuck cares? I am on the verge of being too drunk to worry about it at this moment in time.

I quickly respond: *Love you too. See you in a few hours xxxx.*

My iphone beeps and I notice that my battery is running low. Shit! I must remember to put it on charge. Life without a mobile, is like life without air!

And with that, the iphone is back in my clutch bag and we head off, in convoy, to the Palais du Roscoff.

Chapter Twenty-One

The party is in full swing. The band, Blah, are loud and the KAYSO employees are loving it, the dance floor is rocking. The bar is rammed, but thankfully the venue has set up cocktail and champagne points, from where you can simply grab a drink without having to queue. That's the route for us!

We all congregate at a drinks point and grab a couple of glasses each. The first one, we knock back in one, after yet another toast and the other, is held on to tightly, as we start to dance around, to the sounds of the band, which we can clearly hear, from within the foyer.

Some of the crew have wandered off towards the dance floor. Hugo has met up with Eleanor and is in deep conversation, seated on one of the foyer sofas. Ellie is dancing with Dan and Mel, has been swept onto the dance floor by Hans. Belinda is dancing with Mickey and then there's me. Hell, I'm feeling like a spare part, but hopefully not for long. I am sure that Howard will spot me soon enough.

I rummage through my clutch bag to check whether Alexandre has sent me any further messages and whilst doing so, I sense the presence of someone standing in front of me. Ah, could this be Howard? I look up and rather disappointingly it's not Howard. No, it's definitely not Howard. It's Danny Dickbrain Mendosa.

I look down on him, as I stand approximately two inches taller in these killer heels. He just stands there and looks at me and says nothing. "What?" I eventually ask.

"Nothing, I just wanted to come over and say it hasn't been easy and we didn't really hit it off and yeah, maybe I have been a little heavy on you, so I just wanted to say no hard feelings," says Danny, with a little genuine feeling.

Fucking hell! I wasn't expecting that, far from it! And in fairness, I don't really know how to respond. After all, the guy is still fundamentally, a prick. No doubt about it. So, should I accept his apology? I think it over for a moment or two, smile and then respond. "Fuck off!"

I turn on my heels and head for the dance floor, in the hope that I might spot Howard, or, possibly Theo and Jefferson. My heart is beating fast, as I mull over my response. What did he expect? Was I really going to let him off and think that everything is OK again? I don't think so. Nice that he apologised and yes, in fairness, I should have accepted his apology, so perhaps I was a little out of order, but let's not forget the simple fact that he has made my life hell for the past week. Hell, to the point of despair. Hell, to the point of questioning my own ability in what I do and what I've done for several years. No, my response was definitely justified. And the best way to describe him is still WANKER!

I spot Rochelle on the dance floor and she motions for me, to join her. I quickly down my drink and head over, only to see that she is dancing with Howard. My Howard. Howard Johnson III. How dare she? Bloody bitch!

She embraces me and Howard kisses me on the cheek, giving my arm a little squeeze, at the same time. Ha, he's definitely mine and not hers!

We dance to a couple of songs and then Rochelle wanders off, in need of a drink. Howard and I, remain on the dance floor. Thankfully, he knows how to move. After all, let's face it girls, there is nothing worse than a man who can't dance, is there?

It's the sheer embarrassment of dancing with someone who truly believes themselves to be a good mover, when quite clearly, they are not. I recall a chap I met who was good looking, single, funny and he had a great job—he was a pilot. Good boyfriend material, or so I thought!

On our third date we went to a salsa club in Oxford. The evening had started off well. We had dinner in one of my favourite restaurants. We drank champagne and then he gave me a present. The excitement of opening the present was short lived. Of course, I wasn't expecting an engagement ring, well maybe I was, but well he had given me a brooch. Nice, you might think, but it was a brooch made up of enamel roses. Something that perhaps that my grandmother might have worn, many moons ago. But hey let's get back to the story. So yes, we had dinner, we had champagne, I had a gift; so we decide to go salsa dancing. A night is not complete without the involvement of a few dance moves now, is it?

The club is within walking distance. I am drunk by this point, but hey I can dance sober, or, drunk. As soon as we walk into the club, I make for the dance floor and start dancing to the vibrant, sexy music. I turn and I twist and then I spot 'pilot man' strutting his stuff. Suddenly, I am gripped by horror. He can no more dance salsa, than I can fit into a size six pair of skinny jeans. Oh my God! The embarrassment. Not my embarrassment, but the embarrassment I suddenly felt for him. I suppose I should have realised when he said "Lets go and throw some shapes on the dance floor!" Little did I realise he meant shapes like somebody who is being electrocuted. After that little exhibition, our romance was to be short lived.

After another dance, Howard and I grab more champagne. "Boy that was brilliant. What a fantastic party. You must be in seventh heaven!" I shout, after all, the music is loud.

"This is a fantastic party and we've had a great event. You and the Angel crew have been perfect. I especially enjoyed the porn show; that will definitely remain a highlight," he smiles.

I have an overwhelming desire to kiss him, but in view of so many people around, that would be totally inappropriate. I lean in close. "Might I suggest I have a brief meeting with you, in the Fleur suite please?" I ask.

"Yes of course. Remind me, is that the crew catering suite on the first floor?" he asks.

"Indeed. I'll meet you there in five," I say, as I sway off towards the Ladies.

On route to the powder room, I bump into Jefferson, who is already looking worse for wear. "Oh Mr Jefferson, have you had a little too much of that good old liquor?" I ask.

"Sure thing. I just never know when to say 'no'," he laughs, hugging me tightly.

"Theo told me to wait here. He's taking a pee and then I think we are heading back to the hotel. I've blown it for the night and anyway I'm exhausted," he continues.

Theo appears and gives me a hug. "Cara mia, you see what I have to put up with? He never knows when to stop," laughs Theo.

"But just how boring would your lives be without alcohol?" I ask.

"You're right. Come here and give me a goodnight kiss, so that I can get him to bed," says Theo.

"When are you leaving for the UK? Is it tomorrow?"

"Yes, I've got an afternoon flight. What about you two, where are you off to next?" I ask, with a tad of green eye!

"The plan is to go to Monaco for a few days and then back to the States, but I will be in the UK in a couple of weeks, so I will see you and the rest of the clan then. Organise a party, we need to have fun whilst I am in England," continues Theo.

"Consider it done. I'll speak to you in the morning. Sweet dreams." I say, as I head off to the cloakroom.

Whilst in the cloakroom, I bump into Mel, who is sweating profusely. "Fucking hell girl, what happened to you?" I ask.

"I have been thrown around that dance floor like a rag doll. Hans' has the stamina of an ox—he is out of this world. Fuck! I'm exhausted," she pants. I try fanning her with my clutch bag, in the hope that I can help cool her down. But perhaps I'm a little more drunk than I think I am, as I manage to whack her nose rather than create an airflow.

"What the fuck are you trying to do? It's not bad enough that I am on the verge of collapse, but then you hit me with your bag. Are you nuts girl, fuck off and leave me alone?" responds Mel, pushing me away.

"Nuts? Me? Absolutely not. Drunk? I think so. So everything is going well with Hans then?" I ask.

"Totally. In fact he has suggested that we meet up next month. Just for a long weekend," says Mel, with a huge smile.

"I sense you're smitten with this man. Am I right or am I right?" I ask.

"You're right. He's just... oh I don't know... he's just so easy. He doesn't question my weight and he likes me for who I am. And you know what? He's just full of life. God! I've missed that in a man," continues Mel.

"So, when you said and I quote: 'what happens on tour stays on tour,' you were fibbing. You are planning to continue this long distance love affair. Well, you know what Mel? Life is for living and we are only here once," I say, hugging her and kissing her moist cheek.

"You're right. And he's good for me and as long as it lasts, it lasts. Come on, let's get back to the party!" she replies.

"In a minute. I need to pee and then I'm meeting Howard." I giggle.

"What, you leaving the party already?" asks Mel, anxiously.

"No, no, no, I'm meeting Mr Howard Johnson III for a secret snog. But don't tell anyone, because it's a secret." I say raising my finger to my lips.

"You little slapper. Enjoy and I'll see you later." And with that, she walks out of the Ladies.

I feel total excitement. I think I definitely like him more than I am admitting to myself. Arriving at the Fleur Suite, I open the door, slowly. He has his back to me and is talking on his mobile. I listen for a few moments. I know it's rude but hey, he is potential boyfriend material, so it's allowed. But now I'm wishing I hadn't listened to his conversation because I am hearing 'yes I've missed you too,' and 'of course I know it's difficult when I'm not there with you' and 'yes, I love you too'. Oh my God! He has another woman! Another fucking woman! But he obviously thinks its OK to shag me whilst in Cannes. Well, God damn him! And there's me worrying about my conflict of interest, namely Alexandre. Fuck! He is a dark horse and quite clearly has no intention of seeing me again.

He still has his back to the door and so I quietly close it. What do I do now? Walk away and forget him? Have it out with him? Text him to tell him it's over? I think for a moment or two and then decide, that I am going to have it out with him. Yep, that's right. If he thinks he can screw me behind his girlfriend's back, then he is sorely mistaken.

A deep intake of breath and I walk back into the room. He turns around as he ends the call. "Hey you startled me," he smiles. He'll be smiling on the other side of his fucking face, when I've finished with him.

"So, are you looking forward to going back to the States?" I ask in a direct tone.

"Yes and no. Yes in the sense that there are a lot of interesting things happening within KAYSO and no, because I've had the most amazing time with you," he says, walking towards me.

Shit! He thinks he can simply walk over and kiss me now and everything will be OK. Well you know what? It's not OK. It's far from OK. He's a fraud.

"Are you OK? You seem a little distant. Everything OK?" he asks.

"Everything is fine thank you," I respond, curtly.

He is standing directly in front of me, but I sense that he doesn't know what to do with me. My mood has changed. He takes a step back.

"I was just on the phone to the States," he continues.

"Oh were you? To anyone in particular?" I ask.

"Yeah, one of the loves of my life," he says, with a wink. Can you believe that? He gives me a wink when he tells me that there is someone else in his life. Fuck! He is definitely another bastard. Why, oh why, do I pick them? Well, actually they pick me!

"Tell me more..." I encourage, with anger rising from the pit of my stomach.

"Yeah, she's beautiful, kind and has always been there for me, through thick and thin. In fact, I think she would love you. You should come out and meet her," he continues.

I stand there with my mouth agog. He is inviting me to visit his girlfriend! Is he positively stupid? I look at him in utter bewilderment and eventually say "So, this love of your life, into a threesome is she?" I ask, as coldly as my quivering voice will allow me to.

"Threesome? Are you crazy? I'm talking about my dear old mom," he responds. "Oh my God! Martha, did you think I was talking about another woman? A girlfriend? Do you think I would be such a bastard as to do that to you? No way!" he says, with a hint of annoyance in his voice.

The relief is overwhelming. But how the fuck could I have got it so wrong? Serves me right for listening in on his phone call! I don't know whether to laugh or cry. But suddenly I start to giggle. "So, I think it's quite sensible that perhaps we don't engage in a threesome with your mother. It would definitely be inappropriate."

He holds me close and kisses me passionately. I can feel him becoming aroused. The chemistry between us is overwhelming. I want to fuck him right here, right now, but of course I won't. Can you imagine the implications of someone walking in? Not good.

For the next fifteen minutes we kiss, we touch, we laugh and above all, we desire.

Eventually, we pull away from one another. "So, your place or mine?" he asks.

"Oh definitely yours. After all, I think they stock Krug in your room. I've only got Moet in mine. But I don't think you should leave the party just yet. Your employees want to enjoy themselves, with you, for a little bit longer. So why don't we go and rock this party some more?" I suggest, giving him one last kiss.

"You're right. Let's go party and then I'll rock your world later," smiles Howard, escorting me out of the suite.

The party is definitely in full swing. The band are amazing. Everyone is dancing, either on the dance floor, or, in the foyer. No one, but no one, is standing still. I think practically everyone is drunk too. The champagne and cocktails have flowed all night.

I look over to the stage and spot Mel, who is with Mickey, Dan and Belinda. I head over to them. "Hey guys, how's it going?" I ask.

"Where you been? I been looking for you everywhere!" asks Mickey.

"I've been dancing with Rochelle, boy she can move!" I say, winking at Mel.

"Hey Belinda, where's Ellie and young Hugo? Where have they disappeared to?" I ask. Normally Belinda and Ellie are joined at the hip.

"Well, you're never going to believe this. But Ingrid has made an appearance. I think forty winks and a bout of sickness rendered her well again, so she turned up and now she's dancing with Ellie. Look over there!" Belinda turns me round, so that I am facing the dance floor and sure enough, I spot Ellie, dancing awkwardly with Ingrid, who has definitely got her second wind!

"Wonders will never cease" I laugh. Come on, let's all go and join them. And Hugo, where's he?" I ask.

"He had business to attend to, didn't he? In the guise of that beautiful bird Eleanor," responds Dan.

"Count me out slapper. The witching hour is fast approaching, so I, for one, am going to continue this party back at the hotel with my beau, so if you'll excuse me..." says Mel, hugging us all and with that, she staggers off for her night of fun with Hans.

"Come on then, let's get on that dance floor and show 'em 'ow it's done!" shouts out Mickey.

Within moments we are all on the dance floor, encircling Ingrid who is (a) still drunk, but more importantly (b) loving every minute of this party. We continue dancing for a good twenty minutes. People join us and then disappear again, but without doubt, Ingrid is the centre of attention. Her moves are quite unbelievable, but we are in no position to try to calm her down, after all, she's paying us to be here!

I see Howard and motion for him to come over, which he does, reluctantly. After all, he surely knows that I am going to encourage him to dance with Ingrid now. We clap and we whoop and Ingrid is now gyrating behind Howard. Thankfully, he laughs it off

The time is fast approaching one am and although the party is still in full flow, I've had enough. I am drunk, very drunk, as are the rest of the crew, so we decide to head back to the hotel. Both Ellie and Belinda are now in deep conversation with a couple of guys from KAYSO's French office and so they decide to stay on.

Howard is speaking to Mary-Jo, but I head over all the same, to thank them for a wonderful party.

"Sorry to interrupt, but I just wanted to thank you both for a wonderful party. I think we're all heading back now, before we become too unruly," I smile.

"Martha, it's been an absolute pleasure working with you and the rest of the crew. Do thank them for me and I am sure we'll be working together again, very soon. You take care now," replies Mary-Jo, giving me a big hug and kiss on the cheek.

"Well, just what can I say? Thanks for all your hard work," says Howard, bending down to kiss my cheek. Close by my ear, he whispers "I'll text you when I'm back."

The short distance between the Palais du Roscoff and the Maritime hotel seems to take an age to walk, but eventually, we arrive. "I think we should have one last drink, before we retire for the evening," I suggest.

"Sounds like a plan to me Martha," replies Ingrid, leading the way to the bar.

We order champagne and once again, toast each other. Ingrid at this point, is emotional. Her bottom lip is quivering, but nothing is going to stop her saying her piece. "I know I'm not the easiest person to work with, but that's because I want perfection, but honestly, I really do enjoy working with you all. Thank you for all the hard work this week. And Dan, I have to say, the porno movie mistake, will go down in conference production history. That truly was a classic—just a shame it was on my show—but luckily for all of us, the client saw the funny side. So let's raise our glasses and applaud us all!" she slurs.

Cheers vibrate around the bar and eventually she slumps into a chair. We've lost her again, she's fallen into a deep drunken sleep. "Come on Dan, give me an 'and and we'll get the old bird back to her room." says Mickey, lifting Ingrid underneath her arms. As quick as a flash, Dan is the other side of her and they are literally dragging her through the bar. "Hey boys, don't forget her handbag, it'll have her room key in it!" I shout after them.

"Do us a favour and come up with us, you can be our witness that we don't touch her inappropriately!" laughs Dan.

Grabbing Ingrid's handbag, I follow the boys to the lift. We press the fourth floor button and head up to the executive suites. Arriving at Ingrid's room, I open her handbag and start to rummage for her room key. "Bloody hell, she has so much junk in here. I can't find the key!" I say.

"Hurry up girl she's starting to weigh a ton. Tip the bag out on the floor, it'll be easier to find," suggests Mickey.

I duly tip the contents of Ingrid's bag on the floor. She has everything in there, including: purse, phone, tissues, face powder, a furry rabbit's foot, an attack alarm, a stop watch, a stress ball and wait for it, a packet of condoms together with an Ann Summers vibrating bullet! Boy, she's a dark horse. Who would have thought it? Ingrid has sex. I bet she wishes she was having sex with Hugo tonight, but clearly she's not having sex with anyone this evening. On the other hand, with that bullet, may be she'll be having sex with herself! I can't believe she has a vibrator in her handbag, priceless!

I eventually locate the key and open the door. I return everything back into her handbag and head into the bedroom, leaving the door open. I dump her bag onto the coffee table, taking her phone out and placing it on her bedside table. Come on let's face it, who goes to bed without their mobile? That's right, nobody.

The boys have dumped Ingrid onto the bed. "So, what do you reckon Martha, should you undress her?" asks Mickey.

"Absolutely not. We'll take her shoes off and any restrictive jewellery and she can then safely sleep it off," I say, taking off her sparkly sandals, followed by her choker necklace and bangle.

"Rights, that's it. No wait, actually I think we should turn her onto her side and then put pillows, behind her back. Just in case she vomits. After all, we don't want her choking. We're the last people to have then seen her alive!" I say.

"Good idea, Mart!" says Mickey.

Startled, we all look round, for there in the door way is Howard. For a moment, all three of us simply stand there, saying and doing nothing.

Finally Mickey is the first to speak. "Hi there 'oward. Listen, it's not what it looks like. We definitely ain't breaking into her room. Ingrid drank too much and we was just trying to get her to bed. On her own of course," mumbles Mickey.

"Mickey, I wouldn't think for one moment that you were trying to break into her room. I was simply walking past the door and noticed it open. So don't worry, I'm on your side," responds Howard, with a smile.

"Martha's right though, we do need to get Ingrid on her side with pillows behind her back. In that position, if she is sick during the night, it will project forward, rather than down her throat. What a vile thought!" grimaces Howard.

We put all the pillows behind Ingrid's back. She is now wedged in that position, definitely no chance of her rolling onto her back now.

"Job well done boys and girls, now let's leave her in peace to catch up on her, much needed beauty sleep," laughs Howard.

We all creep out of Ingrid's room, switching off the light as we go.

"Well goodnight all and once again, thanks for all your hard work. It's been a blast!" says Howard, shaking the hands of Dan and Mickey and kissing me on my cheek.

"Absolute pleasure mate. It's been a good 'un." adds Mickey, as we head off to the lift.

"Goodnight now," says Howard, walking down the corridor to his room.

The lift arrives and we go down to the first floor. "He's alright for a corporate waller, ain't he?" says Dan.

"Yeah. No airs and graces like some of 'em. No, nice bloke," adds Mickey.

Arriving at the first floor, I kiss Dan and Mickey and head for my room. "Listen, I'll see you both in the morning, at some point. Sweet dreams and thank you for a brilliant week."

The boys head off in the opposite direction. Needless to say, I don't actually get undressed for bed, no, once in my room, I quickly brush my teeth, swill a mouthful of mouthwash, count to ten and then I head back to the lift, for my short journey to ecstasy.

Back up on the fourth floor, I head to Suite 444. I knock, and within seconds the door is opened. There, in front of me, is a vision of beauty. Howard, with a towel wrapped around his waist. "Come on in young lady. Help yourself to champagne, Krug I believe and I'll just finish up in the bathroom, coz boy it was hot at that party," says Howard.

"You take your time. After all I'm not going anywhere," I say, walking over to the champagne bucket and pouring a marvellous glass of Krug. Pure nectar.

I suddenly think that I should really have taken a shower. But bloody hell, how many showers can one person have in a day? I have a sniff of my armpits and thankfully, they smell absolutely fine. I know, totally unladylike, but just every once in a while... I walk out onto the terrace and take in the night air. There is a slight breeze. The stars are shining and the moonlight has lit up the still waters beautifully.

Within minutes, Howard has joined me out on the terrace. He is wearing a robe, which almost certainly has nothing beneath it. He comes up and wraps his arms around my waist. Not a word is spoken. We simply enjoy the moment. This gorgeous moment.

"Martha, I have a proposition for you," he says, breaking the silence.

For a split second, I think he is about to ask me to marry him. I feel unsteady on my feet. Could this be it? Could this be the moment that changes my life forever?

I turn around to face him. I sense my breasts are moving up and down through my heavy breathing and I catch his gaze move to my boobs. I try to stop breathing, but of course I can't! "So fire away, what's your proposition?" I ask.

"Well, I don't actually have to return to the States until Sunday, via London Heathrow airport on an evening flight. So, I was wondering whether, of course if your diary allows, you would like to join me in Monaco tomorrow. I have a private plane flying to Heathrow late afternoon on Sunday, so that

I can connect with the international flight. What do you think?" he asks, smiling.

What do I think? What do I think? You just try stopping me! Play it cool girl...

"Well, I do have plans for Sunday," I start, slightly disappointed that he hasn't asked me to marry him. Okay, so I've known him a week! But you tell me when a girl knows—she just knows!

"It was just a thought. Might have been fun, to hit the casinos in Monaco, you could have been my lucky lady!" replies Howard, quickly.

"Let me finish!" I say raising my hand. "As I was saying, I do have plans for Sunday, but almost certainly, they are plans that can be changed. So yes, I would very much like to spend the weekend in Monaco with you," I smile.

Fucking fantastic! Monaco, my favourite place in the whole wide world, for the weekend, with the man of my dreams! What more could I possibly wish for?

"Fantastic. I was planning heading over there mid afternoon tomorrow, as I have a series of meetings during the morning. Would it suit you, if we left the Maritime around three pm? I'll phone reception and get a late check out for you," he continues.

"Three pm is fine and don't worry about reception, I can call them, after all, I think the concierge has a soft spot for me—long stemmed roses, if you don't mind. And I'll tell the crew that I've decided to extend my stay, as I want to visit friends in Monaco. After all, they know that I have lots of friends in the South of France, so they won't think it unusual." I smile. "But for now, I think my glass is almost empty, so surely my suitor should be filling it up for me." I say, excitedly.

"I'm on it right away ma'm. And by the way, I don't think it was the concierge who sent the flowers..." winks Howard.

"You shatter my illusion of Mr Concierge. Profuse apologies, I meant to thank you earlier, but of course, with such a brilliant party, I clean forgot. So thank you, they are gorgeous." I smile, finally knowing who sent the flowers.

We remain out on the terrace, chatting incessantly until the bottle of Krug is empty, together with a bag of chocolate Brazil nuts and a jar of cashew nuts.

"Come on Martha, let me get you to bed," says Howard, pulling me up off the terrace recliner. "And then maybe, just maybe, if you are a very good girl, I'll give you your present."

"Oh yes, well remembered. I'd actually forgotten that you have a present for me. So come on then, where is it?" I ask, bounding back into the Suite, banging into the doorframe en route; Fuck! Pissed again.

We head into the bedroom. I have a quick look around, but can't see anything resembling a present. "Mr Johnson, I hope you're not teasing me. Oh, how I love presents!" I say, giggling.

"First, young lady, I suggest you make yourself comfortable, as I don't think I can resist you for too much longer," smiles Howard.

Howard has de-robed himself and is indeed, naked beneath it. This erection is clearly visible. He is simply magnificent.

I slowly allow my dress to fall to the floor and then unfasten my bra, which I throw toward him. His face is eager. I watch him as he strokes his cock. I roll my knickers down and leave my shoes on. I crawl onto the bed lingering over his cock. I take it between my breasts and slowly move up and down, providing him with his much desired 'titty wank.' His breathing is now very deep and suddenly, I find myself underneath him. He's pushed me onto my back, kissing me passionately and thrusting himself into me. Our bodies join in unison. His tongue finds my erect nipples and I cry out in pure ecstasy. We come within moments of one another. He holds me tightly. "I don't ever want this moment to pass," he says and I think he means it.

"You know you're perfect. I don't quite know how I'm going to cope without you back in the States," he says.

"Well, there's nothing stopping you from inviting me over, for the odd few days, every now and then," I respond.

"True, but where do we go from there? I don't know if I can cope with you on a part time basis. It's just that I have such a connection with you Martha. We feel good together, but why is that? I mean let's face it, I don't really know a lot about you, other than the fact, you have a brother who is sleeping with my brother. Hell, I don't even know if you have a partner," he continues.

"Likewise. I know nothing about you, but what I do know, I like. So, for the moment I suggest we open up another bottle of Krug, have a toast to the future and whatever it holds and also open any presents that happen to be lying around," I say.

"Perfect idea!" he responds, heading out to the sitting room.

I follow him out, having grabbed his bathrobe to drape around me. I must look like a slut—borrowed bathroom robe and five inch heels! The cork pops and we toast the future and indeed, whatever it holds.

After a couple of glasses, Howard finally hands over my present. Without doubt, it's jewellery. The box is deep red velvet, around it is tied a black bow, which I undo and slowly lift the lid.

I am spellbound. For there inside, is the beautiful necklace worn by Summer, the model, who wore the stunning cream evening gown during the fashion show.

Words escape me. I have never seen anything so beautiful. I look up at Howard and feel tears start to spring in my eyes.

"Hey what's up? Don't you like it?" he asks, a concerned look, spreading across his face.

For a moment, or, two, I try to compose myself. And finally, I say, "Like it? I absolutely love it. It's the most gorgeous necklace I've ever seen. But, as gorgeous as it is, I can't possibly accept this. It must be worth a fortune and far too precious."

"Its value is not important. What is important is that you truly like it and promise to wear it," continues Howard.

"Howard, I absolutely love it. It's, it's just perfect. Oh, thank you so much. I just don't know what to say," I stammer.

"Say nothing. But here, let me put it on for you. Might I suggest you take off the robe, way too big for you anyway," he smiles.

I slide off the robe and naked, turn around, so that Howard can affix the necklace clasp. I rush to the bedroom to look at myself. What can I say? A stunning necklace and five inch heels. You get the picture. Well how would you feel? I feel like a princess.

I rush back into the sitting room. "I love it. I absolutely love it. Thank you from the bottom of my heart. It's the best present ever!" I say, touching the necklace lovingly.

It's now three thirty am and we are still in the sitting room. We talk about our likes and dislikes and think nothing of opening a third bottle of Krug. In fact, I am now so drunk, that I don't even bother with a glass and drink straight from the bottle, as does Howard.

"Howard, before I get too drunk, tell me where you would like me to make love to you next," I slur.

"Here, might be good," he responds, as he pats the big squidgy sofa, on which we are both sitting.

"Perfect!" I respond. "The sofa it is then. But first another swig of champagne."

Chapter Twenty-Two

Fucking hell! Ouch! What happened to me, last night? I am lying in bed on my stomach, unable to move. My head feels as if I've been in a car crash, although in all honesty, I am not sure what it feels like, to have been in a proper full on car crash as thankfully, touch wood, and lots of it, I've never had one.

It's still dark, so that's good because it means, that I don't need to get up yet. I remember the KAYSO party, which was rocking, but after that, my mind is fuzzy. I need sleep and lots of it. I stretch my arm out and pat the bed. I am alone. I try to lift my head off the pillow, but I can't. I need to find my iphone. It helps me to keep in contact with the world, but more importantly, it tells me the time. I pat around the bed, but alas, it is not within reach.

I can stand the pain no more, so I close my eyes and fall into a deep, joyous sleep. And time passes.

Fuck! I need water. "Help! Can anybody hear me?" I whisper, as I try to open my eyes. I try to lift my head off the pillow, but it feels as if it's weighted down. What the fuck happened to me last night? Where am I?

I muster all the strength I can, to hoist myself up onto all fours. I am sweating and shaking. Boy, I'm not well. But, so far, so good. I am on all fours, which is a start. I start to shuffle backwards, as I want to make it to the end of bed and lower myself off.

I finally reach the bottom of the bed and flop down on my belly again. I am exhausted. How long have I been in this bedroom? What if I've been here for days? I slowly shuffle off the end of the bed. My head is spinning, but finally, I am on the floor. But being on the floor, is not good for me. As you know, I cannot stand hotel bedroom carpets. The sheer thought of someone else having walked, bare foot on this carpet repulses me. I quickly pull myself up, back onto the bed.

With my head in my hands, I start to cry. I don't feel well. In fact, now, I feel positively sick. I touch my body, not in a sexual way, but in a way that determines if I am clothed, or, not. I am not. Well, I say not; I am not wearing any clothes, nothing at all, not even knickers. But rather weirdly, I am wearing a pair of high heels and a necklace. What the fuck is all that about then? The only saving grace of course, is that I can now walk to the bathroom and not worry about touching the carpet with my feet!

This room is so dark, I need light to see where I am going. I eventually manage to leave the bed and stand, in an upright position. To the left of me, I can just about make out curtained windows, so I head to the right and pat the wall to find a light switch. Flicking the switch, the room is suddenly enveloped in brightness. So bright in fact I cannot stand it so I quickly turn it off. Shit! What is wrong with me?

I need to get to the bathroom, as I am going to be sick, but I can't get there without light, as I don't know where I am! I squint my eyes and flick the light switch on again. Ouch! It hurts like hell. I look around the bedroom. Nope, this is definitely not my room. I head towards the double doors and open one quietly, in the hope that I don't disturb anyone, should there be anybody there of course.

The shaft of light that filters through, as I open the door, is too much to bear and so I quickly shut it again. I look around the room and note to my left, there is another door; hopefully this might lead to the bathroom. I open it, but it's not a bathroom, it's a walk in closet. Fucking hell! Am I in someone's home?

On the right hand side, past the windows, I spot another door. 'Please God, for all the good I have done throughout my life, let that door lead to the bathroom.' I pray out loud.

I stagger, yes, actually stagger, across the room and finally make it to the door. My eyes are shut, as I am terrified as to what I might find. As I open it slowly, my heart is filled with joy, for there before me is a bathroom. Thank you God.

I quickly rush in, well as quickly as my pounding head will allow me and make for the toilet, hitting the light switch on the way through. I pee, with my head in my hands. Now, I don't always pee with my head in my hands, it's just that my head is likely to fall off my shoulders, if I don't hold it. I start to pray. 'Dear Lord, I love you more today, than I did yesterday. Please show me where I went wrong yesterday, as I have no recollection of what happened and also please give me an indication of where I am today. Thank you. Amen'

I get up to wash my hands and clock myself in the mirror. Good Lord! I think someone has put green make up on my face. I move a little closer and rub my cheek, checking my finger tips for any residue. No! It's my skin. I've turned green.

Suddenly I start retching. I can't hold on any longer. I turn around and vomit repeatedly into the toilet. My stomach feels as if it's leaving its home and taking a short cut, through my throat. I remain in this position for a good ten minutes, until such time as I am able to stand up again.

Now I've been sick I actually feel a million times better, but of course desperately need to brush my teeth. I hunt around the bathroom and locate toothpaste and mouthwash. I brush my teeth with my finger and rinse four times with mouthwash. I am now starting to feel a little more human.

So, let's try to piece this together. I remember having dinner with the crew at the hotel and then going to the KAYSO party and drinking rather a lot; but after that, nothing. Water. That's what I need, If I drink water and rehydrate myself, I'll remember everything.

I head out of the bathroom and back into the bedroom. I look around for a robe, or, something to wrap around me, but see nothing. (hardly surprising really suffering from alcohol induced double vision)

I head back towards the double doors. Pushing these open, the brightness is overwhelming. There is light streaming in through the terrace doors. Bright, bright sunlight. I am starting to remember the terrace from last night, Yes, I was on that terrace with Howard. Fuck! I must still be in Howard's Suite. I need to get out of here. A chilling feeling shivers down my spine. Fuck! Fuck! Fuckety fuck! Alexandre is coming by this morning! He can't be here yet, because he hasn't called. Thank God!

I head over to the bar and open the fridge, making a grab for a bottle of still mineral water, which I down in one. I spy a bar of chocolate in the fridge, which I think will probably do me the world of good. I take it out and savour four squares. Perfect. Finishing my second bottle of water, I look around and spot two bottles of Krug in the sitting room and one bottle, out on the terrace. No wonder I am feeling like shit! I am so going to make an effort to halt my drinking. I just don't know when I've had enough!

I rush into the bedroom to grab my iphone, but I can't find it anywhere. I move back out into the sitting room to find my bag; I must have arrived with a bag last night for fuck's sake! And there, sure enough, I spot my gorgeous clutch bag on the floor. On the floor—I must have been really pissed, because I would never, ever, in a million years, put a Lulu Guinness clutch bag, on the floor.

I open it up and the relief at spotting my iphone is overwhelming. Boy it's like having your hands chopped off, if your mobile can't be found. But there it is. Thank you God.

I pull it out and to my utter horror it's switched off. My iphone is never, ever off, unless I am in a show and it's causing interference.

I hold down the button to switch it back on, but nothing happens. Why is nothing happening? Fuck! Is it broken? And then I remember, it was almost out of charge last night and through the night it's zapped itself of any life. I hunt around to find my clothes. Nothing in the sitting room; well, at least I made it to the bedroom, before I disgraced myself. I rush into the bedroom and thankfully, find my dress crumpled on the floor. I pull it on and scout around for underwear, but I can't see any. Never mind, at least I am respectable. After all, I have a dress and a pair of shoes.

I enter the bathroom and try to tidy up my face a little, my now white face, at least I am no longer green! I wipe away the black kohl around my eyes and fluff up my hair, which of course, is looking like Medusa at the moment. What I need to do now, is get back to my room, to wait for Alexandre's arrival. Why do I do this to myself? I am so bloody foolish sometimes. But no point in beating myself up now, is there? What's done is done.

I rush back out into the sitting room and look around for a clock, or, something that will, at least, tell me the time. I can hear voices, so I head out onto the terrace. I look down and there are already sunbathers down on the beach front. Fuck! They must be Germans; after all, they are always the early birds aren't they?

As I head back in, I spot a large clock on the terrace wall. It reads eleven forty five. I keep looking at it. It must be wrong, as I know full well that it most definitely is not eleven forty five.

I poke my head out of the suite just to make sure the coast is clear and then I bolt down the corridor to the stairs. I can't chance the lifts, just in case I bump into anybody.

I rush down the three flights of stairs and eventually, make it to the first floor. I poke my head out of the stairwell door, to make sure the coast is clear and then make a run for it. I finally get to my room, but I can't find my room key. Fuck! Please let me find it. I hear a door open and I look up. It's Hans coming out of Mel's room and he's blowing kisses to her and before he can close the door, I make a lunge for it and get myself into her room.

"Thanks Hans. Sorry to interrupt, but I am having a crisis," I say, as I shut the door, behind me.

"Slapper, what the heck are you doing here?" asks Mel.

"Mel. Concentrate OK. Tell me the time. The time right now in Cannes?" I ask, slowly.

"Why are you talking to me as if I'm a fucked up foreigner?" she asks.

"I'm not. I just need to know the time please," I respond, a little agitated now

"The time Martha is now eleven fifty two. That means it is eight minutes before noon. Is that OK?" she says once again, very slowly.

"No way! Don't tell me I've missed Alexandre. Oh shit no! I drank so much last night and then fell asleep in Howard's Suite and Alexandre was calling by this morning. Quick, I need to find my room key, please Mel can you find it for me?" I ask, throwing her my clutch bag. I am now close to tears.

"Just calm down, he's probably already let himself in, like he normally does. If he has, I'm not quite sure how you're going to explain this one away!" she laughs.

"Explain what exactly?" I ask in a stern voice.

"Well, the fact that it's noon and you are just returning to your room in last night's dress, looking like you've had sex all night," laughs Mel out loud.

"You're right. I need to calm down," I say, taking a few deep breaths.

"Anyway wouldn't Alexandre simply call you, if he had already arrived?" she asks.

"Yes he would, but for the fact that my iphone is out of juice," I respond.

"Oh shit! Well, anyway here's your room key now, go sort yourself out and don't forget, we are leaving here at one pm on the dot," says Mel.

I suddenly remember part of the conversation last night with Howard. I think, no, in fact I know, he invited me to stay in Monaco with him today. Yes, I am quite sure he did. And also, oh my God, the necklace. He gave me the necklace, which Summer wore during the fashion show. Oh thank God! My memory is coming back to me again. Perfect.

"Mel, I'm not going back to the UK today. Howard invited me to stay with him in Monaco and return to the UK on Sunday. And also, look at this necklace he gave me last night," I stammer.

"What the fuck do you mean, you are not going back to England today? Are you mad?" asks Mel.

"No, I'm not mad. It's only another day. And anyway, it will be nice to spend time with him. I think Jefferson and Theo, are also stopping over so I won't exactly be on my own," I reply.

"Hang on a minute. Not thirty seconds ago you were freaking out because you thought you had missed Alexandre and now you are spending the rest of the weekend with Howard, in the same city where Alexandre lives. Have I fucking missed something here?" shouts Mel.

"No, of course not. And stop shouting. Look, I just don't know what is going through my mind at the moment. I don't know whether it's Alexandre, or, Howard I want... but... but, well... I don't know!" I respond.

"But for now, I've got to see if Alexandre is in my room and if he is, then I'm going to tell him that I fell asleep in your room. Is that OK?" I ask.

"Oh go on, get out of here and make sure you text me later. And one last thing, make sure you don't bump into Alexandre when you are in Monaco, after all, it's a tiny place. I'll tell the crew that you've had a better offer from Alexandre OK? I do wish you would dump this prat!" laughs Mel.

She clambers out of bed and walks over to hug me. "Text me later alright?" And with that, she is pushing me out of the door.

I hurry over to my room and open the door. The room is in darkness. I rush over to the curtains and pull them open. Sunlight comes streaming through. I look around but there is definitely no sign of Alexandre. I rush to the bathroom, but no, he's definitely not in there either.

I pull my iphone from my bag and pull the charger from my suitcase and insert it into the mobile's socket. I keep pressing my finger on the ON button, but still, this bastard handset, has no life. Oh fuck! Please don't let it be broken.

I start to become very anxious, but, as if by magic, my darling iphone suddenly springs to life. Thank you God, thank you. It takes a few moments, but finally, I am checking my messages.

I have three missed calls—Theo, Howard and Theo again.

I check my text messages and I have four—Theo, Howard, Amelia and Alexandre.

I quickly open Alexandre's message: *Baby, I'm sorry something came up this morning. I'll see you soon, love you xxx.*

I re-read the message several times and feel the tears rolling down my cheeks. Obviously it's a good thing that he's not here this morning, but in my heart of hearts, I honestly did think that he would come to see me again, before I return to the UK.

I listen to my messages. Theo is trying to track me down to say goodbye, although now he doesn't need to, because I'm going to be in Monaco with him.

I send him a text: *Guess whose coming to Monaco? That's right. Me xxx.*

I send Howard a text: *I feel like death. Were you trying to kill me last night? Am back in my room dying xxx.*

I send Amelia a text: *Hi darling, am staying on for a day or so. Let's catch up on Monday. Love you xxx.*

I then remember to phone reception, to advise them that I won't be checking out before three pm, with which, they are fine.

I strip off my dress and shoes and take off my beautiful necklace. I head into the bathroom and stand under the shower, hair and all. I allow the water to jump off my skin, to help me feel human again. I wash my face and my hair. OK, I know it's going to take a fair time to dry, but I'm off to Monaco, so I need to look good, don't I? Especially if I am to be on the arm of Howard Johnson III!

I am now feeling a whole lot better. After applying my Prada body moisturiser, I start the long and horrible process of drying my hair. For the next forty-five minutes, with my head bent down, I dry my hair and when eventually it's dry and I resemble a shaggy sheep, all curly and wild, I let out a sigh of relief.

I check my mobile. I've got five text messages.

Text from Amelia: *Am totally jealous. Have a wonderful time. See you on Monday. xx.*

Text from Howard: *Glad to hear you're alive. You had me worried. Which is your favourite hotel in Monaco? xx.*

To which I respond: *Hermitage. I love it there! xx.*

Text from Theo: *Fantastic news cara mia xx.*

Text from Howard: *I can't get you out of my mind! xx.*

Text from Alexandre: *Baby, did you get my message?* xx.

I respond to Alexandre's text: *Yes got your message. Thanks for nothing and up yours!*

He'll know that I am now well and truly pissed off with him. He promised that he would come over and then just couldn't be bothered. Well fuck him!

I look around the bedroom and decide to pack, because once packed, I can then have a little sleep! I pull out a pair of black jeans, black vest top and mules for my journey to Monaco and the rest goes into the case. The time is now one twenty three pm. The rest of the crew will now have started their journey to the airport. I feel a little sad not travelling home with them, but we'll all be working together again soon enough.

My mobile beeps and I have another message from Alexandre: *Don't be angry. It doesn't suit you. Things happen sometimes. Love you.xx.*

Before I know what I am doing, I have responded to his message: *If you truly loved me you wouldn't fuck me off all the time would you? Don't bother in future.*

I re-read the message I have sent to him. I can't believe I have sent it. I do want him to bother. I want him to bother because I love him. But, I now know, that he doesn't really love me. I'm a distraction, albeit a fun distraction, but I know for sure, that his love for me is not strong enough to make a full commitment. Well, all I can say is that it is he who is living the lie, not me.

My iphone beeps again. This time a message from Howard: *Two suites booked at the Hermitage. Theo grumpy as he prefers the Hotel de Paris! See you at three xx.*

Theo has always preferred the Hotel de Paris, which don't get me wrong, is absolutely fantastic, but there is just something rather special about the Hermitage. Now, if I was visiting Monaco with girlfriends I wouldn't stay at the Hermitage, no, the Hermitage is for love. With girlfriends I stay at the Port Palace Hotel, which is young and funky.

My iphone beeps again. Not another message from Howard? No. Another message from Alexandre: *I do love you. Believe me xxx.*

Oh my God, I can't bear this. Does he really love me, or, is he just playing me? When we are together, there is definitely a connection, there is no doubt about it and if ultimately, I had to make the choice between Alexandre and Howard, in my heart of hearts, I know it would be Alexandre. Howard is wonderful. He's kind, caring, loving and attentive. But Alexandre? Well, he is something else. He's also loving and attentive sometimes, but he's just the ultimate bad boy, which is why I love him so much. But these types of guys just fuck your life up, don't they?

My iphone beeps again. This time it's from Mel: *Slapper, we are homeward bound. Everyone sends their love. We miss you xxx.*

I respond quickly: *I love and miss you all too. See you in Blighty xxx.*

Right, now I need to lie down for an hour. I'm tired and totally hungover. As I rest my head upon the pillow, my mobile vibrates again. Enough now. I pick it up and see a message from Theo: *Hermitage? You are nuts x.*

I don't even respond. I simply drift off into a deep sleep, but not before setting my phone alarm for two thirty pm.

I can hear the beep, beep, beep, but somehow my eyes refuse to open. Perhaps the sleep was a big mistake? I lie still for a few minutes and then force myself up. I head into the bathroom and brush my teeth and then apply some make up.

Time is now two forty eight pm. Soon, I will be heading down to Monaco with Howard, for twenty four hours of fun and laughter. It's just what I need, to get Alexandre well, and truly, out of my life.

I quickly dress. Pack the rest of my toiletries away, put my phone charger in my bag and have a quick squirt of perfume.

I check my messages. No missed calls, but three text messages.

Text message one from Mickey: *See you on the next gig Mart. Be good x.*

Text message two from Alexandre*: Can I visit you in UK xxx.*

Text message three also from Alexandre*: So?xx.*

I respond to Mickey*: Aren't I always? xxx.*

And then I respond to Alexandre: *Why don't I visit you in Monaco instead, as I'll be sure to turn up.*

I pop my mobile in my bag and make my way downstairs to reception where I ask the concierge to collect my luggage from room 102, which he duly organises. I spot Theo in the bar and join him. He is talking to someone and as soon as spots me, he shakes his head, ever so discretely. I quickly dart behind a plant and sneak a peek as to who it is he's talking to. Oh Jesus! It's Ingrid! Bloody hell! I forgot she was leaving on a later flight. Fuck! Now, what am I to do? Francois, the concierge is watching me intently. I put my finger up to my lips and mouth 'sush.' I quickly rush over to his desk and ask to hide, in his office.

"Miss Martha, what iz zee matter?" asks Francois.

"It's nothing, I'm simply hiding from Ingrid, the lady sitting at the bar with my brother," I smile.

"Listen, I need to settle my bill. Can I do it in here, or, do I need to go out to the main reception desk?" I ask, quietly, not that Ingrid can hear me, from where she is sitting.

"Let me go gazer your bill now and I will bring it to you. We can settle zee account in here," he smiles.

"Perfect. Thank you."

Within moments, Francois has returned with said bill. I glance at it and then wonder how I have managed to spend in excess of seven hundred Euros on alcohol alone. After all, my room costs have been placed against the final company account, this bill is simply for my extras. Note to self, must learn to be more frugal!

I hand Francois my credit card and within moments, I am seven hundred Euros poorer, but I think it was worth it!

My mobile is ringing. It's Theo, to tell met that Ingrid has left the building.

I thank Francois for his help and handshake a fifty Euro note into his palm; after all, he has been a life saver! Even if he didn't send me flowers...

Out in reception again and I am met by Howard, Jefferson and Theo. My luggage has been loaded into the gleaming black limo and our next stop is Monaco and more specifically, the Hermitage Hotel.

As we walk towards the car, Howard whispers in my ear, "This weekend is going to be amazing. I promise." And with that, we all pile in, crack open the Krug and start our journey towards a weekend of fun.

Chapter Twenty-Three

I only manage one glass of champagne, before my eyes start to feel heavy. I am shattered. I don't think I've had more than ten hours sleep all week and even by my standards, that's pretty poor! I rest my weary head on Howard's shoulder and close my eyes. I feel him pull me closer, wrapping his arm around me and softly stroking the nape of my neck. I drift off into blissful sleep.

I have been back and forth to Monaco for years. Initially for good times with girlfriends and then visiting boyfriends. I was first lured here on a hen weekend many years ago and the fascination and wonderment of this mini principality, has remained forever.

I wake up just as we are driving through the heavy traffic on the Avenue d'Ostende. Howard still has his arm around me and I have to admit I am starting to feel a whole lot better than a few hours ago.

Finally, we arrive in the Square Beaumarchais, where the beautiful belle époque Hermitage hotel is situated. There is something simply amazing about this hotel. It cultivates a refined atmosphere of intimacy, charm and luxury, all rolled into one and I am totally besotted by its beauty.

Entering the hotel, we are immediately besieged by the hotel manager and the hotel's senior concierge. After introductions, we are escorted to our suites, both located on the top floor, affording fantastic views of Monaco and the Mediterranean.

Our bags arrive within minutes, together with the obligatory butler, who I assume has come to pour champagne and make us feel settled. After all, when guests are paying a small fortune for rooms, they are always made to feel special.

"Madame, permettez-moi de décompresser vos sacs?" asks Henri (our butler). I have to think quickly—what has he just said? I don't think for a moment he'd ask if I would like a cucumber sandwich. No shit! He's asking to unpack my case. No way Jose! Oh my God! There's a weeks worth of dirty washing in there. Quick, quick, how do I respond in my poor French? Oh bollocks! Here goes. "Merci, mais pas." I respond and smile, rather hoping that I haven't made a fool of myself.

I think I've got away with it, as he smiles, steps back and proceeds to ask Howard the same question. He too declines, but in English, rather than French.

I am indeed right, with regards to the champagne though. There is a selection in the bar and Howard has indicated that Krug is the favoured brand. Within moments, we have been handed champagne and beautiful canapés have been delivered. Fuck! I want to be wealthy!

It's late afternoon and I am exhausted. We step out onto the terrace to admire the view, which of course, is utterly gorgeous. I look across to my right and who do I see? Of course, Jefferson and Theo, already in their shorts and not a lot else. Without having to disgrace myself by shouting too loudly, I am able to speak to them, as they are quite literally, next door to us. "Sunbathing already?" I ask.

They both look up. "Well, well, well, if it isn't Ms Martha. How's the suite honey?" asks Jefferson.

"Glorious!" I respond.

"Not as good as the Hotel du Paris," responds Theo, sullenly.

"But this one's not full of Russians is it?" I respond. "And anyway, for the little time you'll be spending in the hotel, does it really matter where we sleep?"

"Enough children. We are here to have a good time and a good time, we are going to have. I suggest that we have a lazy afternoon, as I have bit of work to do and then we can hook up for drinks, dinner, casino and maybe a club later. What do you reckon?" asks Howard, who has now joined me on the terrace.

"Sounds good to me. I am sure Martha could do with a couple of hours of sleep, you look exhausted cara mia," replies Theo.

"Great, well in that case, shall we meet in the bar at eight thirty?" suggests Howard.

"Sure thing bro'," answers Jefferson.

I wander back inside. I am so tired, but don't want to sleep through fear of missing this glorious place. I want to stay awake for the next twenty-four hours and wander through the streets, taking in the sights, but you know what, it just isn't going to happen. I need to sleep!

"Howard, as you have a little bit of work to do, would it be rude of me to grab forty winks?" I ask, quietly.

"You carry on. You must be exhausted. We've worked you hard this past week and you've managed to party well too!" he laughs.

Howard follows me into the bedroom and like a child, starts to undress me. I stand there, in just my knickers I know the inevitable is going to happen. He kisses me tenderly and soon his hands are firmly on my breasts. Just his touch sends shivers down my spine. Our kisses become more passionate, as Howard quickly works to undress himself. As he pushes me gently down onto the bed I hear my iphone ringing. "Leave it, it can wait." he says in a husky 'I have an erection' type voice, as he pulls my knickers down. I roll on top of him and slowly start to gyrate. His eyes are closed and he is biting down on his lip. His hands are on my hips and gently, he eases me onto his cock. We start slowly and then soon build up momentum; we can't resist each other any more and we come within seconds. Howard letting out a deep moan and me wondering if Theo can hear us from his terrace! Fuck! I hope not. Can you begin to imagine just how embarrassing that would be?

I eventually move away and visit the bathroom to take a quick shower. He follows me in. "Martha, I was wondering, what's your workload like when you get back to the UK?"

"Well, I've got a couple of days at home, followed by a couple of small jobs and a possible road show, so neither hectically busy, nor quiet," I respond.

"Why do you ask?" I continue.

"Well, I've got two weeks of hell when I get back to the States, but then I was wondering if you would like to come out for a visit, for a few days?" he asks.

"Why? What's up Mr Johnson, are you missing me already?" I smile.

"Of course I am. Life hasn't been easy over the past few months, but suddenly I feel good again," he smiles.

"Well, if I can get over, then I will. No promises. I would love to come for a visit and of course, whenever you are in Europe, be sure to drop by." I say, all the while wanting him to drop to one knee and ask me to marry him. Which of course he doesn't, but I think it's simply a question of time.

As I step into the shower I smile to myself. I am really happy, after all, I am in a suite at the Hermitage hotel in Monaco and I have a gorgeous, kind and extremely wealthy man, to entertain me for the next twenty four hours. Life really can't get any better, or, can it?

Wrapped in a towel after my luxurious shower, (boy I want one of those at home) I head off to find my iphone, as I suddenly remember the missed call during our romp.

Howard is on the phone at the desk, laptop open, dressed only in his boxers. He turns his head and winks. I blow him a kiss. Grabbing my handbag, I head back into the bedroom. I am Miss Popular again. I have one missed call and four text messages. I open up the text messages, one by one.

Text message one from Mel: *You did well to stay on. Right fuck up at the airport but now on plane. Have a good time slapper x.*

Text message two from Alexandre (oh my God): *When can I see you again? I miss you babe xx.*

Text message three from Alexandre (again): *We need to talk. Call me xx.*

Text message four from yep you've guessed it, Alexandre: *Have a safe flight; call me when you can xx.*

And a missed call from Mr Alexandre himself, but no message. He's got it bad. I am in two minds whether to call him or not, but I am so tired that I'm not in the mood to talk and also, it would be a little awkward with Howard in the next room. I decide to text him. But I am not sure whether, or not, I should still be angry with him. I suppose, I should be, but obviously he is trying to make an effort, as he's upset me so much. Short and sweet that's what I decide: *I'll be in touch soon xx.*

I lay my weary head on the pillow and I am out for the count. It seems like only five minutes have passed, as I feel myself being gently shaken. "Go away and leave me alone!" I say, absentmindedly.

"Martha, hey honey its quarter of eight. We're meeting the guys in forty five minutes, you going to wake up?" says Howard, quietly.

I can hear Howard's voice, but I refuse to open my eyes. "Just five more minutes," I mumble.

Howard rolls me onto my stomach and starts to give me a back massage. It feels wonderful and of course, it makes me feel horny. He gently parts my legs and his fingers enter me. I writhe in pure ecstasy across the bed. He stops and turns me over, pulling me up on all fours. He penetrates me. This man is fantastic! Our bodies move in unison and then he comes inside me and calls out my name. (Well, his actual words are 'Horny Bitch' which I assume is me!) He lies down beside me and lifts his arm over his head. "You're amazing Martha DiPinto. I think I am falling in love with you, you little minx."

"I wondered how long it would take, but now, I think you are definitely mine!" I laugh, as I tickle his stomach and get out of bed and head towards the bathroom, yet again.

At eight thirty five precisely, we are both dressed, Howard in a navy linen suit with white shirt and me in my gorgeous black jumpsuit, ridiculously high strappy sandals and of course, wearing the exquisite necklace, which was given to me by the rather generous Mr Howard Johnson. Howard Johnson III no less. We are heading down to the hotel's bar and I feel a million dollars. I am walking hand in hand with a man who is handsome, generous, but more importantly, says he thinks he's in love with me. Fantastic!

Theo and Jefferson are already in the bar when we finally arrive. Both jump up to greet us. "Wow! You look amazing!" says Jefferson.

"Hang fire now, the only reason my sister is looking so amazing, is that she seems to be wearing our fabulous necklace. How did you get hold of that?" asks Theo, incredulously.

I look at Howard. Shit! I am not supposed to have this? "Boys let me explain. A beautiful piece of jewellery deserves a beautiful neck and that's the reason why Martha is wearing it. I gave it to her, as a token of our appreciation for all her hard work this week," he smiles.

"Make sure you look after that, otherwise you'll have me to answer to! Understand cara mia?" instructs Theo, touching the necklace delicately.

"I will guard it with my life. Now who's drinking what?" I ask, as a waiter approaches.

We all decide on champagne cocktails. I love this decadent lifestyle. We have three rounds of cocktails and then decide to head off to the Café de Paris for dinner. The restaurant is literally situated around the corner, in the Place du Casino, across the road from the world famous Casino de Monte-Carlo. It's well within walking distance, as is everywhere in Monaco. The square is lined with every supercar imaginable and tourists are egging each other on, to have their photographs taken standing next to them. Why? I have absolutely no idea.

As we enter The Café du Paris, Howard and Jefferson are both greeted like long lost friends by the maitre'd. Immediately, we are escorted to a private table away from the hustle and bustle of the tourists.

For the next couple of hours we chatter incessantly. The food is fabulous, the alcohol is plentiful and the laughter is infectious. Theo and Jefferson are holding court this evening and are recounting tales of horror, surrounding the fashion industry.

A few 'locals' have spied Howard during dinner and have stopped by, to say hello. Howard is definitely no stranger to Monaco that is clearly obvious.

During coffee and liqueurs, we try to decide what our plans are for the remainder of the evening. The boys, as in Jefferson and Theo, are anxious to hit the nightclubs, but Howard would like to hedge his bets in the Casino. We finally decide that we'll have another drink, after all, it would be rude not to and then Jefferson and Theo will head off to the Sass Club and we'll join them later; once we've made our millions on the roulette tables!

As we raise our glasses, Theo quips in "If you win, we'll take half, but if you lose you're by yourselves." We all laugh and I quickly reflect on just how perfect my life is at this very moment. Great company, fabulous surroundings, brilliant conversation and total happiness. I never want it to end, that much is for sure.

Howard settles the bill and we go our separate ways. The time is fast approaching eleven thirty pm and I am feeling a tiny bit tired and also a little bit drunk. At this stage in the evening, I have absolutely no intention of retiring after all, the night is still definitely young. Howard takes my hand, as we walk out of the restaurant.

Walking through the crowds making our way outside, I am suddenly gripped by the most overwhelming sensation. I don't know whether to display fear, or, sheer delight. I can't breathe and can't I move. Oh my God! What am I going to do? Howard immediately senses something is wrong. "Martha, what's the matter, are you OK honey?" he asks, with concern.

I look at him and smile and then think of the first thing to come into my mind. "Nothing, sorry, sorry, I was being stupid," I say in a whisper. "It's just that I thought I saw Danny, as in Danny Mendosa over the other side of the restaurant, but of course it's not him, as he's on his way back to the States now, isn't he?" I stammer.

"Yep, that's right, well at least I think he is. Where did you think you saw him?" he asks.

"No, no it's OK, it's definitely not him. I'm quite certain," I reply, quickly.

Now the real reason for my mixed fear and delight is quite simply that to the right of me, three tables way is Alexandre. My perfectly wonderful Alexandre. Together with a female, whom I assume is his wife and two other couples. I feel compelled to look again, but I'm not going to. Instead I push, gently of course, Howard towards the exit, so that I can escape, unseen. Sweet Jesus! What is the probability of Alexandre and his wife (he tells me he never goes out with her) being out this evening and in the same restaurant as me? Why am I so fucking gullible? Why have I listened to Alexandre's lies and promises? Why? Why? Why? What have I done, that is so very bad? I question in my mind.

Once outside, I take a quick glance backwards. I see Alexandre, laughing with the people at the table, suddenly, I wish I was there, sitting by his side, laughing with him.

"Hey Martha, are you ready to hit the casino with me? You'll be my good luck charm. Now make sure you allow me to rub you, when I'm down on my luck. OK?" laughs Howard, leading me up the steps of the Casino de Monte-Carlo.

Howard pays the entrance fee and we both show identity. Initially, we head off into the Salon Europe, purchasing chips, well Howard does and we start to play roulette. I snaffle some chips from Howard, which he relinquishes, without hesitation. He leans into me and whispers "Be lucky." Within the space of twenty minutes the thousand Euros I 'borrowed' from Howard, has become almost three thousand. Howard is placing big bets and I think he's won somewhere in the region of thirty-thousand Euros, from a starting figure of nine thousand. This could be a truly memorable night.

"Let's hit the black jack tables?" he says, taking my hand.

A casino escort gathers up our (how cool is that—'our') chips and escorts us through to the Salons Prives. Only the very wealthy ever really enter the Salons Prives and only the incredibly wealthy will enter Les Super Prives, which I am sure Howard would do, if it wasn't just an evening of fun.

We settle down at the black jack table and soon, my three thousand Euros are down to fifteen hundred. Is lady luck running out on me? No, of course not. I just have to concentrate. Howard has placed his hand on my knee. "And pray Sir, what exactly are you doing?" I ask.

"Well, it seems that luck has eluded you, so I'm giving you a lucky rub. And also, I just wanted to touch the most beautiful woman in this joint," he replies, leaning over to give me a quick kiss.

Well, all I can say is that he must be lucky because for the next seven hands I win, time and again and my winnings are back up to three thousand Euros. Bizarrely, I can quite easily understand how people get hooked on gambling, for the short period of time that I have been in the Casino.

After a couple of hours, we both decide that enough is enough. I have made money and Howard has definitely made money. The casino escort is walking us towards the cashier. A chitty is signed and the money is assigned to Howard's account.

As we leave the Casino, Howard places his arm around my shoulder. "So, exactly how much did you win for me this evening?" he asks.

"You kindly lent me one thousand Euros and I managed to make a profit of two thousand, so therefore, I think you owe me some money," I laugh and ask if we should go and join the boys at the Sass Club

"Sounds good to me. We'll have a couple of drinks there and perhaps head off to Jimmyz for a boogie," replies Howard. "I have something special planned for the morning, so we can't stay out too late," he laughs, looking at his watch—it's already one-fifteen am!

We sail into the Sass club like royalty and spy the boys in the VIP section, which thankfully, is less crowded, than the main part of the club. As soon as they spot us, they become excitable. "Guess what? Rumour has it that JP is in town. Certainly not in here, we've already had a good look around, so he might be over at Jimmyz, so we'll have to go there later. OK?" gushes Theo.

"Who exactly is JP?" I ask.

Theo and Jefferson both look at one another, as if I am completely stupid. I look at Howard. He shrugs his shoulders. "I've no idea who they're referring to either," he says.

"Girlfriend you and I are going to have a little chat," says Jefferson, taking my hand and leading me to a quiet lounge area. We chat for a few minutes and then we head back to Theo and Howard. "OK, I'm with you now. Howard, just in case you were wondering, JP stands for Jean-Paul Gaultier." I say, as if I am totally knowledgeable!

We order champagne cocktails and people watch for a few minutes. The music is pulsating and soon, we are all dancing and loving every moment.

At two-thirty am, having paid the bill, (thank you again Howard) we head off to Jimmyz, it's the premier nightspot in Monaco and part of the luxurious Sporting Club complex. Drinks cost a fortune, so you definitely can't come here on a budget.

The music is loud and uber-trendy. Jefferson and I go off to dance and bump into a few celebs along the way. There is still no sign of JP, but I suspect if he has any sense, he will already be in bed. Do I sound old? After twenty minutes or so, we head back to Howard and Theo. Theo is definitely excitable. "Hey guess what we're doing tomorrow?" he asks.

"No idea, having lunch with JP perhaps?" I suggest.

""Nope stupid. But almost as good," he responds, embracing Howard.

"So go on then, give us a clue?" asks Jefferson.

"Well, Howard has a friend here in Monaco, with a rather beautiful yacht and he's taking us out on it, tomorrow morning. How cool is that?" says Theo, all excited and child like.

"Sounds fantastic!" I respond, genuinely excited.

"I spoke with him earlier and in fact, I invited him to dinner this evening but he already had plans, so we'll hook up in the morning on the yacht," replies Howard.

We remain in Jimmyz until four am. This time Jefferson settles the bill, which is very generous of him, as I know full well we've consumed well over a fifteen hundred Euros of alcohol—how totally obscene. We jump into a chauffeured car and within minutes, we are back at the beautiful Hermitage hotel.

"Shall we have one last drink, before bed?" asks Jefferson.

"Be rude not to," replies Howard, as he leads me into the bar.

A waiter appears immediately. I opt for a cognac and the boys order whiskey. We continue to chatter, quite loudly, but thankfully, we are the only guests remaining in the bar.

After our drinks, we head back to our suites, via the lift, of course. Bidding the boys 'sweet dreams', I eventually kick off my sandals in favour of my flip flops. You see, it's weird, isn't it? Even in this suite, which obviously costs a small fortune, I still cannot walk on carpets without my footwear. Perhaps I need therapy? After all, I spend most of my life staying in hotels, so surely by now, I should be over it?

I quickly undress and feel no embarrassment at walking around the suite naked, in front of Howard. I am totally at ease with him. I head to the bathroom, remove my makeup, brush my teeth, gargle and finally, I get into bed.

Within minutes Howard is lying beside me. "Did you enjoy yourself this evening?" he asks.

"Immensely, I just had the best time ever. Everything was so perfect, especially the company," I answer, God! I am so tired.

We snuggle up to each other and then out of the blue Howard asks me a question, I really am not prepared for:

"Martha, would you ever consider moving to the States?"

How the fuck do I answer that?

"Ask me again in the morning," I respond

I fall into a very deep, drunken sleep. Move to the States? What about Alexandre?

Chapter Twenty-Four

I wake up, to the perfect sensation of Howard touching me delicately, his fingers outlining my breasts. The sunlight is streaming through the windows, with the curtains already having been opened. What a beautiful day. I look across to Howard and immediately wince because I feel as though I have been hit across the head with a mallet.

"Sweet Jesus! Just how much did I drink, last night? I feel like shit, again," I mumble, my mouth is as dry as sandpaper.

"I have to say, you certainly know how to drink and that's for sure," laughs Howard, as he leans forward to kiss me.

"Let's go brush our teeth first," I giggle.

Howard follows me into the bathroom and we stand at our own sinks, smiling at one another in a childish manner.

"You finished?" I ask.

"Yep, I'm done," he replies.

"Good, out of the bathroom now please, as I need a pee," I say.

"Great minds think alike, so do I," he responds.

"Well, in that case Mr Howard Johnson III, might I suggest you use the other bathroom, as this one is earmarked?" I say, shoving him out of the door.

Back in the bedroom I check my iphone. Thankfully, it's only seven-thirty am, which means I've only been asleep for a couple of hours and still have a couple more to go. But somehow, just somehow, I think Howard has alternative ideas. He has an erection the size of the Leaning Tower of Pisa.

"See what you do to me?" he smiles, as we both arrive back into the bedroom.

"Well, I think I might just have a cure for you, Sir," I say, wrapping my hand around his erect cock. I lower myself down onto him and ride him very slowly. His hands encase my hips, as he moves me a little faster. He is biting down on his bottom lip and in one clean move he has rolled me onto my back. Our bodies again become one. All the while all eyes stare at one another, never wanting this moment to end. He penetrates me faster and harder. He mumbles, as he does so. I make out the odd words—it is such a turn on to hear him speak dirty. He comes before me, but I need not worry as he brings me to climax with his expert fingers.

"What a wonderful way to start the day Mr Johnson," I remark and then drift off into a deep sleep once again

"Wakey wakey!" says Howard gently kissing my neck. 'Our yacht awaits.'

"Go without me. I'm way too tired," I respond, sleepily.

"Come on, up you get," he says, as he drags me out of bed. "What you need is a shower, that'll wake you up."

"Don't get my hair wait, it takes an age to dry. And also please put my flip flops on my feet, or, carry me," I mumble.

"OK. Flip flops and shower cap," he repeats, as he pops my flip flops on and guides me to the bathroom. "Right. Let's just pop this little shower cap on," he says. He is struggling to fit all my wild curls into the plastic bag of a shower cap. My eyes are still tight shut, as I sit on the edge of the bath. "Open your eyes and give me a hand here," he says.

"OK, OK. But just don't move my head any more, it's already split in two," I respond, as I pull on the hideous cap.

The shower is sufficiently large enough for both of us. He manages to take my flip flops off, as he props me up against the shower cubicle. Of course, he joins me. I can feel the warm water splashing against my body and it feels wonderful. I then feel Howard's hands exploring my body with shower gel. His hands glide around my neck and then over my breasts. He turns me around, to wash my back and my buttocks. Facing him, again his hands are on my stomach. He's making me feel totally horny again and so, I eventually open my eyes. I help myself to shower gel and gently massage his cock. He is erect, within moments. My hands move up and down his erect shaft and as I lean in close to him, I whisper "Fuck me." And fuck me he does. The animal in him is certainly alive this morning. He thrusts, as if his life depends on it. We are lost in the moment and as we both come he says the words "I love you."

As my orgasm comes to an end, I cup his face with my hands. "Thank you. I think I'm awake now," and I kiss him passionately, ignoring his words for the moment.

We dry ourselves off and then enter the bedroom

"Do we have time for breakfast?" I ask.

"Already dealt with missy. Whilst you were fast asleep, I phoned down and it will be here at precisely nine-fifteen am," he responds.

"God! You really are bloody perfect. Marry me!" I say, without even thinking what I am saying. The words just come tumbling out of my mouth.

"Just say when and I'll be yours," he responds, without hesitation.

"I hope you realise that I might just hold you to that," I laugh. And at that precise moment, there is a knock at the door. It must be breakfast time. Brilliant, I am bloody starving.

"Did you mean what you just said?" he asks, inquisitively.

"Maybe," I say, as I head off towards the door. Nothing comes between me and food and definitely not, a marriage proposal!

Breakfast is amazing and quite literally, I can have whatever I want. I opt for watermelon, as that is my absolute favourite, followed by sausages and scrambled eggs. No bread this morning, as it has a tendency to bloat me and I don't want to be particularly bloated on the yacht now, do I?

"Martha, come here a minute," he says, patting his knee.

Automatically, I walk over to him and sit on his knee, like a little girl.

"You really are something special and I want you to promise me that I'll see you again," he says, looking into my eyes.

"I should hope so!" I say indignantly, but laughing at the same time, 'after all, it's not every day that I sleep with a client for a week.'

"I'm not joking. When I say I want to see you again I mean it and I don't want this to be the end," he says, sincerely.

"I don't think for one moment that this is the end." I say, as I kiss him on his forehead.

I pull away from him. "Come on, otherwise we'll be late." I start to sort out my wardrobe nightmare. What on earth am I going to wear? After all, I came to Cannes to work. I didn't plan on spending the day on a yacht with a millionaire.

In fairness, it's not too much of a nightmare. I've got a brown bikini, brown leather flip flops, a cream halter neck chiffon dress, which sits just above the knee and a pair of D&G sunglasses. A perfect yacht outfit, even if I do say so myself!

I grab my big brown leather handbag, throw in everything I need, which in fairness isn't a lot—iphone, wallet (as if the yacht will have shop on board! lip balm and afro comb (yes, my hair is a nightmare) and I'm ready.

"WOW! Just look at you. And there you are worried about not having anything to wear. You look sensational!" says Howard, smiling.

"Why, thank you kind Sir!" I reply, as I curtsey.

He takes my hand and we head towards the lifts, just as Jefferson and Theo come out of their suite.

"Well, look at you. Quite the princess aren't you?" says Theo, twirling me around.

"Do you approve?" I respond, hugging him, affectionately.

"I for one, think you look stunning. This brother of mine is a very lucky man," says Jefferson.

We head down in the lift and as we walk through reception, heads turn. We are indeed a beautiful bunch of people, there's no denying that. The concierge makes his way over to us.

"Good morning Mr Johnson," he says. "I have a message for you," he continues, as he hands over an envelope. "Is there anything I can do for you?" he asks.

Howard opens the envelope and smiles at the concierge. "Could I trouble you to organise a car to take us to the harbour, on Avenue du President Kennedy please? Also, we are scheduled to take a flight at seven thirty this evening from Nice. Can you organise helicopter transfers for us with a car to take us to the heliport, at around six o'clock?" instructs Howard.

"Certainly, Mr Johnson. Is that all for now?" asks the concierge.

Howard nods and the concierge walks away to make the arrangements.

"What's up? Bad news?" asks Jefferson, pointing to the envelope in Howard's hand.

"No, not at all. AK has some business to deal with this morning, so he's going to meet us on the yacht for lunch. He'll take a speed boat to join us. So come on, let's go and have some fun," says Howard.

We go outside and our car, a Bentley no less, is waiting for us.

Arriving at the port, we are met by the harbour master, who speaks perfect English. "Mr Johnson, good morning. My name is Franco Delotte and I've been asked to direct you to the yacht. Would you all care to follow me?" he says, as he leads us to a beautiful, white and navy cruiser. Now, at this point, I am not even going to try to tell you about the yacht, as I've really no idea. But suffice to say, it is magnificent. It is predominately white with navy bits here and there. It has two tiers and is quite big. There are a crew of five on board and a captain, well, that's what I would call him.

The cruiser is called Whirlwind, which I suspect depicts the life of Howard's friend! I am really excited. There is something quite glamorous, at the thought of going out to sea aboard a private yacht. My only regret of course, is that we are out on board for such little time. How wonderful would it be, if Howard was to hire it, for say, four weeks and we were to sail around the Med? Now, that would really float my boat, as the saying goes!

The captain approaches us. "Good morning. My name is Philippe and I am your captain today. Welcome aboard," he says, as he shakes our hands. 'I understand that Mr Alex will be joining us at lunchtime. So, please allow me to show you around.'

My heart jumps a little beat as the captain says the name 'Alex.' I immediately think of Alexandre and wonder what he is doing right now. How would he react if he knew I was still in Monaco? Still in Monaco, with Howard, my other lover.

We are shown around the yacht, which as I said has two tiers and a small pool and a jet ski on the back. There are four cabins. They are fabulously designed and furnished.

We set sail and head for the open waters. The sea air is fabulous, blowing through my hair. It will be fabulous of course, until such time, as I have to try and comb it, when it will be full of knots, but at the moment, it's worth the pain!

It's now eleven am and as we chat and giggle, amongst ourselves we are offered champagne, delicious canapés and fabulous fruits.

"I would like to propose a toast," says Theo. "To friends and family... may life be as special, as it is today."

We clink our glasses and merrily sip away. Sophie has been assigned to make sure we have everything we need, which of course we do. We have champagne, we have food, we have fabulous company and above all, we are bobbing about the deep blue Mediterranean Sea on a yacht, which is to die for. Life is good.

I decide to discard my dress and head off to the small pool. The water is refreshing. The sun is incredibly hot it must be at least thirty five degrees today. Howard joins me. "So missy, could you get use to this life?" he asks.

"I'm not so sure I could. I mean, after all, how could I possibly get use to lying in the sun, drinking champagne, eating fabulous canapés drifting out at sea with such a special man? Nope, I don't think it's the life for me," I say, as I lean over to kiss him, tenderly on the lips.

"Thank you," I say.

"Thank you, for what? I've not done anything," he replies.

"Oh come off it. You made my week in Cannes totally bearable and then to top it off, you treat me to the Hermitage Hotel and a day out at sea, on a fabulous yacht. I have had the time of my life." I say, and genuinely mean it.

"Martha, you are completely worth it. I've been through some rough times over the past few months. I'm not sure if Theo has told you, but I'm going through a rather acrimonious divorce and it's just killing me. When I married my wife, for me it was for life. For her, I now see, it was for nothing.

She had an affair with another man. OK, one mistake is bad enough, but then I found out, that she's had many affairs during our marriage and it broke me. Infidelity, in my eyes, is the most hurtful sin, one can commit," he says.

I nod, all the while thinking that he would positively despise me, if he knew that I had been sleeping with both him and with Alexandre. Oh my God! Can you imagine? How stupid have I been? I think I can eventually have Howard for keeps and for all the right reasons, including love, but all the while I have been messing about with Alexandre. I need to get Alexandre out of my head and now.

I close my eyes and as I do so, Howard takes my hand and slowly strokes my fingers. His touch makes my skin tingle. I smile. Tenderly his lips find mine and slowly, our tongues explore. How am I going to live without this man in my life? I don't know that I can.

"Martha?" says Howard.

I open my eyes and look at him. "What's up Mr Johnson?" I respond.

"I love you. This just feels so right. I vowed I would never trust another woman again, but you're different. You're genuine and I think you're with me, for the right reasons," he says.

Oh fuck! How do I top that? I think for a moment, but I don't really know what to say, so I waffle! "Howard, as I said, I've had the best week ever and you've made that so special for me. I absolutely adore you and yes, I think I most probably love you too, but we need to be realistic here. After all, we are based on two different continents. Our lives are so different and we've known each other a week. Will you still love me tomorrow, when you're back in the States and into your normal routine again?" I ask.

"Yes, I will still love you tomorrow and I think that's a cue for a song," he says, smiling.

Howard leans in close to kiss me and I respond passionately. Our tongues fight one another and slowly his hand works its way into my bikini bottoms. His fingers slowly stroke me as we continue kissing. I feel myself moving in time with his fingers, as my breathing quickens. Within moments I come and I sigh a sigh of pure ecstasy.

I savour the moment and then say: "Come on then, let's join the boys," I raise myself up, but Howard pulls me back down.

"Can't at the moment," he says.

"Why ever not?" I ask.

"Well, I've just had a sensational moment with a beautiful woman and my body reacted to it, if you know what I mean," he says, laughing.

"Ah. Let me just see if I can remedy this situation," I say as I slide my hand into his trunks. I wrap my fingers around his cock. "How about I make you come?" I whisper.

"Yes, but make it quick, I don't think I can hold on much longer," he rasps.

"I'm not quite sure that you ejaculating in your friend's yacht pool is correct etiquette, so how about I sit on you and you can come in me?" I say.

"Perfect idea," he responds, with a wink.

I casually straddle him making polite conversation, so that it doesn't look too obvious that we about to have sex. I move my bikini aside and he slides into me, with ease. I clench tightly and sure enough I hear a low groan, as his warm fluid enters my body.

"A well thought out plan," he says, as we both head out of the pool and jump into the sea.

For the next half an hour we swim, we dunk each other, we splash and we laugh. By the time we get out, I am totally exhausted, so I retire to the sun lounger for a snooze. Jefferson joins me. "So have you had a good time?" he says.

"Totally," I respond. "I don't think I've ever had as much fun on a job in all my working years. I simply don't want it to end."

"Why should it have to?" asks Jefferson. "After all, big bro' has got it bad for you. What will you guys do?"

"I don't know. The problem is, I can't just move to the States. I have commitments in the UK and you know, I really do like your brother and I mean that, but it's still very early days. I mean, it might be a short lived romance, or, it may work out, but either way I won't deny that Howard is special," I add.

"Martha, this other guy who you hooked up with whilst in Cannes, is he special?" asks Jefferson.

"He was special. I thought that we would be together forever, but it wasn't to be. I've been kidding myself," I respond, suddenly feeling a little sad.

We say no more and simply close our eyes. The warmth of the sun beating down on my skin is glorious. Within minutes, I drift off into a slumber.

"Time for lunch sleepy head," says Jefferson, as he shakes me gently.

"I'm not hungry," I respond. "I'm tired."

"Theo said you would say that, but as soon as you check out this food you'll change your mind," he continues.

"OK. I give in. Help me up and lead me to the feast," I say, as I swing my legs off the sun lounger.

"Also, you'll be able to meet the yacht's owner and his wife, as they've joined us now," says Jefferson.

"You go on, I just want to freshen up," I say. I locate my dress and pull it on over my head, after all, I am sure complete strangers don't want to see me munching away at their dining table, in my bikini, do they?

I ruffle my hair, which has taken on a life of its own and clip it up and as I head towards the dining area, Theo is running, quite literally running, towards me. His eyes are wide and I can sense real concern.

He grabs my wrist and leads me away from the dining area. "Whatever is the matter with you? You look as though you've seen a ghost," I ask, laughing.

"This is no laughing matter Martha," he says a little out of breath.

"Theo, what is it? Tell me. Tell me now!" I say.

"Shit! I can't believe this is happening. Oh fuck!" he continues pacing about.

"Theo, pull yourself together and tell me what is going on. What is it? Come on, for Christ's sake, just spit it out!" I say angrily, as he is really starting to scare me.

He opens his mouth to speak and then closes it. He tries again, but still nothing. We are now face to face. Our noses are almost touching. "Theo, tell me what the bloody hell is the matter, or, so help me God, I'm going to slap you!" I say.

"It's Alexandre. It's fucking Alexandre!" he stammers.

I am immediately gripped by fear. "What do you mean it's Alexandre? Has something happened to him? Tell me. Please tell me, what is it?" I say, close to tears.

"Alexandre owns this fucking yacht and he's now on board, with his wife, talking to Howard. What the hell are you going to do?" says Theo, in a hushed whisper.

"SHIT! FUCK! BOLLOCKS!" is all I can muster.

Chapter Twenty-Five

I am in a complete state of panic. Should I simply jump overboard and swim back to shore? We are in the middle of the fucking ocean; how in God's name, am I going to swim back to the shore? Oh sweet Jesus! This is not happening to me! What the fuck am I going to do? I am on board a yacht, with my future boyfriend, Howard and my 'bastard' Alexandre, is on board too. They know one another. Oh my God! They know one another, which is absolutely fine, but now they are going to know about me. Has Alexandre ever mentioned me to Howard? Has Howard mentioned me to Alexandre?

What am I going to do? Please God! Help me! This isn't happening to me right now. It's all a dream. But no, it's not a dream, it's a fucking nightmare, a HUGE fucking nightmare and soon enough, I am going to wake up.

"Oh God Theo! Please tell me this is one of your sick jokes?" I say with my head in my hands.

Theo shakes his head. "You think I would joke about this, you stupid girl? There has to be someway of getting you off of this yacht. Can you use a jet ski?" he asks and I don't think he's joking either.

"No Theo. This is me you're talking to. I can't fucking use a jet ski. Have you gone mad? Do you expect me to jet-ski back to Monaco?" I respond.

"Cara mia, you've got to think of something, otherwise, you are so busted!" he continues, pacing about.

"Theo. Will you please stop pacing and let me think?" I snarl, as I feel my lips curling.

I look around anxiously, looking for my handbag. I need to text Alexandre, to tell him that I am on board his yacht, at this precise moment and that World War Three, is about to erupt.

Suddenly, Theo and I look at each other. Howard is calling.

"Hey guys, come on up, this food is delicious and come meet Alexandre and his wife, Monica!"

"We'll be up in a moment!" responds Theo, rather shakily.

"Oh my God! Theo, what are we going to do? Jesus! Last time you saw Alexandre, you wanted to punch him and now we're on board his yacht, about to eat his food. Fuck! Fuck! Fuck!" I whisper.

I finally locate my handbag, which has been placed in one of the cabins. I quickly text Alexandre: *I am on board your yacht right now sitting in a cabin—be discreet but come find me IMMEDIATELY.*

I don't bother with kisses, as I really don't think it appropriate!

"Listen. As soon as Alexandre arrives, you need to go to the others and act as if nothing has happened. OK? Do you understand me? Act as if everything is perfect."

"You are completely fucking mad. You have your two lovers upstairs and they know one another and you want me, to act as if everything is perfect?

Cara mia, you have definitely lost it! This is one holy fucking mess!" responds Theo, a little too aggressively.

"Don't get angry. Just do as I say. Quickly. Go. No wait, let me text Alexandre again," I respond.

I text again: *Meet me now I am in one of the yacht's cabins, a red one.*

A few moments pass and suddenly we hear someone approaching. Oh please dear God, let this be Alexandre and not his wife, or Howard.

"Hello, where are you guys?" It's Jefferson's voice.

"No! Quickly Theo, go and explain what is happening here. I can't cope with Jefferson, just at the moment," I say, as I shove him out of the cabin door.

I wait anxiously, in the hope that Alexandre arrives before Howard comes looking for me. And, as if by magic, the cabin door opens and there he is. He doesn't say a word—he simply stands there, staring.

"Oh my God what are we going to do? I didn't know this was your yacht and of course, if I had known, I wouldn't be on it, would I? Oh my God Alexandre, help me, what are we going to do to sort this mess out?" I ramble.

Alexandre steps into the room and after a few moments of silence, he simply asks "Martha, what the fuck is going on? You are supposed to be back in the UK. What are you doing on my yacht with Howard Johnson?"

"Boo listen. It's simple. OK? Howard invited me to stay on another day after the show, as Theo was staying on and he thought it might be nice for me to spend some time with my brother. Obviously, at no point did I think that he would bring me on board your cruiser! Shit! This is such a nightmare. I just wish I had returned to the UK yesterday," I stammer.

"So... Are you and Howard an item?" asks Alexandre, with a hint of jealously and sarcasm in his voice.

Shit! I have to think on my feet here, or else I'm going to be busted big time. Who do I really want? Howard or Alexandre. At this moment in time, I genuinely don't know. Howard is the safer bet, but I'm not going to push my luck, after all if I come out of this mess unscathed, then I'll be happy to be single for the rest of my life!

"No, of course I'm not with Howard. As I said, he thought it would be nice for me to spend time with Theo. There is nothing going on between the two of us. Jesus Christ! He's my client after all." I continue, all the while knowing that I am a compulsive liar, and not a particularly good one, it feels.

Alexandre is sitting on the end of the bed now. I crouch down beside him. "Listen if we're smart, we can get through this, can't we? We just need to pretend that we've never met before. And of course, as you know, Theo is on board too. You two need to act as if you don't know one another so, no fighting. Please, promise me no fighting," I continue.

My hand is on Alexandre's knee. Not really as a sign of affection, but my thighs are hurting as I'm crouching down and I need to steady myself!

"Martha, do you know how good it is to see you? I really thought I'd fucked up by not coming by yesterday morning, but something came up, so I just couldn't make it. Honestly, I wanted to see you, but things happen," he says.

I stand up and look at Alexandre in total amazement. "Are you fucking deranged?" I start. "Your wife is on board and all you can do is tell me how good it is to see me! Pull yourself together and for fuck's sake act as if you don't know me. OK?" I say, a little agitated.

Alexandre is now standing in front of me. His hands are on my waist and suddenly he pulls me towards him. Our faces are close, too close for the inevitable not to happen. His lips are on mine. His tongue is circling the inside of my mouth, as only his tongue can and I feel the throb of his cock against me. I start to melt. I have an overwhelming desire to shag him senseless and bugger the consequences, but no. I push him away. "Are you completely fucking mad? Stop this right now!" I hiss.

"Nope, just horny baby. Calm down. It's just a kiss, but maybe we'll make time for more, later. Now come on, let's pretend we don't know one another, which is kind of difficult with this hard on," he laughs, touching his crotch.

I watch as he readjusts himself and then he leads me out of the cabin and up to the dining area.

"I've found her. I suspect this is Martha and if it's not, then she's a stow-away," laughs Alexandre. "Martha, this is Monica and of course, everyone else you already know."

I lean over to shake Monica's hand, but instead she stands up and kisses me on both cheeks. "Come sit wiz me and leave zee boyz to zemselves," she says, in a heavy French accent.

I duly sit next to her and feel so awkward that I don't quite know what to do with myself. She is indeed the woman from the restaurant last night, where I nearly had a seizure at seeing my darling Alexandre out with another female, who just happens to be his wife. His wife that supposedly he never goes out with. Explain that one away, shit-head!

"So, tell me 'ow you know deez boyz?" asks Monica.

"Theo is my brother, who works for KAYSO and I was working on their conference this last week, where I met Howard and Jefferson," I stammer.

"Which one of zee beautiful brothers do you 'ave your eye on?" she asks.

OH NO! How do I respond to that? Well, it's actually your husband I love more than anything or anyone in the world... I think not...

"Well truth be told, I would find it way too difficult to decide who would be the better catch, so, for now, I'll opt to stay single instead," I smile.

"Well I zink Howard has a, now 'ow you say, a twinkle in 'is eye for you. Howard, would you like me to play zee cupid wiz you and zee lovely Marta?" asks Monica.

"If you could wave your magic wand and encourage her to come to the States with me that would be good," replies Howard.

Oh shit! Why doesn't he just give the States a rest now? Alexandre throws me a side ways glance. Shit! He is suspecting something already and I haven't even managed to eat a morsel yet. I feel myself redden.

"Martha, please help yourself," encourages Alexandre, with a wry smile.

Jefferson and Theo make lots of polite conversation and practically every time Howard tries to speak, they speak over him.

"Jeez boys, give me a chance to speak, will you?" he eventually pipes up.

The boys laugh off the situation and thankfully, after about forty minutes of small talk and an understandably 'difficult to eat lunch,' Monica pipes up: "Right zen, who wants a tour of zee boat?"

"Yacht, yacht, not boat. How many times?" says Alexandre, laughing.

"Sounds good to me!" replies Jefferson. "Theo why don't you come along too? Come on let's check out the fabrics." Monica, Howard, Theo and Jefferson make for the lower deck, leaving Alexandre and me alone.

"Has Howard been sniffing around you?" asks Alexandre.

"No, of course he hasn't. He simply suggested that I might like to spend some time in the States with Theo. There is absolutely nothing going on between us," I lie.

Alexandre is now sitting beside me. I can feel the warmth of his thigh against mine. My mouth is dry and I am genuinely nervous.

Moments pass in silence. Alexandre brushes a stray hair from my cheek and then gently kisses my neck. I want to shout 'No' but I don't. I allow his tongue to find my ear and I allow his hand to wander beneath my dress. Suddenly his mobile rings. He ignores it. His hand feels good, but I know that I must stop this now, right now. I move away.

"Alexandre you should answer that," I say unable to look at him, because I know that I want him to continue. He has total power over me.

"It can wait," he says. "Now come back here." He pats the seat next to him.

"Boo listen. Your wife is downstairs, as is Theo. Come on let's play this cool, OK?" I suggest, my heart beating furiously.

"As cool as you want baby, but for now, come here," he continues.

Suddenly, he's behind me. I can feel his breath on my neck. "What are you thinking?" he asks.

"Nothing," I respond.

"What, nothing? I don't believe you. I think you want me to touch you. I think you want me to fuck you," he says, slowly, quietly.

I turn around to face him. "Well I think you're fucking mental. For the millionth time, your wife is here, but you still think it's OK to flirt with me. What is wrong with you?" I say, shaking my head.

"Nothing wrong with me baby. Now, when shall I come to the UK to see you? Shall I come tomorrow? Or the next day? When do you want me to come? Want me to come now?" he asks, right before his lips meet mine. Initially I struggle, but it's futile. I put my arms around his neck and kiss him passionately. "I love you Boo but it has to stop," I say. But he ignores my pleas.

"I love you too. Now, one of us needs to pull away, you've given me a hard on again," laughs Alexandre.

We both head back to the dining table.

Unbeknown to me, our embrace is witnessed. It is witnessed by Howard, who was eagerly making his way to find me, so that he could tell me all about one of the cabins he has just seen. But, before he is about to shout out my name, he sees me in the arms of Alexandre and hears those three little words—'I love you.' He stands there confused, devastated and totally betrayed. He says nothing about what he has witnessed, as he approaches us both.

"Hey there you two. Have you been getting to know one another?" he asks, as if nothing is wrong.

"I'll tell you what Howard, if I wasn't a married man, I would be making a play for this lovely lady," laughs Alexandre.

"Out of my league I'm afraid. I don't know if I could tame her," responds Howard.

I simply smile. I feel awkward sitting next to Alexandre, whilst across the way is Howard my new potential and available boyfriend.

"Well, you can always try, I'll be gentle with you," I giggle.

Howard doesn't respond. I sense something is amiss, but I don't know what.

Monica returns, with Jefferson and Theo.

"Well zee boyz like zee boat, so zat is good because zay is designers, so if zay say is good, zen it must be good." She puts her arms around her husband's neck and kisses him.

I feel sick to the pit of my stomach. How dare she snuggle up to my gorgeous man? But he is not my man is he? He belongs to her. I am simply someone he turns to, whenever he feels like it.

Theo and Jefferson chatter away, telling us all about the cabins. I look across to Howard, our gaze locks and then he looks away. No smile. Nothing.

"So, what time is it?" I ask, unable to think of anything else to say.

"It is now twenty past zee three," replies Monica.

"Time is pushing on, perhaps we should head back to dry land, after all, we have planes to catch," says Howard.

"Entirely up to you my friend," says Alexandre. 'Of course, I would love you all to stay, but if you've got to go, then you've got to go. Let me tell Philippe to head back to the harbour. Excuse me.'

"Now boyz, you promise to come and visit again. It is no time since I get to know you and already you are leaving me, come on let's go and 'ave zee drink." she says, to Theo and Jefferson.

So that leaves only myself and Howard. I smile across to him. But he doesn't respond. I move round, so that I am hovering next to him.

"Howard, sweetheart is there something wrong?" I ask, none the wiser that he has seen me kissing Alexandre.

"No. Nothing wrong," he responds, coldly.

"I think there is, so perhaps you should tell me."

"As I said Martha, there is nothing wrong." And with that, Howard gets up and walks towards the boys, who are enjoying drinks with Monica.

I don't know what to do with myself. Should I follow Howard, or stay here? Clearly, he is pissed off or upset about something, but God only knows what.

Alexandre returns and ruffles my hair, as he walks by.

"Come on, come and have a drink," he says, taking my arm and leading me to where the others are seated.

"What will it be?" asks Alexandre.

"Champagne, I think is in order," I respond, rather shakily.

"Krug?" he asks.

"Now then, just how would you know that the lady drinks Krug?" asks Howard, directly.

Alexandre shoots me a look. I look away.

"Simple. A beautiful lady will always drink beautiful champagne. She is definitely a Krug girl," responds Alexandre, with a chuckle.

We chatter amongst ourselves for the next twenty minutes or so, until we arrive into the harbour. The captain has already phoned ahead to the Hermitage Hotel, to request a car.

"Well I 'ave to say for zee little time that we was together, it was a good time for me, so come back soon please," says Monica, kissing us all, in turn. 'Especially you Marta, we will 'ave good fun.'

"Martha, it was good to meet you. Next time you are in Monaco, let us know, it would be good to catch up again," says Alexandre, as he kisses me on both cheeks and whispers, "I love you."

I feel myself blush. "Of course, I'll be in touch. Lovely to meet you both and thank you so much for allowing us on board your beautiful yacht," I respond.

I feel a stab of guilt. Monica is a truly lovely woman and I can see that she genuinely loves Alexandre and loves him for who he is, not what he has. Why did God make me such a bitch and him such a bastard?

We head off to the waiting car. The silence is deafening.

"Brilliant day bro, thanks for organising that," says Jefferson, breaking the silence.

"Yes absolutely perfect," I say. I am sitting next to Howard, but he is simply looking out of the window. We arrive at the Hermitage Hotel and all pile out of the car. Howard's phone rings, so he excuses himself to take the call.

In reception, Jefferson turns to me.

"Martha, all is not well. Big bro' has gone very quiet. I reckon he's kind of sad to be leaving the South of France and of course you—you've been a great distraction for him. So what do you reckon, will you guys hook up again?" asks Jefferson.

"Of course I would really like to see him again. I've had such a perfect time. It's a pity that we don't both live in the same country, let alone the same continent, but we'll sort something out. After all, who knows, this could be the start of something special," I add, quite believing that it could be.

I spot Howard walking back into reception and I wave, as he heads over.

"Right then, I suppose we should get packed, we haven't got too long left now," he says, as he strides off towards the lift.

Once into the suite, nothing is said. Total silence. Howard pours himself a Scotch and walks onto the terrace. I feel like a child, not knowing what to do. Should I go and sit with him, or, should I go and pack? I decide to pack, it seems like the easier option, but try as I might I simply stand there and stare at my case, unable to engage my brain, to function correctly.

No, it's no good; I need to speak to him, to determine what's wrong. I head out to the terrace and sit on the chair, beside him.

"Howard, would you like to tell me what's wrong please?" I ask, in a sympathetic voice.

"Nothing," he responds, coldly.

"I'll ask again. What's wrong? And please don't tell me 'nothing' because from where I'm sitting there is definitely something. You've been quiet since lunch. So, what is it? I promise I'll be over to see you very soon, I just need to get a few things sorted out in the UK," I say, as I get up to kiss him.

But rather than responding to my kiss, he turns his head away. I step back. What the fuck is going on?

"Right. OK. Obviously there IS something very wrong. Are you going to actually tell me what's bothering you?" I ask, sternly.

"Leave it will you?" he responds, raising his voice.

"No, I will not leave it! Fucking hell! This morning you were declaring undying love and now you won't even give me the time of day. So just spit it out!"

My voice is starting to quiver.

"I saw you. I saw you and Alexandre, in an embrace and if I'm perfectly honest, I cannot bear to look at you right now. You barely know him? Well that's a complete lie! You were kissing him and telling him that you love him! For fucks sake Martha!" he shouts.

I am frozen to the spot. I cannot believe that Howard witnessed my kiss with Alexandre. What am I going to do now?

I desperately need to be honest with this man. It's not fair that I've strung him along, without an explanation. Sweet Jesus! What have I done to deserve all this shit in my life?

"Alright. What I'm going to tell you is the truth. Just sit there and listen, please. I've known Alexandre for a few years..." I start.

"What do you mean you've known him for a few years? You acted like complete strangers today."

"Please Howard, let me finish. This is difficult enough. As I was saying, I've known Alexandre for a few years and in the past we've had some intimacy and if I'm honest, I thought that he was going to leave his wife for me, but he didn't. I've never met this wife before, so today was a tad difficult for me. When I knew it was Alexandre's yacht, I told him to act as if we were strangers, as I, for one, didn't want to upset you and equally, I didn't want his wife asking questions. It was obvious to me that they are still very much a couple, so he's has been pulling my strings, I am so sorry. I am really desperately sorry. That kiss you witnessed was nothing more than the good old times. I did love him once upon a time, but today, it was evident that we will never be a couple. You've GOT to believe me. There is nothing between us now. Nothing. Please, Howard it's you I want. Not Alexandre. He has simply used me and I fell for it. You've got to believe me!" I say, tears springing to my eyes.

I am not quite sure why I feel like crying. Is it because I love Howard, or, is it because I love Alexandre, or, is it because this is all such a fucking mess? Once again there is silence.

"Jesus Martha! Wouldn't it have just been easier to tell me the truth from the start? What did you have to lose?" asks Howard, speaking quietly.

"I wanted to tell you, but how could I blurt out in front of his wife, that I know Alexandre? She would want to know from where and when, and then what would have happened? The shit would have hit the fan, that's what!" I respond, angrily.

Howard is now sitting with his head in his hands. Eventually he looks up.

"I told you this morning, that infidelity is the worse thing ever Martha. I then witness you, in the arms of another man. Don't you get it? I love you. Can't you understand what you've done to me?" he asks, in a whisper.

"I can say sorry a million times, but you've got to believe me, I am genuinely sorry. There is nothing between him and me, any more. Please Howard, I am asking you, no begging you, to forgive me," I say, as I kneel beside him. I lift up his face and see tears in his eyes.

Oh shit! I am not good with crying men. It's just not natural. Tears are for women and children only.

I wipe away his tears. And cup his face tenderly.

"Howard, please believe me, this will never happen again and I do love you. Honestly I love you," I say, because I don't know what else to say. We slowly move closer and he kisses me tenderly on the lips. Very tenderly and very softly.

"You've got to promise that you'll never hurt me again. That episode tore me in two. I love you so very much, but I won't go through that again," says Howard, kissing me again.

"I promise I'll never intentionally hurt you," I respond, knowing that I am lying...

Howard stands up and leads me into the bedroom. Without words, he slips off my dress and unfastens my bikini top. Soon his hands and tongue savour my breasts. We fall onto the bed and my bikini bottoms and his trunks, are discarded. I straddle him and mouth the words 'I love you.' Our sex is fast and animalistic and very soon, we both pant wildly.

We lie in silence for a few moments. Howard is the first to speak.

"Martha, now for me to have fallen in love with you within the space of a week is unreal, but somehow you've definitely gotten under my skin. You are a genuinely amazing woman and we happened to meet at the right place and right time. Now get up and shower. I'll pack in the meantime," he says, rolling out of bed.

Howard walks off and I quickly find my iphone. I have two text messages and I know that they will both be from Alexandre.

Text message one: *I'll be over to see you next week. This hard on is even too much for me to handle xxx.*

Text message two: L*ove you Baby xxx.*

I quickly respond: *Next week is perfect. I'll administer oral on your complaint! Xxx.*

I press send and quickly start packing, leaving out jeans, a shirt, sandals and a leather jacket, because after all, it's going to be cold when we land in England, it always is!

I swop places with Howard and jump into the shower.

"Do you need a hand?" he asks.

His face is up against the shower glass.

"Go away you pervert, otherwise I'll call security," I giggle.

"Are you sure you don't want me to come in and give you a hand?" he asks.

"No thank you. I'm almost done, so be out with you!" I respond, with a grin.

Once dry and moisturised, I head into the bedroom, to get dressed.

Howard has packed and is part way through getting dressed.

"What's the rush? Shall we stay here for a few more days?" he asks.

I can't stay here! I can't stay here in Monaco, knowing that Alexandre is close by. As much as I want to, the answer is definitely 'no.'

"Nice idea, but I need to get back to sort out a few things," I say, as I blow him a kiss. "Now, hurry up and finish getting dressed."

With the time fast approaching six pm, we just about have time for a drink out on the terrace, before our car arrives.

"What do you fancy?" asks Howard.

"You of course!" I respond, with a smile.

"Aside from me. Fancy some Krug?" he asks, smiling.

"As much as I would love to, I'll just take a juice please. I've got to drive back from the airport, when we land at Heathrow," I say.

We watch the hustle and bustle of Monaco down below and kiss like lovers, soon to be separated.

There is a knock at the door, which indicates that our porters and car have arrived. One final kiss before we head downstairs.

Howard settles the bill and thanks the concierge, with a five hundred Euro tip. I think I might quite like to be a concierge, in another life! Theo and Jefferson join us in reception, clearly running late.

Soon we are on our way to the Heliport in Fontevielle, to transfer to Nice Airport, for our onward flights.

I feel like a movie star. The car takes us directly to the helicopter, our bags are loaded and we are off, for the seven minute transfer between Monaco and Nice Airport.

At the airport, our passports are taken and within minutes, we are boarding the steps of a private Lear jet. Our passports are handed back and our pilot, co-pilot and stewardess, welcome us on board.

Moments later, we are taxing to the runway and then we leave the South of France. I am leaving with great sadness. I look across to Howard and smile. He leans over and kisses me, tenderly.

The stewardess provides us with drinks, which I decline. I have had so much to drink in the past week that I'm going to explode and of course, I am just too bloody exhausted, to drink anymore.

I look across to Jefferson and Theo and both have fallen asleep.

"Howard, do you mind if I grab a little shut eye?" I ask.

"Come, snuggle into me," he says, as I lay my head on his lap and drift off into a very deep sleep.

I feel the sensation of being rocked. "Martha. Come on cara mia, we're about to land. Seat belt on," says Theo.

"It feels as if, I spend my life being woken up," I say, with a sleepy head.

Howard is now sitting opposite Jefferson and Theo is opposite me. How that happened I am not quite sure.

Within five minutes, we have landed and are being taxied to our disembarkation point.

Once through private Passport Control, we are then just a few metres away from the throbbing crowds, housed within the terminal building. People are scurrying around, children are crying and lovers are kissing one another goodbye, just as Howard and I will do in a moment.

An airport representative approaches, wheeling my suitcase behind her.

"Good evening. Are you all with Mr Johnson's party?" she asks.

"Yes. I'm Howard Johnson and these two passengers will be flying onto the States with me this evening," replies Howard.

"Excellent. I have a case for Miss Martha DiPinto," she says, wheeling my suitcase towards me.

"Thank you. That's very kind," I say.

"Gentlemen, if you would like to follow me, your transfer time is very limited," she smiles, hastily making for the door.

Theo is the first to embrace me.

"Cara mia, it's been an amazing week, thank you. I'll call over the next few days," he says, kissing me on both cheeks.

"Likewise girlfriend, it's been awesome. Can't wait to hook up again," says Jefferson, giving me a bear hug.

And finally Howard. He steps forward and tenderly kisses me, on the lips.

"I'll be in touch," he says. And with that, all three turn and walk away.

Well, I was rather expecting slightly more than just a peck on the lips, but I suppose we're out in public and there might be paparazzi around and we don't want his soon to be ex-wife, knowing that he's got a girlfriend, now, do we?

I am feeling sad and totally deflated. My life is normal again and I am, once again all alone. I head off to the car park. Now, where the hell did I park my car? I am just too tired to think straight. Eventually, I find it and throw my bags into the boot. I get into the car and look into the mirror. Not a good look, I can tell you! Never mind, I'll soon be home. I pay at the exit barrier and in what seems like no time at all, I am on the M40, heading back towards the rolling countryside of Oxfordshire.

Suddenly I have a thought. I can't remember turning off my iphone during the flight and I certainly don't remember turning it to Flight Mode, simply because I can't remember how to! I stop at the first service area and rummage around in my bag to find the handset. It's switched off. In that case, I must have remembered to turn if off.

I arrive home within the hour and after opening the front door and wading through the mail, which is piled up behind the front door, I drag my luggage up the staircase. If there is one thing I need to do, the moment I arrive home, it's to empty the suitcase and get the washing on. Once that's done, I flick through my post. It's mainly bills, yep, usually is and then check my iphone.

Nothing from Howard, but then I suppose he's up in the air and not allowed to text his girlfriend. Ah, girlfriend, that's me! I smile at the thought of my gorgeous man and all that has happened in such a short space of time.

I click on the text messages from Alexandre. I want to read those words again, those words that tell me he loves me and that he is coming to visit. I scan down, but there seems to be two additional text messages.

Text message one: *Baby, have a safe flight.xxx*.

Text message two: *I'll be over on Wednesday. Arriving Heathrow at noon. Love you xxx.*

I don't remember reading those. Bloody hell! Was I that tired that I read them subconsciously?

Weird, totally weird! I head into the kitchen to pour myself a much needed cup of tea and then decide I need sleep and plenty of it. I don't set my alarm for the morning. I'll wake up, when I wake up.

I fall asleep quickly. Initially, I think of Howard and then I move my affections onto Alexandre, my darling Boo.

Morning arrives, all too quickly. I grab my iphone, to see what the time is. Jesus! I don't think I've slept this late, in such a long time. It's eleven-thirty am. I check my voice messages. There isn't one—not one!

So, instead, I check my text messages and I have two.

The first is from Howard: *Martha please forgive me. Your phone was on during our flight to Heathrow receiving messages, so I turned it off, but not before reading Alexandre's messages to you. Enjoy your time with him on Wednesday*.

The second text is from Alexandre: *Baby, something has come up on Wednesday, so I need to re-arrange. I'll call you xx.*

I look down in horror. I feel sick. What the fuck have I done? Oh Jesus! I am shaking. I can't take this anymore. I need him in my life, but how, just how, do I win back my true love?

About The Authors

Michelle Shingler

Michelle has spent over 20 years working backstage as a teleprompter, on various conferences and events all over the world.

She has worked with Royalty, Heads of State, Politicians, Movie Stars, TV and Sports Personalities, Rock Stars and many, corporate directors and managers. She has listened to hundreds of speeches: some have made history, some have changed the world, some of course have not (but they had hoped to) some have been enlightening, some have been hysterical and others have been well ...

With the state of the global economy being as it is, there's not a huge amount for people to laugh about. Therefore she feels the time is right to share the laughter, tears and ups and downs of conference crew life.

Michelle lives in deepest, rural England and has three daughters. They describe their mother as: 'outrageous, funny and a complete nightmare, but she is actually quite fit and they wouldn't swap her!' (Their words not hers!)

Her favourite places are; New York, Bermuda, Baden- Baden in Germany and Abersoch in North Wales.

Her mother, on reading the manuscript said: "Oh, my goodness! I hope you are using a pseudonym!'

Vincenza Astone

Having arrived into the live events and conference industry some twenty years ago to do 'just the one small live show at Silverstone, Vincenza has yet to escape the intoxicating world of demanding clients, impossibly tight deadlines, ridiculously unimaginative budgets and total sleep deprivation, but somehow she still manages to love it. Having stepped out of the highly glamorous world of motor-racing (no, not as a racing driver…) life has never quite stood still for her.

Event lows followed by amazing highs – worldwide travel allows the creative juices to flow and sometimes, exceptional events are born.

Yet to be married (not through lack of trying) and certainly not your typical spinster she is ever hopeful. However, as her mother points out on a regular basis "he's yet to be born and his mother is dead!'

Vincenza originates from Italy but has made England her home and has a love of all things English including gin and tonics, strawberries and cream and pimms on the lawn.